Dear Friends Who Read and Readers Who Are Friends,

If you're reading this greeting, you're either in an airport or on an airplane. You're embarking on a journey.

And so I'm jealous.

It's not merely that I love to travel; I love the miracle of aviation. Even when I'm in the middle seat in row twenty-eight, I never forget the fact that I am, quite literally, flying.

The book you're holding wouldn't exist if it weren't for air travel. I had just flown into New York from Armenia, and I was meeting a friend for dinner in Manhattan. I was an hour early, and so I went to the bar and ordered arak, an anise-flavored alcoholic beverage from the Middle East: imagine weaponized ouzo. As I sipped my drink, three ingredients combined alchemically into this novel.

First, I had just landed after a transatlantic flight. I had had breakfast in Yerevan, and I was having dinner in New York. Those two cities are eight time zones apart: that's what I mean by the miracle of aviation.

Likewise, I've always been awed by those people who choose to become pilots and flight attendants, especially these days—an era of airline consolidation, regional jets, and passengers willing to wrestle for space in the overhead bins. Some people assume that a flight attendant's life is a glamorous world of escape to faraway lands, but it's not. Maybe in 1965 it was more romantic because the layovers were longer, but it was never a world of bacchanalian splendor. While researching this novel, the more I learned about flight attendants, the more I grew to respect them.

Second, there was the booze before me. I was at a handsome

bar, and I was jet-lagged just enough to see the aesthetic beauty in the rituals around which we drink: the colors, the bottles, the labels, the glasses.

And third, there was Russia. I had changed planes in Moscow. I've always been fascinated by the country that gave us Tchaikovsky, Dostoevsky, and the Bolshoi Ballet but has—almost without exception—a James Bond villain running the show in the Kremlin.

I asked the bartender for scrap paper and started to write, scribbling for the next half hour. I completed the first three pages of the novel you have in your hands.

You may know this from personal experience, but we're more likely to cry on airplanes than we are on the ground. We get more emotional. It's the idea that we're alone. Or we're leaving home or we're going home. Or we're not alone, but we're going or coming from someplace special. A funeral. A wedding. A business deal.

I think that's why a plane is the perfect place for a book and why I love to read at thirty-five thousand feet. I hope you enjoy *The Flight Attendant*.

Thanks so much for your faith in my work—and in what stories can mean to the soul.

All the best,
Chris Bohjalian

For more exclusive content from Chris Bohjalian, please go to www.hudsonbooksellers.com/chris-bohjalian.

Praise for Chris Bohjalian's

THE FLIGHT ATTENDANT

"Filled with turbulence and sudden plunges in altitude, *The Flight Attendant* is a very rare thriller whose penultimate chapter made me think to myself, 'I didn't see that coming.' The novel—Bohjalian's twentieth—is also enhanced by his deftness in sketching out vivid characters and locales and by his obvious research into the realities of airline work."　　　　—Maureen Corrigan,
The Washington Post

"[An] expertly turned thriller. . . . An assured novel about reckoning not just with some ruthless bad guys, but private sadness as well. . . . [Bohjalian]'s developed a graceful hand at thriller mechanics, smoothly shifting from Cassie's private paranoia to the intricacies of spycraft and mercenaries to the public tabloid sensation she's become. . . . He's back-loaded the story with twists, from ones that were hinted at early to left-field surprises. And the brisk and busy ending is a fireworks show of redemption, revelation and old-fashioned gunplay."　　　　—*USA Today*

"Flight attendant Cassie Bowden: a self-destructive alcoholic who favors one-night stands, a gifted liar, a petty thief. But she's also someone we can relate to: a soul damaged during childhood, terribly alone, and desperate for love. . . . Readers who enjoyed the imperfect heroine in Paula Hawkins's *The Girl on the Train* and the anxiety-ridden paranoia of Fyodor Dostoyevsky's *Crime and Punishment* will be hooked by this murder mystery."
—*Library Journal* (starred review)

"Bohjalian is an unfaltering storyteller who crosses genres with fluidity, from historical fiction to literary thrillers. . . . A read-in-one-sitting escapade that is as intellectually satisfying as it is emotionally entertaining."
—*Booklist* (starred review)

"The author provides enough twists for a roller coaster fan. . . . The beauty of the book is that, along with the politics of the plot, Cassie's humanity comes through. . . . The last hundred pages . . . turn tense as you try to follow the unexpected but believable surprises Bohjalian has in store and answers whether Cassie can find salvation."
—*St. Louis Post-Dispatch*

"A high-octane thriller that will have you holding your breath with every . . . page. As if ripped from today's headlines, Bohjalian paints a vivid portrait of death and despair on a canvas of Russian espionage."
—*The Free Lance-Star* (Fredericksburg, VA)

"A magnificent book. . . . Sleek and gorgeous. . . . This is a master class in fiction."
—Augusten Burroughs

"The stakes couldn't be higher (literally) as Cassandra pieces together a mystery while working forty thousand feet above ground. . . . Read it before Kaley Cuoco stars in the upcoming series!"
—*Cosmopolitan*

Chris Bohjalian

THE FLIGHT ATTENDANT

Chris Bohjalian is the author of twenty books, including such *New York Times* bestsellers as *The Guest Room*, *The Light in the Ruins*, *The Sandcastle Girls*, *The Double Bind*, and *Skeletons at the Feast*. His novel *Midwives* was a number one *New York Times* bestseller and a selection of Oprah's Book Club. His work has been translated into more than thirty languages, and three of his books have become movies (*Secrets of Eden*, *Midwives*, and *Past the Bleachers*). His novels have been chosen as best books of the year by *The Washington Post*, *St. Louis Post-Dispatch*, *Hartford Courant*, *Milwaukee Journal Sentinel*, *Publishers Weekly*, *Library Journal*, *Kirkus Reviews*, *BookPage*, and *Salon*. He lives in Vermont. Visit him at www.chrisbohjalian.com or on Facebook or Twitter.

Also by Chris Bohjalian

The Sleepwalker
The Guest Room
Close Your Eyes, Hold Hands
The Light in the Ruins
The Sandcastle Girls
The Night Strangers
Secrets of Eden
Skeletons at the Feast
The Double Bind
Before You Know Kindness
Idyll Banter
The Buffalo Soldier
Trans-Sister Radio
The Law of Similars
Midwives
Water Witches
Past the Bleachers
Hangman
A Killing in the Real World

The
FLIGHT ATTENDANT

》

A NOVEL

》

CHRIS BOHJALIAN

VINTAGE CONTEMPORARIES

Vintage Books

A Division of Penguin Random House LLC

New York

FIRST VINTAGE CONTEMPORARIES EDITION, JANUARY 2019

The Library of Congress has cataloged the Doubleday edition as follows:
Names: Bohjalian, Chris, 1962– author.
Title: The flight attendant : a novel / Chris Bohjalian.
Description: First edition. | New York : Doubleday, 2018.
Identifiers: LCCN 2017034159
Subjects: LCSH: Flight attendants—Fiction. | Murder—Investigation—Fiction. |
BISAC: FICTION / Suspense. | FICTION / Mystery & Detective. /
Women Sleuths. | GSAFD: Suspense fiction. | Mystery fiction.
Classification: LCC PS3552.O495 F58 2018 | DDC 813/.54—dc23
LC record available at https://lccn.loc.gov/2017034159

Hudson Premium Edition ISBN: 978-0-525-56697-7

Book design by Maria Carella

www.vintagebooks.com

Printed in the United States of America
10 9 8 7 6 5 4 3 2 1

For Anne Messitte,
twelve books together

Men are afraid that women will laugh at them.
Women are afraid that men will kill them.

—*Margaret Atwood*

Part One

BRACE FOR IMPACT

«

1

She was aware first of the scent of the hotel shampoo, a Middle Eastern aroma reminiscent of anise, and then—when she opened her eyes—the way the light from the window was different from the light in the rooms in the hotel where the crew usually stayed. The morning sun was oozing through one slender line from the ceiling to the floor where the drapes, plush as they were, didn't quite meet and blanching a strip of carpet. She blinked, not against the light but against the thumping spikes of pain behind her eyes. She needed water, but it would take a tsunami to avert the hangover that awaited. She needed Advil, but she feared the red pills that she popped like M&M's at moments like this were distant. They were in the medicine bag in her own hotel room. In her own hotel.

And this definitely wasn't her hotel. It was his. Had she come back here? Apparently she had. She was sure she had left. She thought she had returned to the airline's considerably more modest accommodations. At least that had been her plan. After all, she had a plane to catch this morning.

Her mind slowly began to tackle the questions she would need to answer when she rolled over, the principal one being the most prosaic: what time was it? It seemed that the clock was on his side of the bed, because it wasn't on hers. On her nightstand was the phone and a china tray with date and sugar cookies and three perfectly cubed Turkish delight candies, each skewered with a toothpick-sized silver spear. Time mattered, because she had to be in the lobby of the correct hotel—her hotel—with the rest of the crew by eleven fifteen, to climb with them all into the shuttle to the airport and then the flight to Paris. Everything else, including how she was going to find the courage inside her to swing her legs over the side of the bed and sit up—a task that, given how she felt, would demand the fearlessness of an Olympic gymnast—was secondary. She breathed in slowly and deeply through her nose, the noise a soft whistle, this time inhaling a smell more pronounced than the anise: sex. Yes, the room was rich with the unmistakable scent of a luxury hotel shampoo, but she could also smell herself and she could smell him, the evidential secretions from the night before. He was still there, an absolutely silent sleeper, and she would see him once she rolled over. Once she sat up.

God, if only she'd brought him back to her room. But at dinner he had slipped her a room key, telling her he would be back by nine and to please be waiting for him there. She had. His room was a suite. It was massive, impeccably decorated and bigger than her apartment in Manhattan. The coffee table in the living room was inlaid with mother-of-pearl, the wood polished to the point that it reflected the light like a full moon. There was a bottle of Scotch in the bar—this was a real bar, not a minibar or campus fridge with a couple cans of Coke Zero on the lone shelf—that might cost more than the monthly maintenance on her apartment back in New York.

She closed her eyes against the shame, the disgust. She tried to remind herself that this was just who she was—how she was—and to ratchet down at least a little bit the self-loathing. Hadn't they had fun last night? Of course they had. At least she presumed they had. When she had first opened her eyes, she had hoped for a moment that she had only been passed-out drunk, but no, it was clear that she had been blackout drunk. Again. The difference was not semantics. She experienced both. Passed-out drunk was more humiliating when it happened: she was the woman with her face half buried in the throw pillows on the couch, oblivious to the party moving on without her. Blackout drunk was more embarrassing the next morning, when she woke up in strange beds with strange men, and not a clue how she'd gotten there. She could recall this hotel room and this man, and that was a good sign, but clearly there were chasm-like gaps in her memory. The last thing she could recall was leaving. In her memory, she was dressed and she was exiting this suite, and he was in one of those marvelous hotel room robes, black and white zebra stripes on the exterior, terrycloth on the inside, and joking about the broken bottle of Stoli they had yet to clean up. He'd mumbled that he would deal with it—the spilled vodka, the dagger-like shards—in the morning.

And yet here she was. Back in his bed.

She sighed slowly, carefully, so as not to exacerbate her looming headache. Finally she lifted her head and felt a wave of nausea as the room spun. Instantly she sank back into the pillow's voluptuous, downy welcome.

On the plane, he had been wearing cologne, something woody that she liked and he had told her was Russian. He loved the Russians, he said. Yes, he was an American, a southern boy, he joked, but he was descended from Russians and felt he still had a Russian soul. Pushkin. *Eugene Onegin*. Something about the gleamings of an empty heart. The Russians poured money into his hedge fund, he beamed—and it was a beam, not a boast, it was so childlike—and the crazy oligarchs were like uncles to him. They were like teddy bears, not Russian bears, in his hands.

She couldn't smell the cologne now, and then she remembered showering with him. It was a large, elegant shower of black-and-white-striped marble, including a marble bench, where he had sat down and pulled her onto his lap as he washed her hair with that anise shampoo.

His name was Alexander Sokolov, and he was probably seven or eight years her junior: early thirties, she guessed. He liked to be called Alex because he said Al sounded too American. In a perfect world, he confessed, he would be called Alexander because that sounded Russian. But when he started work, his bosses had suggested he stick with Alex: it was internationally neutral, which was important given the amount of time he spent overseas. He had grown up in Virginia, though he had no trace of a southern accent at all, and lived now on Manhattan's Upper West Side, running a fund at Unisphere Asset Management. He was a math geek, which he said was the secret to his success and why his fund delivered the sorts of returns that kept everyone on both sides of the Atlantic so happy. It was evident that he enjoyed the work, though he insisted that in reality there were few things duller than managing other people's money, and so mostly he wanted to talk about what she did. Her war stories. He was utterly fascinated.

He had been in 2C on the flight to Dubai and he hadn't slept much on the plane—if at all. He had worked on his laptop, he had watched movies, and he had flirted with her. He had gotten to know her much better than she had gotten to know him. Before landing, they'd agreed they'd each take a catnap and then rendezvous for dinner. They were going to meet in his hotel lobby. They'd both known that dinner would be mere foreplay. She rolled his name over again in her mind one more time before bracing herself to turn over and face the whitecap breakers of pain. To face him. One more time she thought of how much arak she had drunk last night. One hundred and twenty proof. The clear liquid becoming the color of watery milk once they added the ice. And then there was the vodka, the Stolichnaya his friend had brought later that night. She'd drunk arak before; she drank it whenever she flew into Beirut, Istanbul, or Dubai. But had she ever drunk this much? She told herself no, but she was kidding herself. She had. Of course she had. One of these days she was going to get busted by the airline; one of these days she was going to fly too close to the sun and fail a drug test, and that would be the beginning of the end. It would be the beginning of the end of everything. She would be following the trail her father had hewn, and she knew where that ended.

No, it wasn't her father's trail, precisely, because he was male and she was female. She knew the truth of men and women and booze: it rarely ended well for either gender, but it was the women who wound up raped.

She sighed. It was too bad the airline didn't fly into Riyadh. The hotel minibars in Saudi didn't even have alcohol. She'd have to wear an ankle-length abaya. She wouldn't be out alone, ever, so she wouldn't be out picking up men, ever. Meeting them in their hotel lobbies. Ever.

She thought she might have been fine right now if Alex hadn't taken that call from his friend and had them get dressed. The woman—and Cassie believed that her name was Miranda, but even if this hadn't been one of her blackout benders, her memory this morning was still pretty damn foggy—had phoned just after they'd emerged from the shower, clean and postcoital and still a little drunk, and said she was going to stop by the hotel room for a nightcap. Cassie thought she was somehow involved in the hedge fund, too, and was going to be in the same meetings with Alex tomorrow. She may also have had something to do with Dubai real estate, but Cassie wasn't sure where she had gotten this idea.

When Miranda arrived at the suite, it was clear that she and Alex really had very little history together, and were actually meeting for the first time. And yet they had a past that transcended work: it seemed they had mutual friends and business connections in the construction that was everywhere in this science fiction–like city by the sea. She was his age, with dark almond eyes and deep auburn hair that she had pulled back into an impeccable French twist. She was wearing baggy black slacks and an elegant but modest red and black tunic. And she sure as hell could hold her booze. The three of them had sat in the suite's sumptuous living room for perhaps an hour, maybe a little longer, as they drained the vodka Miranda had brought. It crossed Cassie's mind that this was some sort of planned threesome, and while she wasn't about to initiate it herself, she knew she'd be game if either Alex or Miranda did. Something about the moment—the booze, the banter, the suite— had her aroused once again. Alex and Miranda were in chairs on opposite sides of that exquisite coffee table and she was alone on the couch, and somehow the fact that the three of them were a few feet apart made the moment feel even more heated. But, in the end, this wasn't about a threesome. Miranda left, giving both her and Alex only air kisses beside their cheeks before Alex shut the door behind her. Still, Miranda couldn't even have reached the elevator down some distant corridor before Alex was stripping off her clothes, then his, and they were making love again, this time in the bedroom on that magnificent king with the massive headboard that was shaped like an Arabian arch.

But then she had gotten dressed. She had. She knew she had. She was going to return to the airline's hotel. Hadn't she said goodbye to him at the entrance to his suite? Hadn't she even gotten as far as the elevator, wherever it was, on his floor?

Maybe. Maybe not.

It really didn't matter, because clearly she had come back to his room and climbed back into his bed.

Assuming, of course, that she had even really left. Maybe she was remembering the walk alone from the restaurant to his hotel room after dinner, when Alex had said he had a brief meeting with an investor. He'd told her he wanted her waiting for him naked in his room. She'd obliged.

And now here she was, naked again.

Finally she took a breath, cringing against the spikes behind her eyes, and turned 180 degrees in the bed to face Alex.

And there he was. For a split second, her mind registered only the idea that something was wrong. It may have been the body's utter stillness, but it may also have been the way she could sense the amphibian cold. But then she saw the blood. She saw the great crimson stain on the pillow, and a slick, still wet pool on the crisp white sheets. He was flat on his back. She saw his neck, the yawning red trench from one side of his jaw to the other, and how the blood had geysered onto his chest and up against the bottom of his chin, smothering the black stubble like honey.

Reflexively, despite the pain, she threw off the sheet and leapt from the bed, retreating into those drapes against the window. It was while standing there, her arms wrapped around her chest like a straitjacket, that she noticed there was blood on her, too. It was in her hair and on her shoulder. It was on her hands. (Later, when she was in the elevator, she would surmise that the only reason she hadn't screamed was self-preservation. Given the way her head was pulsating, the sound of her own desperate, panicked shriek might have killed her.)

Had she ever seen so much blood? Not from a human. A deer, maybe, back when she was a kid in Kentucky. But not a person. Never.

On the other side of the body, on the far side of the bed, was the clock. It was digital. It read 9:51. She had not quite ninety minutes to be in the lobby of another hotel and ready to leave for the airport and the flight back to Paris and then, tomorrow, home to JFK.

Her back against the drapes, she slid first into a baseball catcher's pose and then onto the floor. She tried to focus, to make decisions. Her mind only slowed when she spotted the swath of broken glass on the floor, a constellation on the carpet between the foot of the bed and the elegant credenza inside which was the TV. Once upon a time, it had been the bottle of Stoli that Miranda had brought; now it was mostly slivers and triangular fragments that were almost pretty, though the neck was still attached to the shoulder and the shoulder was a jagged edge. And then, when she realized what that might mean, she felt the nausea rising up inside her. She raced to the bathroom with her hands on her mouth, as if her fingers really had any chance—any chance at all—of damming such a gravity-defying waterfall, and made it to the toilet. But just barely.

She sat with her back against the bidet, facing the shower, and watched the nozzles from the ceiling and the walls sway. She started to make a list in her mind of all she could remember from last night, but she was beginning to realize just how much was on the far side of that curtain of arak and vodka and whatever else they had drunk. She tried to imagine what might have led her to take a broken bottle and slash open the guy's neck as if she and her father were gutting a deer. She wasn't a barroom brawler. She'd never hurt anyone—at least not physically. But her behavior when she was drinking, when she had drowned all reason in tequila or gin, was legendary. In theory, there was a first for everything, though it made no sense to her that she would have killed him. Most of what people told her she did during blackouts was degrading and caustic and (on occasion) dangerous to herself. But it wasn't violent.

She realized that the very first thing she had to do was make sure that the "Do Not Disturb" sign was on the hotel room door. She needed to keep housekeeping at bay while she figured out what the hell to do. She blinked. She blinked again. She was astonished at how fast the body of Alex Sokolov had sobered her up and made the pain of yet another tectonic hangover and the remorse from yet another one-night hookup seem rather inconsequential.

«   «

She stared for a moment at the hotel phone in the living room of the suite, and the button for the front desk. In the end, she didn't pick it up.

Instead she showered. She shampooed the blood from her hair and scrubbed it off her shoulder and hands as if it was tar. She didn't know the specifics of the death penalty in the United Arab Emirates, but presumed it was more civilized than next door in Saudi Arabia. (She had a vague sense from the TV news that public beheadings were only a little less popular than soccer in Saudi.) Still, she didn't want to find out.

She really had two choices: either she called someone the moment she emerged from the shower or she didn't. She was either here for a long time—a very long time—or she was on the flight to France in a couple of hours. The words echoed inside her: *a very long time.* Good Lord, she recalled some poor American college student who spent years in a prison in Italy awaiting trial for a murder she swore she didn't commit. She shuddered to think what loomed for her here in the Middle East, especially since she presumed no one would believe that someone else had come into the suite, nearly decapitated Alex Sokolov, and spared her. And if she did choose the first option, alerting people to the corpse in the bed where she'd slept, did she call the front desk or did she call the airline? Did she call the American embassy?

The choice hinged in part on whether she really had killed this young hedge fund manager. Despite the evidence, a part of her—the biggest part of her—honestly believed that she hadn't. Certainly she had done other batshit crazy things when she was in the blotto zone: when she was blackout crazy drunk. She'd hear the next morning about the things she had said. She'd hear the next day about the things she had done. Sometimes she'd hear when she was back at a particular bar.

You were doing this insanely provocative, pretend karaoke—without music, Cassie, without music! There was no karaoke machine!—while standing on a stool in the corner.

Oh, God, you had an epic face plant just outside the ladies' room. How did you not break your nose?

You were taking off your clothes and trying to get the bartender to do naked yoga with you.

It was only dumb luck that she had no DUIs, no crimes and misdemeanors in her history, and thus was still allowed to fly. She thought once more of her father. As she dried herself—quickly, roughly—she recalled the men and the mistakes in her own past, and she counted once more all the different countries in which she had slept with strangers and woken up sick in unfamiliar beds. Even now, probably no one in the crew was thinking anything about the fact that she was not with them at their own hotel. Most of them barely knew her, but most of them knew women and men just like her. Her behavior might have been extreme, but it was not uncommon.

If she hadn't slashed the throat of the man who had tenderly washed her hair in the shower, she guessed she should be deeply grateful that whoever did hadn't bothered to kill her. And that, in turn, suggested either a respect for human life or a distaste for collateral damage that was rather at odds with the ferocity with which he (or she or they) had murdered last night's drunken dalliance. It also might mean that she was being set up. Someone—perhaps even that woman who had come to their room for a drink—wanted her to be blamed for this crime. Two thoughts crossed her mind, and she was unsure whether to categorize them as paranoid or uncharacteristically clearheaded: the first was that she hadn't killed Sokolov, but her fingerprints were nevertheless all over the neck of the broken bottle. The second was the notion that it wasn't the arak that had put her out so thoroughly: she'd been drugged. They'd been drugged. Maybe it was the vodka in that very bottle that Miranda had brought. The woman claimed she'd brought it because she wasn't sure if the minibars at the Royal Phoenician had liquor; in Dubai, some hotel minibars did, some didn't. Perhaps there was no more to the gift than that; perhaps there was.

She took a little comfort in the fact that no one she knew had any idea that she was here in room 511 at the Royal Phoenician. Sure, Megan and Shane had seen her flirting with Alex in 2C, but she'd never told the two flight attendants that she was going to see him. She and Alex had been discreet when they'd discussed where and when they would meet. She hadn't given him her cell because he hadn't asked for it—which meant that she wouldn't be in his phone.

There was only Miranda.

But Miranda knew a lot. Miranda knew that she was a flight attendant. Miranda knew her name—at least her first name. Miranda would, Cassie assumed, be the one to call the hotel when Alex missed whatever meeting he was supposed to be in and didn't answer his cell.

In the end, she told herself that she did problematic things when she drank, but slashing people's throats wasn't among them.

At least she didn't think it was. But she also wasn't going to take the bait and call the front desk. She was going to get as far away from Dubai and the Arabian Peninsula as she could, and she would deal with Miranda's allegations—and, yes, her own guilt—when she was back in the United States.

And so she put the soap and washcloth she had used in the shower into her shoulder bag. She would take the towel, too, though she imagined that her DNA was all over the bedsheets. Nevertheless, after she was dressed she ran a second washcloth over everything she could recall handling in the bedroom, the bathroom, and the living room, hoping to expunge her prints. She wiped down the glasses, the minibar, and the bottles—all those empty bottles. The remote to the entertainment system. Then, because much of the night before was a blur with yawning black holes in between, she ran the washcloth over everything she was even likely to have touched. The hotel room's doorknobs and closet handles, its hangers, the footboard to the bed. That beautiful headboard, too.

When she was done, she picked up all the pieces of the bottle she could find. She gazed for a moment at the jagged edge of the bottle's shoulder. Could this thing have really cut open Alex Sokolov's neck with the thoroughness of an autopsy scalpel? She had no idea. Then she took it, too, rolling it up in the towel.

She pulled aside the drapes and blinked at the sun and the flat blue water a few blocks distant. Though their room was only on the fifth floor, the lobby was as tall and cavernous as a casino, and they had had an unobstructed view of the azure sea.

She told herself that when she was safely back in the United States—assuming she made it back there—she would talk to a lawyer. One step at a time. The important thing right now was to get back to her own hotel, make up a man from the night before if anyone asked, and be in the lobby at eleven fifteen. She had a feeling that she wasn't going to breathe easy until the plane lifted off the runway. No, she knew in her heart that she wasn't going to relax even then. At least not completely. Of all the horrible things she had done when she was drunk, nothing topped leaving behind a body that had bled out in the bed beside her.

And, much to her dismay, she was doing this sober.

« «

She left the "Do Not Disturb" sign dangling by its elegant gold braid around the hotel room doorknob to keep Alex's body undiscovered for as long as possible, and stood for a moment trying to remember where the hell the elevator was. The hotel was massive, with corridors that seemed to snake in all directions. Finally she started off, walking quickly down empty hallways, and eventually she found the elevator bank. The lift seemed to take forever to arrive, but she reassured herself that time was just passing slowly because she was nervous. No, not nervous: she was terrified. She calmed herself by thinking how she could still tell someone at the front desk what had happened and tell them—insist—that she had done nothing wrong. After all, at this point, she had done nothing irrevocable: she was simply getting into the elevator (which was empty, too, a good omen). But then she was crossing the magnificent lobby with its palm trees and oriental carpets and opulent Moorish canopies (and, yes, security cameras), her face hidden behind her sunglasses and the scarf that she'd bought before leaving the Dubai airport yesterday, and then she was passing the row of stores inside the hotel. The shop for Christian Louboutin shoes. The one that sold nothing but Hermès scarves. A rather elegant arts and trinkets boutique. She remembered now, the images a fog, that she had ventured into all three of them. It was after dinner, on her way to the elevator. When she was waiting for Alex to return from his meeting. In one of the stores she had seen a leopard-print scarf—luminous, black and yellow swirls of spots, gold beading along the borders—that she had longed for but knew she couldn't afford.

And now she walked ever faster, risking eye contact with no

one, ignoring the concierge and the bellmen and the gree
ing tea, and then she was back outside in the world of bu.
desert heat and the hotel's line of fountains around twin reflecting
pools. She almost climbed into a cab, but then stopped herself. Why
give anyone additional proof that she had ever been at this hotel
since, it seemed now, she had made her choice? She was outside.
She was leaving. And with every step she took the idea of turning
around grew more problematic—if not impossible—because every
step took her from perceived innocence to perceived guilt. She was
corroborating the allegations that this Miranda person was sure to
make.

She checked her watch: she guessed she was a ten-minute walk
from her own hotel, which would give her perhaps fifteen minutes to change into her uniform and get downstairs to the lobby.
Maybe even twenty, because obviously they wouldn't leave without her. She started to text Megan that she was on her way, but
then stopped herself. Texts left a trail. For a moment, she took
comfort in the fact that Megan hadn't texted her, but then she was
hit hard by a revelation: she disappeared in foreign cities, even here
in the Middle East, with such disturbing frequency that Megan,
the person she had flown with most often over the years, didn't
seem at all worried by her absence.

God, she was a mess. An absolute mess.

And yet she moved forward because like the planes on which she
lived so much of her life, that was the only direction that allowed
for survival. Think shark. She turned right, down the great oval of
the hotel's driveway. She gazed one last time at the palms and the
fountains and the long line of town cars with their bulletproof glass
windows, and started toward the airline's less opulent accommodations. She sighed. She had made her choice—just one more bad
choice in a life riddled with them—and there was no turning back.

2

"You could film science fiction here. Crazy science fiction. Imagine giving a filmmaker like Tarkovsky this palette. Look out a window on the ninety-ninth floor of the Burj Khalifa, especially when the fog is just right in the morning. The spikes are above the clouds. The spires are in the sky—literally in the sky. They're growing from the mist. The best new buildings in this city? I tell you, they were built for the Martians."

Elena nodded. She'd seen plenty of pictures of Dubai before arriving and watched hours of video. She'd had a window seat on her flight, and though she hadn't been able to glimpse those massive man-made harbors that were shaped like palms as the plane descended, on their final approach she'd enjoyed the *Blade Runner*-esque skyscrapers. Even this hotel bar was a series of futuristic black columns, glass obelisks, and chandeliers that fell from the ceiling like slender icicles. The barstools were the highest she'd ever seen in her life. Dubai was a vertical world between the flatness of sand and the flatness of sea, a cutting-edge outpost just across the Persian Gulf from Iran. It was utterly different from Gaziantep, the Turkish city where she'd spent most of the last month stalking her prey. Parts of that city still felt like B-roll footage from a movie set in the Middle East during the First World War. She half expected to see Peter O'Toole in his *Lawrence of Arabia* garb in the souk.

"How was your meeting?" she asked Viktor. He'd just come from NovaSkies.

"They have a drone that hunts drones," he said, not really

answering her question, and she couldn't decide if he was dismissing what he saw or whether he was still ruminating on its potential for Syria. Then: "Any trouble with Alex's computer?" He was wearing a black suit and a white oxford shirt without a necktie. The bar was air-conditioned—it was easily a hundred degrees outside, though no more than sixty-five inside the lounge—but he had seemed utterly impervious to the heat when they had walked here. She had nearly wilted. But then she had been melting ever since the moment she had first emerged from the airport terminal.

"Not at all," she said, handing him a flash drive that masqueraded as the sort of tiny toothpaste tube that came with an airline travel kit. "The Dubai police are good. They'll presume it was some angry investor. They know we have a tendency to overreact."

"You are an angry investor. At least you should be. He was stealing from you, too."

"I know."

She was drinking iced tea because of all the Stoli she'd had to drink last night to keep up with that pair of idiot Americans. But, then, she rarely drank at lunch. Viktor was savoring a cocktail made with rye and Arabian bitters. The bar was on the first floor, and she gazed out at the midday sun. "Yes, the Dubai police are good. Very good," he said, echoing her darkly. "Excellent, really. So are the security forces. I was thinking of that story from a couple of years ago, when that Hamas leader was murdered in his hotel room."

She nodded. She knew the story; they all did. The Dubai authorities were able to track the executioners with the cameras they had placed across the city. They followed them from the airport to a tennis club, where they rendezvoused, and then to the hotel where they executed the military commander. It was Mossad, of course—and Dubai was so furious that no one had told them the hit was coming that they had burned the agents. They'd published the security camera footage and outed them all. "It was more than a couple years ago. More like ten. I was still in college," she corrected him.

"Of course you were. Of course. Your father was still alive," he said, and he offered a smile tinged ever so slightly with meanness. Not outright cruelty, but spite: he didn't like to be corrected. He knew how much she had loved her father, and reminding her of his death was a small rebuke. But once he had made his point, his face changed: "And Alex was asleep?"

"He was. Passed out would be more accurate."

"You didn't shoot him?"

"I brought the twenty-two and a silencer, but no, in the end I didn't. I saw no reason to risk any noise at all. And, I imagine, this will be viewed in some circles as especially Arabian justice—and a more dramatic message."

He dabbed at his mouth with the back of his hand, and then glanced at his watch. "I don't like drama."

On some level, she knew this. It was why she hadn't yet told him about the flight attendant. She'd planned to, but couldn't decide now whether she should. After all, the woman had been hammered; she'd barely remember anything from her one-night hookup with Sokolov. Besides, who would she tell? Why would she tell? When the woman announced that she was going to leave—return to her own hotel—because she had a flight to Paris the next morning, Elena had decided to wait. She'd leave, too, and return later to take care of Sokolov. He was at least as drunk as his new acquaintance, and so it had been easy to slide one of his room keys off the side table and into her purse.

"I was efficient," she said. "Don't worry." She watched the bartender mixing chocolate liqueur and raspberries, and tried to pick out the lightweight in the bar who it was for. She decided the likely recipient was the American blonde with a man twice her age. In a moment, she saw she was right.

"I do worry. You should, too. It's when we stop worrying that we grow careless and bad things happen."

She hated it when he lectured her, but it never made sense to try and defend oneself to a man like Viktor—especially after a comment that was pretty damn innocuous by his standards. He was capable of far worse. He'd come of age in the Spetsnaz, the Soviet army's special forces, in Afghanistan in the 1980s, and had proven particularly adept at convincing Mujahideen to talk. In places like Kunduz and Faizabad, her father told her, Viktor's superiors had often had to look the other way: he got results, but his methods were reminiscent of the Lubyanka basement in the 1950s. Today he was among those who didn't give a damn about the Chemical Weapons Convention, and shrugged at the dead children of Khan Sheikhoun. Before traveling back to Dubai, he'd been in Damascus.

Moreover, it was certainly possible that she had been careless—though not in the way he was suggesting. The truth was, when she had discovered that Sokolov had company, she simply couldn't bring herself to execute the pathetic, inebriated flight attendant who just happened to be in the wrong place at the wrong time. That wasn't what she did; that wasn't who she was. Besides, there would have been blowback from that decision, too. "You're right," she said contritely. "I know you are."

"And so Alex had been drinking when you met him. I imagine he did not make a very good first impression."

"No, not really."

He smiled ever so slightly. "You don't approve of sloppy drunks, do you?"

"I don't," she replied. "I don't approve of sloppiness, period."

3

Cassie bought a bottle of Advil in a pharmacy on the way back to her own hotel and swallowed three pills without water. She didn't want to wait until she got back to her room to start treatment. She put the washcloth and soap from the hotel into the trash can on the corner. In another one she threw away the towel and the remnants of the Stolichnaya bottle, including the broken shoulder. But then she realized that the bottom of her shoulder bag was still dotted with shards and smaller pieces of glass. The lining, no doubt, had yet more traces of Sokolov's DNA. The bag itself was evidence. And so she removed her wallet and passport, her apartment keys and her phone. Her hairbrush. She retrieved her foundation and her mascara, and had a moment of panic when she rooted around inside it and couldn't find her lipstick. But she couldn't focus on that now, it was too late. She obviously wasn't returning to the suite to see if she had left it there. Then she dropped everything she had retrieved into the plastic bag from the pharmacy. A block away, she tossed her shoulder bag into yet a third trash can.

As she walked, she wished she were one of the women lost but for their eyes in the dark folds of their abayas. She thought she might puddle in this crazy desert heat; she wondered if she might liquefy like a Popsicle.

She had been back in her own hotel room barely a moment—she had taken off her scarf and sunglasses and lifted her suitcase onto one of the two queen beds to begin packing, but that was all—when there was a knock on her door and her heart stopped.

This was it: Hotel security. The Dubai police. Someone from the American embassy. When she peeked through the peephole, however, there was Megan, the flight attendant already in her uniform. Cassie was relieved, but felt a pang: Was this how she would feel for the rest of her life when there was a knock on her door or the phone rang? Once again she considered returning to room 511 at the Royal Phoenician and pushing restart.

But she didn't. She opened the door and Megan stared at her for a long moment, studying her, before breezing past her into the room. Inside, the woman leaned against the dresser, appraising her yet again. Then she smiled ever so slightly.

"You know, Cassie, I kind of expected you to look worse," Megan said. "Can I ask where you were? Dare I ask? I was actually getting worried."

Cassie shrugged, pulling off her scarf and wedging it into a pocket in her suitcase. She kicked off her heels. Lord, what did it say about her that she continued to wear heels, even when she was planning (or, at least, expecting) to get sloshed? How many times had the combination of sangria and slingbacks turned a flight of stairs into Everest's Hillary Step? "Seriously?" she asked, trying to make light of Megan's concern. She stepped out of her skirt and began to unbutton her blouse. "Why were you worried?"

Instead of answering, Megan asked, "Were you with that young guy from the flight here?" She noticed Megan's use of the word *young*. He was young. At least he had been. Megan was fifty-one, twelve years older than she was and at least a decade and a half—and very likely two—older than Alex Sokolov. "You know who I mean," she went on. "The guy in two C."

Cassie couldn't risk the transparency of eye contact. Instead she rolled her blouse into a tight tube on the bed, folding it in half and pressing the air out, and placed it in the section of her suitcase she reserved for her dirty clothes. "Two C? God, no. Didn't he say he worked for some kind of hedge fund? Sounds kind of boring. Not exactly my type."

"Rich isn't your type?"

"I have no problem with rich. But aren't those guys crazy alpha?"

"You two were chatting each other up pretty seriously—especially before we started our descent."

She sat down on the bed she had napped in yesterday afternoon to climb into the airline's requisite black pantyhose. "Not really," she said casually.

"So you weren't with him?"

"I told you: no."

"You hungover?"

"I'd nod, but it would hurt too much. Yes."

"You going to be okay?"

"Of course." She stood, adjusted her pantyhose, and leaned over gingerly, reaching into her suitcase for her return uniform. When she stood up, she stood up slowly, hoping to avoid (or at least minimize) the wave of nausea that tended to accompany moving her head at moments like this.

"Want an aspirin?"

"I'm good. I had some with me."

"Of course you did. Can I ask you something?"

"Who was I with if it wasn't that guy from the plane?"

"No. I wasn't going to ask that."

She waited.

"Why?" Megan asked. "Why do you always do this to yourself? One of these days you're going to get yourself killed. I know Dubai is safe. I get it. But we're still in the Middle East. You're still a woman. This isn't Paris and this isn't New York." She sat down on the bed, watching as Cassie stepped into the black uniform dress with the slimming blue and red stripes. The word *killed* echoed inside Cassie in ways that made her shudder. When else, before this morning, had she seen a corpse? At funerals. Not her father's, because the car crash had necessitated a closed casket. But at her mother's. And at the pair of funerals for her grandparents who had died and chosen not to be cremated. She recalled Alex Sokolov's neck. She thought his eyes had been shut, if only because she would have remembered if they had been open, but that did not diminish in her mind the violence of his death.

"I'm fine," she lied. "I'm fine." She hoped saying it twice might make it true. Walk the talk.

"You're not fine," Megan said, her eyes skeptical. "People who are fine don't do—"

"Don't do what?" she snapped, the three syllables lash-like and defensive. Her pique surprised her. "What precisely have I done wrong?"

Megan leaned forward, her hands on her knees, wondering what to say. Cassie couldn't decide whether her friend—no, she was a work acquaintance really, *friend* would suggest they were much closer than they actually were—would begin with the drinking or the sex. When she remained silent, Cassie told her, "Don't judge me. I mean that. You have a great husband and two sweet kids—"

"They're sixteen and thirteen. They stopped being sweet years ago," Megan said, a peace offering of sorts.

"But my life isn't your life. My choices aren't yours."

"I know. I get it. Just reassure me: you're completely sober?"

"Yes. Of course."

"Okay, then, I'll bite. Who was it? Who were you with?"

"Just a guy I met at the bar."

"I didn't see you downstairs."

Though Megan's room was next to hers, Cassie was confident that the other flight attendant had still been dozing when she had left their hotel the previous evening. The slightest subterfuge would do. "We met quickly and we left quickly. We went back to his hotel. What did you do?" She reached into the suitcase for the airline's neck scarf and belt.

"I had dinner with Shane and Victoria and Jada. We went to a Japanese restaurant Shane knows. It was nice. Then we all went back to our rooms and we slept. We rested," Megan said.

Cassie had the sense that the woman hadn't meant to sound sanctimonious, but that last, two-word sentence had rubbed her the wrong way. "Good," she said simply. As she started to tie the scarf around her neck, she stopped. She couldn't help but recall the horrific gash across Alex Sokolov's throat. She shivered ever so slightly at the neck's sheer vulnerability.

Megan saw the involuntary quiver and misread its meaning. She stood up and took both of Cassie's hands in hers. "Do yourself a favor," she began.

Cassie said nothing, but felt herself starting to coil inside, prepared to bite back if Megan said something—anything— judgmental.

"Start again," the other flight attendant said simply, her tone motherly and kind. "Getting dressed, I mean. Put on clean under-wear this time. I'll make sure they hold the van." Then she released Cassie's fingers and left her alone in her hotel room.

《 《

Stewart, their first officer, was chattering away in the first row of the van as they worked their way through Dubai traffic to the airport. Cassie would have preferred to have the air conditioning on a little higher to help combat her queasiness, but she didn't want to draw any more attention to herself than necessary. Their flight didn't leave for a couple of hours, but just in case she thought she better make sure that she had Dramamine in her kit before they boarded.

"Remember, this is Hamburg, and we all know that ground control there is, well, German," the first officer was saying. He had turned around so he could speak to all of them. The van had four-teen seats, including the driver's, and every seat but his was taken with the flight crew. She was in the very back row with Megan and Shane, burrowing as best she could against the window in the corner.

The captain, though he and his family had lived in the Mid-west forever, was descended from Germans, and Cassie wondered whether the first officer was having fun at his expense or German would somehow be relevant to this story. This was the first time she had flown with Stewart, so she had no idea. She knew only that he was a very big talker.

"And that means what, precisely?" the captain asked, his tone good-natured. He was in his midfifties, balding, but still lean and handsome in a classic, right stuff sort of way. She'd flown with him perhaps half a dozen times over the last five years, since she had begun flying internationally, and enjoyed watching the passengers nod approvingly when they peered into the flight deck and spotted pilots like him as they boarded.

"All business," Stewart answered. "You don't screw around. And the plane's on the ground now. We're talking British Airways, so the call sign is Speedbird. Ground control tells Speedbird to taxi to gate alpha two-seven. But the plane? Stops. Stops completely. So ground says, 'Speedbird, are you having a problem finding the gate?' And Speedbird replies, 'Looking it up now.'"

"God, I see where this is going," the captain said, chuckling.

"Yup. Ground is seriously bent out of shape, seriously impatient. They ask, 'Speedbird, have you really never been to Hamburg before?' And the Speedbird captain replies, his voice this icy British, 'I have. Twice. But it was 1943, so I didn't land.'"

Megan and Shane both laughed politely. Megan even nodded a little knowingly. But the captain, who had been Air Force, shook his head and asked, "On what canceled sitcom did you hear that ancient joke?"

"You think it's apocryphal?"

"Yes. I think it's . . . apocryphal. And older than sand. Usually the joke is set in Frankfurt."

"I don't know," Megan chimed in, and she started to say something about a German friend who flew with Lufthansa, but all Cassie could feel now was the impatience of that German controller, real or imagined, in the tower. The van was hardly moving. No one around her seemed all that alarmed since the plane wasn't going to leave without them, and in the end they would probably get to the airport with plenty of time to spare. But the longer they were here in traffic, the more likely it was that she would still be in Dubai when Sokolov's body was found. That "Do Not Disturb" sign had bought her a couple of hours, no more. For all she knew, people—including Miranda—had been texting the fellow for ninety minutes, wondering why he wasn't at some meeting. Any moment now, they might send hotel security upstairs to open the door.

She gazed out the window and saw a police car—one of the force's new Lamborghinis—stuck in traffic right beside them. The cops here wore dark-green berets and short-sleeved olive shirts. The driver looked up and saw her. He was a young guy with a thick mustache. He tipped his beret and smiled in a way that struck Cassie as more chivalrous than flirtatious. She gave him a small wave in return but was glad she was wearing her sunglasses and scarf. She told herself that perhaps she could still go back to the hotel. Even now. Maybe it wasn't too late, and in her head she heard herself shouting to the driver to stop here, please, just let her out.

Though that assumed that she really hadn't killed Sokolov. She didn't believe that she had—that just wasn't who she was—but who else could have done it? The self-doubt had been inflating like a balloon for nearly two hours.

And so she said nothing, and the van inched forward and the police car inched forward, and Stewart continued to prattle on, and other small conversations began to bubble up among the crew.

"Do we even need pilots in bombers anymore? I guess we use them, right? But don't we do most of our damage with drones?" wondered Shane.

"Ask Cassie," murmured Megan. "Her brother-in-law is in the military."

"Really? Air Force? Drones? I love drones. I think it's so cool when there's a drone at a wedding."

"He has nothing to do with drones, at least as far as I know," she answered. "He's in the Army, not the Air Force."

"Oh? Where's he stationed? America or overseas?"

"These days he's right where my sister and I grew up: Kentucky. That's how they met. He's a major at the Blue Grass Army Depot."

"Sounds almost pastoral," said Jada.

"Hah! It's an old chemical weapons facility," Cassie corrected her.

"An engineer at a chemical weapons plant? That sounds scary," Shane murmured.

"I think he helps supervise the elimination of things that are scary. Our stockpile," she answered, but she honestly had no idea. They didn't talk about it. For all she knew, he supervised the production of sarin gas. Then, just as the traffic was finally starting to move, she heard the sirens. They all did.

"That can't be good," Stewart said.

"Fire trucks?" asked one of the other flight attendants, a fellow her age with whom she was flying for the first time. She hadn't gotten to know him at all on the two flights here because he was working the economy cabin while she was in first.

"No," the driver said. "Those are police sirens." Almost on cue, the police car beside the van turned on its lights and started trying to extricate itself from the quagmire and perform a U-turn. "They're south of us. They're on Jumeirah."

She felt herself growing flushed because the Royal Phoenician was on Jumeirah, and she had to reassure herself that Jumeirah was a main thoroughfare in the city and the driver was only speculating. All they really knew was that the sirens were heading for a destination behind them.

"I guess I shouldn't have left a box with a little ISIS flag and a ticking clock in the lobby," Stewart said.

"I really wouldn't make jokes like that, Stewart," Jada told him, reproachful and a little appalled. The flight attendant had a beautiful heart for a face, but now it registered only displeasure. "Certainly not these days and certainly not here—and certainly not if you want any of us to be your friend."

"Too soon?" Stewart asked.

"Too tasteless. Too offensive. Too stupid."

Megan turned toward her and whispered, "Did you forget your purse?"

Cassie rubbed her eyes. She couldn't say that she lost it: she still had her passport and wallet and phone. "It's a long story."

"Tell me."

"I spilled a glass of red wine on it. So I pitched it."

"You threw it away?"

"Yes."

"Where?"

"Does it matter? Let it go."

"You okay?"

She nodded. "Of course. Why?"

"You snapped at me."

"I'm sorry."

"And you look a little clammy."

"I'm fine."

Nevertheless, she was relieved when Megan called to the front of the van and asked the driver if he could please get them a little more air here in the back.

« «

The traffic wasn't much better on the Sheikh Zayed, the highway, even when the loudspeakers on the minarets started to broadcast the muezzin's midday call to worship. By the time they arrived at the airport, they had to rush straight to the plane. It was ready and, almost miraculously, they still had a shot at an on-time departure. Megan was the cabin service director on this flight and Shane was the purser. Once more, Cassie would be in first class. Her July bid included both the route (Paris, Dubai) and the cabin (first). The sky marshal, a heavyset American in a nondescript windbreaker with an aisle seat in the last row of the first-class cabin, seemed to be watching her as he settled in for the flight, but she took a breath and told herself that she was being paranoid.

The safety briefing was a video, but she was still expected to remain alert in the front of the aisle to encourage the passengers to actually pay attention. In this cabin, none ever did. Some wouldn't even take off their headphones or look up from their tablets or newspapers. It wasn't merely that they were all frequent flyers and knew the drill, it was that there was a certain machismo to not watching: to look up and listen suggested you were either afraid of flying or an outsider at thirty-five thousand feet. You were a newbie.

She started to turn back to the galley as the unduly cheerful video prattled on and caught the heel of her pump on the tacking strip, and stumbled. A Saudi executive in a pristine white thobe caught her with his left arm before she fell.

"Thank you," she said. She was embarrassed. She couldn't recall ever tripping on a plane when they were still parked at the gate. It was one thing to lose your balance when you were flying and there was turbulence. But on the ground? This was new. "That was unexpected."

"I'm happy I could help," he told her. He had a wide, magnanimous smile. He adjusted the gutra that covered his neck and hair, its iqal a thick, black halo. Then he returned to the business magazine he was reading on his tablet.

When she was back on her feet and standing with the galley and flight deck behind her, the only person watching her was the sky marshal. She wondered if he could sense, rather like a lion, her fear.

》 《

They were held at the gate and lost their on-time departure. She hadn't seen a conga line on the runway, but the minutes ticked by. Then the captain told the crew and then he told the passengers the reason for the delay: thunderstorms across the eastern Mediterranean and southern Europe. They would be here perhaps half an hour. She tried to believe this was the case, that all that was holding them up was the weather. But her anxiety only grew more pronounced. Still she worked. She and Megan brought the first-class cabin drinks and more drinks, and then they brought them mixed nuts they warmed in the ovens. The passengers in economy could only suffer in silence and fret that they would miss their connections at Charles de Gaulle. Cassie would glance out the windows, half expecting to see police vans converging upon the plane from the tunnels that snaked underneath the airport. She would pause before the front cabin door, fearing there was someone on the other side signaling her to open it, open it right now—there in her mind was the captain, emerging from the flight deck, nodding, giving her permission—because airport security was about to pull somebody off the plane. Occasionally she checked her phone to see if there were news stories of a hedge fund manager from America found dead in a Dubai hotel room, but there seemed to be nothing on Twitter or any of the news sites—at least the English sites that she could Google and read.

Finally the jet bridge was retracted and Stewart instructed them to make sure that the cabin was prepared for takeoff. He said it was time to strap in. They began their taxi, and then they were rolling down the runway and she felt the shimmy that suggested they were seconds from wheels up, and then they were. They were climbing, airborne, and they were leaving Dubai. They were, once more, leaving behind the indoor ski resort, the massive, man-made marinas in the shape of palm trees you could see from space, and the skyline with its towering, futuristic needles. The vending machines that sold gold. They were soaring over the endless rows of oil wells and oil rigs—from the sky, they looked like industrious black ants chained in place to the ground—and then the desert, endless, flat, and unfurling in waves and ripples and hillocks to the western horizon.

And with that came the tears. They were as unexpected as they were unstoppable, and she allowed them to slide down her face and muck up her mascara. She cried silently, aware that none of the passengers could see her here in her jump seat. Megan might look over and wonder at what a hot mess she had become, but Megan had flown with her enough to know that she would rally. She cried, she guessed, in some small way because she was so deeply relieved: she was leaving the Arabian Peninsula, where it was hard enough to be a woman and probably a disaster if you were a woman that men believed had nearly decapitated some poor money manager in an inexplicable fit of arak-fueled postcoital madness. But she was crying mostly, she realized, out of grief and sorrow and loss. Now that the self-preservation that had gotten her this far had begun to dissolve, she thought about the man she had left behind, and for the first time—the shock evaporating like the morning haze she'd recall as the sun would rise over the Cumberland Mountains—she began to feel the despair that walks hand in hand with bereavement.

She made a litany in her mind of the little she knew of Alex Sokolov's personal life: He was an only child. His parents in Charlottesville were starting to toy with the idea of retirement, though it was still a good ways off. (God, that only reminded her of how young he was: his parents had yet to retire.) He said he had been with the fund nearly four years—and that's what he called it whenever it came up, "the fund"—and before that he'd worked for Goldman Sachs. But he had worked in money management since getting some sort of master's in math—quantitative something and finance something—in Durham. (In the same way that he only offered the name of his employer when she asked, he only said Duke when she pressed for more details.) He preferred Tolstoy and Turgenev to Dostoevsky, but encouraged her to reread all three writers "as an adult, instead of as a student pulling an all-nighter."

He had not simply gotten them a table for two at the French bistro a couple of blocks from his hotel, he had paid off the maître d' to seat them in a corner and not seat anyone else at the table beside them. At first she'd viewed the move as pretentious male swagger, but as they were approaching their table he had whispered into her ear that he viewed romance as a totally private matter, and he wanted to romance her that night. Later he would pick up a tab that dwarfed what she usually spent over three nights in Paris and Dubai; it was more than she spent most months on groceries. He had ordered the blanquette de veau and she had ordered the coq au vin, joking that after all the arak they had consumed, it only made sense for her to eat chicken in wine (though of course, he reminded her, the alcohol would have cooked away). They had enjoyed their meal, savoring the seclusion, and taken their time. They finished a bottle of wine and then ordered still more arak. And yet despite how far down the alcohol rabbit hole they fell there, they never lost sight of the fact they were in Dubai. They both had been here before and knew that the penalties for public drunkenness were not pretty. The two of them were far from raucous. They flirted in their own little alcove, but didn't touch. He kept his voice low as he told her the things he wanted to do to her in his hotel room once he joined her there. He slid his room key across the tablecloth, and she shivered ever so slightly when their fingertips touched.

When the police would follow his credit card to the restaurant, people would recall he had been with a woman who was likely from America because the two of them had spoken English like Americans. Someone might recall that she was older than he was. But had they stood out? A bit, yes, because they had indeed ordered arak and wine and then more arak. But she was confident that at least half, perhaps even two-thirds, of the diners in the restaurant were Westerners. They hadn't made a scene.

He liked soccer, she remembered, and had played it at college. He liked squash even more, and played it still.

The notion that he, too, was a boozer—at least for one night—caused her to feel a deep, wistful ache in her heart. Everyone who drank the way she did had a reason, she supposed, and she had never pressed him for his. Did he have one? Now she'd never know. Certainly he had never wondered about her own private pain.

He smoked. She hadn't kissed a man in a while who did, and with Alex it hadn't been like kissing an ashtray. It had felt decadent in all the right ways. He said he only smoked when he traveled overseas.

In his hotel room, they had started on the bed as soon as he'd returned, atop the crimson bedspread, but then he had brought her to the shower. She'd been surprised, unsure whether she should be more stunned by his astonishing willpower that moment or insulted in some way that she didn't quite want to parse, but she had gone along and she was glad. They had made love there, her knees on that marble bench, his hands and fingers around her, between her legs, and then he had washed her hair.

And that recollection made her choke on a small, audible sob right there in her jump seat.

"God, you're crying," Megan whispered, her tone walking the tightrope between solicitous and annoyed. "Can I do something?"

"No."

"Then what's wrong?"

Cassie sniffed and wiped her face with her fingers. "I don't know," she lied. "I swear I don't. But I'm fine. Or I'll be fine."

Afterward, Miranda had arrived. Then Miranda had left and Cassie had planned to leave, too. But Alex had led her instead back to that astonishing bedroom, where they had made love again. They polished off the little bottle of arak they found in the mini-bar. (At least she believed at the time they had finished it; when she had wiped the blue glass down with the washcloth in the morning, she had heard some liquid sloshing around the bottom.) Then they went back to the vodka. For some reason, he'd had trouble unscrewing the cap and accidentally broken the bottle on the side of the nightstand. (Or had he smashed it on purpose in frustration?) Instead of cleaning it up, they'd just laughed. She thought she had gotten dressed to leave. But it was less than a blur, it was a void. She'd been naked when she awoke. What the hell happened to climbing back into her skirt and blouse and returning to her hotel?

God, it was just like so many of the other times she had woken up naked and hungover in bed with a guy, with only the slightest idea how she had gotten there—except this time the guy was dead.

She took stock once more, trying to make sense of what she

had done. What she might have done. Had he attacked her and she had defended herself? Possibly, but not likely. They'd had sex twice that she could recall. Still, no means no. Passed out isn't consent. What if behind the blackout is this: He is trying to have sex with her and she is resisting? They're drunk, they're both drunk. He is upon her, he won't stop, and she is pounding him on his head, his face, his back. She is trying to scratch him, and he is just growing angrier and more violent. She sees nearby the remnants of that bottle of Stoli. Perhaps some of the broken pieces are even on the nightstand. She reaches for one—that jagged shoulder, maybe, gripping the neck like a knife—and she lashes out at him. She slashes him across his throat. She can see in her mind the backhand motion, the resultant gash.

And then she falls back to sleep.

She wished she had looked more closely at the body that morning. She hadn't. She saw Alex's neck and that was enough. She had seen his eyes were closed, but otherwise she hadn't studied his head or his back or his arms. She honestly didn't know precisely where else she might have stabbed him.

And yet when she looked back on her history, it just didn't make sense that she would have attacked him if he was trying once again to have sex with her. A part of her life was—dear God—blackout sex. It happened. She knew from too many mornings with too many creepy guys that it did. She presumed (and the idea caused her stomach once more to churn) that she was more likely to allow herself to be raped.

To. Be. Raped. The awfulness of the expression led her to groan softly to herself.

Even if she hadn't killed Alex Sokolov, however, she had cut and run. That was a fact. The poor guy had parents and friends, and he had bled to death in the bed right beside her. And she had left him.

"You're not fine," Megan murmured. "This is different from your other, I don't know, stunts. Something happened."

"Nothing happened."

"People don't cry over nothing."

But then there was the plane's chime and they were above ten thousand feet, and she could no longer cry. She had to start work. She had to wash her face and reapply her makeup. She unstrapped and stood, resolved to be as charming and efficient as ever.

And yet as she stared at herself in the small mirror in the small bathroom, as she looked at the lines she was hiding under her eyes, the lines she artfully concealed beside her eyes, as she noted the way that the blue of her iris seemed a little less vibrant than it had when she was young—even surrounded by the moth-silk lines of hangover red around them—she felt the tears welling up once again. She recalled something her father had said to her when she was a little girl: you bury the dead and move on. It was a few years before he was so hammered that he crashed the Dodge Colt into a telephone pole with his younger daughter in the backseat; it was long before he accidentally (at least she presumed it was accidental) killed himself and a couple of teenagers who were driving home from Lexington and happened to be in the right lane when he—drunk again—was in the wrong one. She'd been eight at the time he'd given her this piece of advice, and she hadn't, as she had hoped, been allowed to ascend to the next-level ballet class with two of her friends. The teacher didn't believe she was ready.

Her father had tried to console her. Well, he said, sometimes you just have to bury the dead and move on.

Her father, alas, never took that advice. After his wife—her mother—died, he only drank more. And Cassie had neither forgotten nor gotten over the counsel he had offered her when she was in the third grade. She would think of it when her mother would die when she was fifteen and when her father would die when she was nineteen, and often after bidding farewell to the men she had seduced or been seduced by, especially those times when she would be so drunk that she hadn't insisted they wear one of the condoms she carried with her wherever she went. The truth was, there was nothing casual about casual sex. When it worked, it was intense. When it didn't, it was particularly unsatisfying. Either way, it left scars, some that were similar to the blackout scars, but some that were different: the violation was less pronounced, but the self-loathing could be fierce. (One time she had shared her father's wisdom with a stranger in bed. It was another morning after, and they were agreeing rather amicably that the night before had been a drunken, God-awful mistake. They might have become friends and should never have slept together. He, in return, had observed that as dark and inappropriate as the advice might have been, it was about what you might expect from a dad who had named his first daughter Cassandra.)

Likewise, there was no longer anything casual about her drinking, and there hadn't been for years.

There was a knock on the bathroom door and then Megan's voice. "Cassie, I hate to be a pain, but you are either okay to work this flight or you're not. This is the last time I am going to ask." Cassie imagined this was what Megan sounded like when she was urging one of her daughters to buck up and behave. The other flight attendant had beautiful children and a husband who was a management consultant in Washington, D.C., and a lovely house in northern Virginia. The woman had it all, she really did. "Cassie?"

She stood up straight in the bathroom. "I'll be right out," she said. "I'll be ready to rock and roll." Then she brushed her mascara back onto her eyelashes and ran the new lipstick she'd bought at the airport over her mouth. Landing lips, they called it. She was quick, but careful. The shade was similar to the one she had lost in Dubai. And then she emerged, promising herself that if somehow this all turned out okay, she was never going to drink again. Never. She made this promise or one like it monthly, but this time—this time—she told herself that she meant it.

4

Elena supposed that among the reasons why she was good at what she did was the simple reality that she was neither beautiful nor homely. She could look pretty when she dressed well and wore the right makeup—and so she tried to do both—but the goal was not to stand out. She was five-foot-four with deep brown eyes and chestnut-brown hair, which she kept parted in the middle when she wasn't working and in a French twist when she was. She rarely wore sunglasses in America and Russia, because she thought that sunglasses made you more noticeable. She realized here in Dubai that the opposite was true: it was the Westerners who didn't wear sunglasses who were the most memorable, and so she bought a first pair soon after landing and a second pair at one of the hotel stores right after finishing her iced tea with Viktor.

She was walking through the souk, her head scarf pulled tight, and she rather liked the absolute anonymity. She stood in a narrow aisle of spices, unsure whether the smell nearest her was the cumin or the merchant. Elena didn't cook much, but she had used cumin just enough to know that the stench could be either. He was standing behind the long buffet of containers rich with the phosphorescent colors of saffron and curry. On the racks behind him were small glass replicas of the most prominent new buildings in Dubai, each a little reminiscent of a chess piece. She'd loved chess as a child. She'd played it at school and at home with her father until she was sent away to a boarding school in Switzerland. She was rather good at it. Beside the trinket buildings were a variety of ornate, ocean-blue hookahs. She appreciated the way the market seemed to cater to both locals and tourists, though she could imagine tourists bringing home spices as well as a souvenir Burj Al Arab, the iconic Dubai hotel that looked like a gigantic—as in fifty-six-story gigantic—sail. She thought of the Eastern Market near the apartment she'd had when she'd been in Washington, D.C., a few years ago, and how you could find there fresh local fruit as well as paper-weight-size Washington Monuments and snow globes of the White House.

Now she looked up because the spice vendor was asking her if she spoke English. She nodded and smiled.

"What would you like?" he inquired. He was an older man, his beard trim and gray. His thobe was spotless: as white as the cherry blossoms and not a stain on it, despite the spices that surrounded him.

There really was nothing here that she wanted, at least today. The apartment they had given her had a tidy kitchen, but she didn't know yet how long she would be in Dubai. A week or two, she expected, but the next few days would tell. They wanted to be sure there was no fallout from Alex Sokolov that she would need to clean up.

God, she thought, imagine if they knew about the flight attendant. She felt a deep pang of disquiet—almost alarm—when she imagined the possible repercussions from her decision not to kill her, too. She took a breath to calm herself. To compartmentalize. It was, she understood, how she functioned. She was capable of focusing acutely on a problem and thinking many steps ahead. It was why she had been such a capable chess player. She could be farsighted to the point of prescience. But her mind also divided and conquered, squirreling away the nuggets she someday might need, while putting the fears that might paralyze her behind a firewall.

"Please," the vendor was saying to her, "a beautiful woman like you? Surely there is something you want."

She looked at him and then she looked around at his wares. In her opinion, the real fun of a place like the souk was not merely how fresh everything was, but the negotiating. The bargaining. It was rather like low-stakes diplomacy. Elena loved it. She was only thirty—barely thirty—but she had spent enough time in cities in the Middle East that she had grown accustomed to the haggling it took to buy a brick of halloumi cheese. So she guessed she would purchase something.

But then her phone vibrated. She thanked the vendor and turned away to read the text. It was from Viktor. Alex Sokolov had indeed missed the meeting that morning with the investors from Russia. They'd called his cell and they'd called the hotel and left messages. Most of the people in the room had no idea why he wasn't there, but there were a few who did and they were grateful.

She took in his praise, but she didn't smile. She knew that while she was indeed proficient—no, she was beyond proficient, she had (to use an expression a roommate from college rather liked) mad skills—second chances were few in her line of work. Especially with these people. Her father's people. She knew the truth of what they had done to him. She wasn't irreplaceable. The last thing she wanted was to be herself among the hunted.

But Viktor's text was reassuring. He had even used the word *grateful*. And so she turned back to the vendor and pointed at a beautiful scarf so gloriously colorful and luminescent that she thought of Joseph's dream coat. "How many dirhams?" she asked.

He told her. She scoffed and rolled her eyes, and he gave her a second price. And they were off.

5

The moment they had touched down at Charles de Gaulle and were taxiing to their gate, Cassie checked her phone for news from Dubai. She found none. It was possible—though unlikely, she believed—that Alex's body had not yet been discovered. It was nearly eight thirty at night in the United Emirates. If his corpse (dear God, what a horrible word) were still in the bed where she had left it, that would mean that the Royal Phoenician house-keeping team had respected the "Do Not Disturb" sign through cleaning and turn-down service. Whoever delivered the compli-mentary fresh fruit and maamoul cookies late that afternoon had seen the sign and returned to the hotel kitchen. It meant that nei-ther Miranda nor some other business associate had gone looking for him or questioned—at least with any resolve—his peculiar and unexplained absence.

In the end, she concluded that by now the macerating remains of Alex Sokolov had most definitely been found. Had to have been. In her mind, as she thanked the passengers as they disembarked, she saw a forensics team scouring the room, that body in the bed gone but the sheets a Rorschach of red.

Normally she would have viewed the scheduling gods as hav-ing been kind to her, because the airline was only required to give them ten hours of rest. But they had had twenty-one hours in Dubai, and they were going to have nearly fifteen here in France. Now, however, the duration only ratcheted up her anxiety. She wanted to be back in the United States. She wanted to be in her apartment on Twenty-Seventh Street in Manhattan, wanted to know that she would have access to American lawyers, if it ever came to that.

This crew—the thirteen of them—had one last leg together, the return to JFK tomorrow morning, and then they would scatter. Their paths might cross again in different combinations, especially she and Megan and Shane because they enjoyed each other's company and occasionally worked their schedules so they could fly together, but this particular chemical arrangement of pilots and flight attendants would never be duplicated. The airline had nearly twelve hundred flight attendants based in New York, all of them bidding monthly on the routes and the cabins, and somehow she and Megan and Shane had all gotten Paris—though, in this sequence, the price had come with Dubai. Two nights ago, on the way east, the three of them had catnapped in the morning and then spent a lovely afternoon and evening at a bistro and then a nightclub with hipsters half their age near the Bastille. The overnight then had been a lot longer than this one. Cassie had drunk that evening, but not to excess, and she hadn't separated from her friends.

It dawned on her that she shouldn't return to Dubai, at least not in the foreseeable future. Probably ever. It wasn't on her schedule next month, and she sure as hell wouldn't bid on it for September.

"I don't think anyone's going into the city this time," Megan was saying, as they emerged from the jet bridge into the concourse. Tonight the airline had them at an airport hotel because it just took too long to get in and out of Paris and the overnight was much shorter. "But there's a pretty nice restaurant near the hotel we can walk to. Brasserie something. Anyway, some of us are meeting in the lobby at seven. Do you want to join us?"

"No. I think I'm going to rest," she said.

"I think that makes sense," Megan agreed. "Be a slam-clicker for a change. Get some sleep."

They passed a Hermès boutique, and she recalled the leopard-print scarf that she had seen in a store last night at the Royal Phoenician. She thought of her neck; she thought of his. Alex's.

"Treat yourself. Order something light from room service. Eat dessert first," Megan went on.

"Yeah, I think that's the plan."

"God, you have no idea how nice it is as a mother of two hormonally insane teenagers sometimes just to have an evening alone in a hotel room. I might not go out, either. I might just Skype Vaughn and call it a night," she said.

Cassie nodded politely. She'd met Megan's husband a couple of times. He seemed nice enough. She remembered mostly the jokes he had made about being a consultant:

You really only need to get two things to be a consultant: Fired. And business cards.

You want to know the definition of a consultant? A guy who borrows your watch to tell you what time it is.

But since the family had moved to Virginia he had worked a lot for defense department contractors, so Cassie presumed he was far more competent than his self-deprecation suggested. And his jokes certainly had been no worse than those of the first officer she was flying with that week. At that moment, Stewart was regaling the captain with yet another story that was, invariably, a little stale.

"Say hi to him for me," she told Megan.

"I will. And you get some rest."

Cassie nodded. She knew she would be tempted to order a glass of wine, but she was also confident that she would be able to resist: she reminded herself that she tended to binge-drink (and, yes, to binge-sex), but she wasn't really a drunk like her father. Sure, that was the motto of unredeemed alcoholics everywhere: I'm not really a drunk. But she wasn't. She went nights all the time without drinking. Hadn't she vowed only hours earlier that she'd never drink again? She had.

Not quite five minutes later they were nearing the exit beside the security queues and the escalator down to the strip of exterior sidewalk where they would wait for the hotel shuttle, when Jada stopped and handed Megan her phone. The entire crew stopped with her, a herd of gazelle on alert.

"Recognize him?" Jada asked.

Megan enlarged the photo with her index finger and thumb. "Oh, my God," she murmured softly, a little stunned. "Wow. He was on the flight with us from Paris to Dubai."

"Yup."

Megan gave the phone to Cassie, but didn't say a word.

For a long moment she stared at the photo, and it was one of those experiences where she was both reacting to it viscerally and reacting to it with the awareness of a performer because she knew that Megan was watching her. There he was. Last night's lover. The story about him was on a site they all visited on occasion that helped international travelers keep up with international crime, a sort of tabloid version of the State Department's travel advisory website. It was brief and to the point: there had been a rather grisly murder at the Royal Phoenician in Dubai. The victim, a hedge fund manager from the United States named Alex Sokolov, had had his throat slashed in his hotel room. He had been found midafternoon when he had missed a meeting he had been expected to attend. Finally hotel security had ignored the "Do Not Disturb" sign and entered the suite. There were no other names in the story, so there was no mention of a woman named Miranda.

"I am so sorry," Cassie said, hoping that her shock that the body now was news would be construed by Megan and the crew as shock that the body existed at all—that the poor guy had been murdered. She scrolled down a little further and learned that the authorities had no serious suspects. A travel and tourism official was insisting that this was an isolated incident and visitors needn't be alarmed, but a police captain seemed to dispute that by arguing that they had not ruled out burglary as a motive.

Megan took the phone and gave it back to Jada, and she in turn handed it to Stewart and the captain to share. It was interesting to all of them that a passenger on their plane had been murdered.

Then Megan leaned in close to Cassie and whispered, "Swear to me you know nothing about this."

"Of course not. Why would I?" She hoped that she sounded offended.

"Okay. It's just that you two were talking a lot on the flight to Dubai. And then you seemed so off your game and so freaking weird when we were on our way to the airport this morning. And then you were crying when we took off."

She shook her head. "Oh, I guess I'm sad that the young man is dead. He seemed like a nice enough guy. But the last time I saw him was when he got off the plane yesterday afternoon."

The herd started to move and she started to move with it. A part of her feared that each lie was going to bury her deeper. But she also told herself that it was far too late to start telling the truth.

« «

Cassie lay on her side in her hotel room bed in the dark, naked but for the white terrycloth robe she had found in the closet. She listened to the sounds of the footsteps and the rolling suitcases along the corridor, flinching whenever she heard a door slam or a lock click shut. She tried once more to recall missing details from the night before, but they were lost. She tried to recall every word she had said to Miranda. But so much of the conversation existed in the murk that shrouded the events and the men and the bars and the beds from so many nights over so many years.

At one point she considered texting her sister in Kentucky. Asking a few harmless questions about her nephew or niece. About her brother-in-law.

She and her sister rarely spoke of their father and mother, because invariably they wound up fighting whenever they did. There was just so much anger and just so much hurt, and they had responded to their parents in ways as different and unique as snow-flakes. They were not close anymore and probably never would be close again, but Rosemary needed Cassie to be at least on the periphery of her family's life to feed her own longing for normalcy. Occasionally, Rosemary and her husband, Dennis, and their two kids would fly in from Kentucky and stay at an inexpensive hotel in Westchester for the weekend, and then take the train or drive a rental car into the city on Saturday and Sunday. Rosemary was an accountant in Lexington. Dennis worked at the military base in Richmond. Sometimes on these family visits to the city Cassie would be granted a brief audience alone with either her nephew or niece. She would be allowed to bring Jessica to the American Girl Store or Tim to the Metropolitan Museum. A few times she had even gotten to take the children to lunch, just the three of them, and she had brought them to restaurants they had adored—the sort of places where there were young waiters and waitresses singing show tunes or the dining room was designed to replicate a haunted house. Cassie cherished those hours: she couldn't imagine she was ever going to have children of her own, a reality that some solitary nights would leave her feeling bereft of the son or daughter she'd never hold. Usually, however, when her sister's family came to New York, she would see the kids and their parents together. The five of them would go to the top of the Empire State Building. The Statue of Liberty. Yankee Stadium when the Royals were in town, so together they could root against the Evil Empire.

These weekends were free of alcohol because Rosemary didn't drink and didn't want to see her sister drink. That's how different they were.

It spoke volumes about what Rosemary really thought of her that the children had never been alone with Cassie in her apartment. She had offered to babysit them at least half a dozen times so Rosemary and Dennis could enjoy a night out alone. See a musical, perhaps, that wasn't Disney. Enjoy a restaurant where the ladies' and men's rooms didn't have signs marked "Witches" and "Warlocks." But her sister had always passed. Said she and Dennis wanted family time with the kids. In truth, Cassie knew, Rosemary didn't trust her at night. It was when their father often (but not always) got into trouble, and it was when Cassie seemed to inflict the most hurt—on herself and on others.

And so she didn't text her sister. There was really no point. She didn't once reach for her phone as it charged on the nightstand. She was afraid that the urge to Google Alex Sokolov would be irresistible, and now that she knew his body had been found and the investigation had begun, she wanted to secrete herself inside a news void. She was afraid that anything she might learn would only make her feel worse. Either it would frighten her, a noose drawing tight, or it would exacerbate her guilt for telling no one that she'd found him dead and then just left the body behind. That night she only got out of bed when she needed water or had to go to the bathroom.

《　《

She awoke, the air dense with the distant remnants of a dream. The room was silent except for the thrum of the cool, forced air, and the details of the dream were all but gone. Her father was in it, that she knew, and so was hunting camp. But that was it.

She rubbed her eyes. Two seasons she had gone hunting with him and one of his few friends, even though it had meant missing dance class. The camp was in the Cumberland Mountains and it belonged to that friend, a carpenter who had a daughter roughly her age. She had come, too. The girl's name was Karly and she went to a different school. The camp was actually a trailer with plumbing that no longer worked, and so the carpenter had built an outhouse. A composting, eco-friendly outhouse. Those two November weekends, a year apart, had been at once unbeliev-ably wholesome and unbelievably squalid. The fathers had viewed themselves as progressive and enlightened: they were bringing their daughters to deer camp. They'd sent them to hunter safety courses and then refined what the instructors had taught them about fire-arms. But the men had drunk and passed out each night, and then each day the four of them had walked forever in the cold of the woods. It didn't snow either year, thank God, but that also meant there hadn't been any tracks.

The second year she'd wounded a deer instead of killing it instantly, which left her sobbing with remorse. Inevitably it had died, but it had died slowly and in excruciating pain. She'd been such a mess that her father hadn't been able to leave her and track down the animal to finish it off.

And Karly? Karly just wanted to drink with her father and with Cassie's dad those weekends, even though the grown-ups wouldn't let her because the girls were still in middle school. She went on and on about how much she loved the foam and fizz of canned beer, and how popping the top turned her on. Whispered to Cassie that it got her hot.

When Cassie finally climbed from the hotel bed, reflexively she rubbed her right shoulder where the rifle's kickback that day in the woods had bruised her soul far worse than her skin. She hadn't touched a gun ever since.

《　《

It was somewhere over the eastern Atlantic, after she had brought the woman in 6G another glass of Riesling and Jada had brought the fellow in 3A a scotch, that the other flight attendant verbalized the truth that, along with so many others, had kept Cassie staring at the pinpricks of light in her hotel room the night before—the radio, the clock, the smoke alarm. The two of them were catching their breath together in the front galley of the Airbus.

"Since he was an American and he was on our flight, do you think they're going to want to talk to us?" Jada asked. Cassie didn't have to ask who *he* was. "And who do you think *they* will be?"

Cassie rubbed Purell roughly onto her hands. She had contemplated this, too, in the small hours of the morning. She had settled on the FBI, but only because she was pretty sure that the CIA didn't investigate crime. She presumed the FBI must have some sort of arrangement with foreign police forces: maybe in this case, because Alex had been a U.S. citizen, they would ask the questions for the police in Dubai. But maybe not. She knew that Dubai did so much business with the West that it was very likely they had a pretty damn impressive police force. She also suspected that most U.S. embassies had some sort of FBI presence, an officer or two. Just in case. God, if only Alex had been as Russian as his cologne or his taste in literature. She guessed in that case that the questioning would have been cursory—if at all. Why would Americans even investigate a dead Russian in Dubai? They wouldn't. It would be none of their business.

In the end, however, by the time she had climbed from the hotel bed and showered, she had convinced herself that even the State Department would be involved. Alex's family would be lobbying the media for justice. People—powerful people—would be paying attention. The idea made her sick. Somewhere Miranda was sharing her story.

"I think it will be the FBI," she told Jada finally. "If it's anyone . . ."

"I'm not sure I've ever been that close to a person who was murdered."

"Me, either," she said, though she thought of her father and briefly her mind dissected the distinctions between manslaughter and murder.

Abruptly Jada looked over Cassie's shoulder, her gaze intense and her dark eyes widening. Cassie felt a sharp spike of fear and turned around, convinced this was it, it was over, an air marshal was about to arrest her, just as Jada pushed past. And there she saw the other flight attendant helping a young mother with a toddler in her arms, lifting up the diaper bag that was twisting upside down on the woman's shoulder, the diapers and wipes and the sippy cup in the shape of a bunny all about to tumble onto the floor of the aircraft right in front of the starboard-side first-class bathroom. The mom thanked her, rolling her eyes at the nearness of the disaster, and the two of them laughed. Jada was asking the little boy's name as Cassie leaned against the wall with the trolleys and the trash bin, at once relieved and appalled. She wondered: was this sort of adrenal overreaction going to be the norm for the rest of her life?

« «

As she was wrapping her shoulder harness around her in the jump seat in the front of the plane, as the Long Island coastline and beaches were racing below them, she thought of the three words she hoped never to say aloud or hear on an aircraft: brace for impact. That was the signal they were about to crash-land or auger in. Those four syllables? They were the cry of the raven. Imminent collision with the ground, best case a belly flop and worst case a head-on, nose-first crash that would cause the aircraft to break apart and explode, the bodies—the pieces of the bodies that were recognizable—small, charred briquettes.

The words came to her because the captain had informed the crew somewhere over New Brunswick that they were going to be met at the gate at JFK by the authorities. He didn't say why and whether by "authorities" he meant airport or TSA officials or some other law enforcement group, and no one on the crew was going to ask him. But they all had their suspicions. Some guessed there was a possible terrorist on board, someone high on the watch list, and the passenger would be arrested the moment they landed, but Cassie had flown long enough to know this wasn't the case: if the captain had been told there might be a terrorist on the plane, he would have informed the crew so they could keep an eye on him every single moment they were in the air. Instead, as they had pre-pared the cabins for arrival, Megan and Jada and Shane had specu-lated aloud that it had something to do with the dead American in Dubai. What else could it possibly be, Megan had asked? He'd been with them on the flight from Paris to the Middle East.

Cassie considered asking Megan to cover for her: not neces-sarily lie, but simply not volunteer the information that Cassandra

Bowden had returned to the crew's Dubai hotel in the morning barely twenty minutes before they had to leave for the airport. Cassie knew it would be easier to simply tell investigators that she had spent the night alone in her own room at the airline's hotel than have to make up a man to account for her absence. But asking that of Megan would only implicate her further in the other woman's eyes: it would convince Megan that she had indeed been with Alex the night he had died and very possibly had killed him. Already Cassie had felt her friend watching her as they had walked up the aisles, the two of them checking to be sure the passengers were belted in and their seatbacks were upright.

And so she focused right now on concocting two possible stories. If she had the sense from the questioning that Miranda had not yet come forward, she would share with the authorities another hotel and another man, molding him in her mind like a golem. She would keep it simple. Give them a name and admit that she was sure the fellow had made it up because she was sure he was married. She was going to say he was some sort of consultant and she thought he was South African. The hotel would be the Armani because it was big and it was in the opposite direction from the Royal Phoenician, and the floor with his room had been somewhere in the middle. Could have been on the sixth and it could have been on the eighth. She would confess sheepishly that she had been drinking, and she couldn't remember very much. Surely there was a single man in a room on one of those floors who spoke English with an accent she could say later (if necessary) she must have mistaken for South African. But otherwise she would say almost nothing. That was what mattered. It would be much easier to keep her story straight if the details were few.

But what if Miranda had now told the Dubai police that she had met a flight attendant named Cassie the night before, and they had already informed the FBI in America? That would demand a very different lie, one that was more dangerous but in some ways a much easier one to pull off. That lie was simply this: Alex Sokolov had been alive when she had left his hotel suite.

Maybe, as a matter of fact, she should say that no matter what, because at some point Miranda would talk to the police, and Cassie knew that her stories should be consistent. So, yes, this was the tale. This was what had happened. This was the lie.

In the meantime, she would brace for impact. It was, she knew, inevitable.

FEDERAL BUREAU OF INVESTIGATION

FD-302 (redacted): CASSANDRA BOWDEN, FLIGHT ATTENDANT

DATE: July 28, 2018

CASSANDRA BOWDEN, date of birth—/—/——, SSN #————, telephone number (—)————, was interviewed by properly identified Special Agents FRANK HAMMOND and JAMES WASHBURN at JFK INTERNATIONAL AIRPORT, immediately upon her flight's arrival in the U.S.

HAMMOND conducted the interview; WASHBURN took these notes.

After being advised of the nature of the interview, BOWDEN provided the following information.

BOWDEN said that she has been with the airline since she finished college 18 years ago, and this is the only job she has ever had.

BOWDEN confirmed that ALEXANDER SOKOLOV was seated in 2C on Flight 4094 on Thursday, July 26, from Paris to Dubai. He introduced himself to her on the plane before they took off. She said they met for the first time when the aircraft was still at the gate and passengers in the economy cabin were still boarding. He drank red wine, coffee, and water on the flight.

She described him as "low-maintenance" and said it was clear that he was traveling alone. She did not recall him speaking to the passenger across the aisle (2D) or to the passenger beside him (2B), but thought it likely if he spoke to anyone it would have been 2B. She based this solely on her experience that passengers are more likely to speak to the person beside them than across the aisle.

She said that she and SOKOLOV spoke mostly during the food service, and talked almost entirely about the wine and entrée and dessert choices.

She characterized him as a polite and "charming" young man. She said he was "a bit of a flirt" and liked the uniform/dress she was wearing. He told her he worked for a hedge fund and had meetings in Dubai. He said something about clients and real estate holdings there, but added that what he did was just too boring to discuss. He did not say with whom he was meeting or where.

SOKOLOV did not sleep on the plane, which she found normal because it was a daylight flight. She said he ate, he watched a movie, and he worked. She reported that she saw documents open on his laptop, but she did not look at them. She saw no papers on his tray table. Likewise, she said that while she was aware that at one point he was watching a movie, she did not observe which one.

Finally, she said he seemed calm and content—not at all agitated. She characterized the flight as completely uneventful.

6

Usually the drug tests were random: not every flight atten-dant and member of the flight crew was tested. One or two people would be singled out by an airline employee as they disem-barked and asked to take what they called the "whiz quiz." This was different. They were all tested: the entire crew. And all of their bags were searched.

Everyone passed the drug test. And nothing illegal was found in any of their rollers or kits.

《 《

It was odd, Cassie thought, it was strange. It was as if the FBI had no interest in knowing her whereabouts during the flight crew's overnight in Dubai. It was as if Frank Hammond and James Washburn had no reason in the world to suspect that she might have been with Alex Sokolov when he was killed. Hammond was a handsome guy roughly her age with a countenance that had seemed slightly bemused—as if he had seen it all. His hair was short, the color of cinnamon, and just starting to recede. Washburn was younger, with pale, perfect skin and rather professorial, rimless eyeglasses. The two of them acted as if they were concerned only with what she had seen of the man on the flight, and whether he had said something that might have been revealing. Did that mean they were hoping somehow to entrap her in a lie? It seemed not, because they never asked anything that would have necessitated one. Rather, it was as if they honestly didn't know that one of Alex's colleagues had come to the suite in Dubai and had a drink with her.

In hindsight, she realized, her fear had been almost comic. They didn't even record the interview. Apparently that was FBI policy. Hammond asked her questions and Washburn wrote down her answers using a ballpoint pen and yellow legal pad as if it were 1955. When she had asked about the lack of a recorder—good God, they didn't even use their phones—Washburn had said later that he'd type it up on some form he called an FD-302.

She wished she had been a little more detailed about Alex's and her flirting during the interview, but only because there was always the chance that one of the other crew members had mentioned it. Even her friend Megan might have said something. But Megan had insisted that her interview had been cursory, too. The agent who had talked to her was a woman named Anne McConnell, and Megan said that she had asked very little about the rest of the crew.

Probably the real suspects were the employees who worked at the hotel. Or, perhaps, the investors he was supposed to see in Dubai. Or maybe it was the desperate underground that risked Arabian justice to prey upon the scads of rich foreigners who descended upon the city daily. These were the sorts of people the Dubai police most likely were interested in.

And, in truth, it probably was one of them who had killed Alex. She could ruminate forever on why they had spared her and probably never figure it out. It was best to let go of that sort of self-scrutiny. It wasn't helpful.

But she couldn't exhale completely because there was still Miranda. At some point, that was the loose end that Cassie feared was going to trip her. As much as the ghost of Alex Sokolov might dog her, she knew if necessary she could drown that specter with an extra shot of Sipsmith or Jose Cuervo. But Miranda? She had shown up in the suite with the bottle of Stoli, glass chips of which were probably still embedded in that plush carpet in a room at the

Royal Phoenician. By now she had almost certainly said something to the Dubai police, and no amount of tequila or gin was going to make Miranda go away.

« «

She left her suitcase in the hallway of her apartment and pressed Frank Hammond's business card onto the refrigerator in her windowless kitchen with a magnet from the animal shelter. She wasn't sure what else to do with it. Then she went to her bedroom. The apartment was a small one bedroom, but it had a valuable asset: it was on the fifteenth floor and had a magnificent, unobstructed view of New York Life's pyramidal gold cone and, a little further away, the Empire State Building. She'd come a long way from the bottom bunk in a crash pad in Queens. She kicked off her shoes and collapsed on her bed and gazed for a moment at the two buildings. The sun was just beginning to set. She fell asleep in her uniform when it was still light out.

« «

Terrain, terrain! Pull up, pull up!
The mechanical female voice on the far side of the flight deck door. The remnants of another dream. She knew the voice from the hundreds, perhaps thousands, of landings when she was in the jump seat nearest the cockpit on certain planes. On some aircraft, the ones where the passengers were staring straight at you, they called it the Sharon Stone Seat. The Basic Instinct Bench.

When she awoke, when she understood they were neither landing nor crashing, it was nighttime and the peak of the Empire State Building was colored red. One time when her sister's family was visiting, she had looked up online what color the building would be that night, hoping she would be allowed to share the view with them and explain to her nephew and niece the reason behind that evening's selection, but Rosemary had made it clear that they would not be going to Murray Hill and she did not want Cassie alone with the kids.

She wasn't hungry, but she figured she should eat something and went to the kitchen. She recalled again how Alex had ordered the blanquette de veau at the restaurant in Dubai. She imagined herself telling the FBI agents that the deceased had no objection to eating veal and was a tender and rather exquisite lover in the shower. He read—no, he reread—doorstop novels by long-dead Russian writers. In her head, she heard herself volunteering that for one night, at least, he drank as much as she did, and that had been a lot—enough for her to black out. What would Frank Hammond have said to any of that? She gazed for a moment at the portion of his business card that peeked out from behind the magnet.

The refrigerator wasn't empty—far from it—but there was still little in there that was edible. It was mostly unfinished Indian take-out that had gone bad, condiments, diet soda, and yogurt that had expired months ago. She found a can of tomato soup in the pantry and some crackers, a little soft with age but edible, and made herself the sort of meal that she recalled her mother might have prepared for her when she was home from school with the flu.

She ate in silence on the living room couch, watching the moon high above the Manhattan skyline. She ate in the dark but for the light from the kitchen. She thought she might look for news stories about Sokolov on her phone when she was finished. She might even boot up the laptop she rarely used. But she feared she wouldn't sleep if she did, and it was going to be hard enough going back to bed after having slept five hours already that evening.

A sentence came to her: *I awoke beside a dead man.*

Then another: *I may have gotten away with murder.*

But then she shook her head because while it was conceivable that she had killed Alex, she continued to feel deep inside that she hadn't. Oh, there had been moments when she had lost faith and felt waves of debilitating self-hatred: her body actually spasmed ever so slightly once in the elevator in her building. But usually she was able to convince herself that she hadn't killed him. She couldn't. She wouldn't. Not even in self-defense. For better or worse, that wasn't how she was wired.

She also reminded herself that it remained highly unlikely that she had gotten away with anything. All she had done so far was make it back to America, where she would at least have a decent lawyer—assuming she could find one who would work for the pittance she really could pay.

Her only definite crime, literal and metaphoric, was leaving the poor guy behind in the hotel room in Dubai. And if she hadn't killed him, then she was relieved now to have so many time zones between herself and whoever had. Either they had misjudged her and assumed she would call the hotel or the police and wind up a suspect in the homicide—perhaps she would even confess to it—or they had figured she would flee and didn't care. In this scenario, whoever had killed Alex had been a pro at this sort of thing—an executioner—and knew that she was just in the wrong bed on the wrong night and spared her. They understood that she was uninvolved in whatever nastiness had led Alex to get himself practically beheaded.

As she was putting her soup bowl into the dishwasher, she pondered how someone gets into a locked hotel room. Perhaps when she had the courage to Google Alex Sokolov, she would Google hotel room security. If whoever killed Alex worked at the Royal Phoenician, it was probably simple to unlock the door.

She had a bottle of unopened red wine, a Chianti she rather liked and was saving for a special occasion, but remembered her vow that she wasn't going to drink. It wasn't quite eleven o'clock. She considered going to one of the late-night drugstores and getting a bottle of a pain reliever with the letters PM on it, or perhaps some flu remedy with a specifically drowsy formulation to knock a person out.

Instead she thought to herself, fuck it, fuck it all, she wasn't going to be able to sleep. All that loomed if she stayed here at home was the prospect of tossing and turning and waiting for the lights on the Empire State Building to finally blink out, and then, at two or two thirty in the morning, when she was desperate, uncorking that Chianti. She swiped across a few of the men who came up in her Tinder account, but none of the faces interested her. She thought of the different women she knew whom she could text and see where they were and what trouble they were getting into, moving in her mind first through her friends who tolerated her drinking (some barely) and then those who applauded it and drank with her. She had an equal number of both and needed both in different ways: the former to protect her and apologize to the party hosts and restaurant patrons and wedding guests she appalled with her behavior and her mouth, the latter to goad her on as she took off her bikini top or hurled a pool cue like a javelin. But she didn't text anyone. Tonight she would be a lone wolf. Sometimes that was best for everyone.

And so—certainly not proud of herself, but not precisely disgusted either—she showered, slipped into a pair of tight, come-hither jeans and a white blouse that was perfect for the last Saturday night in July, and went out into the dark. She wore the shade of lipstick the airline preferred for her, a deep scarlet that would help the hearing impaired read her lips in the event of an emergency.

《　《

Was she too old to have kicked off her heels and danced barefoot on a floor sticky with spilled beer in a dark club in the East Village, courting a noise-induced hearing loss because the band's amps were set to jet engine? Probably. But she wasn't the only woman who was suddenly barefoot. She was merely the oldest. And she didn't care about her age or her feet, because she was doing this sober and that left her unexpectedly pleased. This was the foolishness the heart craved. She'd found a bar with a band and a party, it was still the middle of summer, and the people were beautiful. She was nowhere near Dubai. The guy she was dancing with, an actor with Gregg Allman hair, honey-colored and lush, had just finished doing six weeks of Shakespeare in Virginia. He said he was thirty-five and was here because one of the dudes on the stage that moment had been in a show with him that spring in Brooklyn. The musical had needed someone who could play the guitar as well as sing and act.

"You're sure I can't get you a beer?" he shouted into her ear. His name was Buckley, which she had told him was the best name ever for a Shakespearean actor, and he had agreed, but he was from Westport and that was the name he got—and it hadn't been a great name when he was doing a musical about the 1970s punk scene last year at the Public. And Buck, he had reminded her, was far worse: if you were a performer named Buck, you were either a cowboy or a porn star.

"Positive!" she reassured him. She jumped and spun and had both of her hands over her head, the bass from the stage thrumming inside her, and then Buckley's fingers were on the small of her waist, pulling her into him, and when she brought her hands down she rested them on the back of his neck and suddenly they were kissing and it was electric.

When they were at the bar catching their breath a few minutes later, she asked one of the bartenders, a young thing in a tight denim shirt and straight black hair that fell to her waist, to bring him a shot of tequila.

"Oh, man, I shouldn't," he said, laughing, his cheeks flushed, but he took the small glass.

"Of course, you should," Cassie told him. "It's well after midnight."

"What does that have to do with anything?"

"Witching hour."

He took one of the drapes of his hair and pushed it back behind his ear. "Seriously?" He had asked the question sincerely, as if he expected he was about to learn something. It was almost sweet.

Still, she was surprised at his reluctance to go from tipsy to drunk. It was a shot of tequila. One shot. They weren't talking about heating a spoonful of crack. She expected more from an actor, even one who had grown up in Fairfield County, Connecticut. She was holding her shoes, and she put them down on the seat of the empty barstool near them. Then with one hand she reached out and took a rope of that magnificent mane of his, not at all surprised at how soft it was. With the other she took the small glass she'd ordered for him and swallowed the shot of tequila. The burn was deep and hot and seemed to ooze out from her chest like an oil spill. It was heavenly. So much for not drinking tonight.

"And yet you passed on the beer," he said, smiling. His grin was childlike, his eyes impish.

"I like tequila."

"But not beer."

"I'm a flight attendant, remember? The uniform is unforgiving."

"Do airlines still worry about weight? Can they do that?"

"It's vague. Weight must be proportional to height. But you really can't do your job if you're fat. I'll be in the gym again tomorrow."

"Because you fly?"

"Because I'm vain."

"Tell me the craziest thing you've ever seen."

"As a flight attendant?"

"Yes. You hear stories that are just insane."

She nodded. She honestly couldn't say whether flying made people weird, or whether people were inherently weird and a closed cabin just made it more apparent.

"You hear them," she said. "We live them."

"I know! Tell me some. Tell me one."

She closed her eyes and saw Alex Sokolov in the bed beside her. She saw once again the deep, wet furrow across his neck. She saw herself crouched against the drapes in the hotel room in Dubai, naked, his blood on her shoulder and in her hair.

"You should have a shot, first," she said.

"That bad?"

"I'll have another one with you." She slipped her shoes back on, trying not to focus on how filthy her feet had become, and took his hand and led him to the bar. She wasn't going to share with him the tale of the young hedge fund manager who had died in the bed beside her on the Arabian Peninsula. There wasn't enough tequila in the world to get her to tell him that nightmare. And so instead, as they dared each other to keep downing shots—a second, a third, a fourth—she told him of the passengers who had tried to open exit doors at thirty-five thousand feet and the couples who honestly believed they were being discreet when their hands were under the blankets while the rest of the cabin was asleep. She told him of the man who had tried to climb over the beverage cart—he got as far as one knee on the top and his foot on the bag of ice on the shelf—because he wanted to get to the bathroom and couldn't (or wouldn't) wait.

She shared with him her encounter with the rock star who purchased the entire first-class cabin for himself and his entourage: "I wasn't allowed to speak to him. I had to whisper the drink and menu options into his bodyguard's ear. I wasn't even allowed to make eye contact with him. The flight was an overnight to Berlin and he didn't sleep a wink. Even though the lights were dimmed and his party was sound asleep—his bodyguard, too—he went into the lavatory and changed his clothes three times, each outfit more outrageous than the one before it. For about an hour and a half he was in a gold sequin jumpsuit and platform heels, and his only audience was me."

She told him the different locales on the plane where they tended to stow the tough cuffs, and the different occasions when she had needed them to restrain a passenger.

And then she told him about Hugo Fournier. She wasn't sure he would know the name, but he would know the story. He probably presumed it was an urban legend. But it wasn't. She'd been there. She'd been on the flight.

"So, we're flying from Paris to JFK. It's a route I bid on a lot. I was younger then and so I got it less often. This was eight years ago. And when I got it, I usually had business class."

"That's a bad thing?"

"No, it's just that sometimes it can be a difficult cabin. On some aircraft, in first everyone has a flat bed and is out like a light pretty soon into the flight. In coach, there's really not a whole lot you ever have to do. But business has thirty-two seats and there's almost the same cabin service as first. And they sleep less. So, some flight attendants feel it's a little less desirable, which means that whoever's working in it might have less seniority."

"Okay."

"So, this particular flight is packed. Not a single empty seat. Maybe an hour west of Ireland, when we're on dessert in business, this guy who has been flying with the airline forever pushes past me to get to the chief purser, who is working in first. He is oozing adrenaline, and the idea crosses my mind that there is some mechanical disaster. I literally think, an engine is on fire. No more than thirty seconds later, I hear the chief purser on the intercom asking if there is a doctor or nurse on board. She sounds pretty cool, but I hear just a quiver of desperation. Of course, I'm also relieved that we're not about to ditch in the ocean."

"Of course."

"There is a doctor. There are, in fact, two. One in coach and one in business, and they both rush to seat twenty-four E, where Hugo Fournier, old and diabetic and obese, has just had a massive heart attack. The doctors, one female and one male, and the flight attendants lay him out on the floor in front of the galley and emergency exit row, because that's where they can find the most room. They get out the defib and work on the guy, and they work him hard. The doctors try everything, and they don't call it for at least forty minutes. Everyone in the cabin knows what's going on. His wife is freaking out. She is shrieking and pleading and crying. Can you blame her? It's not a dignified performance, but it's a real one."

"God . . ."

"Yup. But now we—you know, the crew—have to do something with the body. We can't put him back where he was. He's in the middle of economy and while those are the cheap seats, people still don't expect to sit next to a corpse. Plus, he's covered in vomit, and while we could clean that off his shirt and pants, we couldn't clean off the stench. And the body did what bodies do when they die. Poor Hugo Fournier had crapped his pants."

Buckley put his hands on his face and shook his head. "I do know this story."

"Of course you do."

"You put him in the bathroom for the rest of the flight."

"Well, I didn't. But, yes, the crew did. I actually lobbied that we try and get one of the people in first to give up their flat bed, but our chief purser wouldn't have it. I suggested we put him in one A or one L, so almost no one would see him or smell him. But she wouldn't even ask. So, yes, one of the doctors and two of the male flight attendants wedged him into the starboard, midcabin lavatory. The doctor—a pretty judgmental guy, in hindsight—said it was like getting a size ten foot into a size eight shoe."

"And you didn't turn around."

"The plane? No. We were already over the mid-Atlantic. We didn't want to inconvenience two hundred and fifty-eight people. And so instead we inconvenienced one. She just happened to be a widow. A loud widow."

"Amazing."

"Or appalling."

"You got that Scheherazade thing down," he said.

"Most of us are pretty good storytellers," she agreed. "We are the kings and queens of the degrading."

"Where did you say you just flew in from? I can't remember."

"I didn't say."

"Okay, then: where?"

Such a simple question. It demanded but a one-word answer. Two syllables. And yet she couldn't bring herself to say it right now: it would be like waking in the middle of the night in a dark room and switching on klieg lights. "Berlin," she lied. She was prepared to embellish the trip, if she had to. If it came to that. But it didn't.

"And you still like the job?" he asked.

She rolled back her head, lolling in the heaviness that came with the fourth shot. Perhaps because she'd just lied, she felt an acute need to admit something—to give him something real. The need to confess was irresistible. "When you start as young as I did—right out of college—it's usually because you're running from something. You just have to get out. To get away. It wasn't a career change for me. It wasn't even a choice, in some ways. It was just a road somewhere."

"An escape?"

"You could say that."

"From?"

They were sitting down now and it was a quarter to one. They were on stools side by side at the bar, but they were facing each other. She reached over and hooked her fingers just inside the front pockets of his jeans, locking him gamically to her. His eyes had the fuzzy drunk stare she liked. She wouldn't have been surprised if hers were a little loopy, too.

"There's a town at the edge of the Cumberland Mountains in Kentucky called Grover's Mill. Pretty quaint, right?"

"Whereabouts?"

She shook her head and purred, "Shhhh," her voice the wind in the night. Then: "I'm Scheherazade."

He nodded.

"It's small and quiet," she continued. "Not a lot happens there. Imagine a girl in sixth grade with strawberry blond hair. It's up in a bun because she fancies herself a dancer and she does nothing in moderation. Never has and, alas, never will."

"This is you."

"So it would seem. And today is her birthday. And while Grover's Mill doesn't have much, it has a creamery that makes ice cream. Really good ice cream, at least this eleven-year-old thinks so. And so her mom has a big idea for her birthday, because they really can't afford a whole lot in the way of presents and her birthday has fallen smack in the middle of the week, and so there sure as hell isn't going to be a party. Of course, there probably wouldn't have been a party even if her birthday had fallen on a Friday or a Saturday, because you just didn't dare bring kids over to the house on the weekend, because that was usually when Dad was most likely to get seriously and impressively hammered. Anyway, Mom goes to the creamery and buys a tub of her daughter's favorite flavor."

"Rum raisin?"

"Cute. But, no. Chocolate chip cookie dough. And she buys her daughter a two-gallon tub. Do you how many pints that is? Sixteen. She stops by the creamery on her way home from work— she's a receptionist at this creepy electrical wire factory in this otherwise forgotten ghost town next door to Grover's Mill—and buys this restaurant-size two-gallon tub of ice cream. Just so you know, the girl's birthday is in September and it was one freaking hot September that year. You can look it up."

"I trust you."

She dug her fingers a little deeper into his pants pockets, kneading the flesh of his thighs ever so slightly. "So Mom has all this ice cream in a bag, along with some groceries, in the trunk of her car. She's going to get home just about the same time as her husband. Her eleven-year-old kid is already home, a kind of classic latchkey little despot. She has a kid sister who's eight, but that day the kid sister was at her weekly Brownie meeting. Their father was picking her up on his way home from the high school where he was a P.E. coach and driver's ed teacher. As Mom is nearing the street where her family lives, she sees a police car. It's maybe a quarter mile from her house. It's parked, but its lights are on. And then she sees her daughter."

"You." Even in that one syllable, she could hear the slight catch in his throat as she teased him through the thin strip of fabric that comprised the inside of his pants pocket.

"No, silly. That eleven-year-old is home, remember? She sees the eight-year-old. The child is still wearing her Brownie sash with all of these very colorful badges. And then she sees her husband's crappy Dodge Colt. Robin's-egg blue. A hatchback. And it's wrapped around a telephone pole. She stops, absolutely terrified, her heart sinking. But thankfully no one's injured. Her little girl is stunned, scared, but mostly fine. A couple of bruises on her arm. And her husband? He's in the backseat of the police cruiser. Handcuffed. Drunk. So she follows the police car to the police station and uses all the money in their pathetic little savings account at their pathetic little bank to bail him out. This takes a while."

"Of course it does."

"And by the time she gets home with her drunk of a husband and their adorable Brownie of a daughter . . . by the time they pull into the driveway and pop the trunk . . . all that ice cream for the older girl's birthday is gone."

He reached down and lifted her fingers from his pockets and held them tenderly in his hands. "Someone stole the ice cream? At the police station?"

"Nope. It melted. It melted through the cardboard tub and then through the paper bag. Some of it seeped into the fabric of the trunk and some of it just sloshed around the back of the car like the fluid inside a snow globe."

"God, that's so sad."

She raised an eyebrow. Sharing with him the moment hadn't made her sad at all. It actually had made her rather happy. It was something to get off her chest. It was a memory from a place she'd never, ever see again. She looked at the other bartender, a young guy with a string of silver piercings the length of his ear on the other side of Buckley. She gazed at the neon signs for beer and the white lights over the ice trays behind the thick mahogany counter, and she found herself smiling.

"Nah," she said to him. He was gently rubbing the part of her hand between her thumb and her index finger. "Sad is when the Easter Bunny comes on a Monday. That was way worse."

"How is that possible?"

She hesitated. Just how much could she wallow in this before it really would ruin their buzz? But then she decided that she didn't care and plowed ahead. "The Easter Bunny arriving the day after Easter? One year my grandfather had a stroke and my mom had to race to the hospital in Louisville. She was gone the Friday and Saturday before Easter, then Easter Sunday and Monday. And my dad just . . . just didn't cope. The good news? With all the chocolate and jelly beans on sale the next day—you know, half and two-thirds off—he bought my sister and me a hell of a lot more candy than the Easter Bunny was ever going to bring."

Buckley lifted her hands and kissed her fingertips.

"So," she said. "Are we going to my place or yours?"

« «

In the morning she awoke and saw a strip of the Empire State Building through the vertical blinds of her bedroom window. She sensed Buckley beside her in bed, and for a moment she held her breath to listen. She recalled initiating their retreat to his place or hers at the bar, viewing it as a dare of sorts: regardless of where they wound up, she wanted to see if she had become some sort of alcoholic assassin as forty neared, and suddenly she was killing the men with whom she slept. It had been a private challenge of sorts, a deliberate provocation of the soul.

He exhaled and she felt him move, and a little wave of relief left her momentarily giddy. He reached his arm across her hips and belly and pulled her against him.

"Good morning," he murmured. "But don't roll over. I have a feeling I have serious morning breath. Serious hangover breath."

"I probably do, too," she said, and rose to get them both Advil. She knew he was watching her.

"You're beautiful naked," he said.

"I'm glad you think so."

In the bathroom mirror she looked at the red lines in her eyes and the bags below them. She didn't feel beautiful. But at least this hangover was a piker compared to the one that had welcomed the morning after in Dubai. She wondered if Buckley would want to go to brunch. She rather hoped not. She liked him, but she really wasn't hungry. The fact was, she was almost never all that hungry.

After years of boozing it up, it was as if her body craved its calories from alcohol. There was a reason she was likely to have canned soup and stale crackers for dinner.

She considered bringing him two or three of the red pills, but then wondered if he was similar to her and downed them like peanuts or the sort who followed the instructions on the label and would begin with just one. So she brought the whole bottle along with a glass of water. She opened the blinds and squinted at the way the cone of the New York Life Building shimmered in the sun, and then crawled back under the sheets. She watched a plane as it crossed the skyline outside her window, flying north before banking east to LaGuardia.

"Hungry?" he asked.

"No."

"You sound sad."

"One syllable gave all that away? Nah. Just not hungry."

She heard him put the glass and the bottle down on the nightstand on his side of the bed.

"When you're in Germany, do you ever begin the day with eggs in mustard sauce?"

"No. Never. And what in the name of God made you think of Germany just now?"

"You were in Berlin yesterday."

"Oh. Right."

"Doesn't sound like you're a fan of eggs."

"Not with mustard."

"They're hard-boiled. And delicious," he insisted. Then: "I like your apartment."

She wished she could will into existence the woman she had been last night. The one who danced barefoot and made this very gentle actor happy. The one who wasn't repulsed by the idea of brunch and his hints about eggs and food. But that person didn't exist in the morning. Most of the time, that person didn't exist sober. It was almost fascinating how rapidly her resolve not to drink could dissipate: it was like the thin coat of ice on a Kentucky pond in late January, there one day and just gone the next. And yet she knew in her heart that she wouldn't drink today. That wasn't how it worked for her. She'd send Buckley on his way, go to the animal shelter and nurture the depressed cats—the new arrivals that had just been deserted by their owners for one reason or another and were shocked to be living in a cage in a loud, strange world—and then finish the day at the gym. Tonight she would cocoon, her body clock happily adjusted once again to Eastern Daylight Time. She would read and she would watch TV. She would see no one tonight. She would be fine. She had until Tuesday here. Then, with a crew full of strangers—not even Megan and Shane would be on the plane—she would fly to Italy. The August routes she had bid on were Rome and Istanbul. Both were direct flights from JFK. No Dubai.

"Can I tell you something?" she asked. She needed to scare him away to get on with her day and, more importantly, with her life.

"Sure. But this sounds ominous. Will it be as sad as all that melted ice cream?"

"No. Maybe. I'm not sure. I don't know yet what I'm going to tell you."

"Wow. It sounded like you had something in mind. Usually when a person begins, 'Can I tell you something?' they're thinking of some pretty specific revelation or pretty specific bit of news."

She was still on her side. She brought her knees closer to her stomach and rested her hands together under the pillow as if she were praying. "I was just thinking about my day and what I'm going to do this afternoon. The main thing is I'm going to the animal shelter. I love the shelter. I go when I'm home because my mother wouldn't let me have pets as a girl, and now I've managed to pick a career where I travel too much to have one—at least in good conscience."

A moment ago, he had sat up to swallow the Advil and drink

the water. She imagined if she rolled over, she would see he was watching her. Perhaps he was propped up on his elbow, looking down at her.

"I mean, we did have a pet when I was little. Very little. We had a dog. My parents had gotten him before I was born. Years before I was born. But when I was five, my father ran him over. The dog was old and asleep in the grass beside the driveway, and my dad was so drunk when he came home that afternoon, he missed the pavement and—quite literally—ran him over. Didn't just hit him. Crushed him. And so we never had pets after that. My mom was afraid something would happen to them."

She recalled her parents' fights about pets—about cats and dogs. She and her sister would cry, and her father would lobby with slurred words on their behalf. And he would fail. Did her father feel demeaned? Emasculated? She assumed so now. Her mother once said if her father stopped drinking, they could consider a cat or a dog, but that was never going to happen, even after his DUI or after the high school fired him as the driver's ed teacher. (Much to everyone's astonishment, he was still allowed to teach P.E.) As a girl, she had felt only the unfairness of her mother's edict. It was as if she and her sister were being punished for their father's mis-behavior.

"I think it's really sweet that you go to the shelter on your day off," said Buckley.

"I guess I do it for me."

"And for them."

"I should get dressed," she told him.

"Is that a hint?"

"Yes."

"Got it. You know, if you want me to leave, there are easier ways than dredging up a horrible memory about a dead dog. I'm pretty chill, trust me."

She didn't roll over. "Oh, I never seem to do things the easy way."

"No?"

"No." Then: "And I'm sure you have someplace you need to be, too. Right?"

She felt him swinging his feet over the bed. She expected him to stand up. But he didn't. He sat there a long moment and then said softly, "Just so you know, I don't usually do this. I don't sleep with strangers when I'm on tour or in a theater out of state, and I don't when I'm home here in the city."

She sighed. "I do."

"Okay, of all the things you've told me in the last twelve or whatever hours, that's got to be the saddest."

And with that he finally stood. He picked up his clothes from the floor by her closet, his body angular and taut. She heard him go into the bathroom to throw some water on his face before going home, but she kept her hands under her pillow, her knees bent, and tried to lie there as quiet and fixed as a corpse.

« «

And in the night, she wept. It was, she tried to convince herself, because of the cats. They always got to her. The thirteen-year-old calicos that had lived together their whole lives, discarded because their owner had a new boyfriend and he insisted he was allergic to them. The rough and ruddy orange tom, dropped off because the family was moving. He probably weighed twenty pounds, all muscle, and now was unwilling to lift his head and emerge from his cage. There were rail-thin black cats from a crazy hoarder, one with her ear half gone from a fight, all of them awash in fleas and ticks when they arrived.

She was too depressed for the gym. Instead she went to a bookstore and browsed the shelves of paperback fiction, pausing in the aisles that held Chekhov and Pushkin and Tolstoy. She considered a Turgenev collection because Alex had mentioned him and she was unfamiliar with his work, but the only title the store had was *Fathers and Sons,* and that relationship held little allure for her that afternoon. Eventually she bought a small book by Tolstoy (small for Tolstoy, but still nearly four hundred pages), because the first story in it was called "Happy Ever After." She suspected the title was likely ironic, but she could hope.

At home, however, she discovered the book was quite possibly the worst choice she could have made (which perhaps shouldn't have surprised her, given her predilection for bad choices). At least the first story started out badly given her own personal history. On the very first page the narrator, a seventeen-year-old woman named Masha, shares that she is mourning the death of her mother. Cassie had been a teenager, too, when her mother had died. Masha also has a younger sister. Cassie didn't get beyond the fourth page before putting the book down and taking a lint brush to her clothes, removing the evidence of her day at the shelter. But she didn't change. Nor that night did she drink. Not a drop.

And so she was still dressed and sober and sad when she got the call from a fellow who introduced himself as Derek Mayes. She couldn't put a face to the name, and she presumed it was a lover or Tinder score who didn't realize or didn't understand that she didn't want to see him again and confront what they'd done, but hadn't wanted to hurt his feelings.

"I'm with the union," he explained, his tone clipped, a trace of a New York accent. He said that two other members of the cabin crew on the flight to Dubai had reached out to him and he had already met with one of them: Megan Briscoe. He, in turn, had called the FBI, and it was clear that he needed to see her, too, and get up to speed fast on whatever she knew about the passenger in 2C. "I want to know what really went on between you two on the flight and what really happened in Dubai," he said.

And with that there was a sudden ringing in her ears, her legs grew wobbly, and she wondered if this—this, not waking up beside the cold, still body of Alex Sokolov—was the demarcation between before and after. This, she thought with a terrible certainty, might really be the moment she would look back upon as the point where it all began to unravel.

Part Two

BURN THE CARBONS

《

FEDERAL BUREAU OF INVESTIGATION

FD-302 (redacted): MEGAN BRISCOE, FLIGHT ATTENDANT

DATE: July 28, 2018

MEGAN BRISCOE, date of birth—/—/——, SSN #————, telephone number (—)————, was interviewed by properly identified Special Agents ANNE McCONNELL and BRUCE ZIMMERUSKI at JFK INTERNATIONAL AIRPORT, immediately upon her flight's arrival in the U.S.

McCONNELL conducted the interview; ZIMMERUSKI took these notes.

After being advised of the nature of the interview, BRISCOE provided the following information.

BRISCOE said that she has been with the airline for 24 years. Prior to that, she had worked in guest services for DOVER STAR hotels in Washington, D.C., Baltimore, MD, and Pittsburgh, PA.

BRISCOE said that she had very little contact with ALEXANDER SOKOLOV on Flight 4094: he was being cared for by flight attendant CASSANDRA BOWDEN. She thought BOWDEN and SOKOLOV had flirted, but she said BOWDEN "was always a bit of a flirt." She had seen BOWDEN flirt with other passengers on other flights. BRISCOE explained that she and BOWDEN are friends and sometimes work their schedules so they share the same routes and can fly together. Though she lives now in Virginia, her base remains JFK.

She did not know what BOWDEN and SOKOLOV may have discussed.

When asked whether she and BOWDEN saw each other in Dubai, she said no, they did not. She said there were thirteen crew members on the flight and they separated into different groups, which was normal. She herself went out to dinner at a Japanese restaurant with JADA MORRIS, SHANE HEBERT, and VICTORIA MORGAN.

She did not explain why she did not have dinner with her friend, CASSANDRA BOWDEN.

7

Elena's mother always had corgis. These days she had three, one of which was a descendant of the two dogs she'd had when she divorced Elena's father. She trained the animals to come with an antique silver summoner patterned after the onion-shaped domes that adorned St. Basil's in Moscow or the Church of Our Savior on Spilled Blood in St. Petersburg. It predated the First World War and, thus, the revolution. According to the antique dealer, it may have belonged once to the Romanovs. (Elena presumed he was lying and her mother probably did, too. But that never stopped her mother from telling people that the summoner had resided once at the Winter Palace.) The nails on the dogs' paws would click along the hardwood floors when they scampered to her across her palatial apartment near the Kremlin. If her mother was seated, they would stand up on their hind legs and put their front legs onto her lap, exactly the way she had taught them: her own lady-with-lapdog moment, but played to oligarchic excess.

The animals traveled with her on the plane she bought after the divorce. She had special in-seat safety harnesses created for them for the flights. The straps were lined with the same mink that adorned the safety belts on the Art Deco–inspired Manhattan airship seats she'd had designed for the humans.

Her mother never remarried. Neither did her father. Sometimes Elena would see her mother on the gossip or society pages in an evening gown with waterfalls of jewelry dangling from her ears and around her neck, a Moscow robber baron on her arm.

Sometimes she would see a photo of her on the social networks that someone had taken at the Bolshoi or the botanical garden.

She knew that one of her father's friends had suggested poisoning the dogs after the divorce. Now that gentleman assisted the Syrian government in Damascus; he'd helped Assad squirrel away sarin in 2013, when the international monitors were destroying the rest of the stockpile. But her father had refused to kill the animals. Unlike some of his friends—now, she guessed, some of hers—her father didn't approve of incidental killing or the slaughter of noncombatants.

Elena had inherited that trait from him, she supposed. Certainly that was one reason why the flight attendant was still alive. In some ways, her mother had a far more entrenched killer instinct than her father. Exhibit A? The divorce settlement. She was ruthless.

And her mother had realized early on that her daughter was a daddy's girl—though maybe that was inevitable given the woman's disinterest in child-rearing. Or maybe that had been the plan all along. Her mother had visited her just the one time when she was a teenager in Switzerland, and she'd never once come to Boston when Elena went there for college. The truth was, Elena hadn't seen her mother in years and really didn't miss her. She doubted her mother missed her either.

She looked down once more at the Moscow newspaper she had opened a few minutes ago. More violence in Donetsk. The continued rebound of the ruble. An American drone strike in Yemen. She knew it was this last story that was most likely to catch Viktor's interest: America and China remained the only countries in the world that had successfully weaponized drones, and America's were far beyond China's. It was among the reasons why the Russians had such pathologic drone envy and why Russian military intelligence was obsessed with the American program. It was why Viktor was spending so much time with the Emirates drone manufacturer. ISIS used toy drones as IEDs. Imagine a stealth drone or even a jet drone with a chemical payload.

She finished her tea and recalled her father's samovar. It was rare, a tombac bronze, and once it had belonged to his great-grandmother. Somehow the family had retained it through both revolution and world war. Through Stalin and Malenkov and Khrushchev. It resided now with her mother. Of course. Somehow the woman had gotten even that, the samovar that neither the Bolsheviks nor the Nazis had been able to wrest from the Orlovs.

8

Cassie met the union official for breakfast at a diner on the corner of Twenty-Sixth and Third. Derek Mayes had chubby salt-and-pepper caterpillars above his eyes, the brows shading tortoiseshell eyeglasses and a face just starting to grow jowly. He was mostly bald and his seersucker blazer had blotches of black city dust, but the blue matched his eyes. His wedding band was thick like his fingers. She pegged him for his late sixties.

"I went through your records," he was saying. He was eating scrambled eggs and home fries and bacon. She was nursing a bowl of oatmeal, both because she wasn't especially hungry and because her anxiety had made her queasy. "You were on the Hugo Fournier flight. Infamous."

"I guess."

"Man, some of you were in deep water on that one. Stowing a dead guy in the bathroom? That widow was pissed. And, oh my God, what a PR nightmare for the airline. For the union. Remember *The Tonight Show*? Conan? The *New York Post*? I remember the comics trotted out all the terms: Trolley dolly. Air mattress. Sky muffin. It's like it was 1967 and you were all 'stewardesses' again—like there were no male flight attendants."

"The female terms are all about sex. The male ones are degrading in a different way. A lot end with 'boy.'"

He nodded. "Juice boy. Cart boy."

"Anyway, I really wasn't involved in the decision about what to do with the body."

"I know. We would have met then if you had been. But we had that purser's back and everything turned out okay. And it was never a criminal thing."

"Like this."

"Yeah. Like this. At least I think like this. It's just so typical of the FBI. So typical. They don't call the union, they don't tell you to get a lawyer. It's infuriating. If they were going to meet the plane, they should have told us so we could make sure there was someone in the room with you."

"Are you going to meet with every employee who was on the plane?"

"Oh, yeah," he said, almost chuckling at the certainty as he spoke. "Look, every person the guy met the last couple of days is of interest now. Someone in Dubai or someone in America is going to want to talk to every single bellhop and waitress and concierge and, yes, flight attendant he might have said boo to. Every single one. Of course, it's really only you and Megan and Jada I'm worried about. You're the three."

"Because . . ."

"Because you were the ones handling first class and you were the ones who were in direct contact with Sokolov."

"And you said they both called you?"

"Damn right, they did. You should have called me, too," he said, and she felt chastised.

"You live in the city?" she asked. After she spoke, she wondered if she should have apologized to him for not reaching out to the union on Saturday. But she had been so relieved when the FBI's Frank Hammond hadn't even asked about her whereabouts in Dubai that it hadn't crossed her mind to contact them. She had been in something like shock at the way she thought she might have dodged a bullet.

Mayes nodded as he chewed. Then: "I live about ten blocks

south of here. My wife and I always figured we'd move out to Long Island when we had children, but we never did, so we just stayed. And we like the neighborhood. Lot of NYU kids. Makes us feel younger than we are."

"I like that area, too. Especially in September when the freshmen arrive. They are just so young."

He smiled. "And they get younger every year."

"So, what did Megan say? Or Jada?" It felt like she was feeling her way in the dark. So far she and Derek had discussed her path to the airline, but the most revealing thing she had shared was that she had made it through the University of Kentucky on financial aid and a work-study job at the college switchboard. She'd manned the console, an antique as the twenty-first century loomed, from midnight to eight a.m. two nights a week. Almost no one ever called. Mostly she alerted campus security when students locked themselves out of their rooms or when women wanted a safe ride back to their dorms. Mostly she wrote papers and worried about her kid sister and the foster home where Rosemary was parked until she finished high school. Cassie didn't drink then. She guessed this was irony, given the way that so many of her peers seemed to live on keg beer and boxed wine.

He wiped his mouth with the paper napkin, and then used it on his fingers. "They said they barely spoke to him. Hi and bye. Jada thinks she may have brought him the basket of breads midway through the lunch service and asked if he wanted another roll. She may have offered him a newspaper and asked if he wanted English or French. But they both said—when I asked—that you spoke to him a lot."

"Why did you ask?"

"Because I needed to know who was taking care of the guy and talking to him, if they weren't. And they both said it was you. Jada said he chatted you up pretty seriously."

For a second she said nothing. She was grateful that Jada had told Mayes that Alex had been chatting her up, the implication being that he had paid more attention to her than she had paid to him. The truth was somewhere closer to the middle. Still, she wondered: Was this the moment when she should confess? Tell this union official that she needed a lawyer and the union's help? Tell him that there was a woman in this world named Miranda who may have had something to do with Alex's hedge fund, and had seen her in Alex's hotel suite at the Royal Phoenician that night? But she let the moment pass, as she had every other opportunity she'd had to start over. Derek Mayes wanted to help her, but she rather doubted there was any variant on attorney-client privilege between the two of them that could withstand a court of law. Whatever she told him could come back to haunt her. "I told the FBI everything I knew when we landed," she said firmly. "I know it wasn't very much. But he was just one more passenger on just one more flight."

"Yes and no."

She waited. It took control not to sit back in the seat and fold her arms across her chest. The waitress refilled their coffee, and Mayes poured the last of the milk in the small, tinny creamer into his mug.

"What does that mean?" she asked.

"Yes, to you he was just one more passenger on just one more flight," he said carefully, and for a moment she began to relax. His construction suggested that no one really knew anything about her involvement with the man. "But I don't think he was just a hedge fund guy. Yesterday was busier than I like for a Sunday in the summer. I think the FBI is going to want to speak to you again."

"Me or the cabin crew?" she asked. She heard the quiver in her voice. Her mouth had gone dry.

"Cabin crew."

"The FBI told you that?"

"They did."

"Why?"

"I don't know. They wouldn't tell me." He leaned in conspiratorially. "Look, you spent the most time with the guy on the plane. That's a fact."

"So?"

"He was part of your section in first class. You were the one serving him. Don't get me wrong, the other flight attendants aren't throwing you under the bus. But both Megan and Jada said you two were yakking it up every time you brought the guy a glass of wine or refilled his coffee cup. You spent a hell of a lot more time with two C than you did with, I don't know, four C."

"That's not true."

"You two weren't yakking it up?"

"No."

He shrugged. "Look, even if it were true, why would that be a problem?"

"I was polite to him."

"I'm serious, Cassie. Even if you were flirting with the guy, why would that be an issue?"

"Because it would be unprofessional."

He chuckled, but it was a mean laugh. "Yeah, flight attendants never flirt with passengers—or pilots. Never." He rolled his eyes. "You know how high the divorce rate is in your profession. I guess that's why flight attendants and pilots only wind up married to . . . each other. You're away from home all the time, you're flirting all the time, you're in hotels all the time. And . . ."

"And what?"

"And no one gets you except people like you. No one gets the weirdness of the lifestyle. No one else could possibly understand."

She sighed. "It's inevitable we wind up together. It's simply because we all work together. I'm sure ad people marry ad people, and lawyers marry lawyers. All professions have office romances."

"Yeah, but you don't all work together. You don't. That's the thing. You almost never have the same people on the same crew. I mean, you and Megan are bid buddies, and I guess she and Shane are bid buddies. But there were ten flight attendants on that airplane to Dubai, and seven of you had never seen each other before that JFK/Dubai sequence and may never, ever see each other again. Or, if you do, it will be years from now. And that's just the cabin crew.

Add in the folks in the cockpit. When will you fly next with any of those pilots? A year from now? Two? Ten? No, Cassie, sorry: you don't work together."

"Where is this going? I thought you wanted to help me."

"I do. And that's why I need to be sure that this Sokolov character didn't tell you something meaningful or you didn't learn something about him that you should be sharing with a lawyer or just maybe the FBI."

"Nope."

"Because by now the FBI knows you were flirting with him. And by now they know that you were not having dinner that night in Dubai with any member of the crew, including your friend Megan. If I know that from my limited conversations, then they do from their interviews."

"Why does that matter?"

"Maybe it doesn't. But just in case: anything you want to tell me about that night in Dubai?"

"I went to bed."

"In the airline's hotel?"

"Yes!"

"Did you go out to eat?"

"No," she answered, wondering the moment the syllable had escaped her lips whether she had spoken too quickly. There surely were witnesses at the restaurant. But she also knew instantly that his next question would be about room service—and it was.

"So you had something sent up to your room?"

"No."

"You didn't eat?"

"I wasn't feeling great. I ate some peanuts from the minibar. I fell asleep." She couldn't imagine they could actually check such a thing. How accurate really was hotel monitoring of the minibar?

"So you didn't go out?"

"Did someone say I did?"

"Not to me."

"Okay, then."

"But according to two airline employees in the cabin with you, you were flirting with Alex Sokolov. And then, it seems, you weren't hanging out with anyone from the flight crew that night. No one. You just disappeared—"

"Into my hotel room!" she snapped, cutting him off. She saw over Mayes's shoulder that she had spoken so harshly that the two older men having breakfast together at the next table turned, their heads swiveling like owls'.

Mayes opened his hands, palms up, and sat back. "Got it," he said. "Got it. But for all we know, the FBI is going to talk to the passengers who were seated near Sokolov on the flight, and it's possible that one or more of them is going to say you and the guy were friendly. I don't know yet if Sokolov was from some wealthy or well-connected family, or whether he just wasn't what he said he was. I don't know what he was really doing in Dubai. Maybe it really was just a meeting with investors. But this story has legs, so I want to be sure you do three things. Okay?"

"Fine. Tell me." She hoped that her lies and her fear would be misconstrued for aggravation.

"I want you to get a lawyer."

"I can't afford a lawyer!" she said, even though she recalled vividly her vow in the hotel suite in Dubai that she would find one if somehow she made it back to America. "I can barely afford my apartment. You know what I make. I'm broke. We're all broke. We all need more money than we have."

"So does everyone, so relax. I can help you find a lawyer you can afford. Not a big deal. It's what we do."

"I'm not saying yes—because I don't see why I need one—but what else?"

"Two, I want you to keep me informed with exactly what's going on. Again, this is so we can help you."

"Fine."

"And, three, I want you to tell me the second a reporter calls you."

She hadn't imagined a reporter contacting her. But she realized that was naïve. Of course one might, especially if Sokolov was from a prominent family or wasn't really a hedge fund manager. "I can do all of that, sure," she agreed. And perhaps because of the specter of a news camera in her face or the proximity of the *New York Post* that a fellow at another table was reading, she added, "And if you have a name for a lawyer, that would be great. Cheap, but good. But tell me something."

"Name it."

"If Sokolov wasn't a money manager of some sort, then what was he? A spy?"

"He had a job that demanded he travel. That's a great cover for a lot of things."

"Is that a yes? He might have been an American spy?"

"Or Russian. Or German. Or Israeli. Or South African. I don't know. Maybe he was some kind of go-between or courier."

She thought of the paperback she'd bought yesterday. "He was into his Russian DNA—at least a little bit." When she said the word DNA, she felt another one of those pinpricks of misgiving and fear: it was her lipstick. The lipstick she had lost somewhere in Dubai; the lipstick she had possibly left behind in room 511. She imagined a police tech lifting it off the hotel room floor with tongs and dropping it into a clear plastic bag. There it was, the smoking gun.

And there was something else: a lip balm. A lip balm with her airline's logo. Sure, it was a generic, but she liked it and she used it, too. It had a coconut scent. When she had been emptying her purse before throwing it away in Dubai, she hadn't seen it either. Sometimes she moisturized her lips with the balm before applying her lipstick. Had she done that in 511? Was there a lip balm somewhere in that room that had both her airline's logo and her DNA?

"Maybe it's just that simple," Derek was saying about Sokolov. "Maybe he's FSB."

"I don't know what that is."

"What used to be the KGB. Federal Security Service of the Russian Federation. Counterintelligence. Spy stuff. Often very nasty spy stuff."

"But he still seemed awfully American to me," she told him, hoping Mayes hadn't heard the small tremor in her voice.

"Means nothing. If you're undercover, you want to seem American. But what do I know? He could just as easily be CIA. Or maybe he was a seriously nasty crook selling arms. Or girls. Or drugs. You know, whatever he was doing may have had nothing to do with espionage. I'm just saying, he may not have been what he said he was, given the way he was killed."

"Didn't some Dubai police officer say it was a robbery?"

"It wasn't."

"Really?"

"Nothing was stolen."

"How do you know that?"

He shrugged. "I asked. I asked the FBI agent who interviewed Megan. The woman wouldn't tell me much, but she said nothing was stolen. At least they don't think anything was stolen. His wallet, his watch, his credit cards were all there, according to the FBI chief in the Emirates. His computer was still there. His briefcase was still there."

She wanted to kick herself for not stealing Sokolov's wallet and wristwatch and dumping them in the very same trash can in Dubai where she had tossed the washcloth and soap and the shards of the bottle of Stoli. It hadn't crossed her mind to suggest that the poor guy's death had been part of a robbery. But then she recalled an expression that a philosophy class had debated ad nauseam in college: you can't prove a negative. In the end, the class as a whole had decided that you could. But the expression had stayed with her.

"Well, if something was stolen, it wouldn't be in the hotel room, so you wouldn't know it was gone," she said.

"Agreed. I'm sure the authorities in Dubai, ours and theirs, will compile an inventory as best they can of what he had brought with him. I'm sure they're talking to everyone at the hotel. I'm sure they're talking to everyone who was supposed to be in the meeting with him—assuming there really was a meeting. In any case, the vibe I'm getting is pretty clear: this wasn't a hotel room robbery that went bad. This was an execution."

The word lingered in the air. She looked down at the last of the runny eggs and toast crumbs on the union official's plate. Mayes was probably—almost certainly—correct. She had reminded herself dozens of times how easy it would have been for someone to slash her throat, too. And yet they hadn't. They'd spared her. Still, she would never be able to erase the memory of that body in the bed, so cold and still. She would never forget all that blood.

"Cassie?"

She looked up.

"I thought I'd lost you there for a minute," Mayes was saying. "I was about to snap my fingers. You know, wake you up from your trance."

"I'm sorry."

"You're okay?"

"Yeah. I'm okay."

He sat back in his chair and smiled. He folded his arms in front of his chest. "I'm not completely sure you are," he said. "But you know what?"

She waited.

"I got a feeling some poor dead guy you met one time on an airplane is the least of your problems."

"I think I should be insulted."

"Nah. I'm speaking as an old guy who wanted to be a dad and never was." He picked up the bill the waitress had left on the table—Cassie wondered when that happened, because she couldn't recall the waitress returning—and watched Mayes head for the cashier to pay it.

« «

That night Cassie opened the Chianti alone in her apartment, swirling it in a hand-painted wineglass. It was one of a pair that

Rosemary had given her years before she had realized that she probably shouldn't encourage her older sister's drinking. The glasses had white orchids rising from the base of the bowl to the rim, the petals erotic and lush. As she was swallowing her first sip, her phone pinged and she saw that she had a text from Buckley. He was asking how she was. He added that he regretted how short they had been with each other before he'd left Sunday morning, and hoped he'd see her when she was back in New York. She didn't reply, but neither did she delete it. Usually she would have. Usually when she picked up a guy in a bar like that, there would have been a gap in her memory—an hour or two or ten—that she didn't want to hear about on a second date. Maybe she didn't delete the text this time, she thought, because while she had gotten drunk with Buckley, she hadn't accelerated when she hit her drunken V1 and then broken the blackout barrier with a concussive, window-rattling boom. So, maybe tomorrow she would text something back. Maybe not. Probably not. Still, she kept the text on her phone and told herself that this suggested evolution, a supposed impossibility at midlife when, in theory, no one changed. She thought it was rather kind of him to suggest they had been short with each other on Sunday morning. In reality, she had only been short with him.

The irony of blackouts was this: you had to have a spectacular alcohol tolerance to black out. Amateur drinkers passed out long before they put the hippocampus—those folds in the gray matter where memories are made—to sleep. She was a pro. Partial blackouts happened when the blood alcohol hit the magic 0.2; en bloc or total blackouts occurred when you ratcheted up the number to an undeniably impressive 0.3. The bar for drunk driving, by comparison, was a fraction of those numbers: a mere 0.08.

She considered calling Paula, one of her friends who could keep up with her drink for drink, whether the drink of the day was wine or tequila or Drambuie. Paula had a weird thing for Drambuie: it was her Proustian madeleine from a ninth and tenth grade spent getting sloshed on her father's MacKinnon. When Cassie was with Paula, dullness disappeared and it was like they were skydiving. They might create chaos for the women and men around them—sharing too much, dancing too aggressively, berating a hostess or a bartender for the music that was playing or the fact it was raining outside—but they also dialed up the energy, didn't they? Maybe they did. But in her lucid moments the next morning, she wondered if in fact they just sucked the energy from the room.

Which was why she also had friends like Gillian. Gillian drank, but only like a reasonable person. She didn't get drunk, and so it was Gillian who would grab Cassie's purse at the end of the night when she left it dangling over the back of the bar stool or tell the strange, aggressive guy with the face tats that Cassie wasn't going home with him.

In the end, however, she called no one and texted no one. Not tonight. Instead she booted up her laptop on the kitchen counter and stood before it as she drank. It was time to learn all that she could about the dead American in Dubai. It was time to search for Miranda. She decided to begin with the social networks. There she could read about Alex Sokolov and perhaps discover Miranda among his followers or friends.

Alex had mentioned that he had Facebook, Twitter, and Insta- gram accounts, though he said that he rarely used them. She dis- covered right away that they were gone, if they had ever existed at all. She found no trace of him on LinkedIn and Tinder. She presumed his family had deleted the pages, but she also thought if Derek Mayes had been correct and Sokolov had indeed been a spy, then it might have been just as likely that some government agency (one of ours or one of theirs, she thought cryptically) had made the pages disappear.

Unfortunately, this also meant that she couldn't search among the man's Facebook friends or Twitter followers for this other woman. This was going to demand more digging. And so she switched gears and started to surf among different travel and news websites for stories about the murder. There were plenty, though none were long and they merely corroborated what he had told her about his family life: He was an only child. He had parents in Virginia. They described his job with the hedge fund. The strangest part of the articles? None of them mentioned another Unisphere employee or investor named Miranda having seen a woman with Alex in his suite hours before he was executed.

She recalled him mentioning that his mother's name was Harper, and Cassie was able to find her Facebook page quickly. She half expected to see a photo of Alex and a desperately sad in memoriam from a mother about her son. But there wasn't. Harper Sokolov hadn't posted anything in a week, since she had added a photo of herself, her husband, and another couple in tennis whites on the terrace of a country club. She looked wholesome and athletic and fit in the short dress. Cassie saw Alex in her smile. She searched among the woman's friends for Miranda, though she wasn't confident she'd be there: if Alex was meeting her for the first time that night in Dubai, why in the world would his mother know her? But she had to check. And as she expected, there was no one named Miranda among Harper's friends.

Next Cassie visited the Unisphere website and typed the word "Miranda" into the search box. Nothing came up. The company was too big to include an employee directory. But there was a list of offices around the world, and while they didn't have individual websites, they did list phone numbers. She glanced at the clock on the oven and saw that even eight time zones to the east no one would be in the Dubai office yet. But she could call them later and ask for Miranda. See what happened.

She refilled her glass a third time and placed Mayes's business card directly beside Frank Hammond's on her refrigerator. She had scribbled on it the phone number of the lawyer he had recommended, a woman with the melodious name of Ani Mouradian. She hadn't heard from any reporters. The FBI hadn't contacted her again. She tried to convince herself that Derek Mayes was wrong and she would never hear from the FBI again and she would never need to call this Ani Mouradian. But she guessed she would have to be a good deal drunker to believe that, and so she ran herself a bath and brought the bottle and the glass and her phone into the bathroom with her. There was no reason to be sober: she was alone, and she hadn't touched alcohol since the small hours of Sunday morning. Forty-two hours. Almost two days ago now.

When she was settled under the bubbles, she closed her eyes and tried to lose herself in her ablutions—clearing her mind was of more importance to her tonight than cleaning her body—but it was impossible. She kept thinking of Alex and she kept wondering what would have happened if she had called the front desk at the hotel. But she knew. At least she thought she knew. Everyone would believe that she had killed the poor bastard—which, she had to admit, would be very difficult to refute—and she would be in jail in Dubai. She would know someone from the U.S. embassy very, very well, probably having grown acquainted with him or her from behind bars.

She noticed that the polish on her nails was reminiscent of the Chianti and that it was starting to chip. She would have to get a manicure tomorrow. The flight to Rome didn't leave until seven p.m., so she could sleep late and still go to the gym and the salon. Easy.

She reached down and put her wineglass on the floor beside the tub and grabbed her phone. She decided to search Twitter for news stories about Sokolov, see if there was anything she might have missed, and scrolled through the ones that had been online for a day that she'd scanned just a few minutes ago in the kitchen. But then she saw a tweet from a news agency in Dubai that was only seconds old. She clicked the link and instantly felt her stomach lurch as if she were on a plane that had just dropped a thousand feet in a wind shear. There she was. There she was twice, as a matter of fact. There were two images of her. She wasn't recognizable—at least not really recognizable, because the photos were grainy stills taken from the Dubai hotel's security camera footage, and because in both images she was wearing sunglasses and the scarf she had bought at the airport when they had landed. In the first she was in the lobby, meeting Sokolov before they went out to dinner; they were near the entrance and she had hooked her arm around his elbow. She was smiling; they both were. In the second she was alone, exiting the hotel the next day. This time, her jaw was set. It was the scarf that had likely led the investigators to pick her out the second time.

The sunglasses were pretty common Ray-Bans—one of their classic black frames.

But the scarf? It was distinct. It was a red and blue arabesque with one large cluster of tendrils and palmettes in the center, and then a series of smaller versions framed along the four sides. Also, it had a series of small red tassels. The footage was black and white, but the pattern was vivid.

She'd been with Megan and Jada when she bought it. She'd been wearing it when she'd returned to the airline's hotel. She'd been wearing it in the van with the entire crew Friday morning.

The article said the woman was not considered a suspect, but was merely wanted for questioning. Not a suspect? Ridiculous. Of course, she was. There was an image of her with Sokolov at the hotel at night and then another one of her leaving the hotel alone the next morning.

Almost desperately she reached for her wine, and in her haste, as she transferred the goblet from her left hand to her right, she managed to clang it against the porcelain soap dish built into the tile wall, shattering the glass and spilling the wine into the water. The soap bubbles had long vanished, and so she watched, absolutely immobile, as the red wine spread and then dissipated, leaving the water and the shards of glass—some resting on her thigh, some on her abdomen, some sunk to the bottom where she could feel the edges like pinpricks or rough sand—a soft, almost soothing pink.

It was only as she started to carefully pick the glass from her body that she saw the two long cuts on the side of her hand.

9

Elena watched half a dozen U.S. sailors laughing and cavorting on the sidewalk from Viktor's window on the fifth floor—the top floor—of the nondescript little office building, and knew right away they were lost. This neighborhood had a Sikh temple, a Coptic Orthodox church, a Greek Orthodox parish, and the Dubai Evangelical Center. It also had dentists and accountants. It did not have the gold or jewelry or electronics stores that usually drew the sailors north from the port at Mina Jebel Ali. The carrier battle group was due in tomorrow, and so the day after tomorrow the city would be awash with American seamen and women.

Now she turned away from the window and leaned against Viktor's credenza. His office here was an amalgam of the nineteenth and twenty-first centuries. There was dark wood paneling on the walls and a silver tray with crystal cognac snifters emblazoned with the two-headed eagle on a side table, but there was also a flip-top panel for video conferences and a touch-screen computer built into a chrome and walnut desk. "She wasn't there. I swept the room," she said to him, hoping she didn't sound defensive. She was just stating the facts. Unfortunately, this was getting messy and had the potential to spin wildly out of control. One's vision was always crisper in hindsight, but Elena knew now that she'd made an egregious mistake. It would have been terrible, but perhaps she should have killed the flight attendant with Alex when she'd had the chance—when she'd come to the room and found that Alex had brought a little arm candy from the airline upstairs. If she'd wanted, she could have made it look like a murder suicide. A crime of passion. She could have left behind the knife.

But she hadn't, because this flight attendant wasn't her usual sort of game. She didn't kill bystanders. She didn't kill innocent people.

And now Viktor was furious. She knew that look. He was rather like her father when her father felt that someone had failed: he didn't rant, he didn't vent, he didn't throw tantrums. He seethed. It was far more unsettling. But the ramifications for whoever had screwed up? Just as deadly.

"Oh, I believe you. I believe you swept the room. But the security photos on the news sites are clear. You've seen them, Elena. The woman was definitely at the hotel in the morning and she was wearing the exact same clothes from the night before," Viktor reminded her. "Alex never told you he had company when you called?"

"No. I wouldn't have gone to his room if he had."

Viktor seemed to think about this. "Had he done this sort of thing in the past?"

"If he did, no one told me. He was never part of a honey pot."

"That's true."

She heard the sailors outside on the street laughing a little too boisterously. If the latch mechanism on the window weren't so complicated, she would have opened it and pointed them in the right direction for the sorts of stores they were after. "Look, I almost took care of business then and there. When we were drinking. But I didn't want to risk a scene. I didn't want to risk the noise. Two people? Who knows what could go wrong. The woman said something about going back to her own hotel because of her flight the next day, and so I left and waited for her to leave."

"And then you returned to Alex's suite," Viktor murmured.

"Yes."

He sighed and she felt a flicker of unease. It grew more pronounced when he said, "Obviously it would have been better if you'd taken that risk, Elena. If he was as drunk as you say he was, who knows what he told her. Who knows what she knows now."

"I don't think we need to worry," she tried to reassure him, but she could feel his disapproval. She knew how much trouble she was in.

"I do worry. And, frankly, I am"—and he paused, allowing the moment to grow ominous as he pretended merely to be searching for the right word—"vexed by the fact that you didn't tell me there had been someone with him in the first place."

"I should have," she admitted. "I know."

"Yes. You should have."

"I'm sorry."

"So what did you find? When you returned to his hotel room?" he asked.

"Alex was already passed out in his bed. He was out like a light. The suite was even worse than it had been when I'd stopped by earlier in the evening. Both rooms. It was squalid, it really was. He or that idiot woman had managed to break the bottle of vodka I'd brought and one of the hotel's glasses."

"This was after you left."

"Correct."

"But she definitely wasn't present when you took care of our Mr. Sokolov."

"I'm positive."

"So, it would seem that she did indeed return to his room afterward and find him dead," said Viktor.

"But she didn't call the front desk or the embassy. She just . . . what? Found the body and did nothing? Spent the night with a corpse?"

He gave her a dark, lopsided smile, but remained silent.

"The suite was pretty large," Elena told him, but she knew she was grasping a little desperately for vines around the quicksand. "Maybe she only went back to the living room. Maybe she forgot something in the living room and didn't even peer into the bedroom."

Viktor folded his arms across his chest dismissively and rocked back in the chair. "You can't possibly believe that. The surveillance cameras suggest she was there all night. She knows he was dead. She saw the body."

"In that case, is it actually possible that she believes she killed him?" Elena asked, thinking aloud.

"Oh, come on."

"I'm serious. This flight attendant struck me as a pretty serious party girl. Think 'Chandelier.'"

"I suppose that's a club drug?"

"It's a pop song. Sia. I wouldn't be surprised if she has serious memory problems when she drinks."

He steepled together his fingers. "I guess it's conceivable."

"So maybe this works to our favor. It shouldn't take long for the police to figure out that she was in the room with Alex and pin the murder on her. My impression of the woman is that she's a disaster, she lacks all common sense."

"Maybe. But it's complicated. I spoke with our lawyer here."

She waited.

"Alex wasn't a citizen of the United Emirates," he continued. "He was an American. It would take a lot of work to bring this woman back to Dubai and put her on trial, and the authorities here don't have an especially vested interest in this case."

Outside one of the sailors screamed something in frustration about how lost he was and how his phone wasn't helping. She realized they, too, had been drinking. How was it that Russians had been saddled with the reputation for inebriation? "Is there any chance she might be tried in the U.S.?"

"Only if someone thought Alex's death was a terrorist act," he replied, and then he scoffed. "Can you imagine? A terrorist stewardess."

"Flight attendant," she corrected him reflexively.

There was a long beat as he raised one eyebrow. "Flight attendant," he repeated finally.

"No one will view his death as a terrorist act," she said. "No one will view this flight attendant as a terrorist."

"I agree. Which is fine. Frankly, a trial does no one any good. Not us. Not them. And speaking frankly, Elena, not you."

"I understand." She couldn't bear the ruckus outside on the street any longer. She vowed that when this meeting was over, she was going to march downstairs and tell the sailors precisely where to go.

"I'm not sure you do. The problem, as you have made very clear from your time with Sokolov, is that he was drunk. Peasant drunk. The toxicology report will confirm that, I'm sure. God knows what he might have shared. I think we all need to move forward on the assumption that he said something—that he told her something. You've said yourself that she's an irresponsible drinker, too."

She knew this was coming, but still her heart sank. "Does she have any family?" she asked.

"Have you grown a conscience, Elena Orlov?"

"I simply want to understand what we have to contain," she said.

"No. She has no children and no husband. Not even an ex-husband. It should be very easy for you to fix this. She should have an accident. A terrible, unforeseen, but eminently realistic accident."

"I just . . ."

"You just what?"

"I just feel bad. She did nothing wrong. She's just a pathetic drunk who got in bed with the wrong man on the wrong night."

"She's dangerous," Viktor reminded her.

"Perhaps."

"Perhaps? You should have taken care of them both when you found them together. You know that. I know you do. Besides . . ."

"Besides what?"

"She saw you, Elena. She saw you. Be realistic: one of you has to die." He shrugged. "I think it's your choice."

10

The cuts looked far worse than they were. She wouldn't need stitches, Cassie decided. In the end, she stood naked over the bathroom sink, sobered by the photos she had seen of herself on her phone, and pressed a cold, damp washcloth on each gash until the blood slowed. Then she pressed a couple of cotton balls along the wounds and held them in place with Scotch tape she wrapped around her left hand as if she were a mummy. It looked like a kindergartner had attempted the first aid. Tomorrow morning she would have to buy Band-Aids.

She climbed into her sleep shirt and tried to convince herself that the rest of the crew wasn't searching out stories about Alex Sokolov the way she was, and so they might never see the images of her at the Royal Phoenician in Dubai. But she failed. Of course they were Googling him: He'd been on their flight. He'd been in her and Megan's and Jada's cabin. She lay in bed waiting for the lights of the Empire State Building—the tower was the signature white tonight—to blink out. Eventually someone in the crew would spot the photos. By now the grainy stills had no doubt been shared with the FBI here in the United States and it was inevitable that eventually investigators would explore whether the woman beside Sokolov had been on the plane. First they would rule out friends and acquaintances and clients and hotel employees, but then they would work their way back to the flight. Who had he sat with? Who had he seen? They would ask the crew (They would ask her!) if she recognized the person walking beside the dead man.

What would finally give her away, the scarf? The sunglasses? The sharp slope of her aquiline nose?

In the morning, she told herself, she would call Derek Mayes and tell him that she did indeed need that lawyer named Ani. She was going to phone her, but it couldn't hurt if Derek made a call, too. So much for the manicure. She would buy Band-Aids and retain an attorney. It was time.

« «

In the morning, she called the Unisphere office in Dubai. It was seven a.m. in New York, three p.m. there. In her mind she saw all of those hotel lobbies and all of those airport corridors that used antique clocks to offer the time in, for instance, Tokyo and Moscow and L. A. Her plan, as much as she had one, was first to learn if the woman was actually employed there. If she was, Cassie would ask to speak with her, claiming to be an American expat who was thinking of moving some assets to Unisphere and wanted to set up an appointment. The employee would either agree to meet with her if she was a money manager of some sort or she would direct her to the right person if she wasn't. She planned to introduce herself as Jane Brown, because as a little girl she had looked up her family's last name one day in a Kentucky phonebook, desirous of seeing it in print, and she'd seen whole columns of Browns.

The receptionist spoke English with no trace of an accent, and Cassie asked for Miranda.

"Miranda," the woman said, drawing the name out, clearly expecting as she did that Cassie would offer a surname. She didn't. She would wait this out. And so the receptionist continued. "What is Miranda's last name, please?"

"I'm honestly not sure. We met at a dinner party this weekend."

"This is a small office. I don't believe we have a Miranda here," she continued. "Is it possible she works for another firm?"

"It is," Cassie agreed, and then she got off the phone as quickly as she could.

« «

As Ani Mouradian walked her from the lobby to a meeting room, Cassie found herself wondering how in the name of God Derek Mayes thought she would be able to afford a lawyer like this. The practice was midway up the Seagram Building, a Park Avenue icon between Fifty-Second and Fifty-Third. She wasn't sure whether to laugh or cry. A part of her viewed the location of Ani's firm as one more small, horrid joke the universe was playing on her: sending the daughter of a drunk who, admittedly, drank too much herself, into a building named after a renowned distiller. The reception area was windowless, but the couches were plush and deep and the wood paneling a dark mahogany that belonged in a British library or university club. She could almost see her reflection in the lacquer. The firm had the northwest corner, however, and most of the offices along the exterior walls were awash in morning summer light.

"How many people work here?" she asked Ani.

"We're not all that big. I believe, counting paralegals and assistants, there are maybe sixty of us."

"You know I'm just a flight attendant."

"Meaning?"

"I probably can't afford you. I don't know what Derek was thinking."

"Everyone thinks your life is so glamorous," the lawyer said, ushering her into a small, interior conference room, and then shutting the door behind her. The table was round and modern and would seat no more than four people. The walls had white bookcases filled with law books. "But I know better. Derek Mayes is my uncle. Please, sit down."

She did. Ani took the chair beside her. Cassie guessed that Ani was ten years younger than she was. A part of her was relieved because she guessed a young person had a lower hourly rate;

another part of her, however, fretted that she needed all the help and all the experience she could get. She knew she preferred older pilots to younger ones. A new pilot was every bit as competent as a seasoned one when a flight was uneventful. But when something went horribly wrong—when the engines stalled as you descended in a snowstorm, when geese clogged your engines on takeoff— you wanted as much experience as possible. Everyone who flew knew the only reason that US Airways flight 1549 landed safely in the Hudson River one January afternoon in 2009 was because the pilot, Sully Sullenberger, was an unflappable former fighter jock who was days away from his fifty-eighth birthday when a bird strike disabled both of the Airbus's engines. The guy had white hair. He had years and years (and years) in the air.

"Are you sure you don't want coffee?" Ani was asking.

"Positive. Your receptionist offered me some. I'm fine."

"What happened to your hand?"

"I dropped a glass. Not a big deal."

Ani smiled enigmatically, and Cassie couldn't read the woman's face. Did she not believe her? The lawyer had creosote hair that fell to her shoulders, dark eyes, and dark, pencil-thin eyebrows. She was slender—almost slight—and was wearing an impeccably tailored gray suit. Her blouse was a conservative shade of pink.

"So," she said after a moment, "we do a lot of things here. Some of us specialize in employment law. Labor law, collective bargaining."

"You have pretty nice digs for a bunch of union lawyers."

She chuckled. "What makes you think we represent the unions?"

"Well, your uncle—"

"I'm teasing you," Ani said, cutting her off. "But, yes, the firm makes considerably more money representing the Fortune 500. A lot of my billable hours come from an oil company. We also do criminal defense work, especially white-collar crime. I gather my uncle thinks you might be in need of a little help."

Cassie wondered just how much her uncle actually knew. She had a feeling he must have suspected more than he had revealed at breakfast. "He does."

"Go on."

"I'm curious: what area of your expertise did he think I needed?"

She shook her head. "I have no idea. My uncle gives out my business cards like the Easter Bunny gives out jellybeans. I'm the daughter he never had. You called me this morning. Let's start there."

Cassie glanced down at the Band-Aids on her left hand. There were five of them on the two cuts. Did they make her look hapless or inept? "You probably assume I have some labor issue with the airline."

"I assume nothing."

"Did your uncle tell you about the FBI?"

"He said they met a flight you were on when it landed. That's all."

She looked at the books over Ani's shoulder. They were beautiful, leather the color of a saddle, lettering the gold of a general's epaulets. Inside, she knew, were pages and pages that could probably substitute for the melatonin tabs she took on occasion when she was combating jet lag. Behind her, on the other side of the door, she was aware of a distant, faraway-seeming conversation. She heard, she thought, a copy machine. She thought of the two photos of her that were online, and then she thought once more of Sokolov's body in the bed. She saw it from the vantage point of the hotel room drapes as she sunk, hungover, to the lushly carpeted floor. This was probably her last chance. And so she spoke.

"I called you because the other day I woke up in a hotel room really far away from here, and the man beside me was dead." It was just that simple.

Ani raised one of those immaculate eyebrows but didn't say a word. And so Cassie went back to the beginning, starting with the flight from Paris to Dubai last week when she first met Sokolov and ending with the broken wineglass last night in a Murray Hill bathtub. She told her about Miranda. She showed her the two security camera images of her from the Dubai news story on her phone. She admitted to trying to wipe the suite of her fingerprints as best she could before leaving but said she may have left behind her lipstick and a lip balm in one of the rooms. Occasionally Ani interrupted her with a question, though none of them seemed tinged with judgment, and sometimes she asked her to pause while she jotted down a lengthier note on the yellow legal pad in her lap. When Cassie was done, she said, "I honestly can't say how much trouble you're really in—and I'm working on the assumption that you didn't kill this man."

"That's correct. Well, it's mostly correct. I'm pretty sure I didn't kill him, but I'm not one hundred percent sure."

"You're not one hundred percent sure?" Ani asked, the surprise evident on her face.

"That's right. I can't be completely confident," Cassie said, and then she explained her tendency to drink and even, on occasion, to succumb to—or, arguably, to court—the no-man's-land where memory hadn't a chance. "And then there was the bottle," she said when she had finished.

"The bottle?"

"In the morning, I found a broken bottle of Stolichnaya vodka. I vaguely remember when we broke it the night before. It was the vodka Miranda had brought. Alex was having trouble with the top. Anyway, the shoulder—you know, the neck and the shoulder of the bottle—were intact. Sort of. The top of the bottle was like a weapon and it was by the bed. I took all the pieces I could find and threw them away after I'd left the hotel."

"So, are you telling me that you might have killed him? You used the broken bottle as a weapon and cut his throat?" Her voice was flat. Toneless.

"Here's the thing," Cassie murmured. She recalled how when

people had something utterly ridiculous to explain, they always seemed to begin, *It's complicated.* She took comfort in the fact that she hadn't begun with those two words. "I'm not violent when I black out. I've never been told I hurt someone. I may do stupid things and risk my own life, but I don't attack people. If sometime in the night Alex had tried to have sex with me again, I don't think I would have stopped him. It's probably happened to me before. I mean, I know it has."

"Men having sex with you without your consent."

She nodded. "Look, I know it's not a gray area. I just know that when I'm that drunk, I'm not prone to say no. Or, I'm sorry to say, care."

"You're right, it's not a gray area. It's rape."

"But I don't think Alex would ever have tried to rape me. Either I was so drunk I was oblivious—"

"That's not consent, Cassie!"

"Let me finish. Please. Either I was so drunk I was oblivious, or I was happy with whatever was happening. But if I did ask Alex to stop, I believe he would have. He was a really gentle guy. I mean, he washed my hair in the shower. So, why would I have taken the broken bottle and fought him?"

"Is it possible that you killed him while he was sleeping? Is that where this is going?"

"It's possible, but . . ."

"But . . ."

"But I don't think so," Cassie said. "That's not me. And I've thought about this a lot since it happened. And . . ."

"Go on."

"And I thought I left. I have this memory of leaving that's pretty distinct."

"Leaving the hotel room."

"Yes. The suite."

"But you woke up beside him in bed."

"When I have a blackout, there are gaps. At first I thought I was going to leave with Miranda. Go back to the airline hotel. I mean, I was dressed when Miranda was there. Obviously."

"Obviously," Ani said, but her inflection was tinged with sarcasm.

"But I didn't leave. Miranda left and I didn't go with her. I stayed. And Alex and I went to the bedroom and made love. After that, however, I got dressed again. I know I did. Or I almost know I did. I have this memory of being at the hotel room door and saying good-bye to him. I really do."

"I just want to confirm: you were there when he broke the vodka bottle?"

"Yes."

"So, do you believe it might have been this Miranda person?"

"Who killed him? It's crossed my mind," Cassie answered. "This is the first time I've verbalized any of this, so I'm almost thinking out loud. Working it through. I guess it's possible. I left. Miranda came back. Then I came back."

"And you were so drunk that you didn't notice that Alex was dead?"

"The room's dark. Maybe."

"When Miranda arrived at the suite, she knocked on the door?"

"Yes. Why?"

"I was wondering if she had a key. But even if she didn't already have one, she steals a key while the three of you are having your little party."

Cassie hadn't thought of this, but it would certainly explain how someone had gotten into the room.

"But," Ani continued, "if Alex knows it's Miranda, she doesn't need a key. He just lets her in. How long do you think you were gone?"

"If I was gone? No idea."

"Why would you have come back?"

"I probably forgot something in the room and went back for it. That's happened before."

Ani looked down at her notes and then said, "It's also possible it was someone who worked at the hotel or knew someone who worked at the hotel."

"Yes, I agree that's a possibility."

"And while I personally have no idea how to break into a locked hotel room, I'm sure there are ways."

"I guess."

"This guy told you that he used to work for Goldman Sachs and now has a hedge fund. What else did he say about his job?"

"Nothing."

"Why was he in Dubai?"

"Meetings," Cassie answered.

"About?"

"He didn't say. All I know is what I read online, which really wasn't very much."

The lawyer leaned in. "He was a guy. A young guy. My age. When guys my age hit on me, they always talk about work. It's that alpha male thing to show me how important they are. So, think hard: surely he said something."

"He really didn't."

"And you didn't ask?"

"No."

"Well, the fact he didn't talk about work is revealing, too. Maybe it suggests he had something to hide."

"Maybe. Your uncle thinks he may have been a spy for some country."

Ani smiled. "My uncle loves a good spy story. So tell me: what did you two talk about?"

"We talked about my work. He seemed really interested in what I did. Flying. Passenger craziness. He seemed to get a real kick out of the stories."

"What else?"

"We talked about growing up in Kentucky and Virginia. We talked about food. We talked about drinking. But . . ."

"Go on."

"We both got toasted pretty quickly. It's not that we can't hold our booze. It's just that we drank so much," Cassie explained. It sounded as squalid and confessional as ever.

"What about when Miranda came? What did the three of you talk about then?"

"I don't remember much. It was late."

"Why did you think she was there?"

"When she first arrived? I assumed she and Alex worked together or he managed her money. I assumed they were friends."

"Forgive me, but what kind of friends? Were they lovers? Ex-lovers?"

Cassie looked down at the table for a moment as she answered, because it was getting harder and harder to maintain eye contact with the lawyer. "I thought so at first. I assumed she was there to have sex with us."

"The three of you," said Ani evenly.

"I guess."

"But you didn't."

"No. It never even came up. She brought that bottle of vodka, we all drank some, and mostly the two of them talked. I didn't really pay attention."

"They talked about his work? Her work, maybe?"

"I remember something about a meeting they were going to have together the next morning. That's all. Late morning, I think. There would be other people at the meeting."

"Who?"

"Dubai investors in the fund, I guess. I think it was going to be downtown. But I also got the sense that they really didn't know each other all that well. They may have been meeting for the first time. I think she was maybe somebody's daughter."

"Someone he knew."

"Or someone important in his life somewhere. But I can tell you this: I learned this morning that if she does work for Unisphere, it's not in their Dubai office."

"And you know this how?"

"I called them."

"Dubai."

"Yes," Cassie answered, and she recounted her brief conversation with the receptionist.

Ani sighed deeply. Epically. Cassie knew that exhalation well: it was the Sigh of Judgment. "Okay," she said finally. "Here's the good news. The crime occurred in the United Arab Emirates and the United States has no extradition treaty with them. The Emirates would have to bring you back via a judicial summons—a letters rogatory request or whatever the Emirates equivalent is of a letters rogatory request. And those go through the courts and can take years."

Cassie felt a flutter of relief and it must have been visible in her face, because almost instantly Ani held up a finger to stop the emotion from taking root.

"But that doesn't mean you're home free. There's an amendment to the U.S. law that allows us to extradite a person who has committed a crime against an American citizen overseas. I want to check to see if an American citizen is exempt from the extradition."

"If that's the case, am I okay?"

"Maybe. But there are other issues in play. Even if the U.S. won't send you back to Dubai, Sokolov's family could still go after you in civil court: a wrongful death suit. Think O. J. Simpson. The criminal court acquitted him. The civil court held him responsible and the judgment was thirty-plus million dollars."

"Oh, my God!"

"The families ended up getting nowhere near that. I heard they wound up with maybe half a million."

"Still, I don't have anything like that. All I have is my apartment."

"That's something. But none of this may even matter. On the other hand, those photos of you? Any day now they'll be in the U.S. media. And pretty soon after that, you will be, so to speak, outed."

"Am I that recognizable in the pictures?"

"I don't know. I'd have to see them blown up. I'd have to see the originals. But from what you tell me, someone on the plane with you—one of the crew—will make the connection that it could be you. So will the FBI. What are your plans today and tomorrow?"

"I'm supposed to fly to Rome tonight."

"Not Dubai?"

"No."

"Good. Never go back there."

"I wasn't planning on it."

"I mean that."

"I understand."

"And after Rome?" asked Ani.

"I fly back here. We arrive in Italy tomorrow morning, Tuesday, overnight in the city, and fly back to the U.S. on Wednesday just before lunch. We're there a little more than twenty-four hours."

"Pretty cushy compared to what some flight attendants endure."

She shrugged. "I did my time on the regionals. I've been doing this a lot of years."

"Oh, I know the drill. I know how it works."

"We still haven't discussed how in the world I'm going to pay you."

Ani put her yellow pad on the table and sat forward. She looked almost kindly at Cassie and said, "Look, it's not yet time to burn the carbons—"

"Burn the carbons?" she asked, interrupting the lawyer.

"Just an expression. Do you know what carbon paper is?"

"Of course."

"Hey, I've never actually seen a piece. But I gather people overseas in the foreign services or the CIA used to have a saying: when the world was completely falling apart and the embassy was being overrun, that's when it was time to burn the carbons. You know, to make sure that the Soviets or the jihadists or whoever wouldn't get the state secrets. Anyway, it's not yet time to burn the carbons, okay? So, breathe."

"And as for payment?"

"My sense is you might come home to a shitstorm on Wednesday. Not a burn-the-carbons shitstorm, but it could feel . . . distressing. It could be distressing. So, I want you to go ahead and fly to Rome because I want to be sure you remain in the airline's good graces, and because I want to be sure you've behaved in no way that suggests guilt. Forgive me, no additional way. The existence of those security camera photos is likely to give this story legs in the tabloid media here in the U.S. You watch. It may be as soon as tomorrow or the day after. The police in Dubai are going to bring better photos of you—good photos of you—to the Royal Phoenician and ask around. They'll show the pictures to the bellmen and the hostesses and the people who work in the gift shops, and ask if you might have been the woman with Alex Sokolov. I have no idea if this Sokolov guy might have been a CIA spook or a Russian spook or whatever. Doesn't matter. The family might simply be very well connected. Either way, I am quite sure that the FBI is going to want to talk to you again and this story could be around for a while."

"I see."

"But here's the good news. I am also confident that my firm will represent you pro bono. You're attractive and you work in a job that most people still believe—I know mistakenly—is kind of sexy. I don't like to advertise the fact that we're media ghouls, but we are. We really are. Years ago this place was pretty white shoe, but no more. So, we can help prevent your extradition, if it actually comes to that—which I doubt it will. We can help if there is ever a civil case—which, yes, is a little more likely, but still not something to lose any sleep over just yet. And we can help if the airline ever gives you any grief."

"I hadn't thought about that."

"The airline? Oh, they might be a royal pain. My sense is the union will have your back if that ever happens. But we will, too."

"And you'd do this just for the press?"

"The free press. Operative word is free. We may no longer be white shoe, but we also don't pay for subway ads."

And then they were done and Ani walked her to the elevator. There Cassie went to shake the lawyer's hand. Instead Ani hugged her, and inside Cassie wanted to cry with gratitude.

« «

Most of the time, airlines booked the overnights for the Long Island airports at Long Island hotels. If you only had twelve hours, it made no sense to go into Manhattan, especially since Manhattan lodging rarely came with a free courtesy van: the airports were too far away and the traffic too unpredictable.

But not all of the time. If the overnight was long enough, even the U.S. carriers would send their crews into midtown and provide a van to and from the airport. Certainly many of the foreign carriers did. It was a very civilized perk for an out-of-town crew to get a night a few blocks from Times Square or a subway ride from Greenwich Village instead of one where your room overlooked the lights of Runway 4R.

Cassie knew the departures for most of her airline's overseas JFK flights by heart, and even which domestic sequences were likely to have a layover long enough that the crew would be staying in midtown. And she knew that frequently the airline used the Dickinson on Lexington and Forty-Ninth. So whenever she could, she would take the subway from her apartment three stops north to the hotel and hitch a ride with a flight crew to the airport. The alternative? Get off at Grand Central and take the Airporter bus. The Airporter only cost ten bucks with her airline discount, which was about what she could afford. But in the summer she would sweat like a marathon runner—the polyester uniform didn't help—and her makeup would melt on her way to the subway. In the winter, she would freeze or her suitcase and clothing would be sprayed with road salt and slush. There were flight attendants who thought she was insane to live in Manhattan when her base was JFK, but Manhattan was everything that her childhood home in rural Kentucky wasn't. She was never going to give up that apartment. Never. Besides, she knew lots of flight attendants who would waste a valuable day off or have to get up early commuting from Buffalo or Boston or Detroit to their base—including Megan, who came in from D.C.—and then spend a half day or an overnight in some squalid crash pad near the airport. She'd lived in one once, the bottom bunk in a basement bedroom in a ramshackle townhouse in Ozone Park, Queens. There were at least a dozen other flight attendants who lived there—or, to be precise, crashed there for a few nights or few days or few hours a month.

Today she didn't waste time on a manicure, not after spending so much of the morning with the lawyer. But the subway was delayed, and the crowd on the platform grew as she stood there, her roller beside her and her phone in her hand. It wasn't near rush hour, so the hordes from New York Life hadn't yet descended into the tunnel, but still there were droves because this was Manhattan. And it was when she had been standing there nearly ten minutes that the claustrophobia was replaced by something deeper: unease. She began to inventory the people around her. There were the young mothers with their small children, the high school kids and the college students, the white collar and the blue collar and all manner of delivery women and men. It was just another midsummer melting pot of the aged and the youthful, an abstract of smileless faces above polo shirts and summer dresses, above blazers and sweats and tees for the local sports teams.

But she had the sense, real or imagined, that in this crush was someone who was there just for her. There was someone watching her. She could tell herself that this was mere paranoia, absolutely understandable after what she had seen in Dubai. It was, perhaps, an inevitable if mean-spirited trick of the mind.

But she couldn't shake the feeling. She was a woman, and she had spent enough time alone on subway platforms or streets late at night to know when something was wrong. When someone approaching was sketchy. When it was time to move and to move fast.

And so she did. She put her phone in her purse and grabbed the handle of her suitcase and began to push her way through the throngs, plowing forward with her head up and alert, scanning for that single individual who saw her and knew her and . . .

And what? Was someone actually going to attack her?

She couldn't say. Maybe she was just being watched. Maybe it was all in her head. But she wasn't going to risk that.

As she struggled to pull her suitcase through the revolving bars, she glanced behind her to see if anyone else was trying to fight their way upstream on the platform. She checked again as she lugged her suitcase up the stairs. But a train hadn't arrived at the station, and so she was all alone as she made her way back up to the sunlight on the street. There was a cab across Park Avenue, heading north and slowing for the red light at the corner. It hadn't a passenger, and so she raced for it, climbing into it from the street side.

"The Dickinson, please," she told the driver, and looked back at the subway entrance as the light changed and the vehicle started north. There, emerging onto the sidewalk was a solitary figure in shades and a black ball cap, the brim pulled low on his head. A man. She couldn't see his face; already they were too far away. But he seemed to be scanning the sidewalks, and then his gaze paused on her cab.

She told herself it was nothing; it was a coincidence that someone else had grown impatient and decided to walk or take a cab rather than wait for the next train.

But she didn't believe that.

《 《

By the time she got to the Dickinson, her own airline's shuttle had left. She had missed it by no more than five minutes.

Fortunately, Lufthansa used the Dickinson as well. So, as she had at least three or four times in the past, she slipped the shuttle driver a ten and thumbed a ride with a German crew that was about to leave.

It was awkward: the pilots ignored her and the flight attendants whispered a few jokes to each other at her expense, but no one really cared. Mostly they understood because their salaries were as unimpressive as hers. A ride to the airport for a fellow flight attendant? Really, not that big a deal. Still, she stared out the window, half expecting to see a faceless man in a ball cap on the sidewalk snapping a cell phone picture of her in the van. When they left the stop-and-start traffic of Manhattan, she read the paperback Tolstoy she had with her and tried not to be envious of the fact that she was not a part of the flock. She tried not to think paranoid thoughts, but she was sure she overheard one woman say something about Dubai to another. She feared she heard the syllable *mord* multiple times, and when she looked it up on her phone using Google Translate, it meant—as she suspected—"murder." But she told herself that it was unlikely she had heard the word correctly. Why would they even be aware of Sokolov's death? It would mean that someone in the shuttle had flown to Dubai recently, too, or would be flying there soon.

Which, alas, was possible. Very possible.

Before leaving her apartment, she had checked her computer one last time to see if the photos of her from the Royal Phoenician had gone viral. She'd done this every twenty minutes that day when she was home, it seemed. They hadn't. At least not yet. But she knew that Ani was right and they would. She knew any moment she would get a text from Megan or Jada, because she had to believe that they were following the story, too—though, of course, not with her own vested interest.

She breathed in slowly and deeply and almost managed to convince herself that no one had been watching her on the subway platform. Almost. She took comfort in the fact that now she had a lawyer. She definitely felt better. But as the van inched its way along the Long Island Expressway, she sure as hell didn't feel good.

« «

For a moment she paused before the window and watched the winking light at the edge of the wing, the distinct blink-blink of an Airbus. She shook her head, coming back to herself before she grew lost in the slow, rhythmic strobe. She had coach on this flight because it was Rome and she didn't yet have quite enough seniority to always hold business or first class en route to the Eternal City. Of course, a lot of flight attendants preferred coach. These days, no one felt entitled to anything in economy, and so the passengers—especially on an overnight flight to Europe— were rather docile: the airlines had beaten out of them the idea that they had virtually any rights at all. Moreover, most people checked their suitcases on international flights, unlike on domestic ones, and so there was far less stress as people fought and jockeyed for space in the overhead compartments. Her only issue with coach? You really couldn't flirt. There were too many people and the aisles were too thin and there were just too many families. Of course, she wasn't in the mood to flirt. Not tonight. She wanted a drink—she *needed* a drink—and so when most of the cabin was sleeping or reading or watching movies on their laptops or tablets and she had a moment alone in the rear galley, she did something she almost never did: she took a plastic Cutty Sark single and downed it in one shot. Then she filled her mouth with Altoids, crunching them into bits and using her tongue to run the sand over her teeth.

« «

When they landed in Rome, it was still the middle of the night in America, and she had neither e-mails nor texts that were alarming. Mostly, she had e-mails from clothing and lingerie companies. The world had stood still.

《   《

In the van, traveling from Fiumicino Airport into Rome, some of the crew made plans to meet in the lobby and stroll to the Spanish Steps. Apparently the Spanish Steps weren't far from their hotel, and the Steps, in turn, weren't far from some pretty tony shopping. The extra, a young flight attendant who had been called up from reserve to work the route, had never been to Rome and was so excited to be there that he was orchestrating a group visit to the Vatican. He was at once so enthusiastic and so charismatic that even one of the pilots said he might go.

"God, it's been years since I've been to the Vatican," that captain said. He was an older guy who commuted to work from West Palm Beach. His hair was the silver she liked in a pilot, and his skin was dark and leathery from years in the Florida sun. "Sign me up."

"I say we do the museum, too," said the young guy masterminding the trip. His name was Jackson, and he had been working coach with her. He was from a small town in Oklahoma near the Texas panhandle—"Nothing but grain elevators, crazy preachers, and people looking for Route 66," he'd said—and couldn't have been more than twenty-four or twenty-five. He was a baby. From their conversations in the galley and while playing Words with Friends on their phones in their jump seats, she had come to believe that his childhood had been a thousand times better than hers, but in some ways just as provincial. Becoming a flight attendant was at once rebellion and escape.

"You know there's a secret room at the museum with nothing but statue penises," the captain added. "My daughter studied abroad in Rome for a semester and said this is no urban legend."

"Yup. I think it was a pope who had their junk broken off and covered with fig leaves," said another flight attendant, a part of the team who had been working the business class cabin. Her name was Erica and she was a grandmother, but that was all Cassie knew about her. "But they actually kept them? Had not heard that. Wow. Who knew?"

"Okay, I have a mission in life. It's probably above my pay grade to get the marble men back their privates, but someday I will see that secret room," Jackson told them.

"Imagine: the Vatican has secrets," Cassie said. She hadn't spoken in a while and found the good cheer in the van infectious. But her pleasure was short-lived.

"Yeah, imagine," said Erica. "God, the whole world has secrets. We all have secrets. Why should the Vatican be any different? A friend of mine was working a flight from Paris to Dubai last week. When they landed at JFK at the end of the sequence, the crew was met by the FBI. Why? A guy on the plane to Dubai was murdered in his freaking hotel room!"

"I'm not following," said Jackson. "A passenger was killed in Dubai. Why did the FBI want to talk to the flight crew?"

"Well, they're saying it was just a robbery that went bad, but my friend doesn't believe that. Not for a second. The FBI asked the flight attendants if they'd seen anything unusual on his laptop or noticed any papers on his tray table or he'd said something that might be helpful. She thinks the fellow was a spy or one of the other flight attendants was a spy. You know, CIA? KGB? Something like that. My point? There are people out there with pretty serious secrets."

"An airline is still a great cover for a spy," said the pilot. "Always has been, always will be. You have a reason to travel. It's easy— easier, anyway—to smuggle whatever you've stolen from the Pentagon or the Kremlin from one side of the planet to the other."

Cassie watched from her seat in the van as several members of the crew started searching their phones for news of a dead man in Dubai. She reached into her purse for her sunglasses. She stared out the window, wishing she had an excuse here in Italy to hide herself in a scarf.

« «

Cassie decided not to join any of the crew on their different excursions. She murmured that she just didn't feel up to much that afternoon, but she told the group that was shopping closer to the hotel to let her know where they were having dinner: she might catch up with them then.

At the hotel, she didn't set the alarm on her phone and she didn't ask the front desk for a wake-up call, and she was sound asleep by eleven in the morning. She opened her eyes on her own a little before two in the afternoon, waking to an almost catlike contentment. She never slept better than those deep, late-morning naps when she landed in Europe. For a long moment she gazed at the large abstract of the Coliseum on the wall beside the bed, and then she watched the thin, laser-like strip of light from the drapes. Eventually her mind wandered back to the last time she had awoken in a hotel room bed and she grew a little queasy. She knew she should reach for her phone on the nightstand.

Still, however, she allowed herself a moment more to linger. She thought of the cats at the shelter and she thought of her nephew and niece. She wanted to fixate on things that she loved and the moments in which she was not a mess.

Finally she stretched out her arm and grasped her phone. She pulled the sheet back over her head and looked at the screen. Was it worse than she expected? Perhaps. Perhaps not. She saw that she had slept through a phone call from Frank Hammond of the FBI and texts—three of them—from Megan. The texts alone told her all that she really needed to know:

Don't know where you are but I saw two photos online. Have you seen them?

Call me when you can. I'm still in U.S. Not flying out til tonight. I have your back.

Guessing you're in Europe. Call me. Jada and Shane have seen the
photos too.

She put her phone down on the pillow beside her and closed her
eyes. It was interesting that Megan had been careful to text nothing
incriminating—or, at least, not irrevocably damning. The short
sentence "I have your back" was the only thing she had written
that might even be problematic, but Cassie had watched enough
legal dramas on TV to know (or, at least, to be able to reassure
herself) that a remark like that could be construed a thousand ways.

But its implication was clear to Cassie: Megan believed that she
was the woman in the security camera photos and likely had spent
the night with Sokolov, and now Megan was willing to cover for
her friend. She was willing to keep to herself the fact that Cassie
had only returned to her hotel room in Dubai moments before the
crew was supposed to be downstairs to leave for the airport. Perhaps she was willing to do even more than that: perhaps she was
willing to be part of an alibi.

Either way, Cassie knew that she had to call Megan back. She
wasn't sure about Hammond. She should probably call Ani instead.
Wasn't that what lawyers were for?

Either way, however, first she needed a drink. She should probably eat something, too.

She climbed from the bed, surprised by how cold the room
was, and saw the small refrigerator in the hotel room was empty.
There wasn't a minibar, which meant that she'd have to go downstairs. And while she guessed it was possible she'd run into someone from the flight, she thought it unlikely. By the time she had
showered and gotten dressed and taken the elevator to the lobby,
they'd be long gone—if they hadn't left already.

« «

When she was dressed, her hair dry and her makeup on, she sat
on the edge of the bed and surveyed the hotel room. She had never

stolen anything from a hotel for herself, but over the years she had taken things for her sister and her nephew and niece. Sometimes she tried to rationalize the thefts: the hotel was overpriced, the stuff was junk anyway, and (of course) everyone else took the soap. She could recall bringing her sister a beautiful black bathrobe from France (which she had actually stolen from the dirty hamper of a maid service cart in the hallway), exotic throw pillows from Vietnam, fancy wooden coat hangers from San Francisco, a Wedgwood blue coffee service from Italy (which was on the corridor floor outside another guest's hotel room), very fluffy towels from Miami, and a brass magazine stand from Germany. For the kids she was most likely to pilfer little decorative sculptures or small but interesting prints or paintings or photos that weren't bolted to the wall. (When she took a photograph or a print, she would always steal it the moment she checked in, calling down right away to the front desk to report the blank spot above the bed or beside the armoire.) She'd brought them images of lighthouses and skyscrapers and the iconic architectural landmarks of Paris and Sydney and Rome. In her hotel rooms, she'd found them trinkets and paperweights of dragons (Hanoi), Vikings (Stockholm), and ballerinas (Moscow).

Did her sister suspect the gifts were stolen? Perhaps. But Cassie always insisted that she had paid for them, in some cases swearing that the objects were sold at the hotel gift shop. She always cleaned them, boxed them, and wrapped them when she was back in New York.

She wasn't searching for gifts for anyone in particular right now, but she noticed a small replica of a famous statue of the mythical twins Romulus and Remus as infants, nursing from the wolf that saved them. It was on a side table, atop the leather-bound guest directory and a magazine for tourists about Rome, and she realized that once upon a time it had been half of a pair of bookends. She stood up and lifted it. The bookend was maybe six inches long and six inches wide, and made of copper. It was hollow, but filled with sand. Her nephew was about to start sixth grade, and she had a vague memory of studying the Greek and Roman myths when she was that age. She associated Diana, the Roman goddess of the hunt, with her beautiful young teacher for sixth grade: Diana Dezzerides. She thought Tim would get a charge out of the sculpture once he had been properly introduced to the great myths. It would be a Christmas present. She would tell Rosemary that she had discovered it in an antique store, and because it was only half the set, she had gotten it for a song. The key would be to find something equally as idiosyncratic for her niece.

The idea of slipping the copper bookend into her suitcase gave her a small rush. The truth was that she didn't loot like this to punish the hotel or because it was the only way she could afford to bring her family gifts; she didn't even really try and convince herself that it wasn't all that different from stealing the soap, because she knew it was. Like almost everything else she did, it was crossing a line that most people wouldn't. She did it because it thrilled her. It was just that simple. She did it because it was, like so much else that made her happy, dangerous and self-destructive and just a little bit sick.

《　《

The hotel bar was quiet in the middle of a weekday afternoon, but it was cozy and dark and warm without being hot. Most people preferred to drink outside in the sunlit piazza, and so Cassie had the place to herself. She brought her paperback with her, though she was never one of those single women who minded eating or drinking—certainly not drinking—alone. She didn't bring the book as a prop or a buffer against intrusion. She thought she might actually see if "The Death of Ivan Ilyich" would offer any spiritual insight into the death of Alex Sokolov. She doubted it, but she'd read a little more of "Happy Ever After" upstairs in her hotel room and found that the story had been a welcome diversion from the maelstrom of her real life. She was starting to like Masha: she was starting to like her a lot.

The bartender was a slim young guy with reddish-brown hair

he slicked back and a trim mustache. His eyes were moonstone, and the uniform here was a white shirt and blue vest that happened to match those eyes perfectly. He smiled at her and she ordered a Negroni, and then took it with her to a leather booth in the back, choosing the one beside a replica of a classic sculpture of Mercury and beneath a Tiffany lamp with a stained-glass shade. She made sure there was cell service before she got comfortable. Then she took a long swallow, savoring the burn of the gin, and sucked for a long moment on the orange peel. When the glass was half empty, she sat back and called Megan. Her friend picked up quickly.

"My overseas plan is fine for texting, but not great for talking," she told Megan, "so we should get right to it."

"See, if you had small children, you'd have a great plan for talking. But if you had teenagers, like me, you wouldn't: the last thing you want is to deal with your daughters' dramas overseas. I'm in the same boat as you."

"Your kids are terrific."

"They're hormonal beasts who love me madly one day and want me locked in the attic the next."

"I read your texts. Are you alone? Can you talk?"

"Yeah, now is fine. The beasts are out," Megan said. Then: "Look, I saw the photos. We've all seen the photos. It is you, isn't it?"

And instantly Cassie understood her mistake: she shouldn't have called Megan back. She should only have phoned Ani. Yes, she and Megan had known each other for years, but in the end Cassie was now going to have to ask Megan to perjure herself. She wasn't quite at that place yet, however—she was still too sober. But the crux of the problem was really very simple: she had told Megan one thing in Dubai and Derek Mayes another at the diner in New York. So far she had told the FBI nothing. If she was to accomplish anything right now, she should see if there was a way to reconcile her two stories and get Megan and Derek on the same page. She swallowed the last of her Negroni, and the bartender, as if he were telepathic, emerged from behind that great, wonderful balustrade of a bar and was at her side, asking if she wanted another drink. She nodded enthusiastically.

"What photos?" she asked Megan, stalling for time by playing dumb.

"You haven't seen them? You really haven't seen them?"

"I don't know what you're talking about."

Cassie could hear the woman's great sigh of exasperation through the phone. "There are two photos on the web of a woman who looks like you and is wearing a scarf that might be the one you bought when we landed in Dubai. You know, at the airport? The photos are from the hotel in Dubai where the guy from two C was killed. The hedge fund guy. In one picture, she's with the dude; in the other, she's alone. Jada is sure it's you. Shane is absolutely positive."

"And you?" Cassie asked. She wished Alex Sokolov were more than the guy from 2C or the hedge fund guy. He deserved better. "What do you think?"

"Tell me, were you with him? I know you didn't kill him. But were you with him? Just tell me that. The FBI has been calling. I'm supposed to meet with them today and I need to know what you want me to say."

What you want me to say. The words echoed in Cassie's mind.

"I guess the FBI will be calling me, too, when I get back," she said, instead of mentioning that she already had a message from an agent herself. She watched the bartender preparing her drink, and tried to will him to hurry up. She needed to ratchet up the pain medication.

"Yeah. I guess," said Megan, her tone equal parts frustration and derision.

"I'm glad I'm in Italy. Where are you this month?"

"Berlin. The seven-thirty flight tonight."

"I like that flight."

"You're not answering my question. Should I read something into that?"

"No. Of course not."

"Then what's going on? What's really going on?"

The bartender returned with her drink and when he placed it on the table, she had an urge to reach out and touch his long, beautiful fingers. Instead she murmured her thanks and plucked the orange peel from the rim, tossing it unceremoniously onto the table beside her small paperback book. Then she drank it down at least an inch and a half. "Here's what I want you to do," she began.

"Go on."

"I want you to forget I ever told you that I picked up a guy at the hotel bar in Dubai. I want you to forget we ever spoke that morning in my hotel room before we left the city. As far as anyone knows, I never left my hotel room that night. I didn't even order up room service. That's all."

There was a long pause and Cassie used the opportunity to drink some more. Her stomach was empty. She knew she would be feeling better soon.

"So you want me to lie," said Megan.

"I doubt it will ever come to that."

"It will."

"Then, yes. Please."

"Can you tell me anything more?"

"Oh, Megan, I just don't want people to get the wrong idea. I just don't want you to get sucked into this. Assume I really did hook up with a guy from our hotel. Why not just believe that, okay?"

"Because you're a spy."

"You're kidding, right?"

"I don't know."

"One more thing," Cassie said. "You haven't told Jada or Shane or anyone about our conversation in my hotel room in Dubai that morning—and what I said, right?"

"That's right."

"Okay, then. Good."

"Send me your schedule for August, so I know when we're

both going to be in the same time zone," Megan asked. "We have a lot to talk about. It would be great if it could even be in person."

"I agree," Cassie said. "I'll send you my schedule. Maybe we'll be at JFK the same day." Then she thanked her—deeply and sincerely—and took the last of her Negroni to the bar. She knew she should call Ani now, but she couldn't cope. She just couldn't. The bartender was leaning back and looking at something on his phone. He had a gold badge with his name: Enrico.

"Another one?" he asked when he noticed her. He had only a trace of an Italian accent.

"Yes, please. You make a good one." She couldn't recall the last time she'd had sex sober, and wondered a little now at the synaptic connection between her body—body image, really—and booze. Between intimacy and intoxicants. She ran her fingers through her hair: she needed another drink to make these sorts of mental gymnastics go away. Some lives, including hers, were best left unexamined. She was buzzed just enough to crave a little shame. To crave this young waiter.

"Campari is an acquired taste," he said.

"Oh, I acquired it a long time ago."

"It couldn't have been all that long."

She shrugged. "You'd be surprised." Then: "Your English is very good."

"I have a grandmother who's American. And we have lots of American guests here."

"Tell me something, Enrico," she said.

"Okay."

"Did they pick the vests here because of your eyes?"

He smiled at her, one side of his mouth curling up a little higher than the other. If he hadn't been so young, she guessed it would have looked rakish. She hoped he only worked until dinner, so she could bring him back to her room and still get a good night's sleep.

FEDERAL BUREAU OF INVESTIGATION

FD-302: MEGAN BRISCOE, FLIGHT ATTENDANT

DATE: August 1, 2018

MEGAN BRISCOE was interviewed by properly identified Special Agents NANCY SAUNDERS and EMORY LEARY at the FBI office in Washington, D.C.

SAUNDERS conducted the interview; LEARY took these notes.

BRISCOE said in her first interview (see FD-302 July 28, 2018, taken at JFK Airport) that she did not see CASSANDRA BOWDEN in Dubai, other than when traveling via the airline van between the airport and the airline's hotel. She said that she assumed BOWDEN spent the night there alone in her hotel room.

When shown the two security camera images of the woman in the sunglasses and scarf at the ROYAL PHOENICIAN HOTEL, she said yes, that could be BOWDEN. She corroborated what flight attendant JADA MORRIS had said: the scarf the woman is wearing in the photo looks like the one that BOWDEN had purchased when they first landed in Dubai on Thursday, July 26.

She then remembered seeing BOWDEN at the airline's hotel on the morning of Friday, July 27. She saw her returning to her own room and they spoke there briefly. In her recollection, BOWDEN said something that suggested to BRISCOE that the woman had spent the night with a man in a different hotel in Dubai.

BRISCOE said this wasn't the first time that BOWDEN had disappeared when she traveled for work. According to BRISCOE, she does this often when she is overseas. And while these may be sexual liaisons, BRISCOE acknowledged that there may be more to them since BRISCOE has never once met any of the men that BOWDEN allegedly is seeing.

She added that the woman was distracted and upset in the van to the airport in Dubai that Friday morning and was crying soon after takeoff. She also said that BOWDEN lost her handbag in the United Arab Emirates, but not her passport or wallet.

11

Elena didn't seriously believe that she had killed her father, but every once in a while, especially in the small hours of the night, she wondered if she had been the last straw. Years earlier, just as she was finishing her second year of college, her father suffered what everyone assumed was a stroke. He'd lived, but he was a frail shell of what he'd once been. He walked slowly and with a limp, the left side of his face sagged like badly bunched drapes, and his words—when he could find them—were barely comprehensible. Now she had flown to Sochi for a visit—the Olympic construction had begun, but his summer estate was on a small lake far from the madness—and had just helped him from the passenger seat of the BMW he could no longer drive, and either he had lost his balance or he had tripped where the asphalt met the first slate step, and suddenly he was falling onto the driveway. She managed to cradle his head just before it would have cracked onto the pavement, and for a moment was relieved at how quickly she had reacted. But certainly his fragile brain inside his fragile skull had been violently shaken. She knew it then and she knew it as the evening progressed. He'd seemed fine at dinner—or, at least, as fine as he ever was at that stage in his life, which meant that he spoke in drooling whispers and ate very little—but it would be later that night that he would be found unresponsive on the floor of the living room. It was his live-in nurse, a Georgian who coincidentally shared the name of a Russian football team her father followed, who had heard the fall, discovered him, and called upstairs to wake her. The nurse was a gentle giant with a chinstrap beard named Spartak. Elena had been nodding off in the very same bedroom she had lived in as a teenager those weeks or weekends when she would be sent to see him after her parents' divorce. (*Get* to see him, really, because she missed him terribly after her parents separated.) He'd die at the hospital a few hours later. Cause of death? A cerebral hemorrhage. A burst blood vessel. Another one. This time his brain had drowned in its own blood.

It might have occurred moments before he fell in the living room. Most likely it did. But maybe not. Perhaps it had been a slow bleed that had commenced when he had nearly hit his head outside on his driveway.

He had always been such an old father: he was fifty-six when Elena was born, her mother thirty-five. She was an only child. Her parents had divorced when she was eight, and it had been nasty. Their marriage couldn't survive the crazy amounts of money he made when, as a former KGB officer with boxes of surveillance files at his disposal, he was allowed to buy thousands of shares of the Yukos oil conglomerate at a fraction of their real value. He'd then invested in real estate in St. Petersburg, New York, Doha, and Dubai. There was the fund, some of which was fueled by all that bricks and mortar and some of it—and she didn't believe this— pilfered from the Russian treasury in a complex tax scam. She didn't believe that because she knew how close her father was to the president of the Russian Federation. The president had been a protégé of her father when they'd both been KGB. But then there were those who hinted that the president, too, had been involved.

Even years later, when she left her Swiss boarding school for college in America, her parents still spoke mostly through their few mutual friends. Neither remarried. And so she was the one who had had to figure out what to do with him when he had that stroke when she was twenty and it was clear he could no longer live alone in the apartment in Moscow or the dacha in Sochi. She'd come home from school and stayed nearly six months. She brought in Spartak and Spartak was wonderful. He was perhaps a decade older than she was, and he had sobbed and sobbed at her father's small memorial for his Black Sea acquaintances in the woods behind the house. (The funeral had been in Moscow and it had been considerably larger. The Russian president himself hadn't attended, but he had sent staff.) Spartak had cried in ways that she hadn't; she had cried only when she was alone, because in public she felt the need to represent the strength of the Orlovs. But alone she had wept. She had loved him the way a girl can love both her father and her grandfather. She had loved him because he had spoiled her as his only child and because he had respected her intellect and her resourcefulness; he saw so much of himself in her and always, no matter what, had been proud of her.

Elena knew instantly why she was thinking of her father this evening, alone in her bed in Dubai. Part of it was the no-win situation that had greeted her when she had gone to Sokolov's hotel room that first time. Yes, she could have killed him and that flight attendant together when she'd had the chance. Just taken the twenty-two and been done with it. The problem was that while Sokolov had to die, the flight attendant didn't. The stakes were high and she probably could have rationalized the double hit. But there certainly would have been fallout from killing Bowden, too. In hindsight, the double bind was unsolvable.

Still, if Bowden hadn't returned, she wouldn't now be facing this fiasco. That was a fact. She honestly wasn't sure how long she could forestall the inevitable.

Moreover, Elena knew there would be consequences for her, as well—mistakes were seldom forgiven in her line of work—and in the end the flight attendant might still be dead.

Be realistic: one of you has to die. I think it's your choice.

Had her father been as cold-blooded as Viktor? Without a doubt. She just never saw that side of the man. She saw the doting father who would deny her nothing.

That afternoon she'd been scrolling through news stories on her phone and come across the assassination of a prominent Russian opposition leader on a sidewalk in Kiev. She had known it was coming. The victim had been a member of the Russian Parliament before defecting. His killer was a little younger than she was: twenty-seven years old. He'd shot the politician and his bodyguard on the street and disappeared. But he'd been recognized by a nearby politician, and a spokesperson for Ukraine's interior ministry alleged that he was a Russian agent. The Russian president said that was absurd.

It wasn't. She knew the executioner.

She turned over her pillow to the cool side, and rolled over. She wanted desperately the escape of sleep. But whenever her mind roamed from the flight attendant, it landed once more on her father. She missed him. She missed him as much as she missed anyone. And she always seemed to think of him when she was given an assignment like this. He was the first person she may have killed.

No, she had only finished him off. Maybe she hadn't even done that.

She knew the real truth of that first stroke. It was why she did what she did. It was why she was who she was.

Nevertheless, memories of her father and the things she had done because she was his daughter kept her tossing and turning into the small hours of the morning.

12

Cassie awoke just before four in the morning, recalled where she was, and reached out to the side of the bed where Enrico had been. She knew she would feel only empty sheets there: he'd been gone for seven hours now. It had been a little before nine at night when she'd been resting beside him, her head on his chest, and she'd heard herself murmuring that she was exhausted and should get some sleep. He was so young that at first he hadn't understood this was her way of gently excusing him. He'd pulled her closer to him. She'd had to explain that she preferred sleeping alone (which wasn't always the case, but was last night). She'd reassured him that she'd see him again in a week or so, when she was back in Rome, but in her heart she doubted she would. The airline would most likely be using the same hotel, but she'd steer clear of the bar. Now that she was sober, she wondered what in the name of God she'd been thinking picking up the bartender at the hotel where she was staying, but she knew the answer: she wasn't thinking. She was on her third Negroni. By the time he had finished his shift and they went upstairs to her room, she'd finished five.

Negronis in Rome. Akvavit in Stockholm. Arak in Dubai. Her life was a drinking tour of the world.

If only she had brought Sokolov back to her hotel room in the Emirates and then kicked him out. If only she had followed through on her intentions to leave his. Instead she had blacked out. That was how much she had drunk that night last week.

And it was last week. God. Somewhere the hyenas were circling . . .

She understood enough about her body clock to know that she probably wasn't going to fall back to sleep now, but she wasn't due downstairs in the lobby for hours. And so she climbed out of bed, switched on the light, and pulled the terrycloth robe from the closet. She didn't mind the sight of her naked body in the mirrors—and this hotel room indeed had a lot of them—but the room was chilly. The digital thermostat was set for Celsius, so she upped it a few digits and hoped she wasn't going to cook herself.

She saw she had phone messages. Her lawyer again. The FBI again. Her sister. She listened only to the one from Rosemary, just to make sure that nothing horrid had happened to her nephew or niece. Nothing had. Rosemary was calling to say hello and remind her that she and her family were coming to New York that weekend. She wanted to know if Cassie could join them at the Bronx Zoo on Saturday and then go to dinner in Chinatown.

She couldn't bring herself to listen to the messages from Ani or Frank Hammond. But she didn't delete them either. Perhaps she should splurge and have some oatmeal and an Irish coffee sent up to her room. The kitchen was open twenty-four hours. Even if they didn't have someone in the kitchen who could properly top the drink at this hour—the thick cream was actually her favorite part—they could toss a shot of Jameson's into the coffee. Then, properly fortified, she could hear what Ani and Frank had to say and take stock of her situation.

《　《

She Googled "trauma" on her tablet as she spooned the oatmeal in small bites and sipped her spiked coffee. She wondered if people who woke beside corpses were scarred for life, though she presumed there was, at best, a very small body of evidence from which to make deductions. For a few minutes she took comfort in the essays and research papers she found that suggested the families of murder victims often needed serious counseling and medication to get over the loss, equating herself with those poor souls, but then she recalled Alex Sokolov's parents and began to imagine what they were experiencing.

Finally she braced herself and listened to the messages from Ani and Frank Hammond. Her lawyer said that she had information on extradition laws she wanted to share. Cassie couldn't decide from the woman's voice whether it was good news or bad. The FBI agent said he was just crossing a few *t*'s and had a couple quick questions, and he was wondering if she'd mind coming downtown to the agency's offices. He sounded casual, but she had a sense—that gift of fear—that he was playing dumb. That he was playing her. Surely he suspected she was the woman in the security camera photos. And if this was just a minor follow-up, why the request that she visit the office in lower Manhattan?

She recalled her moment on the subway platform the day before, her fear that someone was tailing her, and then the figure she had seen at the sidewalk entrance as her cab sped away. Maybe it hadn't been an overreaction. Perhaps this was what FBI surveillance felt like: there was always someone just beyond your peripheral vision. Then again, the FBI knew what they were doing. Would she know she was being watched? Probably not. Maybe this was what paranoia felt like.

Though the sun was rising here, it was still late at night in New York. She couldn't yet call back either Ani or Hammond. And given that the flight's wheels up from Fiumicino was 11:05 a.m., she wouldn't be phoning either of them until the plane landed at JFK. By the time the passengers had deplaned and she was free, it would be close to 3:30 in the afternoon on the East Coast. So be it.

She sent Ani a text that she had heard the message and would connect with her as soon as she had landed in New York. She added that Frank Hammond had called her twice, but she wouldn't ring him back until they had spoken. She pulled the drapes and gazed out the window. She could see a few blocks in the distance the twin bell towers of the Trinità dei Monti, the church that stood atop the Spanish Steps. It dawned on her that any day now Alex Sokolov was probably going to be buried. By now his body had to be back in the United States. She wondered who he was—who he really was. She recalled the way he had gently washed her hair, massaging her scalp rather expertly as she'd sat on his lap on that marble bench in that elegant bathroom, and how that night he had kept up with her drink for drink. Few men could do that.

Likewise, she contemplated Miranda with her serene smile and her French twist, her gift of a bottle of Stoli. Who was she?

Cassie swallowed the last of her coffee, and fantasized traveling to Virginia to say something to Alex's parents. Tell them how sorry she was that their son had died and she had left him behind in the bed. Ask them what they knew of this woman named Miranda. But she understood that she couldn't—or, to be precise, that she shouldn't. And that only made her feel worse. She told herself that her sadness was part of her trauma.

Her guilt. Yes. Guilt.

She wondered if people—ordinary people, not serial killers or Tony Soprano—who got away with murder made promises to be better people. Did they vow they would do good work in the future? Actively search out and find God? Did they . . . atone? She wasn't convinced she had any of that in her. She wished that she did. But she wasn't sure it mattered because she hadn't gotten away with murder: she continued to believe, even if she was pathetically deluding herself, that she hadn't hurt Alex Sokolov. Perhaps no one else would believe that, but she did. Moreover, so far she hadn't gotten away with anything. The FBI still wanted to see her. The photos of her from the Royal Phoenician were now online. Soon she would be exposed, fully and irrevocably.

Below her on the street she watched a blue Vespa race by, the driver a young girl with blond hair and blue jeans. She saw an older woman on the sidewalk with a canvas bag filled with, among other items, a large loaf of bread. There was a delivery truck parked beside a store that sold lighting fixtures, and there were two men unloading large cardboard boxes. And in the apartment building across the street she watched the tenants through the windows: A fellow her age tucked his necktie into his shirt before sipping his espresso from a small cup and gazing down at something on the kitchen counter. A woman in a black blazer and skirt was blow-drying her hair in what looked like a rather petite living room. Another woman vacuumed.

She stripped off her robe and stood naked for a long minute in front of the window. She honestly wasn't sure why. She made eye contact with none of the people in the windows across the street and had no idea whether they noticed her or cared. It was a hotel. They probably witnessed assignations and saw exhibitionists all the time. Then she went to the shower, wiped the tears from her cheeks, and scrubbed a bartender named Enrico off her body.

《 《

Later that morning when she and Jackson, the young flight attendant from Oklahoma, were at the entrance to the aircraft and greeting the passengers as they boarded, he turned to her and said quietly, "I have a big idea."

"I'm all ears."

"I think we should give everyone in coach a Xanax. It should be airline policy. Can you imagine how easy our job would be if we medicated people properly before squishing them into those seats?"

《 《

Cassie heard the passengers shrieking, a small chorus in rows thirty-three and thirty-four, the section of coach that was four seats across sandwiched between two aisles, and for a second she feared that someone had a box cutter or a gun. The panic had what she always speculated was the "this-plane-is-going-down" terror to it. But then, almost as one, the call buttons chimed and she saw the red dots on the ceiling there light up like a bough on a Christmas tree, and the simple reasonableness of passengers pressing their call buttons calmed her. She put down the large plastic bag with the service items—airline-speak for trash—and raced seven rows forward from the rear galley and into the scrum. They were below ten thousand feet now and everyone was supposed to be buckled in as they approached JFK; she herself had only moments before she was supposed to be strapped in as well. Jackson was running up the aisle parallel to her, and the two of them got to row thirty-four at almost the same time. She wasn't sure what to expect, but she was glad there were two of them and that one of them was male.

"No, stop it! Stop it!" was the one sentence among the screams that seemed to register most cogently in her mind. For a moment she thought, *Stop what?*, but then she saw and she knew. There in seat D, one of the two middle seats in the middle section, was a grandmother holding her grandson—or, to be precise, holding her grandson's little penis, grasping it with two fingers as if it were a joint (a roach clip was actually what Cassie saw in her mind)—the child's blue jeans and underpants down around his ankles, as he stood between the rows and urinated into the airsickness bag she was clutching with her other hand.

No, he was only *trying* to urinate into the airsickness bag. Mostly he was missing. Mostly he was spraying the back of seat 33D and into the space between the seats, showering the passengers' arms and laps. And the kid was, apparently, a camel. Cassie and Jackson both commanded the woman to stop the child, and then they yelled at the boy to stop, but this was a tsunami. The grandmother either didn't speak English or was pretending not to speak English, and she did not pull up the boy's pants until, without question, he was done. From the passengers came a cacophony of curses and groans, a choral keening of disgust. The teen girl in seat 33E was in tears as she struggled to extricate herself from a very damp orange hoodie. "Ewwww," she sobbed each time she exhaled, a plaintive, almost biblical ululation.

Cassie chastised the grandmother, telling her that what she had done was absolutely unacceptable. The old woman ignored her, clipped shut the folds at the top of the airsickness bag, and then handed it to her, smiling as if she were presenting Cassie with a bakery bag full of cookies.

« «

Cassie knew that newspapers put stories online well before the actual paper went to print, so she guessed she shouldn't have been surprised when she saw the photo of herself on the *New York Post* website on her phone on the Airporter bus to Grand Central. But she was surprised. She wanted to vomit, and actually feared for a moment that she might. She was the mystery woman, the unnamed "black widow spider" who may have murdered a handsome young American money manager in Dubai. Moreover, someone had spoken with the hotel and restaurant employees, all of whom agreed that the woman they had seen with Sokolov was likely American. For the moment, everyone seemed to presume she was an American who lived in the United Arab Emirates. That's what the waitress at the restaurant had said. She'd told the Dubai police that Alex had said something that made it clear that while he was a visitor to the Emirates, the woman he was with was not. Cassie couldn't imagine what that was, but guessed it must have been some remark between them about how well she knew the city. She'd said something like that, because she had bid on the route often the last year and a half. In any case, the Dubai authorities were scouring the American community there, seeing who might have hooked up with him at the hotel.

She wished that Ani would call her back. She'd called the lawyer the moment she was inside the terminal and left a message.

This was water torture, she decided, this slow, relentless drip. The authorities had to work backward to get to her: they had to rule out all of the women he might have already known in the city and all of the women living there it was possible that he had met.

They had to show those photos to all of his friends and all of his business associates. They were probably showing them to the people he worked with at Unisphere in America. And so it felt like it was taking forever for them to, once and for all, focus only on her.

But she knew this: whatever was coming was getting closer.

« «

When she got home, she finally connected with Ani. She rolled her suitcase into her bedroom and collapsed onto the couch to look up at the Empire State Building through windows speckled with city grime and summer grit. The sky was blue, however, and though it was August now and the days were noticeably shorter than a month ago, the sun was still high.

"How was Rome?" Ani asked.

"Not glamorous. I stayed at the hotel. I didn't feel like going out." She took a breath and said, "I've seen the pictures on the *New York Post* website."

"Yup. They weren't online yet when I called you. But I've seen them, too. I rather doubt it will be a front-page story in the paper edition tomorrow. It was Dubai, after all."

"That's the bright side."

"Yes. But I have good news."

And instantly she knew what Ani was about to say, and she closed her eyes and realized she was crying. Again. And she didn't care. It was as if she had just gotten a call from a doctor about a biopsy and it was negative, and the doctor was explaining that she didn't have cancer. "Go on," she said.

"Highly unlikely you'll be extradited. That amendment I told you about? An American citizen is indeed exempt."

"That means I could only be extradited to Dubai if I weren't American?"

"Correct."

"So, then, what's next?"

"Call back the FBI, but tell them nothing. Nothing. Say things like I don't remember. Let me think about it. If they insist on seeing you—and they might—I'll go with you and we'll meet with them together."

"Why would they do that?"

"Want to see you? I think a lot depends on who Alex Sokolov really was or how well connected the family really is. Frankly, I'm more than a little shocked that the FBI seems to be so deeply involved. I've done my homework now, and Dubai doesn't need the FBI. They're not amateurs. They know what they're doing."

"Okay."

"I've also done a little more research into Sokolov."

Cassie held her phone against her ear with her shoulder and blew her nose almost silently. "And?"

"And everything suggests he really was a hedge fund manager. Yes, he's based in New York, but all the money runs through the Caribbean."

"What does that mean?"

"It could mean nothing. It could mean anything. Whenever the money goes through a place like Grand Cayman, you have to wonder. The U.S. can't track it as easily—if at all. The Treasury Department has something called an OFAC list. It's a whole bunch of seriously sketchy foreign nationals or groups, and American banks or funds can't accept money from any of them. So if you want to work with those characters, you have to work through the Caribbean."

"So he was doing something shady?" Cassie asked. "The FBI believes he was involved with people on that list?"

"Maybe."

"Is that why he was killed?"

"Well, we wouldn't kill him for that. If he was doing something illegal, I kind of think we'd just arrest him."

"So why did . . . they . . . kill him?"

"Maybe he was stealing," Ani answered, and Cassie found herself relieved that the lawyer hadn't begun her response, even in jest, with something along the lines of *Assuming you didn't kill him?* "You know, skimming off the top," she continued. "Or maybe he was running some Ponzi scheme and he went too far. Got in too deep."

"Good God, if no one slashed Bernie Madoff's throat, why would the investors take out poor Alex? What he did had to have been small potatoes by comparison."

"We don't know it was small potatoes. We just don't. There could be a lot of Russian money in that fund. You don't steal from the Russians. I'm Armenian, trust me. I know. They can be seriously badass."

"He just didn't seem like the type."

"When people need money or love money, they sometimes make very bad decisions," she reminded Cassie. Then: "The family published his first full obituary. You can find it online. It's in the *Charlottesville Progress*. Here are a few things I learned that are not in the obit: Grandfather emigrated here from the Soviet Union when Stalin was still Stalin: 1951. Unsure precisely how. He was a soldier in the Second World War. Self-made man after he got here. Settled in Virginia. Became a lawyer and married a good southern girl with money. I've already had a private investigator do a little digging. I'm going to have him do a little more."

"Can I afford that?"

"No. But he won't go crazy. I just want to learn a bit about the family and about Alex. See what sorts of interests he might have had."

"Business interests?"

"Yes. It might be helpful to discover precisely what was in the fund. But I was thinking personal interests, too."

"Can you tell me more?" Cassie asked.

"No, but only because there isn't anything more to tell at this point."

"What about Miranda?"

"What about her?"

"Did you find out anything more about her?"

"Like does she really work with Alex or does she or her family really have money in this magical fund?" asked Ani.

"Yes."

"Unisphere Asset Management has easily six or seven hundred employees in New York, Washington, Moscow, and Dubai. None of them are named Miranda."

"You checked?"

"My investigator did, yes."

"Can he find out if she's an investor?"

"Maybe. But I'm not confident."

"Is it possible she made up the name?"

"If she killed him? Absolutely," said Ani, her tone decisive. Then: "You should call back Frank Hammond. Then call me back. Let's plan on meeting tomorrow, regardless of whether he wants to see you again."

Tomorrow was Friday. She had something on Friday. Maybe. She flipped through the calendar in her mind, trying to recall what it was. Then it came to her: Rosemary. Her nephew and niece. She needed to call Rosemary back because her sister and her family were coming to New York. Her sister had said something about the zoo on Saturday, so she guessed she wasn't going to see them tomorrow.

"Sure," she told Ani. "What time?"

"Come by my office around twelve fifteen. There's a really good falafel cart around the corner on Fifty-Third Street, and it's supposed to be a beautiful day. Do you like falafel? We could eat al fresco."

"That's fine," she said, not really answering the question.

"Okay. But call me after you talk to the FBI."

《 《

"The air marshal on the flight said you and Sokolov were talking a lot. He noticed," Frank Hammond was saying on the phone.

"I don't remember," Cassie said, as she opened her suitcase

and started unpacking. A part of her knew that she shouldn't be multitasking: all her attention should be on the FBI agent. But the unpacking was calming her.

"And the other crew members said he was your guy."

"My guy?"

"Your section."

"Yes, that's true."

"And you two had a lot of interaction."

"I doubt I had any more 'interaction' with him than I did with any other passengers I was serving," she said. It was a lie, but *interaction* struck her as a vague, ridiculous word that was impossible to quantify. She wondered whether the flight crew was volunteering her name so enthusiastically or whether it was only the air marshal. She guessed it was also possible that Hammond had phrased his sentence this way because he was bluffing: he was trying to frighten her into believing that he knew more than he did.

"You know what I mean," he said. "You chatted. A lot. It wasn't just about the wine list."

"I was polite. He was polite."

"You were flirting. He was flirting."

"Maybe he flirted with me a little," she said. "But passengers flirt. They're bored. They flirt with all of us when it's a long flight."

"Got it. Anyway, that's why I'd like you to come in and chat. I want to see if Sokolov might have said something that can help us help the authorities in Dubai. That's all."

"May I bring a lawyer?" she asked. She wished instantly that she hadn't inquired. What if he said no? But he didn't. She dropped a dirty blouse into the hamper.

"That's your right," he answered simply.

"Okay, let me find out when my lawyer is free."

"But we want to see you tomorrow."

There wasn't precisely an edge to his voice, but for the first time he hadn't sounded quite so casual. Quite so laid back. It suddenly felt a lot less like this was busywork to him. And so she called back Ani and then she called back the agent, and they agreed to meet the next day at the FBI offices downtown at Broadway and Worth. She said that she'd be there at two o'clock sharp.

« «

She read the obituary in the newspaper, matching the man recalled in the story with the one who had made love to her in Dubai:

CHARLOTTESVILLE, Alexander Peter Sokolov, 32, died July 27, 2018, while traveling for business in Dubai, the United Arab Emirates. He was born March 15, 1986, in Alexandria, Virginia. Alex, as he liked to be called, graduated Phi Beta Kappa from the University of Virginia, double majoring in mathematics and foreign affairs, and then earned a Master of Quantitative Management at the Fuqua School of Business at Duke University. He helped run the Stalwarts Fund for Unisphere Asset Management out of their Manhattan office. He loved his job because he loved data, but he also loved the fact that his work took him often to Russia, the Middle East, and the Far East. He was fearless, whether he was playing his beloved squash or exploring the world. But he was also a kind and generous friend and son. He loved movies and books, especially Russian literature, but most of all he loved anything surprising and new. He leaves behind a grieving father and mother, Gregory and Harper, as well as an extended family of aunts and uncles and cousins who will miss him dearly.

The funeral was the day after tomorrow, Saturday, at a Presbyterian church in Charlottesville. She imagined it crowded with Alex's classmates from the University of Virginia, his childhood friends, and at least some of the employees he worked with at Unisphere. A part of her wanted to go, but she knew that she shouldn't. She wouldn't.

The obituary was short and actually revealed very little. In the end, that didn't surprise her, either.

« «

She stared at the text from Buckley the actor. He said he had an audition on Friday for a pilot that was going to film in New York in the autumn, and had to get a haircut first thing in the morning. He wanted to know what country she was in, but hoped wherever she was, she was dancing barefoot. She recalled how her tale of the dead passenger in the coach bathroom had made him smile. She hadn't answered his last text, but she decided to answer this one. She told him that she had just flown in from Rome, her feet were killing her, and the last thing she did before strapping in before landing was empty an airsickness bag full of some little boy's pee into the lavatory. She added that the bag wasn't full, because a lot of the urine had wound up on the passengers in the row ahead of the child, and he should take a moment and read the venom about the flight and the airline on Twitter. The hashtag, which already had a life of its own, was #WorstFlightThatDidntCrash. (It was actually a rather high bar, she thought, when she saw the hashtag gaining momentum.)

He suggested a late lunch the next day, after his audition, and she wondered what he would have thought if she had texted back that she was seeing her lawyer and then the FBI right about that time. She thought of the way they had parted the previous Sunday morning and sighed. She knew that most men desired her because she was attractive and she was smart, but also because she was a drunk and she was easy. This one? She hoped for his sake he wasn't as different as he seemed, because she always disappointed those men quickly or broke their hearts over time.

She texted back that she was busy during the day tomorrow and going to the zoo on Saturday with her nephew and niece. She thought it made her seem wholesome—certainly more wholesome than she was. She suggested dinner tomorrow night and he agreed.

She couldn't imagine what condition she'd be in after a second interview with the FBI and the print edition of the *New York Post* hitting the stands. She wondered if he would see the image and recognize her.

At some point she'd kicked off her shoes and pulled off her pantyhose, but she honestly couldn't remember when. She had taken the bookend with Romulus and Remus from her suitcase and placed it on the glass coffee table. She couldn't recall doing that either. It must have been when she was on the phone with the FBI. She stretched her toes; her feet really were killing her. She never had gotten that manicure, and now she needed a pedicure, too. That's what she'd do this August evening. That would be her exciting Thursday night. She'd call neither Paula with her love for Drambuie nor Gillian with her willingness to pick up the pieces of the messes she left behind. (Momentarily she was struck by the ironically sobering revelation that all of her friends always expected the worst from her. But surrounded as she was by far more troubling and immediate realities, the insight passed.) She'd call no one. She'd steer clear of the bars and be level-headed and crisp tomorrow morning when she picked up the *New York Post*, when she met with Ani and Frank, and when—once more—she had to face the ghost of poor Alex Sokolov.

《 《

It was after five on a Thursday afternoon in the summer, but she reminded herself that people were still working. There might be people in the office.

And so that part of her that even sober cavalierly hopscotched across lines most adults had the common sense to respect led her now to the soaring atrium of an office building on the Avenue of the Americas. Here was where Unisphere housed its Manhattan employees and where, once upon a time, Alex Sokolov had worked. The idea had come to her when she had been stripping off her uniform, planning to change into a casual summer slip of a dress for a mani-pedi and then a quiet evening at home. Instead she put on a blouse and skirt and pantyhose, and took a cab to the building on Forty-Ninth Street. She simply had to know more than she was learning on the web, especially with another face-to-face meeting with the FBI tomorrow afternoon.

She told one of the two uniformed men behind the chest-high marble counter that she had a five-thirty appointment with Alex Sokolov, showed them her driver's license, and signed in. But when they asked her to write her name in the book, she scribbled something that looked more like Alessandra than Cassandra and a last name that was indecipherable.

As she expected, after a few minutes a slim, statuesque woman in a black blazer emerged from the elevator bank. She had gray eyes and salt-and-pepper hair, and introduced herself as Jean Miller from Human Resources. "And your name is Cassandra?" she continued.

"Alessandra," Cassie answered. She shrugged. "They sound the same."

"Alessandra . . . what?"

"Ricci. Alessandra Ricci."

The executive motioned toward a marble bench far from the elevators and led Cassie there. "Let's sit down."

"Is everything all right?" Cassie asked. "I thought at first you were Alex's assistant and were going to escort me upstairs. But you said you're with personnel. Has something happened?"

She nodded. "Yes. Something has. I'm so sorry you haven't heard and I'm so sorry I'm the one who has to tell you." She took a breath. Then: "Alex was killed last week in Dubai."

Cassie wrapped her arms around her chest and stared at Jean, hoping that she wasn't overacting. "My God. Killed? How?"

"Someone stabbed him. Or, I guess, cut his throat. In his hotel room."

"That's horrible. Just awful," she murmured, looking down at her shoes and shaking her head. "Why? Have they caught the person? Or the people?"

"No, they haven't. And we don't know why. The motive was probably robbery."

"In Dubai? That city's supposed to be so safe."

"I guess things can happen anywhere," said Jean.

"He was such a sweet guy. Did you know him well?"

"I knew him better than I did some of the other managers."

"How come?"

"He was from Virginia. I'm from North Carolina. Not a lot of southerners in this office. So even though our paths weren't likely to cross all that often for work, we sometimes had coffee. Sometimes we chatted. 'Visited,' as we might say in the South."

Cassie almost said that she was from Kentucky, a reflex. She stopped herself just in time. Instead she said, "He introduced me to Russian literature. I hadn't read Tolstoy, not even in college, until we met."

Jean smiled. "He was weirdly bookish."

"Weirdly?"

"The sort of man who runs a hedge fund isn't usually the sort of man we think of curled up with a book."

"What books did he talk to you about?"

"Oh, you know . . ."

Cassie waited, hoping Jean would elaborate, but she didn't. When she remained silent, Cassie said finally, "He loved Tolstoy and Pushkin. Turgenev. We talked about whatever he was taking with him to read on airplanes all the time."

"I'm glad you two shared that."

"He had a girlfriend in Dubai—a friend who was a girl. Her name was Miranda. Any idea who that might be? He ever mention her when you two would . . . visit?"

"Why?"

"He told me he was going to have dinner with her when he was there. He was looking forward to it. They were just friends, but he was hoping it would become something more. He had a crush on her. You said you knew him a bit. Did he ever talk about her? Miranda?"

Jean looked at her a little more intensely now. "What's her last name?"

"I don't know."

"I don't, either," she said. "But I'll be sure and tell the police about her. The FBI, actually. I think you need to speak to them, too."

"Yes, of course. Absolutely."

"Tell me, why were you supposed to meet with Alex today? His assistant had nothing on his calendar this afternoon. He wasn't even supposed to be in America today. I asked her on my way downstairs."

"Was he supposed to be in Dubai still?"

"Moscow."

"He traveled a lot."

"He did. Was your meeting today a personal thing, Alessandra? Is that why he didn't tell his assistant?"

She shrugged. "We're friends, yes. We *were* friends. Sorry. But I was also a client of his. Of yours." She recalled his obituary. "I'm invested in the Stalwarts Fund."

Jean seemed to take this in, absorbing the information. Cassie considered the possibility that she simply didn't look wealthy enough to be an investor. But then Jean said, shaking her head ever so slightly, "That is such an old boy fund. Such an old man fund. Why did you invest in it?"

"Alex recommended it."

She sighed. "I thought we'd called every one of his clients to tell them what had happened to poor Alex."

"Maybe I have a voice mail I missed."

"Maybe. But we were persistent," Jean said, and for the first time she sounded slightly dubious. "I really was under the impression that we'd spoken with everyone. Everyone."

"I appreciate that."

"Would you like me to schedule a meeting for next week with someone about your account? Or a phone call tomorrow?" She pulled a phone from her blazer pocket and opened a calendar app. "We can do this right now."

"Yes. Certainly. Who would that be?"

"We have a couple of managers who are diving in. You tell me what's convenient for you."

"Okay," she agreed, and she suggested anytime on Tuesday or Wednesday afternoon, and then offered a fake phone number and a fake e-mail address. When Jean stood, Cassie stood with her and exited back into the summer heat, aware that the executive probably was memorizing every detail about her that she could. She guessed the woman would be on the phone with the FBI before she had even crossed the street.

《   《

As she walked south, she inventoried in her mind the little she had learned: Alex was going to Moscow from Dubai and he had never mentioned a person named Miranda to this other Unisphere employee. He ran a fund that, at least in the opinion of this woman from personnel, had a select group of investors: old boys. She couldn't fully translate what that meant, but she had a sense it meant Russian. Old Russians. In her mind, she saw a portrait of the Politburo, circa 1967. A lot of bald white guys with bad haircuts.

It wasn't much, but it was something, and she was glad she had gone there.

It was while crossing Fifth Avenue near the library that she felt it: a prickle of unease along her skin. A shiver along the back of her neck. She knew the word from a psychology course she'd taken in college: *scopaesthesia*. The idea was you could sense when you were being watched. It was a cousin of scopophobia: the fear of being watched. She had the exact feeling now that she had experienced the other day when she had fled from the subway. She looked to her right and saw there in the other crosswalk, also walking east, a fellow in shades and a black ball cap. It wasn't an uncommon look, not

at all, but hadn't the guy watching her on the subway platform—
maybe watching her on the subway platform—been wearing a similar cap and similar shades? Of course he had. She tried to catch his
hair color, but couldn't. She tried to guess his age, but she couldn't
guess that either. He could be twenty and he could be fifty.

She continued walking and considered whether to confront
him. If anyplace was going to be safe for this sort of engagement,
it would be late on a summer afternoon in midtown Manhattan.
She tried to imagine his response, and presumed the sort of denial
she'd get from an FBI agent would be different from the kind she'd
hear from a . . .

A what? An assassin? The person who'd killed Alex Sokolov?

She stopped at the corner of Madison, planning to cross the
street to his side. At the very least, she would get close enough to
see who he was. The idea that this might not be an FBI agent had
given her pause, and she was less confident now that she would
actually ask him why he was following her. But she had been
emboldened by her visit to Unisphere. She'd gone there and was a
little wiser now. Nothing cataclysmic had occurred.

But when she reached the far side of the street he was gone—if
he had ever really been there at all.

FEDERAL BUREAU OF INVESTIGATION

FD-302: JADA MORRIS, FLIGHT ATTENDANT

DATE: August 2, 2018

JADA MORRIS, date of birth—/—/——, SSN #————, telephone number (—)————, was interviewed for a second time by properly identified Special Agents AMARA LINDOR and JON NEWHOUSE at the FBI office in Melville, New York.

LINDOR conducted the interview; NEWHOUSE took these notes.

MORRIS said she was confident that the woman in the two security camera photos from the ROYAL PHOENICIAN HOTEL was CASSANDRA BOWDEN. She said she only learned that BOWDEN's brother-in-law "had something to do with chemical weapons" on the morning of July 27, when the discussion among the cabin crew in the airline shuttle van in Dubai gravitated there.

She reiterated that she had met ALEX SOKOLOV for the first time on July 26, on the flight between Paris and Dubai.

MORRIS said she had bid on Moscow four times in the last year (and gotten the city twice) simply because she had never been to Russia. She claims to know no one there.

Her trip to Dubai on July 26–27 was her fourth visit that month with the airline, but this July marked the first time she had gotten the bid. She was able to account for her whereabouts the full time, including her dinner on Thursday night, July 26, at the KAGAYA Japanese restaurant with three other flight attendants.

She said she has lost touch with ELIZA REDMOND HOUGH, her classmate from Michigan State University, who married drone pilot CAPTAIN DEVIN HOUGH. She said she knows almost nothing about what her cousin, engineer ISAIAH BELL, does with stealth technology at WELKIN AEROSPACE SYSTEMS in Nashua, New Hampshire.

She claimed never to have heard of United Arab Emirates drone designer NOVASKIES.

13

The Dubai restaurant faced the harbor and had floor-to-ceiling casement windows, open now to catch the morning breeze off the gulf. There were white linen tablecloths that were pristine, as were the white leather banquettes on which the guests were sitting. It was part of a hotel with a marina. The buffet of pastries and cheeses and exotic fruits and vegetables was presented on white serving plates on white marble counters that were streaked and dotted with black: they looked to Elena like giant squares of stracciatella gelato. She and Viktor had shared a yogurt and purslane salad, but now he was waiting on the fried eggs and Turkish sausage he had ordered in addition. He had insisted they have breakfast before she followed the flight attendant back to America.

"They tell me the flash drive was worthless," he said to her. "Nothing of value. Nothing NovaSkies can't already do and nothing to help with a new sort of . . . payload."

He wasn't precisely chastising her, but there was more than mere disappointment in his tone. A thought passed through her mind, but she told herself that she was being paranoid and she should not allow it to take root: Did Viktor suspect that she had tampered with the flash drive Sokolov had been given? Did he believe that she had deleted the information they were expecting? "Really, nothing?" she asked.

"Nothing."

"I'm sorry," she said quietly.

"We expected more." He looked around and she saw why. The hostess was about to seat a couple of Western businessmen at the table beside them. Instantly he stood and asked the woman in Arabic if she could please seat them a little further away: he was discussing deeply personal family matters with his daughter and would be grateful for the extra privacy. The young woman, Indian or Pakistani, Elena presumed, smiled and obliged. The business-men didn't seem to care.

"Now I'm your daughter?" she asked Viktor when he sat back down.

He shrugged. "I would be proud to have you as my daughter."

She didn't believe him and rolled her eyes. He and her father had endured each other, little more. She knew, in the end, what Viktor had done to him. "Even after this fiasco?"

"Even after, yes. Even the most successful people in this world make mistakes. Often they're just better at correcting them and moving on."

His eggs and sausages arrived and he smiled happily at the waitress. After she had placed them before him and retreated, he continued. "Our job is to anticipate, and in this case you antici-pated wrong. Now you are responding accordingly."

"Yes. Of course."

He motioned at his plate. "God, this stuff is good. You really should try some." Despite his apparent enthusiasm for the entrée before him, however, almost delicately he sliced off a thin section of one of the sausages. He brought the piece to his mouth, chewed, and smiled a little too rapturously for Elena's taste. If breakfast could make him this happy, she shuddered to think of what he might be like in bed. "I spoke to the police," he said when he had finished chewing. "They interviewed most of us."

"And?"

"It was fine. None of us are American women. But it could have been awkward. Another reason why you should have told me right away about the flight attendant."

"I understand."

"I'm sure you do."

"How much time do I have?" she asked.

"How much time do we have," he corrected her. "Don't feel so alone out there."

"I am so alone out there."

"The woman is either a wild card or something far worse."

"A wild card," she repeated, mulling that over. She considered pressing him about what he meant by something far worse, but she recalled his remark about the worthless flash drive. If he really didn't trust her—if he actually doubted her—the last thing she wanted to do was inadvertently force him to say such a thing aloud. Verbalizing it would make it too real, the accusation irrevocable.

"Yes. A wild card. She's a drunk and, I have come to believe, a little self-destructive."

"You mean in addition to her drinking?"

He put down his fork and looked at her intensely. "I'm not sure what I mean. I just know that I want her gone. It shouldn't be difficult."

"Probably not," Elena said, though she didn't completely agree. It wouldn't be difficult operationally, but it sure as hell would piss people off and it sure as hell would exact a high price on her soul. Killing Bowden wouldn't be like killing Sokolov, an opportunistic fuck who'd agreed to mule American data because he knew he was in deep shit for skimming and had now served his purpose. He clearly couldn't be trusted. Nor would it be like killing that despicable colonel at Incirlik who was playing both sides and getting rich: that prick had just screwed some poor Yazidi girl who couldn't have been more than fourteen or fifteen years old when she shot him. He was a pig. But this flight attendant? Not her usual quarry. It would be like drowning a kitten. But Elena was in survival mode herself, and so she added, "It's mostly the travel that annoys me."

"You really don't like to travel?"

"I was looking forward to spending a little time here. Or going home to Sochi for a bit."

He seemed to relax a little bit. He picked up his fork and gazed down at his breakfast. "You will. All in good time. This is a speed bump, that's all. No, it's a detour. A detour to America. You like America," he said, the last sentence a small, slight dig. "But then you'll come back. Or go home. Whichever you want."

"Okay."

He looked over her shoulder and pointed. She turned and saw a pair of myna birds on an outside railing just behind her, their yellow beaks phosphorescent in the sun. "Even the birds here eavesdrop," he said, smiling. But then his tone grew serious. "You asked me how much time you have," he said. "The fact the flash drive was of no value—no use—doesn't reflect well on you. You should know that no one is happy about that. I am just being honest. So, I think you should move quickly. For your own sake, Elena. For your own good. Soon would be best—for everyone."

14

Cassie saw that she was on page nine of the *New York Post* and page eleven of the *Daily News*. At the same time that she bought the two newspapers at the Rite-Aid a block from her apartment, she bought new sunglasses: big and bulky and a completely different shape from her old ones. The ones in the photograph. On her way back to her building, she threw away the sunglasses she was wearing in Dubai, as well as the scarf with the arabesque patterns. It was pretty and she knew she would miss it. She deposited them into an overflowing trash can on the corner, because the garbage would be collected later that morning.

The article was identical to the version she had read online, and she was rather surprised by how tame it all seemed now that she had read Sokolov's obituary. Usually the *Post* wrote the worst or the wildest things that anyone thought or suspected but would never say aloud. But there was no conjecture that Alex was CIA or KGB, no innuendo at all that he was a spy. Alex was portrayed as just another hedge fund guy who happened to go to places like Moscow and Dubai for work.

On the sidewalk near her apartment, she saw three schoolgirls walking toward her in matching plaid uniform skirts and white blouses, and guessed they were close to her nephew's age: they looked about eleven. Each was using her phone as a compact, flipping the camera lens as if taking a selfie, but she could tell by the anxiety in all of their eyes that they weren't merely checking their makeup—were they wearing anything more than lipstick?—but were instead examining their faces for uncorrectable imperfections. One of the girls had twin constellations of freckles on her cheeks. Another, who looked closest to tears, had a slight bump along the ridge of her nose. They were pretty girls, and their self-doubt and their fear seemed needless. But Cassie understood. She had no idea where they were going because she doubted even private schools started this early in August. Perhaps it was some sort of summer program or summer day trip. It didn't matter. She recalled feeling the way they did herself. She knew her niece would soon. All of Jessica's confidence would disappear like a helium balloon released on a blustery autumn afternoon. Maybe some of it would return, but it would never be as bold and pure as it once was.

When the children were behind her, Cassie looked again at the picture of herself in the tabloid. Utterly disgusted, she shook her head exactly like the girl with the freckles.

《 《

Almost as soon as she was back in her apartment, her phone rang and she saw it was Megan. She paused for a brief moment but then answered it. "Hey, there," she said. "Aren't you in Berlin?"

"I am. The flight's delayed, so I thought I'd check in with you. You okay?"

"Let's see: I'm speaking again to the FBI this afternoon and I'm kind of wigged out by the newspapers. Other than that, what could possibly be wrong?"

"I get it. The FBI talked to me again, too."

She stared at Hammond's business card on her refrigerator. Suddenly she felt as if she had just dodged a bullet not saying anything more to Megan. She told herself that she was being crazy, but an idea came to her: this conversation is being recorded. The FBI was using Megan to get her to incriminate herself. And so, just in case, she responded, "I hope they get to the bottom of this soon. I feel so bad for that poor man's family." She said a small prayer that

Megan wouldn't bring up the fact that she had asked her friend to lie for her when they had spoken last.

"Vaughn feels that way, too," Megan agreed, referring to her husband. "When he read the newspaper stories, he called and said he didn't understand why it's all about the mystery woman and not the guy who was killed."

"How is Vaughn?"

"Good. Same old, same old."

"What's he working on these days?" she asked. She had no interest at all in what Vaughn Briscoe did for a living as a consultant, but the question struck her as innocuous and safe. She felt bad not trusting her friend, but just in case, she had to get this conversation as far from Dubai as she could.

"More government nonsense. He's in Edgewater, Maryland, again. He's happier when he's with private-sector clients, but it makes our life so much easier when he's working in Maryland or inside the Beltway. When the girls were younger and he was working for that pharmaceutical company in Colorado, childcare was a nightmare. He was always away. Always traveling. Kind of like me. Now he's home every night, and this fall he'll be able to pick them up from the ten trillion places they have to be after school when I can't."

"How was Berlin?"

"It was fine. Are you nervous about this afternoon?"

"No," Cassie lied. "How many times and how many ways can they ask me about what Sokolov was like on the flight or whether he said anything of interest?"

"That's all they're asking?"

"So far. Maybe they'll have more interesting questions for me this afternoon."

"Look, Cassie . . ."

"Go on."

"Do you need anything? Is there anything I can do?"

"Like what?"

"I don't know. I just feel so bad for you. I just—"

"I'm fine," Cassie said. She wanted to cut her friend off before she could say something they both might regret. "I need to run. My family's coming to town from Kentucky this weekend, and I have a thousand things to do. But I really appreciate the offer, and I love hearing your voice. I love it. But I'm okay."

"If you change your mind, you know where to find me."

"Yeah. Berlin," she answered, and she laughed ever so slightly. Her friend, if she needed her, probably would be on another continent and in a time zone six hours distant.

« «

To try and take her mind off the newspapers and what loomed that afternoon, she finished "The Death of Ivan Ilyich" on the couch, occasionally glancing up at the Empire State Building when her mind wandered from nineteenth-century Russia. She felt neither virtuous for reading Tolstoy nor relieved by Ilyich's transformation: the way he went from fearing to welcoming that great, ineludible light. Mostly she continued to hope that Alex Sokolov hadn't woke up when his throat was being cut.

« «

It was hot and sunny again that Friday, and so Ani directed Cassie to a glass table in a shady spot of the courtyard, and the two of them brought their street falafel there. The city felt quiet to Cassie, even for the start of a weekend in the middle of the summer.

"This building isn't precisely a ghost town on August Fridays, but a lot of people clear out—especially the businesses on the other floors. Don't even try and schedule a meeting after lunch on a Friday in August," she told Cassie.

"We're getting so Parisian in the two-one-two," Cassie murmured. She was distracted. She hadn't fallen asleep until, almost in desperation near midnight, she had done a couple shots of vodka, popped a pair of Advil PMs, and swallowed a few tabs of melatonin. Normally she didn't need melatonin on this side of the Atlantic. But normally she wasn't meeting with lawyers and then the FBI. She'd been fine—a little fuzzy maybe, but fine—when she had first crawled out of bed and walked to the Rite-Aid for the newspapers.

Ani smiled at her small joke, but Cassie could see concern in her eyes. "You look tired," she said.

"I am." She stared at the falafel and sauce in its pita. The wrap in its wax paper. She had no appetite today, and tried to decide if she was any less hungry than usual.

"Are you going to be okay?"

"I think so."

Ani wiped her fingers on her napkin and reached over and took Cassie's hands. "Try not to worry. You're not in Dubai. No one is going to prosecute you for committing an act that may lure a person to sin."

"That's a thing in the Emirates?"

"It is. So is having consensual sex outside of wedlock."

She looked down at her hands in Ani's. Her skin was so pale compared to the lawyer's. It was August. Why hadn't she been to the beach? Or a lake? Or even, for God's sake, a tanning salon and gotten sprayed? She took back her hands, hoping Ani wouldn't think it was an unfriendly gesture. "We should eat," she added quickly, trying to give a concrete reason for her discomfort with Ani's kindness. With her touch.

"Yes," the lawyer agreed.

"I went by Unisphere yesterday. After you and I spoke."

"You what?"

"I wanted to learn more about Alex," she said, aware of how sheepish she sounded.

"Had you been drinking?"

"No! I think I should be a little insulted you even asked that."

"God. Tell me precisely what happened," Ani commanded, and so Cassie did, sharing her exchange with the woman from personnel and the little she'd gleaned from the encounter.

"They're going to know it's you—if they don't already," the lawyer said when she'd finished.

"I suspected as much. But I had to try."

"Please promise me that you won't do that sort of thing again."

"I promise," she agreed. "Did you find out anything more about Alex at your end?" she asked.

"No. But I called my investigator friend again last night," Ani said. "Did you read Alex's obituary?"

"I did."

"And?"

"I don't know. Doesn't it scream spy to you?"

Ani took a small bite of the wrap and seemed to think carefully before answering. "It doesn't scream that. Maybe it hints at that. I picked up on how brief it was."

"And the cities."

"Lots of people work in Moscow and Dubai who have nothing to do with espionage."

"When will the investigator know something?"

"Next week," Ani answered. "Maybe even early next week."

"Okay."

"Now, this afternoon, the case agent—this Frank Hammond—is going to be sneaky. It's possible you're going to think he's a freaking dunce. But he's not, I assure you. An FBI knife goes in very slowly. FBI agents are trained to get someone to unwittingly tell the truth. Also? I'm sure he knows a lot more than the newspapers do. He knows everything the FBI's legal attaché in the Emirates knows, and they're eight hours ahead of us. There were probably developments today that we know absolutely nothing about."

"God . . ."

"Don't feel that way. A lot depends on whether the Emirates feels like playing ball with the U.S. They may not. It's their country. And while they might be worried about some kind of tourism backlash, the rest of the Muslim Middle East is a hell of a lot scarier to most Americans than Dubai. Besides, it's not like there's a pattern of violent crime against tourists there. The truth is, there's really no reason why Dubai will care all that much about the murder of some money manager in their fair city."

"Unless they actually want to make it clear that he was killed by another American: a drunk flight attendant from New York."

"I guess. But assuming he was just some MBA with Unisphere Asset Management, I really can't understand why the FBI would give a damn. And yet it's clear that they do."

"Do you believe they're still looking for an American woman who lives in Dubai?"

"Nope."

"No?" She heard the fear in her voice.

"I mean, I don't know that for a fact. But by now they've talked to the people Alex knew or might have known. Everyone who was supposed to be in that meeting, everyone with Unisphere. Everyone at the hotel. They're working their way backward. By now every American woman he spoke with on that flight from Paris to Dubai—especially the flight attendant—is under suspicion."

"I see."

Ani put down her wrap and took a breath. "Now, this meeting with the FBI isn't precisely a situation where you can perjure yourself. This isn't a sworn deposition. But they will try and catch you in a lie, and it is a federal offense to lie to an FBI agent. You may not even feel the knife going in until they begin to twist it."

"I had been planning to lie like crazy when we landed. But they never asked me anything that demanded a lie."

"That's good."

"So what am I supposed to do?"

"Well, first of all, don't lie. Just don't. But you can take the Fifth Amendment. Do you know what that is?"

"Yes. But then, of course, I sound like a Mafia wife."

"That is the problem with the Fifth. The FBI may still be fishing—they might in fact have nothing concrete—and if you take the Fifth, that's a pretty serious nibble. So, I want you to look at me before you answer any question. If I nod, tell the truth. If I shake my head, take the Fifth."

Cassie watched a plane flying silently high overhead. Even now, despite her years at thirty-five thousand feet, the miracle of flight continued to move her. "Won't you be sitting next me?"

"Probably. But I don't care if they see me coaching you. That doesn't matter. Good God, if necessary, I will jump in for you and say you're taking the Fifth. The thing is . . ." Ani's voice trailed off.

"Go on."

"I wanted to tell you this in person. You may not be extraditable for murder, but you aren't out of the woods. There are other reasons why you could be prosecuted in the U.S. for Sokolov's death. Terrorism, for instance."

"What?"

"It's unlikely. But here's the chain. The Department of Justice and the OVT: the Office of Justice for Victims of Overseas Terrorism. The OVT reports to National Security. The OVT director meets weekly with the folks in counterterrorism and counter-espionage. Alex Sokolov is an American citizen who was murdered abroad, and his death could be handed over to them—especially if he was someone important to the government."

"That's absurd. Once in a while I may drink too much, but I'm not a terrorist."

"I get it. I just want to be sure you understand the stakes before we go downtown. Now, you should eat. You really should. If you don't like falafel, don't be polite. Tell me. We'll find you something else. I want to coach you for a few minutes, and I want to be sure you have some sustenance inside you before we meet with the FBI."

She nodded and started to eat, and tried to pay attention. Suddenly, she was feeling like a victim herself, and that only made her feel worse. It shamed her to feel that way. After all, she wasn't the body left behind in the bed.

《　《

Cassie rarely got to Wall Street, but when she did, she was always struck by how narrow the streets were compared to Murray Hill and midtown Manhattan. The FBI was in a skyscraper on Broadway, but Broadway this far downtown, this close to the Brooklyn Bridge, was the slender tip of the funnel. Federal Plaza was a little more squat than the Seagram Building, but what made it feel so different was the Wall Street claustrophobia induced by the combination of tall edifices and thin streets. Outside the building was a small park with three tall, dark columns, a sculpture called the Sentinel, and some trees that she guessed were a kind of willow. On the side streets around the plaza were manned guardhouses and black-and-yellow striped metal barricades that police officers raised or lowered to allow select vehicles in and out of the parking garage. She thought of the Fearless Girl standing tall against the Bull a few blocks to the south. Cassie understood that there was nothing heroic about who she was, nothing courageous about what she was doing; she was here because she drank too much and a decade and a half of bad decisions—especially one night in Dubai—was catching up to her. But she thought of that bronze little girl with a ponytail, her hands on her hips and her chest out, facing off against the much larger bull. Cassie wanted now to be just that plucky and do the right thing.

Whatever that was.

"Ready?" Ani asked. They hadn't spoken since they had gotten out of the cab a minute ago and paused in front of the Sentinel.

Cassie shook her head. "No. But I really don't have a choice now, do I?"

Ani looked her in the eye. "You'll be fine. Just remember: whatever you do, don't lie."

《 《

The room was windowless and Cassie didn't care. She was struck by the shiny, fake veneer of the rectangular table, and how the chairs were covered in an orange shade of Naugahyde that belonged only on pumpkins. Once again Frank Hammond was interviewing her and James Washburn was taking the notes.

"Glad you could make it this afternoon," Hammond said after Cassie had introduced Ani to the two agents and everyone was seated. "I really am grateful. I know it's an inconvenience, but we want to help the Emirates and put this part of the investigation to bed. We want to move on."

"Of course," she agreed.

"I just hate to have busywork hanging over my head over the weekend—especially a summer weekend."

"It's fine."

He smiled. She was struck once more by how world weary he seemed for a guy who couldn't have been more than forty or forty-one. Once again she noted Washburn's unblemished skin and rimless eyeglasses, and wondered if he was ever allowed outside. "When do you fly out again?" he asked.

"Sunday."

"Back to Dubai?"

"Rome. I have Rome this month."

"I love Italy."

"I do, too."

He shook his head wistfully and she presumed he was recalling a moment in a beautiful piazza in a Tuscan village or a perfect, endless meal in Florence. "Of course, I've never been there. But I hope to get there someday," he said. "So: I guess I really just love the idea of Italy."

For a moment she was taken aback, but quickly she gathered herself. "I hope you get there, too," she said. "It's beautiful. It lives up to its reputation. It's one of the prettiest places in the world, I think."

"And you've seen a lot of the world."

"I guess."

"Is that why you became a flight attendant? You love to travel?"

She shrugged, unsure whether this was chatter to wear down her reserve or he needed to know for some reason. Washburn's gaze was moving between her and the pad on the table in front of him, but he wasn't writing anything down. "I think so," she answered simply. She remembered her carefully scripted answer during her job interview with the airline eighteen years ago: *I enjoy people. I think customer service is a real art.*

"Ever consider becoming a pilot?"

"Nope."

"How come?"

"Not really my skill set. I kind of think you don't want a person like me ever driving a cab or a school bus." She'd meant it as a joke, but she saw Ani's eyes grow a little wide and she realized that humor—at least humor that acknowledged her more irresponsible tendencies—was a particularly bad idea.

"Oh, why is that?"

"I just meant that I live in the city. I don't even own a car."

Hammond nodded and Washburn started to write.

"So, we're just clearing up a few little things as a courtesy to Dubai," the case agent said. "This shouldn't take very long at all. You said that you and Alex Sokolov spoke during the food service on that last flight—the one from Paris to Dubai on July twenty-sixth."

"That's correct."

"You said he was a flirt."

"Kind of."

"How? What kinds of things did he say?"

"He said he liked our uniforms. We actually have three kinds: A pants suit. A skirt and a blouse. And a dress. I usually wear the dress."

"Why?"

"It's the most flattering on me."

"That's interesting."

"Why?"

"I don't know. I guess I'd wear the one that was most comfortable."

"That's because you're male."

He chuckled and nodded. "Probably true."

"But, to be honest, they're all pretty comfortable."

He seemed to think about this. Then: "What else did he say?"

"Alex Sokolov? I don't remember. I've had"—and Cassie paused to count in her mind—"four flights since then."

"The air marshal recalls you two talking a lot."

"I don't know about that. I try to do a good job, and part of that is making passengers feel relaxed and happy on a flight."

"He tell you anything about himself?"

"Not really. He probably didn't tell me much at all."

"You said he told you that he was a money manager. What else?"

"I can't think of anything."

"You two both talked about living in Manhattan, yes?"

"Yes."

"Another passenger recalled him telling you that he was an only child. You told him you had a sister. Do you remember that?"

"Not really."

"Some other family stuff, maybe?" he asked. "Someone else said you two talked about Kentucky. How your sister and her family still live there."

She glanced at Ani and then at the way that Washburn had suddenly, inconceivably filled almost an entire sheet of paper on the yellow legal pad. "I don't know. It's possible."

"Did he tell you about why he was in Dubai? His work?"

"I don't remember him saying much about that."

"Okay. He said he was a money manager. What else?"

"He said he ran a hedge fund."

"Good. Go on."

"That's all. I don't even know what a hedge fund is precisely," she admitted.

"What meetings did he mention?"

"I know he had a meeting, but we didn't discuss it."

"It was supposed to be the next day?"

"Yes."

"Who was going to be in it?"

"Investors, I suppose."

"So these were investors in Dubai?" he asked.

"I'm just speculating."

"Any names?"

Instantly she recalled Miranda and almost offered that name, but as far as the FBI knew, she hadn't seen Alex once he exited the jet bridge in Dubai. She considered telling Hammond that he brought the woman up on the plane, but she wasn't sure she would be able to manage the questions—the fallout—that would emerge from the revelation. And so she answered, "Not that he told me on the plane."

"Okay. What about friends? Did he say anything about any acquaintances or buddies or women he might have been planning to see while he was in the Emirates?"

"No. He didn't mention anyone."

"I don't think we asked this when you landed. I'm so sorry. Did you see Sokolov in Dubai?"

She thought of how Ani had warned her that she might not feel the knife going in, but she knew she would. Here it was. The question, the third in a string of short sentences, was the blade at the edge of her skin. *Did you see Sokolov in Dubai?* She also recalled how Ani had said that under no circumstances should she lie. It was better to take the Fifth. And so she took a deep breath and she did.

"On my counsel's advice, I am invoking my right under the Fifth Amendment not to answer." It took courage to say those words—not Fearless Girl bravery, not a righteous refusal to be bullied—but it was still a kind of valor she wasn't sure she had. She wanted to lie. It was just easier to lie. So much of her life was lying. Oh, she would have moments of candor, especially when she was forced to face who she was after a particularly deep drunk or when the postcoital revulsion was stifling after a romp with a stranger. But usually she lied. Now she watched Hammond look quickly at Ani, who was absolutely stone-faced, and then back at her. He smiled.

"Really?" he said, his tone almost light. "How could that question possibly incriminate you?"

She said nothing.

"So the last time you ever saw Alex Sokolov was as he was leaving the airplane after you touched down in the Emirates?" he pressed.

"On my counsel's advice, I am taking the Fifth."

Hammond said to Ani, "I'm not sure what you think we're looking for here, Ms. Mouradian, or why in the world you would give Ms. Bowden that advice."

Ani glanced down at her nails and then up at Hammond. Her legs were crossed, and her skirt had ridden up a few inches on her thighs. Her pantyhose were black and sheer, and Cassie recognized the color as one of the shades the airline approved with the uniform. "What are you looking for, Agent Hammond?" she asked him.

"We're just trying to learn all we can about the death of an American citizen in Dubai. We're trying to see what he did there the night before he was killed. A courtesy for another country. A courtesy for a grieving American family in this one. Maybe Alex Sokolov said something to your client that will help us find out who murdered him."

"Why not ask her that?"

He nodded. "Okay." Then he turned back to Cassie: "Did Alex Sokolov say anything to you that might help us find out who murdered him?"

"No," Cassie answered.

"That wasn't so difficult, was it?" Ani asked the agent. He ignored her.

"Did Sokolov tell you where he was going when he landed?"

Ani jumped in: "Agent Hammond, surely you have already asked Unisphere Asset Management that question and they have told you. For the life of me, I can't see why you keep coming back to this line of questioning with my client. I'm sure you know exactly who Alex Sokolov was meeting with in Dubai. I'm sure you know exactly why he was in the city."

"And do you know, Ms. Mouradian?"

"No. Do you care to tell us?"

He looked irked, but he said nothing to the lawyer. Instead he turned back to Cassie and said, "Let's make it easier: did he tell you the name of the hotel where he was staying?"

Ani jumped in again. "We all know that, Agent Hammond. It's been in the newspapers, for God's sake."

"Ah, but did he tell your client? That's my question."

"I invoke my right under the Fifth Amendment not to answer." Cassie noticed that Washburn was writing even that down.

"Do you honestly believe that we or the police in Dubai think you've done something wrong, Ms. Bowden?" He was, Cassie supposed, trying to sound at once astonished and hurt. She might have believed that he actually felt that way if Ani hadn't warned her.

"I'm guessing that's a rhetorical question," Ani said to the case agent.

"It's not. I'm trying to help solve a crime. I'm trying to help a family get justice. And, just maybe, I'm trying to save other lives by catching a killer."

"All noble goals. I want you to succeed," said Ani.

"And there are flight attendants, passengers, and an air marshal on Alex Sokolov's last flight who are quite clear about this: your client was talking to him. A lot. And in their extensive conversations, it is at least remotely possible that he may have told Ms. Bowden something that could be useful."

"So you don't believe she has done anything wrong?"

Cassie was struck by how everyone was suddenly referring to her in the third person, as if she weren't there. *She. Ms. Bowden.* She wanted to raise her hand and remind them that she was here, she wasn't invisible. She recalled a line from an old Beatles song: *I know what it's like to be dead.*

Hammond's brow grew furrowed. "Why would we? Because she went by Unisphere's New York office late yesterday afternoon?"

And then, as if it were only a game of high-stakes poker, no one said anything. She could see that Ani and Hammond were trying to surmise each other's tell, that almost imperceptible behavioral tic that would allow them to gauge their opponent's hand and sense their advantage. It was actually Washburn, the scribe, who broke the silence.

"I just want to confirm," he began quietly, looking at Cassie, "you said Sokolov didn't tell you at which hotel he was staying, correct? You only learned where he was staying from the newspapers, well after the fact." Then he put his head back down and seemed to be staring at the tip of his ballpoint pen as he held it an inch or so above the yellow paper with the thin blue lines.

"I took the Fifth," she said, the words timorous and momentarily caught in her throat. She clasped her fingers together in her lap because otherwise they would be visibly shaking.

"Where were you the night that Alex Sokolov was murdered?" Hammond asked.

"I am taking the Fifth."

"Were you in your room that the airline had booked for you at the Fairmont Hotel? In other words, were you at the same place as the rest of the crew? Or did you spend the night elsewhere?"

"Again, I am taking the Fifth."

"You know the Fifth is not some crazy magical bullet, don't you?" Hammond told her.

She said nothing. She tried to breathe slowly. She tried not to think about the drink she would have when she got out of here, but to focus instead on this poker game, this chess match. Did they somehow know—and know categorically—that she had not been in the room the airline had provided her, or were they just presuming she was not there because of the Royal Phoenician security camera photos?

"No," said Ani, answering for her, "it's not. But it is her constitutional right."

"And I hope you realize," Hammond went on, "that by invoking the Fifth you are only giving me the impression that you really have done something incriminating—that you really do have something to hide."

"I . . ." Cassie stopped. She didn't know what she wanted to say.

"Look," Hammond began, his voice growing a little more gentle. "Let's just clear up the little things. The easy things."

"Okay," she said.

"When did you meet Alex Sokolov?"

For a moment the absurdity of the question confused her, and she had to think about it a second. "On the plane," she said. "When he boarded."

"You never saw him in New York?"

"No."

"It's a weirdly small city. And, of course, you did go by his office yesterday."

She remained silent.

"Anyone tell you he was going to be on the flight?" he asked.

"No. Why would someone? That's . . ."

"That's what?"

"That's not how it works. No one tells us who's on the flight until we get the passenger list before takeoff."

The FBI agent looked at her earnestly. "I'm trying to help you, Ms. Bowden. But I can't help you if you don't help me."

"I think she's being quite helpful," said Ani.

He ignored the lawyer and continued. "The newspapers. I'm sure you've seen them. Is that you in the pictures, Ms. Bowden?"

"What newspapers? What pictures?" she asked. She was stalling and the two FBI agents had to know it—how could she not have seen the newspapers by now?—but her reflex when she couldn't answer with a grandiose lie was to answer with a modest one.

Hammond was clearly going to play along. "Well, let me tell you. Some of the newspapers have published security camera photos from the hotel where Alex Sokolov's body was found. Most have published two. One shows a woman on Sokolov's arm the night before he was killed. The other shows that same woman leaving the hotel the next morning. Alone. She's wearing the same clothes."

Washburn opened a manila folder beside his pad and placed the two photos on the table in front of Cassie. "Here they are," he said.

Ani smiled but didn't glance at the pictures. "A walk of shame? Seriously? Why are we even discussing this?"

Hammond ignored her and elaborated: "The legal attaché in the Emirates says that the woman in these pictures matches the description of the woman—an American—who three different hotel employees say they saw with Sokolov the night before he was murdered. Apparently, she matches the woman with whom he dined at a French restaurant that evening."

The photos were eight by tens. They were crisper than the reproductions in the newspaper or the images she had seen on her phone, but certainly not crystal clear. Was the woman indisputably her? Not indisputably. The first was a grainy, long-range profile. In the second, the woman was wearing sunglasses. In both she was wearing the scarf. But a reasonable person could reasonably suppose it was her.

"Recognize the scarf?" Hammond was asking.

She shrugged. She gazed for a moment at the arabesque, at the almost hypnotic array of tendrils and swirls.

"One of the flight attendants on the plane with you from Paris to Dubai recalls you buying one just like that when you landed," Hammond said. "It was near the duty-free shop at the airport. Maybe even next to it."

She wondered: Was this Megan? Jada? Shane? It could have been any of them or someone else. There were nine other flight attendants. "I may have," she answered simply.

"So: is that you?"

She looked up at him and she looked at Ani. She glanced at Washburn. She held her hands tightly together, but she couldn't stop her legs from shaking under the table. She knew she was supposed to take the Fifth. But, suddenly, she knew also that she wasn't going to. She knew it. She thought once again of that old Beatles lyric, *I know what it's like to be dead,* and understood with certainty that she was going to lie, because that was who she was, and you can no more escape your DNA than you can an Airbus that is pinwheeling into the ocean after (pick one, she thought to herself, just pick one) a cataclysmic mechanical failure, a suicidal pilot, or a bomb in the cargo hold. She was the lightning that brings down the plane, the pilot who panics on the final approach in the blizzard.

They'd probably found her lipstick in Alex's hotel suite already. Or, perhaps, that lip balm. They'd found it where she had left it or where it had fallen out of her purse. They'd found it beside a mirror in the bedroom or the bathroom or on the carpet near the chair where she had tossed her purse. They'd found the incontrovertible evidence that she had been with Alex the night he was killed.

"Well?" Hammond pressed. Ani was mouthing the three syllables *Take the Fifth*, her eyes wide and intense.

Instead, however, Cassie gazed for one long, last moment at the images on the table, savoring these final seconds before the plane hits the earth, unsure whether the next few words would result in a successful crash landing or the aircraft would break apart and explode upon impact. She took a deep breath through her nose, exhaled, and then said, "Of course, it's me. Alex and I met on the plane, we had dinner in Dubai, and then we went back to his hotel room. We made love in the bedroom and in the bathroom—in the shower. And in the morning, when I left, he was still very, very much alive. I can assure you of that. He kissed me once on the forehead before I said good-bye, and then said he was about to get up himself. But I swear to you on my life: when I left the hotel, he was perfectly, totally fine."

FD-302—EXTRACT: CASSANDRA BOWDEN, FLIGHT ATTENDANT

DATE: August 3, 2018

Although BOWDEN had pled the Fifth multiple times in the interview, including one time when asked if SOKOLOV had told her the name of the hotel where he was staying, when shown the hotel security camera photos, she admitted that she was the woman in both of them.

She said that she and SOKOLOV had dined at LA PETITE FERME before returning to his hotel room at the ROYAL PHOENICIAN HOTEL. There they had consensual intercourse two times before going to sleep. She says that when she left his room on the morning of July 27, he was alive. He was awake and kissed her.

She acknowledged leaving about 10:45 a.m. She didn't believe he had any meetings that day until lunchtime, which was why he had suggested she shower and get dressed first, while he "lolled" in bed a few more minutes. He had even joked, "After all, you have a plane to catch. I don't."

Finally, she said that a woman came to SOKOLOV's hotel suite the night before. SOKOLOV introduced her as MIRANDA (LAST NAME UNKNOWN). She seemed to be American, roughly thirty years old, brown eyes, auburn hair, medium height for a woman. No eyeglasses. Baggy black slacks, red and black tunic top. The woman brought a bottle of vodka with her, and the three of them shared it.

At the time, BOWDEN thought MIRANDA had something to do with UNISPHERE ASSET MANAGEMENT. She presumed she was either an employee or she had money invested in a fund. (BOWDEN insisted that she visited UNISPHERE on August 2 hoping to learn more about the woman or about SOKOLOV.) BOWDEN thought that MIRANDA may also have been involved with real estate in Dubai. She said she had a sense that MIRANDA was going to be in the same meeting (or meetings) as SOKOLOV the next day.

She did not believe that SOKOLOV and MIRANDA were close friends or had known each other very long. It was even possible that they were meeting for the first time that evening.

BOWDEN believes that MIRANDA probably stayed less than an hour, but she was intoxicated by then and unsure. She recalled they talked a little about her work as a flight attendant (SOKOLOV and MIRANDA were interested), but not their own work. The conversation was difficult for BOWDEN to recall in any detail because she was drinking.

= = = = = =

FOLLOW-UP: The Office of the Director of National Intelligence (ODNI) has informed us that Alex Sokolov's computer showed seven Russian investors in the Unisphere Stalwarts Fund who have been singled out by OFAC, including Viktor Olenin. Withdrawal and transfer records suggest Sokolov's theft from the fund may have exceeded two million dollars.

ODNI said there were two e-mails with Russian operatives we believe were affiliated with the Syrian chemical weapons program, one of whom is believed to be a COSSACK, but the content was routine business about the fund's returns. There were no specific mentions of sarin, VX, or the compounds at the Blue Grass Army Depot in Kentucky in the e-mails, nor was there any reference to chemical weapons defense tools.

There was no reference to the stealth drone or jet drone projects.

But there was information on the flash drive that seems to have come from the Edgewood Chemical Biological Center (though we cannot yet rule out a source at Blue Grass).

Finally, there were no e-mails or documents or references anywhere on the computer to the flight attendant.

15

Elena really wasn't afraid that the passenger in the lavatory was a terrorist. He was a Sikh in an orange turban. He had to have been close to seventy. But this was a U.S. carrier flying from Dubai to Amsterdam, and a fellow with a beard and cloth on his head had been in the bathroom nearly ten minutes now. The Americans on board were starting to fret. "I am really not going to be happy until that guy gets the heck out of there," she heard one woman saying. A man joked to the passenger beside him, "Yeah, it's a long drive, but right now we're at thirty-five thousand feet and I kind of wish I'd rented a car." Even the flight attendants—a pair of middle-aged guys who were still pretty buff and clearly knew what they were doing—were conferring. Elena was in the bulkhead seat in coach, which was about as good as it got in that cabin, and so she could see and hear the business class passengers trying to encourage the flight attendants to do something, but parsing their words to dial down their racism and paranoia:

"I'm sure he would come out if he knew he was inconveniencing people," said a mother Elena speculated was a decade older than she was and had a son seven or eight years old sitting beside her.

"It's probably just all that Middle Eastern food," said the gentleman across the aisle. She guessed he was the woman's husband given the way that he reached over and patted her arm.

Even the casually dressed dude who Elena was sure was an air marshal had grown sufficiently alarmed that he had unbuckled and was leaning into the aisle, staring, poised to assist the flight attendants if it came to that.

But Elena suspected it wouldn't. Terrorists weren't seventy-year-old Sikhs.

Finally, when she counted five people clogging the front of the cabin, one of the flight attendants knocked on the door and asked the fellow inside if he was all right. When he didn't immediately respond, she watched the heads pop up over the wider, cushier seats in business. Some of those passengers very likely were imagining the explosion that would take out a part of the port-side fuselage and the flight deck, sending them all plummeting to their deaths somewhere over Hungary or Romania. The flight attendant began knocking a little more determinedly, but his voice was still cool. The last thing he wanted was to overreact.

It made her wonder what Cassandra Bowden would do. Had she ever been in a situation like this? No doubt, she had. The woman clearly had a fight-or-flight mechanism that was either uncannily precise or badly off kilter. If Elena had to choose, she would bet on the latter: A broken magnet. A shattered gyroscope.

It was just then that the Sikh emerged, and he looked a little irate that his personal space had been, in his opinion, seriously violated. The air marshal sat back, and one of the flight attendants said to the passengers in first who were watching, "He had something disagreeable for breakfast." The Sikh glared back at him and took his seat.

Elena recalled what Viktor had said about Cassandra Bowden: *She's a drunk and a little self-destructive.* When her father had formed the Cossacks a quarter century ago, choosing the most patriotic (translation: old-school Russian) officers he knew in the KGB, Viktor had been about her age right now. It was Yeltsin who'd seen the iconic power in Cossack culture and first allowed for the rehabilitation of one of the Bolshevik party's fiercest opponents during the early days of the revolution. Now the Cossacks were among the darkest arms in the FSB, the successor to the KGB. They worked often with Russian military intelligence, the GRU, as they were on this project. And, yes, they were among the most corrupt. Elena knew that. Her father had known that. And clearly the Americans knew it. The Cossacks were ruthless and they were rich.

Viktor was smart. He'd probably moved all of his money from Sokolov's fund already. They all had. It had probably disappeared before she had even been dispatched to room 511 at the Royal Phoenician. Oh, the investigators would try and follow the money, but eventually they'd hit a wall, an impenetrable coral reef somewhere in the Caribbean. They might find Sokolov's: she'd left plenty of breadcrumbs on his computer. But not Viktor's.

Elena had a pretty good idea what would happen to her if she didn't kill the flight attendant: Viktor had been eminently clear. But she knew there would also be violent aftershocks even if she did take care of this loose end. She guessed it depended on what—if anything—Sokolov had told Bowden, and what the woman remembered. What she was telling everyone.

But Elena would never forget the rage she had felt when she'd finally understood what the Cossacks had done to her father. Methyl iodide. For years she had thought it was a stroke.

Elena tried to analyze precisely what it was that she herself didn't know, which was a lot. It was all a bit like the wooden nesting doll she'd had as a child. The figure sat on her dresser, first in Moscow but then in Sochi, a smiling peasant in a colorful sarafan. She would separate the top from the bottom, and inside there was a smaller doll, a smaller figure. And inside that doll was a third, more petite peasant still. Altogether, there were four dolls nestled inside Matryona, the tiniest one the only one that wasn't hollow.

She sighed. Viktor would have someone looking over her shoulder in America. She was positive.

Now she gazed down at the in-flight magazine that was open in her lap. Her eyes rested on a photograph of Sylvia Plath and an idea came to her. Bowden's death shouldn't look like an accident. It should look like a suicide. This way everyone on both sides of the Atlantic would have plausible deniability. She should wait for the newspapers and the news channels to out the flight attendant as a drunk and a murderer who wouldn't (at least right away) be extradited to face trial.

Then, publicly shamed, Cassandra Bowden would kill herself.

Part Three

ACT LIKE A GROWN-UP

«

16

Ani waited to rip into Cassie until they were outside Federal Plaza and walking west toward Church Street, where they could find a cab heading north.

"What's the plan, Cassie? To go to prison here or in Dubai? What in the name of God were you thinking?" She was walking so quickly that Cassie was almost jogging to keep up, and she was doing it in high heels.

"It just seemed . . . easier," Cassie said. "Can we get a drink and talk about this?"

"We can talk about it in my office. Not in the cab."

"I could really use a drink."

"You could really use some common sense. It almost doesn't matter if you are innocent: every single thing you've done has suggested you're guilty. You fled the scene. You told no one you were in his hotel room. You lied by omission when you landed—"

"Not really. No one asked me anything."

"Okay, fine. You lied by commission just now."

"I know. I get it. It's just . . ."

Ani stopped and turned to face her. Her eyes were wide with rage. "It's just what?" she asked, her tone accusatory.

"It's just that it was so clearly me in the photographs. It's just that they probably have my lipstick already. And now it doesn't matter, because I've admitted I was there."

"So what? You take the Fifth. Besides, it isn't clearly you. It's likely you. Big difference. Very big difference. And your damn lipstick could be anywhere. Do you know what's going to happen now?"

Cassie shook her head. She waited.

"They are going to confirm the approximate time of death with the coroner in Dubai. They won't know the definitive time, but if they can show it was before ten forty-five in the morning, you are fucked. Pardon my French, Cassie, but you are fucked."

Then they stood in silence for a moment, and Cassie thought she might get sick right there on the street. She looked down at the sidewalk and took a few slow, deep breaths to compose herself. Maybe she was self-destructing because she knew on some level that she had in fact killed him, and she was craving punishment. Justice. Across the street was a bar with a neon sign with a four-leaf clover. "Please," she said, her voice quavering as she pointed at it. "I've got to have a drink. I really, really do."

《 《

In a voice that was quiet but intense, a fioritura of frustration and fury only barely mollified by the gin and tonic she was finishing in great gulps, Ani explained to Cassie what she believed was likely to happen next, all of it contingent only on the time it would take for three people to connect as midnight neared on the Arabian Peninsula: the FBI's legal attaché in the United Emirates, his connection at the Dubai police, and the coroner in that massive city by the sea. Last week, Ani said, after Alex Sokolov was found, the medical examiner had autopsied the body. He—and in Dubai, Ani supposed, it was more likely a male than a female coroner—had seen how much (if any) of the veal from dinner remained in Alex Sokolov's stomach, taken the body's temperature, and checked to see how far rigor mortis had progressed.

"I don't know a hell of a lot about forensic entomology, but I can also see them examining the bugs that are starting to eat at the guy's corpse. There probably weren't beetles and there certainly weren't maggots yet, but there may have been houseflies," Ani said. "In any case, the coroner will have offered an approximate time of death."

Cassie had downed a shot of tequila as soon as they arrived, and the warmth had helped. It was pretty good tequila. Smooth. She was calmer now, at least a little bit. The tequila reminded her of Buckley and dancing barefoot in the bar, a memory that was growing sweeter and fuzzier with time. She was almost done with the margarita she had ordered immediately upon finishing the shot. "You said it would be an approximate time of death. That means there's a window. Do you know how big that window is? Are we talking an hour? Three hours? Five, maybe?" she asked. She sat back in her stool and swiveled so she was facing Ani. Sometimes she really enjoyed a place like this: dark paneling and little light, not quite a dive, but a far cry from Bemelmans at the Carlyle. There was a pair of older men in drab brown suits at the far end of the bar, but they were the only other customers here this time of the afternoon.

"Probably in the neighborhood of two or three," Ani replied. "But decomposition isn't really in my wheelhouse. It could be more. It could be less."

"They found the body late in the afternoon, right?"

"Yes."

A notion was floating just beyond Cassie's reach. She thought she might be able to reel it in if she could talk the idea through. "So let's say Alex was found at five p.m. You and I know he was killed before I woke up, and that was around nine forty-five in the morning. If the window is three hours, let's hope he was killed an hour or so before I first opened my eyes."

"Don't get your hopes up. By eight forty-five in the morning, there were people in the hallways: Housekeeping. Guests checking out. Guests going to breakfast. No one commits a murder in a hotel room if they have to run a gauntlet of guests and maids."

"There was no one around when I left the room about ten forty-five. And even if there were people in the hallways earlier in the day, doesn't that help my case? People coming and going? A crowd? Maybe whoever did it counted on the crowds."

Ani folded her arms across her chest: "I said there would be people. I didn't say there would be crowds. I seriously doubt that the fifth floor of the Royal Phoenician is ever Penn Station."

"Still. All we need is the window to work in our favor."

"And to be big. Really big. Think picture-window big, Cassie."

She nodded hopefully. "And they're going to try and find Miranda now, right?"

"Yes. They will."

Cassie was disturbed by the cadence of Ani's words. "You make it sound like there's a *but* coming."

"There is. We already know there's no woman named Miranda who worked with Sokolov. There's no Miranda at Unisphere Asset Management."

"So?"

"What if there's no Miranda anywhere in his life?"

"Look, I didn't make her up. I'll admit, Alex barely knew her—if at all. I told you, maybe she's just a friend or relative of an investor."

The bartender glanced at the two of them, and Ani grew alert. Cassie understood that her lawyer wanted her to lower her voice.

"Another round?" he asked the two of them.

"No, thank you," Ani told him, and Cassie felt a pang of disappointment. Then her lawyer took a deep breath and said to her, "You drink too much. You pass out. You black out. And you are, by your own admission, a liar. You lie all the time."

The words hung in the air, revealing and hurtful. "I thought you believed me," Cassie murmured. She could hear the devastation, almost childlike, in her response. It was as if Ani had betrayed her.

"You're not even sure you believe you," Ani said quietly.

"Sometimes!" she shot back. "Most of the time I am absolutely confident: I did not kill him."

"Fine," said Ani. "Fine. If it makes you feel any better, I don't think you did, either. Does that help or make a difference? Not at all. Let's hope there is evidence in the hotel room that this Miranda person exists."

"There will be. Won't her DNA be there?"

"It's a hotel room. There's DNA from a hundred—a thousand—guests in there."

"Of course," she agreed, but then an idea came to her. "Her DNA might be on the glass she used. So might her fingerprints. I wiped the glasses down, but who knows how thorough I was. I was kind of panicking."

"Aside from the reality that wiping down a couple of glasses just screams guilt, how do they compare the DNA to a person they can't even find? How do they compare the fingerprints? It's not like there's a database of DNA and fingerprints of people who say their name is Miranda."

"I see . . ."

"I just don't know what you were thinking when you volunteered the information to the FBI that you slept with the guy and spent the night in his suite. I am just . . . incredulous."

"Either I wasn't thinking, or I was thinking they already knew from the photos that I had spent the night with Alex and they were going to find my DNA or my fingerprints or my stupid lipstick in the room somewhere. I honestly don't know which."

"You are making the assumption that you're even going to allow them to swab your cheek to get your DNA. Or take your fingerprints. I will still try and stall that for a very long time, but you have made my job that much more difficult."

"I'm sorry. I really am."

Ani's face went a little pensive. "You said the day we met that the cuts on your hands were from a broken glass. Were they?"

"Yes. What are you suggesting? Do you think I tried to kill myself?"

"No, of course not. They were on your hands, not your wrists. I was thinking defense wounds. You were trying to protect yourself. You were fighting off a knife or that broken bottle. Tell me honestly: did Sokolov attack you at some point that night? Maybe—forgive me, I have to ask—some sort of creepy sex play that got out of hand?"

"He never attacked me, Ani, at least that I can recall. But that doesn't sound like him. He was . . ."

"Go on."

"He was really good in bed. It was our first time, and he was pretty gentle. Those cuts on my hands? I saw a Dubai news article with the two security camera photos of me, and I dropped the wineglass I was holding. It was in my bathroom the night before we met."

"You even drink in the bathroom?"

"I had brought a glass of wine with me into the tub. Not the worst thing I do," Cassie said.

"Okay, so the cuts had nothing to do with an attack," said Ani. "I get it. You told me about Sokolov's neck. Did he have any defense wounds on his hands or his arms? As if he were trying to parry the broken bottle?"

"You mean if I were attacking him?"

"Or someone."

"There was blood everywhere, but I don't think so."

"There was absolutely no evidence of a struggle?"

"If there was a struggle, don't you think I would have remembered it?"

The lawyer replied by raising a single eyebrow.

"No," said Cassie. "You're right. I wouldn't have remembered. But I don't think there was a struggle. I don't recall seeing any cuts on his hands or his arms. Is that a good thing or a bad thing?"

"Well, it's not a good thing. I wish I'd thought to have photographs taken on Monday morning of the cuts on your hands. That's on me, that's my bad. If they do decide you killed him, it would have been nice to claim there was a fight and you were desperately defending yourself."

Cassie looked at her hands. She hadn't even bothered with Band-Aids today. The cuts no longer looked like very much. "I guess it's too late now." Nevertheless, Ani took out her phone and used the camera to take a series of pictures, posing Cassie's fingers and hands on a white paper placemat on the bar.

"These are probably worthless since the wounds are five days old and I'm using a camera phone, but what the hell?" the lawyer said. "By the time I find a photographer on a Friday afternoon in August, the cuts will be completely healed."

"There is one good thing about Alex not having any defense wounds," Cassie said.

"Go on."

"Maybe it means that he didn't feel any pain. I've been hoping he just never woke up."

"That's sweet. But not helpful."

"I know."

"Remind me," Ani asked. "What time did you pass out?"

"It was a blackout. It seems like I was still up and about. Functioning, sort of. I wish I had just passed out."

"Okay. What is the very last thing you remember?"

Cassie put her face in her hands and thought. Her fingers were moist from the perspiration on her glass. Finally she looked up and answered, "Here's the chronology. Miranda is there and I'm dressed and we're drinking. We're in the suite's living room. She says she's going to leave, and I'm going to leave with her."

"But you didn't leave with her, right?" Ani interrupted. "You were there when Alex broke the vodka bottle."

"That's correct. He convinced me to stay, which wasn't that hard. We drank some more and we had sex again, this time in the bedroom. But then I got dressed."

"You're positive?"

"No. But almost positive. I'm pretty sure. I really did plan to return to the airline's hotel. That was my intention, anyway. Miranda had left and now I was going to leave, too."

"Do you know what time Miranda said good night? Perhaps they could find her on the security camera."

"Eleven? Eleven thirty? Midnight?"

"That helps. So you would have left when?"

Cassie shrugged. "Twelve thirty? One? An hour later, I guess."

"Okay."

"But they didn't see me at that time—or, at least, they didn't publish any photos from the lobby security cameras of me leaving in the middle of the night. That would suggest I didn't leave until the morning."

"Or, at least, that you didn't get as far as the lobby."

"Yes," she said, and an idea, fuzzy and inchoate, began to form. She tried to gather it in, to mold it: to imagine where else she might have gone. She focused on the corridor. She saw so many hotel corridors, but few as elegant as the one at the Royal Phoenician. There were the long, endless hallways, which was typical, but the Oriental carpets had been beautiful and the elevator doors—when you got there—were black and gold; there had been the sconces along the walls, at once Aladdin-like and futuristic, as if the genie had instead been a Martian, and there had been the exquisite guest-room doors with their Moorish cross-hatching bordering the panels. There were the divans with the ornate blue and gold upholstery by the elevators and by the windows and in the nooks at the corners. She had stood beside one when she first exited onto Alex's floor with the key he had given her at dinner, enjoying the view out the window on the way to his room. No, it had been beyond his room. She had walked to the end of the corridor to see the city from there.

"Sometimes I make a wrong turn when I leave a hotel room—even when I'm sober," Cassie said. "I am just in so many hotels. We all make that mistake. Pilots, flight attendants. The elevator was to the left and around the corner in Berlin, for instance, but then it's to the right and straight ahead in Istanbul. It happens all the time."

"And?"

"I don't know. This might sound pathetic, but I have a vague memory of panicking in the hallway after leaving his room."

"Because someone was after you?" Ani asked, clearly a little stunned.

"No. Because I was lost. It was the middle of the night and I couldn't find the elevator and I couldn't find his room. I couldn't even remember his room number. I mean, now five-eleven is branded into my brain. But it wasn't then. Think of all the room numbers I see every month of my life. Anyway, I didn't know what to do. I think . . ."

"You think what?"

"I think I collapsed on a divan in one of the corners of the corridor. I think it was by a window that overlooked the city."

"This was after Miranda left."

"Yes. This was after she left. And so there I was alone in the corridor. But I was so drunk—so very, very drunk. Maybe I got lost and gave up. Maybe I just sat down on the thing and tried to figure out what the hell to do. And maybe there I passed out. In other words, I never made it to the lobby. I got lost in the hallway and crashed on the couch for, I don't know, half an hour. An hour. Maybe less, maybe more. But I woke up before anyone from hotel security or room service happened down the hallway."

"And then you found your way back to his room?"

"That's right. I had a key. Maybe the catnap helped me to focus. Or sobered me up just enough that his room number came back to me."

"You wouldn't have to have been gone all that long. I'm guessing even ten minutes would have been enough for someone else to enter his room and kill him."

"Oh, it's very possible I was gone at least ten minutes. Those hotel couches and divans looked really, really comfortable."

"And when you return the room is dark?"

"At least the bedroom is," she answered. "Maybe there was a light on in the living room." She had to believe that even she wasn't ever so drunk that she would knowingly crawl into bed with a corpse. Still, the reality of what she was suggesting was beginning to become clear.

"God, Cassie. What if Alex was killed at one or two in the morning? That's why you take the Fifth." Ani's frustration was evident as she paused to take another long, last swallow of her drink. "I wish I knew more about how precise an autopsy could be at pinpointing a time of death."

"Aren't you glad I told them about Miranda? At least now they have a suspect other than me."

The lawyer stared at her but said nothing.

"Look, I'm sorry," Cassie said. "I am. I'm just built . . . weird."

"Irresponsible would be a more precise word. So would insane."

"Will we know what happens before I fly to Rome?"

Ani put both of her hands on Cassie's knees. "You are assuming that the next time I see you isn't after you've been arrested—at, let's see, a bail hearing. You are assuming that you haven't turned over your passport by then. You are assuming you still have a job."

Cassie picked up her margarita and ran her tongue along the very last of the salt on the rim. The glass was otherwise empty. "I'm taking my niece and nephew to the zoo tomorrow," she said, her voice a little numb in her ears. It was as if she had headphones on. Then: "Will I be fired?"

"The zoo. Your job. Really? Are you hearing a word I'm saying?"

She nodded. "I am."

"The union will have your back. My uncle will have your back. Call him tonight and let him know what's going on. I'll call him, too. I rather doubt the airline can fire you. Presumption of innocence and all. But at some point they may put you on a leave of absence. There is a whole branch of law that studies precisely when you can fire an employee for off-duty conduct—and when you can't."

"I see."

"I'm not sure you do. I'm really not."

"You know what's the damnedest thing?"

"Right now? After you decided to just drop by Unisphere yesterday afternoon? After your performance with the FBI today? That's one hell of a high bar. I don't know. Tell me."

"It's this, that expression you just used. Presumption of innocence. Who knows what I'm capable of when I'm that blotto and the memory's collateral damage. But I really do know in my heart that I didn't kill Alex. I do stupid things when I'm drunk and I do irresponsible things, but I don't do . . . that. I don't cut people's throats. And so if the hammer comes down hard on me this time, it will be a kind of awful irony."

"Cassie?"

She waited.

The waves of Ani's anger were receding now, and in their wake was only sadness and worry. "I promise you: you've done nothing so bad that you deserve what might be coming."

《　《

Cassandra, Troy-born daughter of King Priam and Queen Hecuba, knew the future, and no one believed her. At least most of the time that was what occurred. Apollo gave her the great gift of prophecy because he was confident that she was going to sleep with him; when, in the end, she refused, the god spat in her mouth, leaving behind the curse that no one would ever believe a word that she said. And so she lived with frustration and dread.

Cassandra, Kentucky-born daughter of no one who would ever be construed for royalty, pondered the disbelief that she, too, left in her wake and the apprehension and fear that now marked her every step. The reality of what she had done (and what she had not done) had become incontestable fact in her mind, but she rather doubted the FBI ever would believe it if she were to volunteer the chronological truth: she said good night to Alex Sokolov and left the palatial digs that existed behind the door to room 511 sometime around twelve thirty or one in the morning and then wandered the hallways in search of an elevator. He was most definitely still alive at that point. But she never made it to the elevator. She just never found it. And so she collapsed, an appalling, drunken, boneless marionette on an ornate Middle Eastern divan, and dozed. When she awoke, she still didn't reach the elevator, either because once more she couldn't find it or because she hadn't even remembered that it had been her original destination. Either way, she returned to Alex's suite, stripped naked, and climbed into his bed . . . utterly oblivious to the fact that he was dead. Or almost dead.

No, in the morning she had seen his neck. He had bled out quickly. He was dead.

And she had slept the rest of the night beside his corpse. In the same sheets. Her head on the pillow beside his pillow. His blood clinging to her hair.

This was a spectacular, revolting fail even by her standards for indignity and mortification. She guessed if she weren't already such a lush, the revelation would have driven her to drink.

« «

And yet, for whatever the reason, despite her performance at the FBI office that afternoon, the authorities did not come for her that night. She and Ani shared a cab uptown, Cassie exiting on Twenty-Seventh Street, and she was back in her apartment by a quarter to six. She called Derek Mayes, Ani's uncle at the union, and he actually seemed considerably less shocked by the story she shared—beginning with the body in the bed and building to her confessing to the FBI that she had spent the night with Sokolov—than she might have expected. She attributed this more to his rather low expectations of her as a person than to his experience with flight attendants generally. He assured her that he and Ani would talk and together they would look out for her. He was comforting. He reminded her that she hadn't definitely killed anyone, though he did add, a dig that was more ominous than funny, "at least that's your story this week."

And then, buoyed by Mayes's generally can-do attitude and the Washington State Riesling she opened and poured over ice, she called Buckley. Didn't even text him. The actor suggested they meet for a drink later that evening, after he'd seen a friend's show at the Barrow, and since it was rare for her ever to say no to a drink, she said yes. They picked a bar in the West Village this time, one near the theater.

Then she collapsed onto her couch and stared up at the Empire State Building. She pulled the paperback Tolstoy from her purse and sipped her wine and read, hoping to lose herself in the narrative and escape the reality of her life—and yet somehow also to glean insights into Alex Sokolov's. It was an impossible balancing act: if she was reading to learn more about the man who had died on the sheets on which they'd made love, then certainly she wasn't reading to take her mind off the utter precariousness of her future. Before returning to "Happy Ever After," she paused on one particular paragraph about Ivan Ilyich that had stayed with her: "He had an affair with a lady who threw herself at the elegant young lawyer." But the relationship meant nothing to him, "it all came under the heading of the French saying, 'Il faut que la jeunesse se passé.'" Translation? Youth must have its fling.

It made her feel old. She reminded herself that she had viewed Alex as but a harmless romp, too.

Eventually she phoned her sister, who was already at her hotel in Westchester, and they picked a time to meet tomorrow morning at the zoo. They'd rendezvous at ten thirty at the fountain near the sea lions, just inside the Fordham Road entrance. She was grateful that she wasn't going to be alone with the kids. She was actually relieved. It would be such a disaster if she were alone with her nephew and niece when she was arrested.

« «

Buckley took her hand as they walked from the bar to his apartment. It was only a few minutes after midnight, and so the West Village was still vital and vibrant, the narrow streets crowded, the bistro tables along the sidewalks full.

"You were checking your phone a lot," he murmured. She had

told him nothing, nothing at all. Either he hadn't seen the photos in the newspapers that day or he had looked at them so quickly that the fact they were her hadn't registered.

"I haven't been reserve in years, but the airline asked me to be available," she lied.

"Didn't you say that you're flying to Rome on Sunday night?"

"They might want me for another route tomorrow instead." The air was cool, and she wished that she had brought more than a sleeveless blouse. She felt the hair on her arms rising.

"Would you still get to go to the zoo tomorrow? I'd hate to see you miss the sea lions—and your family."

"We'll see," she said, though in her mind, she imagined herself replying, *If I'm not at the zoo, it's probably because (best case) I'm meeting my lawyer and getting my cheek swabbed for DNA. Worst case? I'm being arrested for murder.* But she didn't say any of that. "Tell me more about your audition," she said. "Tell me more about the pilot. You said it's a drama."

"Sort of. Based on the script, there's also a lot of very dark humor. It's about a Staten Island drug family. Apparently there will be a lot of scenes on the ferry and a lot of nighttime shooting—and shooting during the shooting. It looks crazy violent. I'd be one of the brothers. Think Edmund in *King Lear*. I'd be the younger brother and a bastard—literally and figuratively."

"Do you think you have a chance?"

"Yes, but only because it's a small role. It's a recurring character, but not one of the four major leads." He pointed at a squirrel clinging to a second-story screen window and peering into the apartment. "Peeping Tom," he murmured.

Looking up at the squirrel from the sidewalk was a huge orange tomcat, his fur so thick that Cassie could see only a bit of the collar. His tail was thwapping back and forth, sweeping the concrete. She thought about her cats at the shelter—and so many of them were her cats in her mind, at least until they found permanent homes—and wondered what they would do without her. Oh, there were other volunteers, but she didn't know how diligent they were about sneaking in catnip and treats and toys, and brushing the poor things for hours and hours on end.

"When will you know?" she asked.

"If I got the part? Next week, I guess." Then: "There's lots of great sibling stuff in the script, too. That's the kind of material that fuels my jets. My relationship with my brother and sister in real life is pretty complicated."

"Yeah. Mine, too."

"Are you and your sister close?"

"Not really."

"You wouldn't be friends if you weren't related?"

"Probably not."

"Even after all you two endured together growing up?"

"Even after that."

He asked her what her sister did for a living and then what her brother-in-law did. He found her brother-in-law's work far more interesting. Everyone did. No one asked follow-up questions when you said your sister was an accountant. But an engineer at an army base that disposed of poison gas and nerve agents? People were fascinated—especially men.

"I'll bet he doesn't talk about it much," he said.

"Because it's all so classified?" she asked.

"Because it's all just so dark. Chemical weapons? That's crazy. We've all seen the pictures from Syria."

"I think he's in charge of getting rid of them. Or one of the people in charge, anyway. But, yes, it is classified."

"And not exactly Thanksgiving dinner table conversation, in any case."

"Nope." Then, feeling uncharacteristically defensive of her family, she continued. "He's really not a dark person at all. He's pretty chill. He's very sweet. I get along better with him than I do with Rosemary."

"Well, you and Rosemary have a lot more history together."

"Yeah, we do. And most of it's kind of dark," she said. She asked him to tell her about his family, and he laughed a little bit, but then he started to talk, making jokes about Westport and WASPs and how his family's Thanksgivings would have rivaled Martha Stewart's when it came to detail and production values.

She leaned into him as he regaled her with tales of the crested blazers he would wear as a boy and his mother's impeccable Christmas trees. She was tipsy, and she liked herself best when she was tipsy. She thought she was prettiest when she was just on the cusp of drunk. She'd spied herself (or studied herself) in enough mirrors—at parties, on airplanes, in her compact—to know that her eyes looked a little more wanton and her lips a little more inviting when she was just starting to leave the sadness of sobriety behind. When she was working, when she'd snuck a drink or two on the flight, she knew that men watched her differently, their own eyes more rapacious. She could feel their gaze on her hips, her ass, as she worked her way up and down the thin aisle. And so she stopped walking, which led Buckley to stop. She had to take her mind off this kind man's childhood and the shelter cats and the travel and the liquor—all that she might be about to lose.

She felt no one was following her now. No one.

He stared at her for a long moment, regarding her.

"What is it?" he asked.

"It's you," she said. "It's a starry night in the city." Then, for reasons that she didn't precisely understand, she brought his fingers to her lips and kissed them.

《 《

And in the morning, it seemed, they still weren't looking for her. Or, at least, they hadn't come for her. The only text she had was a brief one from Ani asking if she had heard anything. She texted back that she hadn't, and watched Buckley sleep for another moment more. It crossed her mind that she might never see him again after today. She just didn't know what awaited her in the coming hours. The coming days. The indignities. The accusations. The public and private pain.

He was still asleep when she climbed from beneath the sheet and sat for a moment on the side of his bed. The shade was down, but she could tell it was sunny outside. It would be a delightful day at the zoo.

She checked the weather on her phone, punching in Charlottes-ville, Virginia. She saw it was going to be hot and sunny there, too. It was going to be, as these things went, a perfectly lovely day for a funeral.

《　《

A pair of sea lions popped effortlessly from the water onto the stone platform, spraying the young woman with the bucket of fish as if they were playful black labs that had just come in from the rain. The trainer smiled at them and tossed them each a couple of sardines.

Cassie was standing along the rail beside Rosemary. Next to her sister were her two children, Tim and Jessica. Dennis, Rose-mary's husband, had moved a few dozen yards away from them, photographing the animals from what he believed was going to be a vantage point that would allow him to capture both the animals and his family. Jessica hadn't yet started third grade, so she was still young enough to laugh and squeal at the sea lions' antics, but Cassie observed that Tim was watching with the feigned disinterest of a rising middle-schooler. At least she presumed it was feigned: how could you not enjoy watching sea lions frolic on a Saturday morn-ing in August? Still, he seemed considerably more fascinated by the small drone the zoo had hovering above the sea lions for a video feed inside a nearby gift store. Cassie knew he had one at home that was probably just as sophisticated. Drones were such a guy thing, she thought. It was downright chromosomal.

They were both attractive children: Tim was in the midst of a growth spurt, but he was already lanky and slender, his hair the same reddish blond as hers. His jeans were baggy and his Roy-als T-shirt so faded it looked almost like denim. Jessica was overdressed for the zoo, but Rosemary said the child was overdressed for life: though she was eight and this was Saturday and it was the middle of the summer, she was wearing violet wedge heels, a black skirt that had been part of one of her costumes from her June dance recital, and a red velvet blouse with a scoop neck but very long sleeves. Cassie recognized the blouse from the American Girl store. She recognized as well the rhinestone headband Jessica was using to pull back her hair. Cassie had bought her niece the blouse when she had taken her shopping in the spring, and she had bought her the headband at the grand bazaar in Istanbul. It had cost maybe a buck.

"I want one," Rosemary was saying, smiling at the animals. Her sister had gotten a job a year earlier crunching numbers with a health insurance company in Lexington and had fallen in love with the gym and the spin classes at the headquarters. Cassie thought she'd never looked healthier. "I think a sea lion would make a great pet."

"You know that's ridiculous," Tim chastised his mother, rolling his eyes.

"I do," she said. "But I still want one."

"I kinda do, too," Cassie admitted. She looked at her watch. In Virginia, Alex Sokolov's funeral was under way. She conjured in her mind a southern brick church with a clean steeple, and a sloping, manicured lawn that was a deep green. She thought of his parents and his extended family in the front pew, the wood polished and gleaming in the sun through the stained-glass windows. She saw black clothes and white handkerchiefs. She saw the old and the young, and in her head she heard their occasional, choked sobs. She heard laughter when someone shared a story about Alex that was charming or funny, or hinted at whatever it was that made him special.

Whatever it was . . .

How was it that she knew so little of the man who had died beside her in bed? How was that possible? But she knew the answer.

Of course she did. The proof, as she was wont to joke, was in the proof. All that wine. All that vodka. All that arak.

By now, she supposed, the Sokolov family had been informed that the presumed killer—that alleged black widow—was not an expat American living in the Emirates, but a flight attendant living in the United States. She imagined the father demanding news and progress from the FBI, and someone from the Bureau reassuring him that the noose was tightening. An arrest was imminent.

But was it? The United Emirates couldn't arrest her here. Unless this was deemed a terrorist act, neither could her own country. An extradition could take years. Was it possible that everyone in the world who followed this story would believe she was a killer and there was absolutely nothing they could do?

No, not nothing. There was still a civil sword of Damocles dangling by a thin thread above her. And the FBI was interested. That was a fact. That was why Ani was so worried about her.

She looked at her phone once again. Still nothing from either Frank Hammond or Ani Mouradian.

"Who in the world are you expecting to call you?" Rosemary asked. "You're like a teenager, you're checking your phone so much."

"The airline," she said. She figured she might as well use the same lie on her family that she had used on Buckley last night. "They might need me on the flight to Rome this evening."

"I thought we were all having dinner together." Her sister's lips grew pursed.

"We are," said Cassie. "It's a long shot. I'm sure I'll be here with you." But she wasn't sure. Despite the silence from both her lawyer and the FBI, she in fact wondered if she'd get to have dinner with them tonight. She had a canvas bag over her shoulder, and in it was the Romulus and Remus bookend she had stolen from the hotel in Rome and a pair of her own earrings. They were small gold cats she had bought years ago in an antique store in Frankfurt but had decided when she was back in America were too precious for a grown woman. This morning she had repackaged them in a little box from the greeting card store near her apartment and had brought them as a gift for her niece. She'd decided that she shouldn't wait until Christmas to give her nephew the bookend—today might be her last (her only) chance—and so she wanted to be sure that she had a present for Jessica, too.

The word *present* gave her pause. A memory. Her mother reading aloud to her before bed in Kentucky. Her mother was sitting on the mattress beside her, and Cassie was perhaps six years old and curled against her in the narrow twin bed. They were leaning against Cassie's headboard, and Cassie was already in her pajamas. The story tonight was one of Beverly Cleary's books about Beezus and Ramona.

"Now, you sit here for the present," her mother read aloud. In the book it was the first day of school, and a schoolteacher was telling Ramona to remain in her seat . . . for the moment. And so Ramona absolutely refused to move because she mistakenly believed there was a gift—a *present*—waiting for her if she sat perfectly still. Cassie recalled being so happy that evening. She had been roughly Ramona's age, she was enjoying her own first days at school, and her mother was wearing a floral perfume that smothered the coppery scent that usually stuck to her when she came home from the wire factory where she was the receptionist.

Cassie heard the crowd around them laughing. One of the sea lions was using its flipper to shake the trainer's paw and then gently slapped at the woman's open hand as if giving the trainer a high-five.

"I've got something for you," Cassie said to Jessica. The girl looked up at her. She was beaming. Clearly her niece loved the animals. Cassie noted that today she was wearing the starfish studs that Rosemary had given her when she had gotten her ears pierced at the start of the summer. "Consider it a back-to-school present," she added, handing the girl the small box.

Tim turned toward his sister and smiled. "Oh, good. More stuff you can lose in that mess you call a bedroom." Already the way her niece left her bedroom looking like it had been ransacked by drug addicts was legendary in the family. Apparently, she considered at least three or four outfits before school every day, leaving the rejects scattered on the rug or her bed or the window seat.

"I have something for you, too," she told the boy, handing him the small, wrapped sculpture. "Jessica, I got your gift in Frankfurt. Tim, I got yours in Rome."

"It's heavier than it looks," he said.

"God, your life sounds glamorous. Frankfurt. Rome. If people didn't know better," Rosemary murmured. Over the years, Cassie had shared with her sister dozens of the experiences—some appalling, some merely degrading—that came with the job, so she did know better.

"It does have its moments," she admitted. Tim waited chivalrously for his younger sister to open the box before pulling apart the red tissue paper that swaddled his gift. The girl cooed when she saw the earrings, and Cassie bent over so her niece could hug her.

"I love them!" she said. Then, the words at once strange and precocious coming from a girl so young, she added, "They are perfectly elegant."

Over her shoulder, Tim rolled his eyes.

"I'm glad you like them," Cassie said. "Your turn," she said to her nephew.

Tim pulled off the blue ribbon and then tore off the red tissue. "A sculpture," he said simply, and for a moment Cassie thought of that old joke: When someone opens a gift and says aloud what it is—a juicer, a car vac, napkin rings—they hate it. And she felt bad. But the moment lasted only a second, because then he went on. "I know this story. It was in a book about the myths that was on my summer reading list. No one connects the twins to werewolves, but I think that's the coolest link."

"Is it a paperweight?" Everyone turned at the voice. The children's father had appeared almost out of nowhere and inquired. His camera was around his neck, and he was cleaning his sunglasses with a handkerchief. Dennis McCauley was a big man, not fat and

not muscular, but tall and stocky with a stomach that was just starting to grow bulbous. He was handsome, his hair now more white
than black, but still lustrous and thick. He parted it in the middle
and swept it back, and her sister often teased him about having
movie-star hair and said he looked like an actor when he was in
one of his uniforms. He wasn't wearing a uniform today, however, he was wearing khaki cargo shorts. In Cassie's opinion, that
eliminated instantly any chance at all that he might be mistaken
for an actor. Sometimes her sister called him absentminded, but
Cassie rather doubted that he was ever inattentive at work. He was
an engineer and probably just compartmentalized. Everyone knew
how bloody brilliant he was. She wished that she had told Buckley
that last night. Shown a little more pride in what he did. She'd
said Dennis was sweet; she should have said he was smart. The
guy, after all, helped dispose of chemical weapons. It was work,
Cassie suspected, that was more dangerous than he was ever likely
to admit to his family.

"No, it's a bookend," Cassie answered. "I bought it at an antique
store near the Spanish Steps in Rome."

"They only had half?"

She nodded.

"I love it. A bookend about twins and half has gone missing,"
Dennis said. "That may be the definition of irony. What will you
use it for, son?" he asked Tim.

The boy shrugged. "I don't know. But I like it. It's cool."

"I agree," said Dennis. Then he bent over to look at the earrings that Cassie had brought his daughter, oohing and aahing at
their beauty. When he was done, he stood up straight and put back
on his sunglasses. "You find the damnedest things in your travels,
Cassie."

"I guess."

"No, I mean that. You bring back the most creative things.
Me? Ask these two: the stuff I bring them back when I travel is
way less interesting."

"That's because you only go to places like Maryland and Washington, D.C.," Rosemary tried to reassure him.

"Nah. Cassie has a much better eye," he said. "Really, they're perfect gifts."

"Thank you," she said. She was touched. He was always so much kinder to her than Rosemary was, Cassie thought, even though he knew just as much as Rosemary did about her peccadilloes great and small. But he was less judgmental. She had a feeling that when her name was attached to the dead body in Dubai, he would be far more surprised than his wife.

17

Against the allegations that his people were brutish, Elena's father would smile and bring up the Bolshoi. Chekhov. Tchaikovsky. "We can be merciless," she once heard him remark as he studied the Ararat cognac in his snifter, "but we are no more and no less brutish than anyone else." It was over dinner with his old comrades from the KGB, most of whom now were more focused on their trophy dachas and trophy wives, and the riches that they had found in the rubble of the once iconic wall. He reminded them how much Lenin loved novels, and how literature was a part of the political world in which Lenin grew up. When Lenin wanted to belittle his rivals, he'd refer to them as particularly stupid or especially loathsome characters from Chernyshevsky, Pushkin, and Goncharov. "The biggest difference between an Oblomov and an oligarch?" he asked that night, the setup for what he viewed as a bon mot. "If an oligarch spends the day in bed, it's because he has a hooker and he's getting his money's worth." In his heart, of course, he knew that wasn't the biggest difference. Not at all. The oligarchs now had the wealth of Oblomov, but they weren't lazy and they hadn't inherited their vast fortunes. Most of them were self-made. Corrupt, of course. Corrupt on a positively titanic scale. But they worked hard. And perhaps the only man before whom they would bow was the Russian President. They were alpha males who took no prisoners.

Viktor was, in her mind, a perfect example of that balancing act between barbarism and refinement: he was cold-blooded and feral beneath his crisp black suits, but he had constructed a veneer that compelled him to eat in small bites. He spoke multiple languages fluently and appreciated the aesthetic of films by Tarkovsky.

And he wasn't alone. Supposedly even Stalin, as uncultured as they came and absolutely no fan of art for art's sake, died in 1953 with Russian pianist Maria Yudina's recording of Mozart's Concerto no. 23 playing on the nearby turntable.

《　《

Elena opened the app on her phone and watched the little blue dot beat like a small, tiny heart. A frog's heart. It pulsed, in and out, in and out, sending a fainter blue wave away from it in a perfect circle, before the wave would disappear and a new one would follow. The dot was her prey and her prey was at the zoo.

She put her phone down on the wooden bench and folded her arms across her chest. She looked up once at the Flatiron Building a block and a half to the south, and then at the young parents playing with their toddlers on the grass or walking their dogs along the paths that looped throughout Madison Square Park. The simple normalcy of the tableau was affecting: she felt a forlorn tug at her heart and shook her head ever so slightly, willing the melancholy away. This wasn't her world or her life and it never would be. Not in Moscow and not in Manhattan.

She was wearing nondescript khaki shorts, a sleeveless white blouse, and beige espadrilles. She had a magazine and a bag with a bagel in it, but only so it looked like she had a reason to be sitting on the bench. It was sunny but hot, the air damp and still, and she wished for a breeze.

She really didn't know much about this neighborhood. The section of New York she knew best was midtown west of Fifth, the great wide blocks of skyscrapers where Unisphere had its Manhattan office, and she'd probably only been there four or five times in her life. The family money. The family business—or part of the family business, anyway. The part that came of age after the final collapse in 1991. She'd been but a toddler then. When she thought of this city, she thought first of lunches in the dark oak dining rooms with her father and the American managers of the fund while she was at college—before he was poisoned—the dining rooms packed with administrators and executives who seemed to eat and drink as if it were another era. (The older adults occasionally still called each other *comrade*—they even called the Americans *comrade*—though there was now a trace of irony to the term.) Of dinners alone with her father in nearby restaurants that were largely empty because they timed their meal to begin after the pretheater crowd had left for their shows. Her father enjoyed coming to America, and he loved it when she was a freshman and a sophomore and would come south from Massachusetts to New York to meet him. He enjoyed these people. He probably would have enjoyed Sokolov—or at least gotten a kick out of him until he showed his true colors—because Alex's blood was so rich with Russian DNA. But her father was Russian through and through, and his trips to the United States were brief. He took pride in his accent. (She, by design, had worked hard to lose any trace of hers.)

She'd certainly never been to the Empire State Building or the Metropolitan Museum or the Bronx Zoo.

She rolled her eyes as if she weren't alone. The zoo, she thought. Really? The woman's life was unraveling, and Cassandra Bowden had gone to the zoo. Based on the homework Elena had done on the flight attendant, she was most likely with her sister's family. She'd probably be with them all day, since they were in from Kentucky. Tomorrow night she was supposed to fly out to Rome.

The problem, she had told Viktor now that she was here, was that Bowden lived in a building with doormen and porters. Lots of them. This morning, a Saturday, Elena had watched as many as three different people behind the front desk at the entrance or sweeping the sidewalk or opening the door for residents and waving them politely out into the August heat. There also were cameras filming the reception area and the elevator up from the basement and the parking garage that was attached by an underground, cinder-block corridor. She knew from experience that it was much more difficult to remain invisible from the cameras in a private apartment building than it was in a hotel. There were so many fewer people coming and going in an apartment, and the lobby was dramatically smaller. So it would be difficult to get inside Bowden's apartment, which was unfortunate because home was where most suicides—80 percent—occurred. (A person's place of business accounted for nearly 10 percent, but even Viktor had joked that no one wanted Elena to entertain that possibility. Sure, pilots occasionally brought down whole planes in a fit of selfish, suicidal madness, but no one wanted an Airbus on that side of the ledger.) And if Elena couldn't easily get in and out of Bowden's apartment, then the flight attendant would have to take her life in some private nook in some relatively public space.

The second issue, which Elena knew was painfully clear to everyone, was time. It was absolutely unimaginable what kind of damage a loose cannon like Cassandra Bowden could cause if Alex had told her something or if suddenly she felt compelled to broadcast to anyone who would listen that another woman had come to room 511 that night in Dubai.

And, of course, the clock was running for her, as well. Certainly there were people in Moscow who were shaking their heads at the way that Dmitry's overly Americanized daughter had allowed the flight attendant to leave Dubai. They were at best confused and at worst alarmed. For all they knew, Bowden was CIA. Perhaps she was part of some military intelligence task force. And so they were angry, and these were the Cossacks. She knew what happened to anyone who pissed off this clandestine old guard. Her own father would have been appalled at what she had done—or, to be precise, at what she had failed to do. She knew she was on thin ice. Viktor had made that clear, not even masking the threat in a polite understatement.

A thought came to her. The media still hadn't identified the woman in the sunglasses and scarf in the Royal Phoenician security camera photos. No one in the Dubai police had leaked the name of the flight attendant. Elena decided she would tell Viktor that she needed that reveal before proceeding: Cassandra Bowden's suicide would be considerably more plausible if she'd been publicly shamed.

She picked up her phone and watched the little blue dot. It would be great to take care of this—one way or another—before Bowden flew to Rome tomorrow evening, but now she could wait until the story broke. If Bowden's name wasn't online or in the newspapers by tomorrow morning, she'd go ahead and make the phone call to a newspaper or a cable news network herself. She'd offer an anonymous tip.

And in the meantime? She'd continue to watch Bowden and see if an opportunity of some sort presented itself. She wondered where the flight attendant and her family were having dinner tonight, and whether it might demand that the woman take a subway home.

18

Cassie joined Rosemary and her family for dinner Saturday night at a crowded Cantonese restaurant that Rosemary had discovered online. It was a block south of Canal and closer than she would have liked to the FBI building on Broadway and Worth. She guessed she was only a five-minute walk from yesterday afternoon's debacle.

The restaurant catered to a tourist crowd that wanted to try dim sum. It was massive and loud and packed. But Cassie was surprised at how delicious the dumplings and pan-fried noodles were, and then felt guilty for having experienced a little culinary snobbishness before they had joined the throngs inside. Yes, she traveled a lot and had eaten all around the world, but just because tourists liked something didn't mean it wasn't wonderful. Exhibit A? The peppermint macarons at the bakery near the Eiffel Tower. Besides, she was a flight attendant. It wasn't as if she was dining in La Pergola when she was in Rome.

And she appreciated the sheer ordinariness of her sister and her family—the lack of drama—and the way the four of them knew each other's rhythms so well. There was just such comfort in the predictability. Cassie understood that she would never feel anything like this: love born of certainty and ritual.

"Do you remember that awful Chinese restaurant in Grover's Mill?" Rosemary was asking her now.

She nodded. Her sister rarely brought up their childhood

around Tim and Jessica. There were too many land mines, and you never knew when a memory would trip one. "Of course I do."

"It's now a weirdly expensive clothing boutique. Kind of like Anthropologie. I mean, they had tops in there for two hundred bucks."

"They must need a place to launder their crystal meth money," Cassie said, only half kidding. "That's certainly one possible explanation."

"I agree."

"I don't know what's stranger: the fact the store exists or the fact you know it's there. Were you actually back in Grover's Mill recently?"

"We all were," said Dennis. "It was when we took the kids to that new amusement park that opened at the end of June. It's pretty close."

"They have the steepest water slide in Kentucky," Jessica added. The girl was using her spring roll a bit like a spoon to get as much peanut dipping sauce into her mouth as she could with each bite.

"And then you detoured to Grover's Mill?" Cassie asked.

"We did," her sister answered. "I thought it was time these two saw where their mother grew up."

"I think we got the PG version," Tim said. Cassie couldn't believe how many dumplings the boy had consumed, but he seemed sated now. He was sitting with his elbows on the table, his head in his hands, watching as the waiters wheeled the carts through the narrow spaces between the patrons.

"Maybe," his mother agreed. "But at least you saw the house."

"It was so tiny," said Jessica.

It was, Cassie thought, it really was. It was a small saltbox, shabby with age, on less than half an acre. Their parents kept the booze in a kitchen cabinet, on the bottom shelf, which accommodated the taller bottles. The first time she started watering them down was when she was nine. Her father had come to the elementary school that day in June to watch the end-of-year Field Day contests: The three-legged races. The sack races. The sponge battles. (She never did find out why he wasn't in the high school where he was supposed to be that afternoon, but he must have had an excuse. Wouldn't he have been fired if he'd just disappeared or they'd known he was drunk when he left?) It was right after lunch. He had interfered in the egg race—a relay race—meeting her on the center-field grass where they were playing, and trying to coach her on how best to transfer the egg to her partner's spoon. It was shocking to see her father there, in the midst of the game, instead of with all the other teachers and administrators and a smattering of parents—the other grown-ups—off to the side. As he tried to assist her, breaking the rules in every imaginable way, he accidentally knocked the raw egg in her spoon to the ground, where it broke open, the bright yellow sun of the yolk exploding like a star, a supernova of shame. It had been mortifying, and Cassie hoped desperately that everyone supposed her father was merely clumsy and a cheater—not also a drunk. In her desperate embarrassment, she hoped they thought he was only an idiot.

He had left soon after that, mumbling something about having to get back to the high school.

That night was the first time that Cassie had crept from her bed while everyone else in the house was asleep and opened the cabinet where her parents stored the liquor. There was Jack Daniel's, of course, but Cassie knew that was reserved for "special" occasions. Mostly her father drank a Scotch whiskey called Black Bottle, and the level of liquid was about at the top of the label. It was three-quarters full. She poured out an inch and then added an inch of tap water. She did the same with the vodka and the bourbon and the gin. She wished she could do the same with the beer in the refrigerator, but each can was sealed and so that was impossible.

"But I had my own bedroom there," Rosemary said, and Cassie felt herself wincing inside at the word *there*. Rosemary would go from *there* to the foster home, where she would share a strange bedroom with a strange girl—another teen in the foster care system—who was angry and violent but could dial it down just enough in front of their foster parents to stick around. It was hard to believe that the saltbox with the watered-down gin and their father's drinking and their mother's weeping and their weekly fights about money and booze was a well with sufficiently happy memories that Rosemary wanted to share the house with her children. How many evenings had Cassie tried to drown out their fights by cocooning inside her Walkman headset? How many nights had poor Rosemary crawled into bed with her, sobbing and scared?

"More tea, Cassie?" Dennis was holding the pot near her teacup.

"Yes, please," she said, though she would have preferred a Long Island iced tea: tequila, gin, vodka, rum, triple sec. The whole damn cabinet in a highball glass. At the table beside them, everyone had a bottle of Tsingtao beer. She wanted one of those, too.

"And we actually had a very nice swing set and playhouse in the backyard," Rosemary went on. "It was made of wood—not metal that rusted out as soon as it rained. My friends and I used to play *Little House on the Prairie* on it. The timbers were so thick and sturdy, they looked like they belonged on a log cabin."

"That sounds like the lamest game ever," her son said.

"Oh, it was," Rosemary agreed. "Totally lame. But we were little."

Cassie sipped her tea and recalled that moment after college when she broke her vow of alcohol abstinence. She was twenty-three and was at the swimming pool at a hotel in Miami. There were afternoon thunderstorms in the Northeast and their flight back to New York had been canceled, and so the crew was sent to a hotel. It was in Coral Gables and had a rooftop pool. There were crews late that afternoon from three different carriers because the hotel filled its rooms in the summer—the off-season—with airline employees. Everyone was drinking, except her. The flight attendant on the chaise beside her, a motherly veteran who had been flying twenty-five years, was sipping a piña colada, and it smelled heavenly. Cassie considered ordering a virgin colada, but the waiter wasn't nearby, and the idea of getting up and going to the bar seemed like a lot of work at five in the afternoon, the temperature still in the mid-eighties. And so she had taken a sip. And it was good. Better than a virgin colada, the taste sharper, the tingle deep, deep inside her. She inhaled the aromas of coconut and pineapple, yes, but there was also something else. Something more. Rum. Had there ever been rum in her parents' kitchen in Kentucky? Probably. But she had no memory of watering down a bottle or of her mother cascading rum down the sink. It felt different and new, and though she sensed she was flirting with something so wonderful but—for her—so reckless that it would kill her, she pushed herself to her feet and walked to the pool bar in her bikini. She ordered a piña colada for herself. Did she even bother to nibble on the pineapple wedge? Probably not. She drank it fast because it was sweet and she could feel the way it warmed her insides and made her worries go away. Suddenly, she wasn't fretting about her hips. They were fine. She was fine. She was no longer that girl who was scared in the backseat of the car as her drunken father tried to control their hideous robin's-egg-blue Dodge Colt on the winding road between Landaff and Grover's Mill, her mother yelling at him to please, please, please, for God's sake let her drive. She wasn't that anxious college student, awake at four a.m. at the college switchboard, praying to herself that her kid sister would be okay in the foster home. She wasn't that diligent, joyless, unremittingly responsible twenty-three-year-old flight attendant who strove for perfection in all things, because anything else was the start of the downward slope that would lead her back to the small, sad village where her father drank and her mother cried and she was pouring Black Bottle down the sink. She was . . . free. And she liked that. She enjoyed the taste, sure, but more than that she liked the sound of her laugh when the first officer made a joke (not especially funny, but he was cute) about the way a particular cloud in the sky over Miami looked like a puppy with a cigar. That evening he would seduce her, or she would seduce him; in hindsight—even the next morning—she really hadn't a clue. She learned quickly that music sounded better, people were nicer, and she was prettier when life's rough edges had been smoothed over with a little alcohol. Or, better still, with a lot. What fault could anybody possibly find in any of that? God, it was good, it was all good, and it was all Cassie could do that very moment in the Chinese restaurant not to violate Rosemary's Rules and summon the waiter to bring her a Tsingtao, too. Or, better yet, a gin and tonic made with Beefeater or Sacred or Sipsmith, if they had it.

"I'm reading a book about a pilot," her niece was saying to her, and Cassie turned to her and tried to focus.

"Oh? Tell me about it," she said.

And her niece did and she tried to pay attention, but a part of her was recalling the denial that marked her drinking in her early and midtwenties, and how she convinced herself that she wasn't her father's daughter and she wasn't repeating his mistakes. She wouldn't let alcohol destroy her the way it had destroyed him. And for over a decade and a half—until Dubai—on some level she had even believed that. Because it wasn't until Dubai that she had really become one with her father by allowing her addiction to lead her to the dead. You can repair anything but dead. You can't fix that.

So you buried the dead and moved on.

You burned the carbons.

The proof was in the proof.

And yet she wanted that gin and tonic. Even now. Even as she waited for a phone call from Ani Mouradian or Frank Hammond. She wanted it badly.

"Can I borrow the book when you're done?" she asked Jessica.

"Sure, but it's a kids' book."

She shrugged. "A lot of the best books are kids' books. *Charlotte's Web. The Giver. Matilda.* It's a long list." She smiled at the girl and then told the table that she was going to the ladies' room. She planned to drop a ten with the bartender on the way there, curl her tongue into a funnel, and drain a shot glass of gin.

《 《

Dennis didn't mind driving in New York City. He rather liked it, in fact. His big complaint was the cost of parking. But the hotel where they were staying in White Plains was reasonable, and so he had driven to the Bronx Zoo, which had made it easy for them all to drive to Chinatown. Then, after dinner, he insisted on chauffeuring Cassie back to her apartment. She invited them all upstairs, but it had been a long day and Dennis really didn't want to park again. So she said her good-byes in the car and exited at the corner of Third Avenue and Twenty-Seventh Street, waving at Noah the doorman the moment she emerged from the car. She was in her apartment by eight o'clock.

« «

If she hadn't had a shot of gin at the bar at the restaurant in Chinatown, would she have stayed home once she had settled down inside her apartment? Probably not, because Paula phoned, her siren song drawing Cassie once more toward the rocks: the magical cubes that added such beauty to the luminescent brown of Drambuie and transformed the waters of arak into clouds. Briefly she considered not answering when she saw Paula's name on her phone's screen, but willpower had never been her strong suit. And so she did answer, which meant that by nine she was drinking at the bar at a Mexican restaurant near Union Square with her friend and a woman from Paula's ad agency named Suzanne, and by ten she was telling the two of them a version of her nightmare in Dubai in which Alex Sokolov himself didn't appear, but instead she slept with a fictional commodities trader named Alex Ilyich—a surname she commandeered on the fly from Tolstoy. But she was certainly imagining the real Alex as she spoke, giving her fictional one that same peculiar jones for the Russians and Russian literature. Alex, she said, had told her that he would be back in the States and visiting his parents in Virginia this week. The man, she added, had promised to call her when he was stateside but never had. Never even texted.

Which, perhaps, was why now she was allowing them to prod her to call him at his parents' place in Charlottesville.

"Do it!" Paula said raucously over the sound of the crowd and clinked glasses and the thrum of the bass from the speakers on the far side of the bar. "Do it! Call him! Give him shit for fucking and forgetting!"

Cassie gazed at her friend and at her friend's friend. Their eyes hung heavy with tequila, and their smiles had that Saturday-night smirk, thin-lipped and derisive, but also eager for a rush to cap the weekend with a pulsating vibrato of hilarity and chaos.

"I don't have his number," she said.

"So? Call Charlottesville! Call his parents! How many people there have unpronounceable Russian last names?"

And so to appease them she pretended to search for Ilyich in that Virginia city, but actually looked up Sokolov. She found that name instantly. She pressed in the digits, let it ring once, and then hung up. She felt at once mournful and brutish. She knew she would be unable to endure the sound of Alex's mother's or father's voice on an answering machine, or the voice of whoever was screening calls at the house the night after the funeral.

"Busy," she said.

"Like hell it was!" said Suzanne, rapping her knuckles on the wood of the bar, then laughing and moaning at how she had banged them so hard that she'd hurt herself. "You're a coward and a wimp."

"No, it was busy," she insisted. "It really was!"

"No way!" Paula laughed, rolling back her head. With the speed of an attacking snake she grabbed Cassie's phone and pressed on the number that Cassie had just dialed. Cassie tried to wrestle the phone away, but Suzanne held down her right arm and then her left, and then bear-hugged her and giggled. Cassie didn't struggle, not because she feared making a scene—she never feared making a scene—but because a part of her had to see where this speeding train was going to crash and just how cataclysmic would be the carnage.

"Hi, this is Cassie Bowden," Paula said when someone answered. "I met Alex last week in Dubai and I want to speak to him right now! I want to know why he hasn't called me!"

She watched as Paula's drunken eyes went wide and her jaw actually went slack in disbelief. She said nothing more, nothing at all. She just handed the phone back to Cassie, as Suzanne released her arms.

Cassie looked at the screen and saw the connection was gone.

"He's . . . um . . ." her friend began, but then stopped.

Cassie waited. Suzanne pushed Paula hard on her upper arm, literally prodding her to continue. "What?" Suzanne asked, still smiling at the hilarity of all of this. "What?"

"He's dead," Paula murmured.

"He's what?" Suzanne asked.

"He's dead," Paula repeated. "Someone at the house—not his mom or dad, I'm pretty sure—got really pissed and hung up. So, I don't know any more than that."

"That's so weird and so sad," Suzanne said, her voice softened by the absolute buzzkill of Paula's news. But she was stunned only briefly. "Let's Google how he died," she said. "Maybe there's an obituary."

Cassie took back her phone. It felt radioactive in her hand. Would it ring again soon? Would Alex's mother or father call her back? Probably not. Instead she would probably get a call from Frank Hammond or someone in authority somewhere, telling her not to harass the family. But maybe not. Oh, the family certainly would tell the police she had called. They'd tell the FBI.

And eventually it would get back to Ani.

But the more she thought about it, the more she wondered whether this stupid little stunt would be anything other than one more black mark in her file somewhere.

She sighed. She hoped when Ani called her next, it wouldn't be to say that she'd had enough of her and was dropping the case.

"Don't waste your time Googling it, Suzanne," she said. "I can tell you exactly how he died."

Paula sat up a little straighter on her stool. "Wait, what? You knew he was dead and allowed me to call his parents? Are you crazy?"

"I tried to stop you."

"She did," Suzanne agreed. "She did."

"Not hard enough!"

"He was killed in Dubai at some point after I left his hotel room," Cassie told them. "If you want to read all about it, just go to the *New York Post*. You can even see me. Sort of. His real name was Alex Sokolov. Not Ilyich. Sokolov."

She had been planning to order another margarita and stared a little longingly at the squat, lovely bottle of triple sec behind the bar. But as she glimpsed the faces of her friends as they held their phones before them and read about the death of an American trader in Dubai and the woman of interest in the security cam photos, she had a change of heart. She had a twenty-dollar bill and two ones in her wallet, which wouldn't cover what she probably owed, but she handed it to Paula and said she was sorry—sorry, in truth, about so many things, of which not paying her share of the bar tab was pretty damn inconsequential—and said good night.

« «

The next morning, Sunday, she wasn't sure which surprised her more: the fact she slept through the night or the fact she still hadn't been arrested. Her attorney hadn't called to fire her for phoning Alex Sokolov's family in Virginia.

Of course, the day was young. A lot could still happen.

She got up and went to the animal shelter, as if it were just another Sunday in August. It was a fifteen-minute walk if she strolled, considerably less if she was in a hurry. But as she was passing a supermarket on the avenue, once more she had the distinct sense that she was being followed. She told herself, as she had the other day, that she was being delusional. But she knew also that the FBI had reason to put her under surveillance. And there certainly were other people out there, including whoever had killed Alex, who might want to know more about the woman in the Royal Phoenician photos.

The idea that whoever that was knew who she was caused her to feel a chill, despite the stifling summer heat. She paused and flipped open her compact to look behind her, almost hoping to see Frank Hammond or someone else who just exuded FBI, because she knew she would have preferred that to the faceless man in shades and a black ball cap.

Unless that dude was FBI. And maybe he was. She thought of how casually the air marshals always dressed on her flights.

In her compact she saw no one in particular on the sidewalk. There wasn't a lot of traffic on the streets on a Sunday morning in August, and among the cabs and buses and delivery vehicles she noted nothing suspicious. Still, she trusted her instincts. There again was that gift of the amygdala, the gift of fear. Ahead of her was a corner convenience store with entrances on both the avenue she was on and the cross street she was approaching. She flipped shut her compact and went in. But instead of buying even a cup of coffee, she cut through the store and left through the other exit. A few yards down that cross street was a doorway for a dry cleaner that was closed for the day. She stood flat against the side wall, invisible from the avenue, and waited. She counted slowly to one hundred, adding the word *Mississippi* after each number, the way she'd been taught as a little girl. Then instead of returning to the avenue and continuing north to the shelter, she walked a block west. She'd head north at the next intersection. It was a long detour, but it dialed down her panic.

And she indeed felt safer when she was inside the shelter, though she knew that wasn't rational. If they wanted to arrest her, they would: an animal shelter wasn't an embassy in some faraway land giving her refuge. Likewise, if someone else was after her, they'd find her. Their . . . expertise . . . was evident.

She went straight to the community room where the older cats lived. This morning she counted eight, dozing or draped on the cat condos and the cat trees and on the cat beds on the bookcase. She saw Duchess and Dulci were still there, a pair of eleven-year-olds whose elderly owner had died and his middle-aged son had been unwilling to adopt. (She had never met the man who had brought the animals in, but Cassie loathed him and viewed his behavior as utterly despicable.) The cats recognized her voice and went straight for her lap when she sat on the floor. She brushed them and cooed, and they purred in response, the noise reminiscent of mourning doves, and they nuzzled against her and stretched out their legs and their paws. They looked a little thinner than the last time she was here, and she hoped they weren't so sad that they weren't eating. She reached into her shoulder bag and offered them some of the treats she had brought, and was relieved when their appetites seemed fine.

She sighed. Was there anyplace she was more useful than the shelter? Was there anyplace she was happier when she was sober? She knew the answer to both of those questions. There wasn't.

« «

As she was walking back to her apartment, once again she had the unmistakable feeling that she was being watched. She guessed she probably was. She recalled the way the half brother of the North Korean leader had been killed in broad daylight with a fast-acting nerve agent by a stranger in an airport concourse in Malaysia and found herself giving a wide berth on the sidewalk to anyone approaching her from the other direction.

And yet soon she was home and the walk had been, by any objective standard, uneventful. And still she hadn't been arrested. She sat down on the couch and called Ani.

"Oh, I wish I could tell you that you're off the hook and this all will pass," Ani said. "Maybe it's just taking time."

"In that case, do I report to work and fly back to Rome? If so, I should be out the door in an hour."

"Go."

"Okay. And maybe I should just stay there. Never come back," she said wryly.

"Maybe," Ani agreed, but Cassie understood the lawyer wasn't being serious.

"I did something stupid last night," she confessed, and she told Ani what had occurred at the bar. But instead of firing or even chastising her, Ani sounded as if she had come to expect this sort of bad behavior from her client. There was an edge of disappointment to her response, but mostly she just sounded sad.

"Someday you'll hit bottom," she said. "For most people, that would have been Dubai. Not you, apparently. We'll see."

"How much trouble am I in?" she asked.

"For calling the Sokolov family in Virginia? Oh, probably no more than yesterday. You should be embarrassed, but I'm not sure it's really possible to shame you, Cassie."

"It is," she said. "It really is."

"Just . . ."

"Just what?"

"Just, please, act like a grown-up."

》 《

While packing, Cassie called Derek Mayes.

"Have you heard anything from the airline about, I don't know, their asking me to take a leave of absence?" she asked. "Are there any threats to my job?"

"Not yet," he told her.

"Does the airline know I'm the woman in the photos?"

"They might. If I had to guess, I would guess yes. I'm quite sure that someone from the FBI has contacted them. But no one from the airline has gotten in touch with you?"

"Nope."

"Well, they haven't called me, either."

"Your niece says I should go ahead and fly to Rome."

"My niece is very smart. Listen to her in all things."

"I will," she said, though she instantly recalled how she hadn't with the FBI agents that Friday afternoon.

A half hour later, unsure whether it was the August humidity or that nagging sense that there was always someone just beyond her gaze who was watching her, she said good-bye to Stanley, the doorman. Briefly she considered taking the subway to the Dickinson and hitching a ride with the crew for the Madrid flight, but she couldn't cope. She just couldn't. Instead she hailed the cab nearing her apartment building's awning. Her instinct was to ask him to take her to Grand Central, where she would catch the Airporter bus, but she couldn't face that, either. Not now. Not today. And so even though she couldn't afford a cab to JFK—with tip that would cost seventy-five bucks—she asked him to take her to the airport.

And there in the cab, somewhere in the snarl of traffic that dogged the Van Wyck Expressway even on a Sunday afternoon in August, her phone rang. It was a number she didn't recognize. When the woman said hello and introduced herself as a reporter, Cassie instantly forgot her name and had to ask for it a moment later, because her mind could focus only on the tabloid banner of the writer's newspaper. When she recovered, she said she had nothing to say and hung up, blocked the number on her phone, and called Ani Mouradian.

19

In the end, Elena chose the *New York Post* for the simple reason that the *New York Times* had covered the story responsibly. They understood the death of Alex Sokolov was not an act of terrorism and seemed, as far as she could tell now, to have moved on. They might be preparing a longer story on the hedge fund manager and Unisphere's connections to select members of the Russian political leadership—there might be the usual innuendo about corruption and crime, intimations that the White House was indebted to the Kremlin—but the financial machinations of a hedge fund were at once too complex and too dull to ever elicit much readership or interest. And if they were preparing a story on the utter randomness of dying on a business trip far from home? Elena believed that reportage like that might be compelling and beautiful, but it would never gain traction in the Age of the Troll. In the Age of Mass Shootings. In the Age of the Suicide Bomb in the Crowd.

After planting her seed—her anonymous tip—she phoned Viktor. He was finishing dinner but took the call and went outside the restaurant. She wondered whom he was with and worried when he didn't volunteer the companion's name. Usually he did because most of the time it was someone she knew or at least knew of. It was a further indication of the sort of trouble she herself was in. He didn't trust her. At least not completely.

"Are you going to go with the flight attendant?" he asked.

"Back to Italy?" She heard incredulity instead of obedience in her voice, a reflex, and took a breath to rein in her emotions.

"If that's where she's going, yes."

"No. I hadn't planned on it," she admitted. She wasn't a pilot or a flight attendant, and her body wasn't wild about the idea of flying east to Rome days after flying west from Dubai.

"You might want to consider it."

Might want to. Was there ever a more passive-aggressive phrasing? There was a threat behind it, only thinly veiled, but there was also a message. She was responsible for Bowden. This was a mess of her making. Their patience was almost up.

"Do you want me to finish the job in Rome?" she asked guardedly.

She heard him lighting a cigarette, pulling the smoke deep into his lungs. "Well, I like your idea of a suicide. In some ways, I like it even more in Rome than in New York. Just be sure that she has had time to really feel the pain from the media swarm. You know, cause and effect. But a hotel suicide in Rome the day the story appears in the *New York Post*? Makes perfect sense."

"Then I'll go."

"Just don't be on her flight."

"Viktor?"

"Yes?"

She almost told him that she wasn't born yesterday. She felt the need to defend herself and convey at least a hint of her annoyance at the imposition of another trip across the Atlantic. But she knew that sort of flippancy would be ill advised at the moment. And so instead she said simply, "You're absolutely right. I'll make sure I'm not." It was the politic response, and she loathed herself for saying it.

《 《

She flew out of Newark since Bowden was based at JFK. She didn't want to risk the flight attendant spotting her at the terminal on Long Island.

She was stopped at security, a random pat-down and wanding. The TSA officer opened her leather duffel and commented on both the wig and the straw sun hat with pretend strands of hair attached to the side and rear panels. She volunteered that they were for her sister in Orvieto who was about to begin chemotherapy. On the other side of the full body scanners, people were standing like storks on single legs as they pulled their boots over their shins or slipped back on their sneakers and espadrilles.

A moment later when she was repacking the wig and the sun hat properly—the way she liked, not the way the TSA agent had mashed them inside her bag—she wondered if she wore them in Rome tomorrow or the day after tomorrow whether someone would recall them from a woman's bag back in Newark. Not likely. They were all too busy looking for shoe bombs.

《　《

There were actually a few empty seats in coach on the Sunday-night flight, including the middle seat beside her. She had grown interested in flight attendants in a way that she hadn't been before Bowden had shown up in Alex's hotel room, and now—almost curiously—she watched a slim woman with white hair and athletic calves work the aisles, asking passengers what they would like to drink as she stood behind the cart, but occasionally responding to lengthier questions about when the cabin lights would be dimmed and whether they could have an extra blanket or pillow.

When the beverage cart reached her row, the flight attendant looked down at her. Elena—who had donned the cosmetic tortoiseshell eyeglasses for the flight she'd bought months ago at a costume shop—glanced up from her *Vanity Fair* just enough to be polite, because rudeness was memorable. She asked (please) for a Diet Coke, no ice. From the corner of her eye she watched the woman pouring the can into the plastic cup and noticed that the flight attendant's nails were almost the same shade of red as hers.

She placed her magazine in the seat pocket and unfolded her tray table for her soda. Then she logged on to the aircraft's Wi-Fi and immediately went to the website for the *New York Post*. And there it was. The story was live. She stared for a long moment at Cassandra Bowden's name as if the syllables were an incantation or the two words an eponym: she grew lost in her connection to the flight attendant. She blinked to regain her focus.

Bowden had offered no comment and the FBI had offered no comment, but an anonymous source with the Dubai police had confirmed that Cassandra Bowden of New York City was, at the very least, a person of interest. Another flight attendant could not corroborate the story but had volunteered that Bowden was "a bit of a party girl" and "kind of a wild woman." She'd added something that on the surface sounded contradictory, but Elena understood how it made all the sense in the world and that in fact the woman had probably been coached: "Cassie is sweet and kind of a loner. When she's home, she goes to this animal shelter a lot because she really likes the stray cats. I think sometimes she's as depressed as they are. And when we're working, she's not always out somewhere going crazy until one in the morning. Sometimes she just clicks shut her hotel room door and sleeps. I mean, the job is just too demanding and that's not how she's hardwired." Elena knew the ebb and flow of binge behavior, and the way a person sometimes just wanted to retreat into the bleached white sheets of a Hilton or into the fur of an equally needy, equally wounded cat. But she doubted that Bowden was actually depressed: that was expediency finessing the truth.

The article also quoted her lawyer: a woman named Ani Mouradian said that Bowden was cooperating fully with investigators and had absolutely nothing to do with Alex Sokolov's death. Finally, a representative for the airline said the flight attendant had not been charged with a crime in either the United Arab Emirates or the United States and had violated no airline policy. And so they had no comment.

Nevertheless, the *Post* already had a nickname for Bowden and for the crime. Now that she was no longer a mystery woman, she was no longer a rather generic "black widow spider." They knew she was a flight attendant, and so they had christened her the "Cart Tart Killer."

It wasn't brilliant, Elena thought, but it wasn't bad. It had rhythm and alliteration, and best of all was the way it combined sluttiness and murder.

She closed the page on her phone and sat back in her seat. She thought of her brief time with Bowden back in Dubai: the woman was lit, sure, and dopey with drink. But so was Alex. But she'd also seemed rather kind and funny. And it was at that very moment, like a revelation, that Elena recalled the way Alex had become so attentive when Bowden said something about what her brother-in-law did for a living. It was the name of the army base. The fact, Bowden said, that he was more engineer than soldier.

She grimaced there in her seat at the obviousness of what she had missed. Sokolov already knew that. He knew all about Bowden's brother-in-law. She must have said something on the flight to Dubai, and instantly he had connected the dots. It was why he had brought Bowden back to his room. This may have ended up a drunken romp with a hot mess, but that wasn't how it had begun. She hadn't seduced him; he, in fact, had seduced her. It was a move that simultaneously reflected his brilliance and his naïveté. The courier—whoever it was, because God forbid Viktor should ever violate his "need to know" policies of spy craft and secrecy and tell her—had sensed that the FBI was circling and grown anxious. So Viktor had enlisted Sokolov to make the handoff, an assignment he had gladly accepted because he knew how much trouble he was in with his Russian clients. And into his life walked a flight attendant with connections to Blue Grass who probably needed money. Bowden must have just screamed "recruit" to Sokolov; she was the perfect offering to bring to a Cossack crazy who was trying to weaponize a drone with chemical agents.

Elena's father had one rule that he said had served him well both before and after the collapse: trust your instincts. He said it had saved his life when he was with the KGB, and it had saved his fortune when he was done.

The beverage cart was well behind her now, but another flight attendant appeared out of nowhere and offered to refill her glass. He was a handsome guy with a mane of tapered, coal-colored dreadlocks held back in an immaculate ponytail.

"Thank you," she said.

"Absolutely," he said, smiling. "Let me know if you need anything else."

She raised her glass to him in gratitude, but already her mind was elsewhere. Nothing really was wrong, and nothing really was different, she told herself. But there it was, a beacon from deep inside her, a warning light now flashing red.

20

News spreads like an airborne virus in the digital age, and though Cassie knew not a soul in the crew on the overnight flight to Rome, they knew her. They had all read the story on their phones on the way to the airport or as they waited to pass through security or then as they waited to board. They had been directed to the story by friends and family and coworkers who had seen it on Facebook or Twitter. After all, she worked for their airline.

And while she wasn't wearing a scarlet A—the uniform regulations would have prohibited that sort of accessorizing, Cassie thought darkly to herself—everyone watched her warily and she felt like Hester Prynne. No, the vibe of this madness was Russian. Anna Karenina, she corrected herself. But, of course, Anna hadn't killed anyone. It was only her own life that she'd taken. The cabin service director, a fortysomething fellow named Brendon who was lean and stern and led spin classes in Buffalo when he wasn't flying, asked her if she would be capable of working. She said yes. Of course. She said she knew this was coming. She added—and she said this so many times in the half hour before they walked down the jet bridge to prepare the plane for takeoff that she had begun to believe it herself—that Alex Sokolov had been alive when she had left his hotel room. She had no idea who had murdered him, which she also said with conviction, though mostly she was sure that she did know: it was either Miranda or someone Miranda knew. But somehow Miranda was involved.

Perhaps Miranda was even behind the dude in the black ball cap.

Unfortunately, there were also still those occasional moments when she wondered if, just maybe, she was blaming Miranda needlessly—because she herself had killed Alex Sokolov. Usually she was able to walk herself in from the ledge when her mind would go there. It was just that over the years there had been so many other revelatory and appalling morning-after discoveries of what she had done when she was on the far side of the blackout zone.

Cassie, you really don't remember when you were kicking the jukebox? You were weirdly pissed off because they had nothing by Taylor Swift. Have you looked at your foot this morning?

You were screaming like a porn star, girl. The people in the apartment next to mine were banging on the wall.

You were about to give this homeless guy your credit cards, Cassie—all of them. You were, like, emptying your wallet. It was sweet, but insane.

Houdini Bikini. That's what you called it. You took off your top and were trying to step out of your bottom.

Once when Paula was sober she'd ruminated that one of them was destined to die via "death by misadventure." Apparently that was what coroners wrote on death certificates when people died doing something monumentally stupid, usually while drunk. They drowned or they fell off buildings or they tumbled down long flights of stairs. Paula had joked that it wasn't the worst way to go.

The small talk among the crew grew awkward fast. Usually they all would have chatted casually and gotten to know each other a bit, but how do you make small talk with a person of interest in a murder investigation in Dubai? Cassie got it. She understood. She was by no means a pariah, but no one could quite figure out how to transition from a discussion of the murder of some hedge fund manager to asking if you had any hobbies.

Yes, she would have answered, had they asked. *I drink. Want the secret to a dirty martini? Plop an ice cube and a little water in the glass and place it in the freezer for a couple of minutes before mixing together the gin, the vermouth, and the olive juice.*

And yet somehow she had done her job for three hours now. She was working the business-class cabin with a kind woman her age named Makayla, and it probably helped that the other flight attendant was almost heroically competent. She was always a step ahead of Cassie on the hot towels and warmed nuts, opening the different wines and gently—very gently—helping her remain on task as they warmed the trays with the steaks or the salmon or the risotto. When Cassie introduced herself to the passengers, she used her middle name, Elizabeth, and asked them to call her Ellie. (She had taken off the badge with her name, which was technically a uniform violation, but she didn't care this evening. She just didn't care.) She was pretty sure that the paunchy guy in the ugly, short-sleeve jacquard shirt knew who she really was, but he was traveling alone and hadn't bothered to share his reconnaissance with anyone else on the plane. He just eyed her knowingly, as if he got it, he was in on the joke.

Now for the first time, in the dark over the Atlantic when most of the passengers were starting to sleep, she was able to sit down in her jump seat and stare at her phone. To read and reread the story. To see her "no comment," which seemed profoundly incriminating in the context of this nightmare, but also the deft way that Ani Mouradian managed to defend her and deflect the allegations. She couldn't help but scan the comments from readers that followed the story, most of them fatuous and some accusatory, but all of them hurtful and cruel. She examined the way that the saga was being discussed on the social networks. Finally she returned to her own e-mails, including the ones from Ani and Megan and her sister. Rosemary chastised her, writing that she couldn't understand why Cassie hadn't told her what was going on, either on the phone immediately after she returned to the United States from the Emirates or at some point on Saturday. *After all, we spent all Saturday together,* she reiterated. Her sister was angry and sad and worried about her. The e-mail was as judgmental as ever, and Cassie knew that she had earned every word.

And then there was the e-mail from her friend Gillian: it was a well-meaning but appalling joke about just how bad this guy must have been in bed for her to cut his throat.

Brendon and Makayla and the rest of the crew left her alone, undoubtedly aware of what she was facing.

She honestly wasn't sure what was worse: the online jokes or the online hatred. There were lots of both, all of it mean-spirited and sexist. The news story didn't include her confession (quasi-confession, if she were honest with herself) to the FBI on Friday that she had indeed spent the night with Alex Sokolov; no one at the FBI had leaked that bit of information. But the story certainly suggested that she had, based on both the hotel surveillance camera footage of her and an interview with a hotel employee who said he had seen the flight attendant with the murdered businessman. She was sipping Coke to settle her stomach, but she wanted a drink. She sighed. She didn't dare try and sneak one. Not now.

The strangest part of the news story, she decided, was a quote from Alex's father. It was after his rather straightforward expression of his faith that the FBI and the Dubai police would find his son's killer. It was after his lovely observation about the gentleness of his son's interests, such as Alex's "childlike" fascination with numbers and the way he had built it into a career. After that, however, Gregory Sokolov had volunteered how surprising and unwarranted he found the allegations that his son was a spy. The idea had crossed Cassie's mind numerous times, the seed planted originally by Derek Mayes when they had first had breakfast. But it was almost as if Alex's father was protesting too much. Moreover, she hadn't realized that the notion was out there in the zeitgeist. Sure enough, however, when she Googled Sokolov now she found the innuendo and the rumors that had emerged with the suddenness of dandelions in May. There was plenty of speculation that he worked for the CIA and plenty that he worked for Mossad and MI6 and the FSB. There were even a few conspiracy theorists who argued that he worked for some assassin squad far darker than the CIA or the FSB, and he reported directly to the American or the Russian president. She saw groups with names like Double O (British), Cossacks (Russian), Phoenix (American), and Kidon (Israeli). None of it matched well with the young man she had dined with in Dubai, a gentle fellow from Virginia. The guy was into money and math, for God's sake. He liked to read books from the nineteenth century. She was pretty sure that she knew more about guns than he did.

But he did have a Russian last name. He had Russian interests. Russian cologne and books and alcohol.

A passenger, a slender young woman in leopard tights that were disturbingly reminiscent of those luxurious bathrobes at the Royal Phoenician, smiled down at her, and Cassie assumed that she was about to slide into the lavatory beside her. Her hair was long and dark and parted in the middle. Her eyes looked a little sleepy. But she didn't enter the bathroom. Instead she leaned against the handle beside the exterior door—the one that was attached to the interior of the fuselage and that Cassie was supposed to hold on to in the event of an evacuation so she wouldn't be pushed from the plane in the desperate scrum to get out.

"The bathrooms are free," Cassie said to her.

The woman nodded, but didn't go in. "I just needed to stretch my legs," she murmured. Then: "What's happening in the world?"

"Nothing at the moment. Thank God. Mostly it's just the midterm election madness."

"I like a slow news day. It means some corner of the planet hasn't blown up. A hospital wasn't shelled in the Middle East. A school wasn't attacked by some crazy person with a gun in Kentucky."

"I grew up in Kentucky," said Cassie.

"I've never been there. I hear it's very pretty."

"It is."

"I'm Missy."

"Hi. Ellie."

"Can I ask you something"—and she paused before saying her name—"Ellie?"

Cassie waited. Usually when a passenger asked her a question in the middle of a flight this tranquil, it was an innocuous question about her job. They couldn't sleep and wanted to talk, and sometimes the utter marvel of aviation—of flying—became real for them at moments like this.

"Of course."

"When you refilled my wine during dinner . . ."

"Go ahead. Ask."

"Your hands were trembling. And just now, well, you look kind of like you just want to cry."

"And the question is?"

"Why are you torturing yourself and reading what's out there? I write a style blog for *Enticement*, which isn't exactly hard news, but I still see my share of crap on the web. Maybe I see even more. Crazy fat shaming. Slut shaming. Fashion shaming. I know who you are, and I know what's out there about you. I was probably just reading the same articles and reactions you were. That stuff is absolutely toxic. So why don't you just, I don't know, download a novel and read that instead?"

"I actually have a paperback with me," she said. She had responded automatically.

Missy nodded. "Good. I think you should do yourself a favor and stay off-line for a while."

Cassie couldn't decide whether this was kindness or invasiveness smirking behind kindness. But Missy's gaze was gentle.

"My parents are both shrinks," she went on. "And so I know what a total disaster these well-intentioned little chats can be. So, I'm sorry if this isn't helpful advice at all. But you just looked so . . . so forlorn that I had to say something."

"It's fine," Cassie said, and she felt her eyes welling up. "It's good."

"Do you know people cry on airplanes more than anywhere else?"

"I didn't know it was a fact," she answered, "but I might have suspected as much from my years up here."

"Yeah, you'd probably know better than me. But on a plane, you're often alone. Or you're stressed. Or you've just had some meaningful experience. Movies and books will really get to you at thirty-five thousand feet."

"You're right." She squirted Purell onto her fingers, rubbed it in, and then wiped the tears off her cheeks.

"Have you shut down your Tinder?"

"Not yet."

"Do it. Just shut it down. Shut down Tinder, Facebook, Instagram. Twitter. God, especially Twitter. Whatever you have. Just hit pause."

She sniffled. "That's good advice. I will, thank you."

Missy smiled. It was a beautiful smile. Cassie stood and hugged her, wondering why she didn't have more friends like this younger woman—friends whose interactions with her weren't about either drinking or the fallout from drinking—and wishing she could stay in her arms for the rest of the flight.

« «

After Missy had retaken her seat, Cassie took her advice and hit pause. She didn't merely deactivate most of her accounts on the social networks, she deleted the apps from her phone.

Then she finished the Tolstoy novella she had started days ago but put aside. Much to her surprise, "Happy Ever After" was not an ironic title at all. She wept at the ending. Masha, she thought. Masha. Such a beautiful name.

« «

Many of the flights from the United States landed at Fiumicino in the same window: midmorning. The crush at passport control was not all American, not by a long shot, but in a provincial sort of way it felt like it was. Cassie heard accents in the throng from the South and from New England and from New York.

But the flight crews had their own line and passed through more quickly than the passengers.

Now she was walking beside Makayla, and they were just beyond security, nearing the exit to the baggage carousels (which they did not need), and then the terminal exit, where they would meet the van that would bring them all into Rome. Makayla was telling her about a vegetarian restaurant she liked on the Via Margutta and suggesting they go there for dinner. Cassie was aware that one of the wheels on her roller was not quite right. The bag was dragging ever so slightly. She was trying to listen to the other flight attendant, but her mind kept wandering to what might be going on that moment in the cities of New York and Dubai. Yes, most of New York was still asleep, but perhaps not the FBI. In her mind she envisioned FBI investigators and Dubai detectives e-mailing or texting or sharing encrypted files. Videos of her. Photographs. Her e-mails, perhaps, which they had downloaded from a server. Interviews with hotel employees.

She imagined someone was somehow searching through a central trash repository on the outskirts of Dubai, looking for exactly the sorts of things she had thrown away. She wondered if they would take a screenshot from the security camera footage and enlarge her purse, and look for precisely that bag in the mountains of garbage in the desert somewhere. Or maybe they would look for the missing hotel towels. Or a knife. Could a coroner make a reasonable guess about whether it was a knife or a broken bottle based on the way that Alex's throat had been cut? Probably. She told herself that no one could even begin to find something as small as a shoulder bag or the precise shard of glass in a city as big as Dubai. And so while the idea of a search caused her anxiety, she was mostly able to quell that fear.

And it was then that she stopped. She put her hand on Makayla to stop her, too. There, on the far side of passport control, in the lines and lines of passengers who were not from the European

Union—largely Americans, mostly businesspeople arriving on a Monday morning, though certainly there were also some vacationers and people whose passports were from other non-EU nations—was a woman with auburn hair and a French twist. She was putting a pair of tortoiseshell eyeglasses into her purse, and had a beautiful, calfskin leather duffel slung over her shoulder. When the traveler looked up, Cassie was sure she knew who it was, she hadn't a doubt in the world. And so reflexively she whispered to herself one small expletive and the woman's name: "Fuck. Miranda."

Part Four

NOBODY'S PUSHOVER,
NOBODY'S FOE

«

21

Elena knew that the West viewed the president of the Russian Federation as a Bond villain. The guy took out his political enemies with radioactive tea, for God's sake. He had his intelligence agencies hack and release the e-mail of U.S. political parties to influence presidential elections. He was perceived at once as scary and comic. You took him seriously—very seriously—but you scoffed behind his back.

And she knew that while Canadian citizens had been welcoming Muslim immigrants in the worst of the refugee crisis a couple of years ago, an awful lot of everyday Americans had presumed that Islam was a synonym for ISIS. They were convinced that all mosques, whether they were in Fallujah or Florida, were breeding grounds for suicide bombers, and they armed themselves with semiautomatic weapons. They convinced themselves they were safe if they had guns and walls.

She wished the world were that simple. She thought of something one of her father's FSB friends had said to her back in Sochi, when he was testing the waters with her—seeing if he might be able to recruit her. "It's a terrible era when idiots are allowed to govern the blind," he had said. "I'm paraphrasing Shakespeare—perhaps rather badly—but I'm sure you get my drift. The world is a madhouse, Elena. Always has been, always will be. And it's a complicated madhouse. Now, our country has the potential to be the best, I feel. You know, after all we've been through. All that our people have endured. But it's a very low bar."

And yet there wasn't a Cold War anymore. At least not the way that her father and her grandparents would have understood the term. There certainly wasn't a World War. At least not yet. The United States and Russia had grown as nationalist as ever and, thus, rather testy with one another. At first that hadn't been the case. For a time, the United States had shed great crocodile tears for the people of Aleppo, but they understood that Syria—and obviously Ukraine and Crimea—weren't in their backyard. They were in Russia's. And so other than the op-ed writers, for a long while no one in North America really cared all that much even when the Russian Federation deployed nuclear Iskander missiles in Kaliningrad, or what had been Königsberg forever.

Good Lord, half of America was pretty sure their own president was a Russian puppet.

The truth was, very few men or women on the streets of Indianapolis or Kansas City fretted all that much when the Russians penetrated the country's NSA computer system. No one lost sleep when they turned—converted—another contractor who hoarded boxes of files in his utility shed the way some people held on to old issues of *Life* magazine or plastic Star Wars action models or porcelain figurines of Siamese cats.

No more.

If any patch of sand in the world was capable of creating another world war, she believed, it was Syria. Oh, North Korea had the ICBMs and the nukes while the Syrian army was often—very often—reduced to pushing primitive barrel bombs from helicopters. But the Syrian skies were crowded, and the refugee crisis had the West on the edge. Nations great and small were terrified of the suicidal psychotics, sometimes homegrown and sometimes imports, with bombs strapped to their chests or automatic weapons in their arms or simply a very big truck they would use to plow through a crowd as if the pedestrians were merely raccoons crossing a country road in the still of night. They would appear from nowhere, human land mines, and butcher the unlucky women and men around them in the nightclubs and airports and movie theaters. They killed people by the dozens or by the hundreds. It was random. And then they killed themselves.

Were those crazies any worse than the Syrian soldiers who shoved the barrel bombs out the chopper doors? Perhaps, but only because they were suicidal. The Syrian army would drop a bomb on (for instance) a rebel-held neighborhood, wait twenty minutes for the rescuers to start pulling their neighbors from the rubble, and then drop a second one. The barrel bombs killed tens of thousands more civilians than the chemical weapons.

But it was the chemical weapons that caused voters in places like Munich and Manchester and Minneapolis to pay attention. It was the videos of the children choking to death and the adults vomiting and frothing at the mouth. If you want to get the attention of the White House, kill children with sarin. Send it via a surface-to-surface missile or drop it from a MiG.

The Russian drones moved slowly across the same skies as the Americans'. Distant pilots on the ground would guide them over their targets, and the unmanned machines would send back the video images and coordinates. This was how it worked in Ukraine, and this was how it worked in Syria. The Russian drones certainly weren't low tech, but unlike the American and Chinese models, they were still capable only of surveillance.

Imagine: all that money to protect one pilot from having to fly a plane inside its cockpit. Meanwhile, you're still savaging the civilians with tools as barbaric as barrel bombs and as brutal as sarin.

Sometimes she looked at Viktor or she looked at photos of the presidents in Washington and Moscow and Damascus and thought darkly to herself, this is where it all ends. Here.

But there was, alas, just no turning back.

And so she did what she could, which really wasn't much and probably wasn't worth the toll it exacted upon her mental health.

But unlike the terrorists and anarchists and jihadists, she could still count on one hand the number of people she had executed (though she did need her thumb). Most of what she did—and what she had been hoping to do in Dubai once Sokolov was dead—was rather bureaucratic. She could never tell Viktor or anyone else, but she lived with a certain amount of self-hatred, even if (so far) the dead on her conscience all needed to die. Even, just maybe, Sokolov. Both sides would have agreed.

But he was the least definite. Speaking objectively, he wasn't evil. But he also couldn't be trusted. You didn't steal from Viktor. Still, he wasn't like the slime she had executed in Latakia or the cretin she had executed in Donetsk: he'd simply paddled into white water he thought he could navigate. He was rather like her: a pawn. Square D2 or E2 on the chessboard. The pawn moved out to open clean attack lines for the bishop. Against most players, a pawn didn't last long. He'd done his job and delivered the goods. She had to kill him for one reason and one reason only: because Viktor had asked.

She listened to the soothing hum of the engines in the dark and closed her eyes. She wished she could go back in time. She wished she could go back to the Royal Phoenician that night.

No, she wished she could go back to the moment before she had gone to the hotel. When she had called him.

Alex, hello! Lovely to know we're going to meet tomorrow. Are you alone?

That last question? It hadn't crossed her mind to ask it. She should have. Because then he would have answered, *Actually, I'm not. I have a new friend with me. But, please, come over anyway.*

But this time she wouldn't have come over. She would have waited. Maybe she would have gone to the Royal Phoenician much later that night instead. Maybe not. Maybe she would have taken care of Sokolov the next day. Or the next night.

Alas, she couldn't go back in time. She could only go forward. Do her job. Fix the mess she had made and then survey her options.

FEDERAL BUREAU OF INVESTIGATION

Re: ALEX SOKOLOV

DATE: August 6, 2018

The Dubai Police alerted our legal attaché in the United Arab Emirates that this morning at 9:15 a.m. UAE time, a woman in housekeeping at the Royal Phoenician Hotel found a possible piece of additional evidence in the investigation into the murder of Alex Sokolov.

ILMA BAQRI, a part of the hotel housekeeping staff, was vacuuming on the northeast corridor of the fifth floor. When she moved the round couch there, she saw on the floor behind it a lipstick tube and a lip balm with the logo for CASSANDRA BOWDEN'S airline. It is the sort that is included in the first-class amenity kits.

Without a DNA sample or fingerprints, we cannot determine if either item belonged to CASSANDRA BOWDEN, but the Dubai Police have retained both items.

22

Cassie wasn't averse to chaos when she was drunk; even sober, she knew, she was eminently capable of mind-numbingly bad decisions. Exhibit A? Friday afternoon at Federal Plaza with the FBI. But she realized that she couldn't possibly reach Miranda while the other woman was in the queue at passport control. Crossing back past security wasn't merely swimming against the tide: it was swimming into a wall of steel and glass cubicles, slender corridors, and armed women and men whose job was to spot (and stop) possible terrorists. Though she wanted—and she wanted desperately—to charge into the throng and then fight and claw her way through the crowd to Miranda, she didn't dare. She'd be detained, perhaps even arrested, before she had gotten anywhere close to the woman. But she was almost visibly shaking, she was so agitated. And so she kept her eyes on Miranda and said to Makayla, "Can you ask the crew to stop for a minute? Just wait for me? And can you watch my suitcase?"

"What's going on?" she asked.

"I know someone in passport control: line six. I have to talk to her."

She wondered briefly about the eyeglasses she had spotted Miranda putting into her purse, because Miranda hadn't been wearing them when they had met in Sokolov's hotel room in Dubai. But perhaps she didn't wear contact lenses on overnight flights so she could sleep. Or they were reading glasses. Didn't matter. Cassie speculated that the woman wasn't wearing eyeglasses in her passport photo, and so she didn't want to be wearing them now when the security officer looked up at her and did the obligatory compare-and-contrast with the thumbnail image in her navy blue book.

If it was a navy blue book. For all she knew, it was red or black or green. She realized she had presumed the woman was a regular American with a regular passport. Maybe not. Maybe she wasn't American. Or maybe she was, but she had some sort of diplomatic stature.

"Who?"

It would have taken too long to explain to Makayla specifically who the passenger was, and so Cassie answered simply, "Someone from Dubai. Someone who's part of the shitstorm that's my life right now." All she had to do was say the word *Dubai* and she guessed that everyone in the flight crew would have a pretty solid inkling of what she was talking about. Adding shitstorm had been a reflex, an uncharacteristic flicker of self-pity. But it was also unnecessary: they all had their theories about what might or might not have occurred in Dubai—what she might or might not have done—and if only out of a gawker's curiosity they were not about to desert her right now.

She watched the woman stand before the passport officer, watched him stamp her passport (though the color remained a mystery), and then she raced to the end of the funnel where the passengers exited into baggage, frustrated that it meant taking her eyes off Miranda. But she hadn't a choice: she couldn't risk allowing her to disappear into the hordes of travelers who weren't slowed by lines or checked bags. All her postflight exhaustion was gone, her eyes were alert, and she didn't worry about what she would say or what she would ask. Because she knew. She knew.

While she waited, she sent Ani a text telling her that she understood she was sound asleep in New York, but she was about to confront Miranda at Fiumicino. She was going to ask her who Alex Sokolov really was and who she really was, since the woman sure as hell didn't work for his hedge fund. A part of Cassie understood well that she was playing with fire: if Miranda had killed Alex, who knows what she might do if she felt cornered. But Cassie was ready. She told herself the woman was likely unarmed because she had just disembarked from a transcontinental flight; even if, somehow, she had snuck a weapon onto the aircraft, how could she possibly attack her amidst the baggage carousels in a crowded—packed—international airport?

But the seconds went by, and she didn't emerge. The people kept coming, an endless, steady stream, and there was no sign of Miranda. Cassie considered whether she might have missed her while she was texting, but she didn't believe that. She had only looked down at her phone for milliseconds at a time; she'd always been watching. She craned her neck to see back toward passport control, but there was no sign of her. She scanned the area for a ladies' room where she might have gone, but there wasn't one between security and baggage. There was only one behind her.

Then, however, she saw the bag—that beautiful calfskin leather duffel. It was over the shoulder of a woman who had indeed walked right past her, a woman with blond hair and sunglasses and a wide-brimmed straw sun hat who was already beyond the first baggage carousels. Cassie once more scanned the exit from passport control, and when she didn't see Miranda, she made a decision. She turned and ran after the woman in the sun hat, well aware that she must have looked like a madwoman, but no longer caring.

Cassie reached her well before the passenger had exited. She grabbed her from behind, taking her shoulder and spinning her around to face her. She couldn't see the woman's eyes behind her sunglasses and what she could see of her hair beneath her hat was so much lighter than Miranda's. She couldn't decide if it really was her or not. She tried to recall whether this was the same blouse—white and a little baggy—that Miranda had been wearing a few minutes ago while in line, but it was so drab and nondescript that Cassie wasn't sure.

The woman looked past her, offering not the slightest hint of recognition.

"It is you, isn't it?" Cassie asked, pleading, and though she hadn't shouted, she had the sense that if anyone were listening they would think she was hysterical.

"Pardon me? Have we met?" The tone was light and unflappable. Had Cassie heard it before? Maybe. Maybe not.

"You're Miranda, aren't you? You have to come with me to the police."

"I'm sorry, but my name isn't Miranda. Is there something I can do to help you?" she asked.

"Dubai! Room five-eleven at the Royal Phoenician!" Cassie insisted, her voice almost a wail.

"I don't know what any of that means," she replied. "I've never been to Dubai."

So Cassie shook the woman, not because she still believed that it was Miranda but because she understood that it wasn't. It wasn't. Either she'd never actually seen Miranda or she'd gotten away, and Cassie feared in her heart that it was the former. In her despair, she was more violent with this stranger than she had intended— she was even about to reach for the brim of the woman's hat and whip it aside, one last pathetic gesture, one last hope—when she saw someone else from the corner of her eye, another passenger, and this person was turning a small red tube of lipstick toward her. And even before Cassie could respond, she knew what was going to happen. What was happening already. She felt the spray on her face, the sting more excruciating than a sunburn, and though she had closed her eyes and brought her hands to her face, instantly her eyes were running and her nose was a melting glacier and every breath was a raspy, asthmatic wheeze or a cough. She collapsed to her knees, she used the kerchief around her neck to wipe her face. She tried to call out, to speak, to apologize. Instead she was aware of someone standing over her as if she were a vanquished pro wrestler, and sensed it was the Good Samaritan who had pepper-sprayed her. The passenger was calling out for help, and Cassie heard people running—the tile floor was vibrating beneath her—and then the woman with the pepper spray was pulled away from her.

"She was attacking that lady, I saw it," she was explaining in English, her accent vaguely Boston. Cassie heard Italian, too, police officers, and then she felt hands on her shoulders and rubbing her back, and somewhere very far away she heard Makayla's voice and Brandon the cabin service director's voice, and they were saying something about bringing her to a bathroom right now and irrigating her eyes and finding the airport infirmary. But the police—no, they were actually soldiers—were going to have none of that. They had other plans for her.

"Please, tell her I'm sorry," Cassie begged, "please," but it was already too late. She opened her eyes, despite the pain, and the woman in the sunglasses and the sun hat was nowhere in sight. She'd vanished. And with a pang of despair Cassie realized that if the encounter had been caught on a security camera, it would look like a crazed flight attendant—the one who may have nearly decapitated a young American in Dubai—had attacked a traveler in sunglasses and an elegant straw hat as she emerged from passport control, and someone with a vial of pepper spray in a lipstick tube had come to the poor woman's defense.

« «

Makayla stayed with Cassie, but the rest of the crew went ahead and took the van into Rome. At one point when the dust had settled and Cassie was still kneeling on the floor of the baggage section, she had looked up and through watering, searing eyes seen three tall, trim men in camo fatigues and flak jackets, each with an assault rifle—Italian soldiers—standing like a phalanx around her, and she was reminded of the three-column sculpture outside the FBI building in lower Manhattan. The Sentinel. Then she had blinked shut her eyes and felt Makayla putting her arms around her and asking her if she was capable of walking. She said she was.

Tenderly the other flight attendant helped her to her feet, her arms around Cassie's waist.

Someone had already escorted the Boston woman somewhere else. They had thanked her and said now they needed to get a statement from her. She was, Cassie knew, going to tell the story of her remarkable heroism on her first day in Italy for the rest of her life to anyone who would listen. Cassie hated her.

Makayla and one of the soldiers brought Cassie first to an infirmary, where a nurse with rugged scruff along his cheeks and chin and breath that oozed peppermint numbed her eyes with anesthetic drops and then irrigated them until he believed that the worst of the spray was gone. He washed her face with a solution that he said was actually very much like watered-down dish detergent, and then gave her a skin cream to apply in the evening. One of the soldiers who had brought her there had remained, occasionally speaking to his superiors in Italian on his radio, at one point taking her passport and making a photocopy before returning it to her. When the nurse was done, the soldier escorted her and Makayla to a windowless conference room where they were met by a pair of men in crisp suits and brilliant white shirts. They worked for airport security and offered her water (which she accepted) and coffee (which she declined). If her throat weren't so sore, she might have asked for anything alcoholic and strong. Then they asked Makayla to wait outside while they sat Cassie down in the middle of a long conference table. They both sat opposite her, and one had a laptop open beside him. She couldn't recall their last names, but she remembered that the taller fellow with the meticulously shaved and tanned head—the one who was apparently in charge—was Marco. The other fellow, who seemed to be responsible for the laptop, might have been named Tommaso.

"Please, tell us exactly what happened," Marco was saying. His English was excellent, though his accent was thick. "There were passengers in the area who feared that some sort of attack was in progress—a terrorist attack. One said she expected explosions and gunfire. Another Amsterdam. Another Istanbul."

Cassie had felt the adrenaline draining like water from an unstoppered tub as the nurse had treated her for the pepper spray, and now she wanted nothing more than to go to the airline's hotel and sleep. She had been awake roughly twenty-four hours and the result was the sort of bedlam that she wrought usually when she was drunk—not sober. But she was also anxious to talk to Ani and tell her what had happened. There were three points that she wanted to make: She had seen a woman with an uncanny resemblance to Miranda in passport control, and the woman had vanished before exiting into baggage. She had spotted a second woman with the same carry-on duffel near the luggage carousels, and she had also looked a bit like Miranda, but with different-colored hair. Then she had accosted that second woman by mistake—and wound up pepper-sprayed by a third.

She was not quite ready to admit that she had not seen Miranda at the airport. She thought it unlikely that she had, but a small part of her still believed (or at least tried to believe) that she had indeed spotted her and the woman had managed to disappear. It was that same part of her that had the distinct sense she had been tailed in Manhattan and someone was watching her. And so she wanted to learn if there was any way that Ani could check the passenger manifests of the flights that morning into Fiumicino and see if there was a traveler with that name on a plane. She also wanted to ask Ani this: if it was Miranda, why would she be here? It couldn't be a coincidence. It had to mean that the woman had followed her to Rome.

She tried to recall details of Miranda's face from her visit to Alex's hotel suite—her eyes, her lips, the way she was wearing her hair—piecing them together with the person she had glimpsed that morning in the passport queue. The truth was, she had already been well beyond blitzed by the time she had met Miranda in Dubai. How accurate was her memory, really? And now she had just accosted some poor, innocent woman who simply had a passing resemblance to the individual she'd met one time in circumstances that were (as they frequently were in her life) clouded by alcohol. Meanwhile, it was possible that the actual woman had eluded her and gotten away.

"Late last month," she began, "I spent the night in Dubai with a man I had met on an airplane earlier that day. I was in his hotel room. After I left the next morning to catch my flight to Paris, someone murdered him. And that woman I was trying to talk to in baggage . . . she reminded me of someone who had come to his hotel room the night before."

Marco raised an eyebrow: "She spent the night, too, so it was the three of you?"

"No. Not at all. She just came by for a drink. Then she left."

"What's her name?" he asked.

"I don't know her last name. But she said in Dubai that her first name was Miranda."

"And you attacked a passenger this morning because you thought it was her?"

"I didn't attack anyone. That woman with the pepper spray overreacted and attacked me."

Marco and Tommaso exchanged a glance, and instantly she felt judged. Tommaso looked at something on his laptop. "I will rephrase," said Marco. "And so you approached a passenger this morning because you thought it was her?"

"Yes."

"Why?"

"I was trying to stop her."

"Stop her from what?" Marco inquired.

"From getting away. She—"

Marco put one hand up, palm flat, quieting her. "Please," he said firmly. Then he leaned forward and clasped his hands together on the table. "Please, let's start again. If you don't mind, let's go back to the beginning. To Dubai."

"Do I need to call the American embassy? Do I need a lawyer?"

"Why? We're not arresting you. The woman who you . . .

approached . . . isn't even here. She's probably left by now. She's probably begun her vacation here in Italy."

"She left?"

"Yes."

Again Cassie felt a surge, as if she had just pressed her foot down hard on the treadle that powered her angst. The fact the woman had fled meant something. Wouldn't a normal person have stayed? "Can you find her?"

"I doubt it."

"Will you try? Maybe use the security camera footage and the witness descriptions? You must have both."

"Her back was to the camera in that section. It's not as well lit as we'd like. And she was wearing a beautiful hat and sunglasses. We can't even say for sure what color her hair was."

"It was blond."

"Fine. You think it was blond."

"And you have witnesses. God, you have that nut ball with the pepper spray!" she said, and she heard a quiver in her voice. She knew that sound: it was exhaustion and frustration mixing rather toxically together. She considered adding, *illegal pepper spray,* because pepper spray—especially one disguised as a lipstick—wasn't allowed in a carry-on bag.

"We do," he answered. "And they—including the American with the pepper spray—can describe you beautifully. And, yes, they can describe the way you threw yourself on the lady."

"I didn't throw myself on her."

Again the two men glanced at each other. She realized that while they weren't going to arrest her, neither were they going to help her.

"Can we go back to Dubai?" Marco asked. "Tell us about that night."

"I think I should just go."

"We want to understand what happened."

"Then call the U.S. embassy or let me call them. I'm too

tired to talk to you right now without someone from the embassy with me."

"It will take at least an hour—maybe more—for them to get here. And that assumes someone is available. I'm sure you don't want to wait that long."

"Then I'm just going to leave, thank you very much. You said you're not arresting me."

"No." There was a long beat, and then Marco lifted from the table a photocopy of her passport and waved it almost dismissively. "But we know exactly who you are, Ms. Bowden. Interpol knows exactly who you are."

"Then why did you waste my time asking me about Dubai?" she snapped. "I'm exhausted, and I was just attacked!"

"When people are exhausted, they are often the most cooperative. The most talkative."

"So, what's next? Waterboarding?"

He shrugged. "Your country does that. Not mine."

"I'm leaving."

"As you wish," he said. He asked her for the name of the hotel where she was staying and her cell phone number, which he wrote down on the copy of her passport. Tommaso typed it into the laptop.

"How long will you be in Rome?" he asked.

"Until tomorrow. Late morning."

"Flight two-ten to JFK, right?"

"Right."

He nodded a little smugly. "I know your airline's schedule well. I know most airlines' schedules well." Then he stood and Tommaso stood, and so she rose from her chair as well. "We'll call you today if we need to talk to you again. But Ms. Bowden?"

"Yes?"

"Please, for your own sake, don't attack—pardon me, approach—strange women while you're here." He was smiling, but there was a cloying, ominous lilt to his voice, and she felt his words were more threat than advice.

23

Airports fascinated Elena because of the way everyone was wired when they were there. Everyone was amped. There were the passengers who were nervous and tense, stressed because they were worried—and this was the anxiety spectrum—about their connections or they were white-knuckle flyers or they were on high alert for the heat and light and the eardrum-shattering thunder from a terrorist bomb. There were the more frequent flyers who were fretting about connections or upgrades, and those who were annoyed by the inconveniences of clear plastic three-one-one bags and metal detectors and having to step from their wingtips and sneakers. (Her own frustration? She was always piqued by the idiots who put their filthy shoes in the bins with their coats and bags. She cringed when she'd have to layer a cashmere sweater into a plastic tray that a moment ago had been cheek-to-cheek with soles that regularly stood before urinals.)

Elena had slipped the straw hat back into her duffel even before she had exited baggage. She considered ducking into the ladies' room and pulling on a different wig, but she knew that Bowden wasn't going to be leaving the airport anytime soon. There was nothing more to worry about.

The irony that the flight attendant had spotted her in passport control in Rome was not lost on her. Viktor was certain to say something. He might do more than that. Far more. And yet the possibility of running into Bowden was what had led her to fly out of Newark instead of JFK in the first place.

On the other hand, it was an unexpected little gift that Bowden had seen her and attacked her. And then there was the good fortune that some vigilante from Massachusetts had come to her aid. Elena had been ready with her own pepper spray, but she hadn't needed it. She'd slipped what looked like an elegant Italian fountain pen discreetly back into her purse after Bowden had collapsed to her knees, her hands on her face.

She paused when she caught a whiff of jet fuel as she stood in line outside for a cab. She hated the smell of jet fuel. It nauseated her. But she shook it off because it was sunny and the encounter in baggage was a rather good thing. A rather good thing indeed. She would definitely tell Viktor that. As far as the gaping world was concerned, it was all further proof that the flight attendant was completely unhinged. The cause and effect was clear: Bowden murders Sokolov in Dubai. She is outed by the *New York Post*. She lunges at a strange woman in Fiumicino. Tomorrow morning when her body was found in Rome, everyone would think it was eminently likely—it was downright predictable—that the flight attendant had killed herself.

Assuming, of course, that she went ahead with the plan. First, however, she wanted to understand precisely what this brother-in-law did at the Blue Grass Army Depot and how much Sokolov could have picked up online. She knew what she herself could learn—easily, one call and then one call back—but she had to know what *he* could have learned. That was different. She also wanted to dive into onionland and her dark assets online to see if her instincts about Bowden, her brother-in-law Dennis McCauley, and the courier were correct. Then she had to have a consult with her handler. She knew she couldn't stall very much longer. They knew that, too. She wondered what the next twelve hours would bring. Or, for that matter, the next twenty-four. Either they brought her in or Bowden was dead. It all depended on how badly they wanted to know about Viktor Olenin and his dreams of drones and poison gas.

24

Makayla told Cassie that she was thirty-six while they were seated in the backseat of the small cab into Rome. She and her husband, an ad executive, had a five-year-old daughter who was about to start kindergarten. They lived in Douglaston, Queens, and her in-laws lived nearby, which was a godsend when it came to childcare. She talked and talked, asking almost no questions, which was perfect, because the cab was stifling in the mid-day August heat and Cassie wanted only to listen. She might even have fallen asleep if, once they were inside the Rome traffic ring, the cab hadn't been stopping and starting with unpredictable (and incessant) violence. But Makayla's voice was low and kind, and Cassie imagined that voice reading aloud to her daughter those nights when she wasn't flying to Frankfurt or Rome.

God, Cassie thought, what must it be like to have a daughter? To have children? One time she saw a quote written in blue and yellow chalk on a blackboard outside a clothing shop in the West Village: "Remember that person you wanted to be? There's still time." She wanted to believe that; she wanted to believe it almost desperately. She wanted to be different from what she was—to be anything but what she was. But every day that grew less and less likely. Life, it seemed to her in the back of the cab, was nothing but a narrowing of opportunities. It was a funnel.

"Here's our hotel," Makayla was saying, and before Cassie could reach for her wallet inside her purse, the other flight attendant had paid for the ride.

"Please, let me pay you back," she said. She knew they were staying at the same hotel where the airline had booked them last week, but it still caused her to sigh in frustration when she looked up at the entrance. She thought instantly of how she would have to avoid Enrico. He would see the other crew members in their iconic black and blue and red uniforms and speculate that she was in the hotel, too.

"Not a big deal," said Makayla. "You can buy me a drink tonight. How's that?"

Cassie smiled at the suggestion. The fact that for Makayla alcohol was nothing more than a shorthand for friendship and camaraderie wasn't lost on her. It was for so much of the world. "Okay," she said and hoped that if they did have that drink, the gods would be kind to her and today would be Enrico's day off. The driver lifted their two suitcases from the back of the cab. "Thank you," she said to Makayla. "I mean that. Thank you for everything."

"You're welcome—though I really didn't do anything. Now, you should go get some sleep. I can certainly use a nap."

Cassie nodded and watched a bellman carry her suitcase up half a dozen marble steps and then roll it to the reception desk. She would sleep. But first she would call her lawyer back in New York. It was almost seven a.m. on the East Coast. Ani would most likely be up.

《   《

"You saw her?" It was a question, but Cassie could hear the shock and incredulity in Ani's voice over the phone.

"Maybe," Cassie said. "I'm torn. I thought I did. I was sure at the time I did. But the more I think back on the moment, the more it seems possible I was mistaken. Maybe this is just one more example of the way I'm losing my mind. It's just getting harder and harder to keep it together. That may scare me as much as anything right now." She was perched in the desk chair in her hotel room, one leg underneath her. She feared that if she sat on the bed, she would lie down and fall asleep midconversation. Maybe she'd never get up. She was on a different floor from last week but on the same side of the building, and once more she could see the towers of the Trinità dei Monti outside her window.

"Tell me exactly what happened," Ani demanded, and so Cassie did, including her interview with Fiumicino's airport security.

"Did you just yawn?" Ani asked when she had finished.

"I'm exhausted."

"I get it. But you must realize that going after some poor woman in baggage is exactly the sort of thing that gives the airline a reason to put you on a leave of absence. Today's *New York Post*? Nah. They won't ground the Cart Tart Killer—that's just alleged craziness—but they will ground a flight attendant who is demonstrably unstable in baggage at a major international airport."

The magnitude of that sentence caused Cassie to nod, even though she was alone in the room. "That has crossed my mind," she admitted.

"And obviously you have given the prosecution, when they get around to you, a little more fodder. This is a thousand times worse than calling Sokolov's family in Virginia on Saturday night."

"I know."

"And yet you went up to this lady in the airport just because she had the same duffel bag as the person you saw in line? What did you think, she'd put on a disguise?"

"Yes. Maybe. I don't know. I was just so frustrated that the woman I thought was Miranda was suddenly gone."

"God. I really am worried about you. You are completely out of control."

"I know. I'm a little scared, Ani. I'm scared I'm not thinking straight anymore, even when I'm sober. I mean, I thought I was being followed in New York."

"What?"

"Twice I saw a guy with a black ball cap on the street behind me. He was wearing sunglasses. Another time I was sure he was there."

"But you didn't see him?"

"Not the third time. That's my point. I think I'm losing it."

"Maybe you are. But maybe not. I wouldn't be surprised if the FBI has someone watching you."

"So I'm not crazy?"

"Oh, you are crazy, Cassie. You're an absolute mess. But that doesn't mean you're not being followed. Please view the pepper spray as a wake-up call. A warning. I'm sorry it happened. I really am because I hate to think of your discomfort. But I'm also a little grateful that someone dialed you down before you did something absolutely insane."

"I would never have hurt her. I'm not violent." At least I'm not yet, she thought. "Grabbing her was a reflex."

"Are you still in pain? Uncomfortable?"

Cassie had been careful to avoid the large mirror in the hotel room. She didn't want to see how blotchy her face most likely was. She feared her eyes were still vampire red. The nurse told her she would look much better by dinner. She hoped so. "Not really. But I'm wondering if you or your private investigator can do something for me."

"Go on."

"Can you check the passenger manifests of the planes that arrived in Rome this morning? Can we find out if there was a woman named Miranda on one?"

"I thought you believed you were mistaken."

"I said I'm torn. I seem to go back and forth."

"Well, I can't find that out," said Ani, "but I'll ask my P.I. I doubt he can, either. That kind of sounds like a job for the FBI."

"Okay," Cassie said, though her lawyer's response frightened her. "Has he told you anything more about Alex's background?"

"No. I'll call him after we hang up."

"Thank you. Oh—and I'm sorry I didn't say this right away— thanks also for the way you handled that reporter from the *New York Post*. I really appreciate it."

"I know you do. Trust me, so does my boss," Ani said wryly. Then she asked, "What are you doing this afternoon? And tonight?"

"Worried I'm going to try and find Miranda myself?"

"No."

"But you do believe she exists, right? I mean, maybe she's not in Rome. Maybe I didn't see her. But she is out there somewhere."

Even across the Atlantic Cassie could hear the brief hesitation. "Most of the time I believe that. I really do. But your browbeating a strange woman in an airport doesn't inspire a whole lot of confidence in your mental health."

"I know. I'm sorry."

"Maybe you should just chill. What do you think? Don't go out to dinner. Don't go sightseeing. And for God's sake, don't have a drink. Pretend you're under house arrest."

It may have been the word *arrest,* but she thought of the two FBI agents back at Federal Plaza. Was there no ceiling to the trouble she caused? To the trouble she was in?

"And Cassie?"

She waited.

"Just in case, do yourself a favor: dead-bolt your door tonight."

« «

She didn't sleep nearly as long as she expected. Her body clock was too well conditioned, too predictable, and so she awoke from her catnap around three in the afternoon. She climbed naked from the bed and opened the drapes to the summer sun, and then burrowed back under the sheets on the cool side of the bed. For a while she stared out the window at the blue sky, and then at the walls of her hotel room. At the large, framed black-and-white photograph of the Pietà at St. Peter's. At the television. At the armoire. On the desk she had noticed a pencil cup with a single pen in it with the hotel's name. The pen was crap, but she liked the container. It was designed to resemble an architectural ruin—a remnant of the sort of granite column that held the great portico of the Pantheon. (The columns were Corinthian, she recalled from one visit to Rome or another.) She thought she would steal the pencil cup, probably as a gift for her nephew, but maybe for her brother-in-law instead. It would probably look nice on his desk.

No, she wouldn't take it. She would exert a little self-control. She had been in this hotel just last week and pilfered the bookend. Perhaps housekeeping had noticed it was gone right after she had checked out and her name was now on some sort of hotel watch list. It would be yet one more example of the cruel humor that marked the world if, after all she had drunk over the years, she ended up getting fired by the airline for stealing trinkets from a hotel room in Italy.

Of course, that was the one constant in her life: she drank. Alcohol gave her pleasure and it gave her courage and it gave her comfort. It didn't precisely give her self-esteem (especially not the next morning), but it gave her the faith that whatever she was, was enough. She was no longer the daughter of the driver's-ed drunk in Kentucky. She was no longer the girl alone at the college switchboard at the loneliest hours of the night. Yes, she went days without drinking, but those were mere intermissions between acts. Between acting up. Between the moments when she was most really herself.

And, she knew, those days were growing less and less frequent.

She checked her phone. Nothing from Ani. Nothing from Frank Hammond. Nothing from the airline. Nothing from anyone. That was probably good news.

Finally she swung her legs over the side of the bed and ran her hands through her hair. Fuck it. Perhaps Ani was right that she should dead-bolt the door and pretend she was under house arrest, but she was who she was. She knew as well as anyone that people didn't change. Just look at her father. The lure of the Limoncello—the Negroni, the Bellini, the Rossini, the Cardinale—was irresistible. She would shower. She would put on the cheerful floral sundress she had packed. Then she would apply her makeup and the skin cream the airport nurse had given her and go for a walk. Find a bar where (and the theme from a sitcom from before her time came to her) nobody knew her name.

« «

She saw the note under her door when she emerged from the bathroom. She had just toweled herself dry and was about to get dressed. It was from Enrico, the young bartender, and it was apparent that he spoke English better than he wrote it, and was probably dependent on Google Translate. He had indeed seen the other members of her airline's flight crew at the hotel, and so he had asked a friend in guest services if she was among them. Then he had convinced his pal to look up her room number. He hoped she would view this as "enterprised," not "stalker." He had found someone to cover his shift and was "desirable" of taking her for a walk and to dinner. The note was adorable.

But she thought of Buckley back in New York. Arguably, her relationship with the actor had grown more involved in the last week. They'd slept together again, and it had been more of a date than a random hookup in a bar. Their relationship was, as her Drambuie friend Paula would say, Tinder Plus—the gray zone that was more than Tinder but not yet dating. She and Buckley might not yet be exclusive, but they had a connection that transcended libido and booze and an app for sex with strangers.

Moreover, was there even the remotest possibility of a future with Enrico, given the difference in their ages? Of course there wasn't. But then again, did she have a future with anyone? Of course she didn't. Her future, eventually, was in prison. She looked at the penmanship on the paper in her hands. It was hotel stationery. The ink was blue, and Enrico wrote with careful, thoughtful strokes. He had written that he would be waiting downstairs in the bar, and he could leave with her anytime and go anyplace she liked.

She had no idea where she'd be a year from now—or even a week or a month.

For all she knew, she hadn't heard from Buckley because he had read the *New York Post* and was justifiably appalled. He wanted nothing to do with her. And why should he? God, most of the time she wanted nothing to do with herself. That, too, was one of the reasons why she took solace in the blotto zone. It was just so much easier to look at yourself in the mirror when it took that critical extra second for your eyes to focus and in the morning you wouldn't remember just how awful you looked or how ridiculously you had behaved.

As she was reaching behind her to clasp her bra, she glanced out the window and gazed for a moment at the beauty of the towers of the Trinità dei Monti. She was in Rome, the city where Nero had supposedly fiddled as the buildings around him had burned. She had no idea if it was true. She didn't know if violins even existed in the first century. No matter. She got the point. When in Rome . . .

She'd go downstairs and fiddle.

《 《

As she expected, Enrico was at the bar. But he wasn't working. He was seated on a stool before the beautifully burnished mahogany slab. He was at the near end, across from the hidden sink and the impeccable row of shakers and jiggers and stirrers and spears. He was chatting with a petite young woman in the hotel's requisite white button-down shirt and blue vest, her hair a magnificent dusky mane. She was the bartender on duty. Cassie guessed she was in her early twenties. The world, she thought, was just so young. The bar wasn't deserted this time, because it was nearing late afternoon. But the guests—and she counted a dozen or so people—were at the tables, not that long, inviting counter.

Enrico noticed her right away, as if he had an eye on the entrance, and stood to greet her. He, too, was wearing a white shirt, but he had slithered inside a pair of tight jeans instead of the dressier black pants he had been wearing last week. He was gorgeous. She wondered if as soon as she'd had a drink—oh, maybe two or three or four—she would bring him upstairs to her room.

"I was afraid I wouldn't see you," he said, wrapping his arms around the small of her back and pulling her into him. He kissed both of her cheeks and then leaned back a little, appraising her. She felt the warmth from his fingers through the thin rayon of her dress. "You got more beautiful in the last week."

"I didn't. But I did get a week older."

"And you were outside without sunscreen. Shame on you!"

She nodded sheepishly. It was easier to nod than explain she had been pepper-sprayed at the airport that morning.

"But that dress is perfect on you," he continued.

"I'm probably too old for it."

He released her and smiled. He motioned at the woman behind the bar, who was making Bellinis for a table of Brits in the corner. She had pureed fresh peaches for the drink and the Prosecco looked very good. "This is Sofia. She makes an excellent Negroni, too. I taught her myself. But let me make yours."

She watched Sofia place the flutes on a tray and bring them to the guests' table. When she was silent, Enrico asked, "Is it a Bellini kind of day? Would you prefer that to a Negroni?"

She met his eyes. Yes, she wanted a Bellini. She wanted him. She wanted to get lost in the booze and wrap her naked thighs around his naked ass and feel him inside her. She wanted to forget Alex Sokolov and Frank Hammond and the woman she had thought was Miranda. This was a new thing, this drinking to forget. Usually she just drank to get lost, which may have been a cousin in some way, but was most definitely different.

She heard the chime from her phone that informed her she had a new text.

"Sorry," she told Enrico. "I should see what that's about." She reached into her purse and pulled out the device. The text was from Ani, and the lawyer was asking her to call back right away. Cassie took a long, slow breath to calm herself. She heard a slight ringing in her ears and felt her heart starting to race. "I need to phone my sister," she said to the bartender.

"You look worried. Is everything okay?"

She watched the Brits raising their champagne flutes with their Bellinis and clinking them gently together. My life, she thought, is all hunger. Hunger and want and need. "I guess we'll find out," she answered, and she took her phone and retreated into the anonymity of the hotel lobby.

25

Elena got a spray tan at a salon across the street from Bulgari and Gucci, and she instructed the attendant to think Saint-Tropez. She wanted to look like an old Bain de Soleil ad. Then she went by a pharmacy—choosing one far down the Via Sistina from both her hotel and Bowden's—and bought a pair of plastic gloves and a shade of hair color that was called "natural blue black."

Back in her room, she meticulously worked the dye into her hair and set the timer on her phone for forty-five minutes. She had no gray yet, not a single strand, but she wanted to be sure that the color was solid. She thought she might enjoy having hair the shade of ravens' wings for the rest of the summer and the beginning of autumn.

As she waited, she sat on her bed and used the encrypted network on her laptop to dig deep into Dennis McCauley. See if there was anything new. Anything they'd been unable to tell her. She went underground, hacking into his life through a variety of dark sites she accessed through the Lewis Carroll–like looking glass of RATs and rootkits the Cossacks preferred. She looked at the meetings on his calendar that week at the military base in Kentucky and the one the next week at the Edgewood Chemical Biological Center in Maryland. She noted his predilections in porn, which were far more conventional than a lot of guys in the military or the male defense contractors she had dealt with, and she saw that his fantasy baseball team had done especially well that week. She scanned his family's bank and investment accounts.

But she could find no indication that he was a Cossack asset or that he was getting rich selling them what he knew.

She thought once more of her revelation on the plane last night, the idea that for so long she had had the Dubai seduction backward: she had been assuming that Cassandra Bowden had picked up Sokolov on the flight to the Emirates, when it was quite probably the other way around.

God, he'd been such a rank amateur. He was up against people who'd grown up in a culture in which paranoia was a survival skill.

After she'd killed him, she'd switched flash drives, giving Viktor one with dramatically dumbed-down data. It had specs on the stealth drone, but nothing that Russia probably wouldn't have on its own or through NovaSkies within months. It was, they hoped, just enough to satisfy Viktor. They were wrong. Then she'd left the evidence that Sokolov was stealing from the fund on his laptop. No one could miss it. The CIA would know why he was dead, and eventually National Intelligence would share what they knew with the FBI. But the Dubai police would just see it as Russian business—cold-blooded and unflinching—as usual. The price for a regular hit when a deal went bad was pennies. Her father had once paid an underling a measly fifteen-grand bonus to execute a commodities trader who had tried (and failed) to bilk him out of the steel he'd bought from a Lipetsk mill. Another time, he'd paid a pittance—five thousand dollars—to have some poor British contracts manager in Donetsk killed when his bosses back in London had refused to renegotiate a contract. (They did after that. Right away.) The American agencies weren't thrilled that Sokolov was dead, but he wasn't an especially good egg, and no one wanted to see him on trial. He knew too much. Mostly they were just grateful that no one's cover had been burned. It was weirdly polite. It also wouldn't demand a public escalation, which nobody wanted.

She logged off her computer and tried to slip into place the last pieces of the jigsaw puzzle, but there were too many and she was too tired. And so she willed herself to relax. She thumbed through the Italian and British fashion magazines she had bought at a kiosk on the street and read news stories on her tablet. But she kept coming back to the flight attendant and what she was supposed to do and what she had planned to do. There were just so very many ways to kill yourself. There were pills and there was bleeding out in the bath. There was falling from great heights and falling into oceans or rivers or deep, beautiful chasms. There were streetcars and subways and buses. There was hanging. There were guns—just so many kinds of guns.

She considered it likely that an absolute train wreck such as Cassandra Bowden might have one last surprise for her. If she had to bet, she would bet on the bartender; after all, he combined Bowden's two principal interests in one tidy package. That, of course, would be a disaster. The last thing she wanted was him, too, on her conscience. Unfortunately, a murder-suicide involving Cassandra Bowden and some Italian hookup would look just as plausible to the world as a suicide, and it was possible that they might ask this of her.

She had promised herself a few days alone in Sochi when she was done, though of course she would not be completely alone. No doubt, some of her father's old friends would come by. There would be someone who was long out of the loop and didn't know how badly she had screwed up with the flight attendant. Maybe it would be someone who knew only that Sokolov was dead and wanted to thank her. It was pretty simple: you went for the jugular. It was—to use their old joke—cut and dried.

But she'd have plenty of time to watch the bears from the porch and listen to the owls as she dozed beneath the pergola. She would try to regain her emotional equilibrium after Diyarbakir and Dubai and now Rome.

She sat back against the headboard and closed her eyes, savoring the air conditioning in her hotel room but agitated because of all the things that she didn't know and all the things it was possible they had chosen not to tell her.

26

In the hotel lobby, Cassie took a seat on a plush, ruby-red Renaissance fainting couch, perching herself on the end that was backless. She smiled at the concierge. She smiled at the handsome guy in the dark suit and earpiece who was clearly hotel security.

"So, are you in your room?" Ani was asking.

"Yes," she lied.

"Good. I'm sure there are reporters ferreting out from the airline where you are. Someone will find your hotel. That's another good reason to lay low."

"Really? The crime occurred in Dubai, not Perugia or Rome. Why would an Italian reporter care?"

"Why would any reporter care? Sex and murder."

"Oh. Of course."

"I heard back from my investigator."

"About the passenger manifests?"

"No. He doubts he can get us much there. But he has done some other nosing around."

Cassie listened carefully, trying to focus. "And?"

"Here are a few of the things he learned. Remember what I told you the other day about the sorts of people who invest in that fund?"

"Yes. You said a lot of them are Russian."

"Right. There are a couple on the Treasury Department's OFAC list. Apparently a few are the sort of oligarchs who are just crazy wealthy. Some, he believes, are ex-KGB. Those are guys who made ridiculous amounts of money in the years after the Soviet

Union collapsed. He thinks it's possible that the FBI is investigating Unisphere and that particular fund."

"Because Sokolov was killed?"

"No. In this case, the FBI was already looking into the company because of the investors. Who they are."

"I see."

"But they may have been investigating Sokolov himself. Maybe he was mismanaging the fund: taking a little extra for himself. Or maybe, like I said, it was a Ponzi scheme. Maybe he was only delivering the returns these folks had come to expect by bringing new people into the fund, and he finally went too far."

"Why would the FBI care if he's only stealing from Russians and the money's in the Caribbean?"

"Unisphere is an American company, and Sokolov may have been committing fraud. For all we know, some of the Russian investors live in America and are totally clean."

"And so he thinks it was some Russian thug who killed Alex?"

"Could be," said Ani. "Remember: you mislead those guys or you steal from those guys and you're a dead man."

"The Internet trolls have been saying for days that Alex was a spy. Is that still possible?"

"Yes, very possible. If Sokolov wasn't a crook or playing fast and loose with other people's money, then perhaps he was an embedded operative."

"For us?"

"Or them. If us, Unisphere is his cover because we know who some of the investors are and we know of their connections to the Russian president. If them, Unisphere is his cover because he can live and work easily in the U.S. and then meet without suspicion with these folks. He can be their little messenger boy or—I guess this is the term they use—courier. So that fellow you met in seat two C? He was just as likely one of ours as he was one of theirs. Or maybe he was playing both sides. My guy says that's a possibility, too. Maybe that's how he got himself killed. Nothing's ever really black or white, is it? Maybe he was just a little nasty."

Cassie thought about this, about the man she had slept with in Dubai. "But Ani? He didn't seem like a crook or a nasty guy. I've met my share of—forgive me—pricks, and he didn't seem like one."

"Well, if you're stealing, you don't want to advertise that now, do you? Same with being a spy. You don't exactly give out business cards with your real occupation."

"I guess not," Cassie agreed.

"Now, Sokolov left behind none of the footprints that scream spook. No Langley, no State Department connections, no friends at embassies."

"But he did have family that originally came from the Soviet Union."

"Yes."

"So maybe it's more likely he was a Russian spy," Cassie murmured.

"Maybe. Now"—Ani paused, clearing her throat—"we do have the full coroner's report from Dubai."

Cassie noticed how her lawyer had halted briefly midsentence, the way she had almost reflexively stalled. "It's bad news, isn't it?"

"No, it's actually pretty good. It really is. But there are also some wrinkles that are curious."

She rested her forehead in her hand and closed her eyes. She waited.

"The body was found at five in the afternoon. The blood was mostly dry. Apparently gastric emptying time is four hours, maybe five because of the alcohol, and his stomach was completely empty. So, he was definitely killed before one in the afternoon, and probably before noon. Probably before lunch. But the room was sixty-five degrees. The body really wasn't—forgive me—bubbling up. It wasn't bloated, and it was just starting to decompose."

She shuddered, unsure whether it was general disgust or sadness at the specificity of Sokolov's mortal deterioration. "This all sounds promising," she said, "though forgive me if I can't get overly excited at the vision of the poor guy's body decomposing in the bed where we slept."

"It is promising. Focus on that. If Dubai wants to prosecute or the Sokolov family wants to go after you in civil court, you can argue convincingly that he was still alive when you left the room. They can't prove otherwise."

"Well, okay then," Cassie said, but she knew the truth. If she needed a defense, like so much else in her life, its foundation would be a lie. She wondered if her voice was as dead in reality as it sounded in her head. She understood all too well why this news hadn't made her happier.

"But here's the thing," Ani continued. "According to the report, this was done—and this is my word, not theirs—professionally. Whoever killed Alex slashed the carotid artery. Knew right where it was. They severed the trachea. He was gone in thirty seconds. I'm sure, Cassie, you are completely capable of killing a person with a knife or broken bottle or even a letter opener while he's asleep, but it would not be so—forgive me—efficient. So surgical. It would not happen so fast. Do you even know where the carotid artery is?"

She stared down at the swirls in the Oriental carpet below her. She saw her toes in her sandals. The pink of the nail polish. "No. I really don't."

"I mean, even if this was one of your worst blackout moments ever and you really did kill the guy, I think it would have been pretty damn messy."

"It was pretty damn messy."

"Let me rephrase that. There would have been punctures and gashes and defense wounds on his hands and his arms, because he would have woken up and fought you. There were none. You would have been plunging that broken bottle into his chest, his face. That didn't happen."

"So you're saying I can be absolutely confident that I didn't kill him?"

"Yes, absolutely. One hundred percent," said Ani.

"Huh."

"You don't sound relieved. You've been saying since the beginning you were convinced you didn't do it. I'd think this informa-tion would make you happier. What's going on?"

"It's just . . ."

"It's just what?"

"It's just surreal, I guess. And the poor man is still dead, and I still left him behind in the bed." Vindication, she thought, was not especially gratifying when everything she did was pathetic. She'd had so little faith in herself that she'd run and she'd lied and she hadn't done a whole lot to help find the person who really had killed the interesting fellow who had washed her hair in the shower, and to her, at least, had only been giving and generous and kind.

"Well, unless the FBI or the Dubai police think you're actu-ally a spy or a paid assassin, I can't imagine you're a serious suspect. Whoever killed him was very well trained. A professional. A hit man. Did you see anyone like that when you were at dinner with Sokolov at the restaurant? In the hotel lobby maybe?"

"I have no idea what a hit man looks like."

"You said he went somewhere between dinner and when he returned to his room. You have no idea where?"

"None."

"The only person you saw him interact with was Miranda?"

"That's right."

"And Miranda doesn't seem to exist," her lawyer said. "The security cameras in the lobby show people using the elevators in the middle of the night. But they all seem to match guests, and they all seem to have reasons for coming or going: an early-morning flight or a late-night party. And none is a single woman matching the description you gave for Miranda."

"What does that mean?"

"I don't know. Maybe she left Alex's room but not the floor. Is that possible?"

"I guess so. It's a huge hotel with at least three wings."

"And multiple elevator banks?"

"I think so," Cassie answered. Then: "Have you heard from the FBI today?"

"No."

"Well, maybe that's good news. Maybe they don't care. Maybe they've decided, just like you, that I didn't kill Alex. Or they're just going to let Dubai take care of it—which, as you've said, could take years. Maybe your investigator's theory is right, and this is all about fraud and angry Russians and I had nothing to do with it. They'll just follow the money."

"That could be. But please don't get your hopes up."

"Why not?"

Enrico had come to the lobby and was leaning against a column, his arms folded across his chest, watching her. He looked concerned. "First of all, it's not even lunchtime here in New York. For all we know, we'll hear from them again in ten minutes. Maybe two hours. Maybe tomorrow. My point? It's early. Besides, this is just how I've interpreted the coroner's report. They may view it very differently."

"And second?"

"Second? The more I think about that report, the less I'm sure the FBI even matters. Whoever killed Alex Sokolov now knows you were in the room after they cut his throat. You were there. You saw the body, and you saw this woman who may or may not be named Miranda. Even if you somehow manage to dodge an FBI bullet, Cassie, you still have to dodge theirs."

》 《

Enrico took her hand, and they started down the street from the hotel toward the Villa Borghese, entering the park by the ancient gates at the Piazzale Brasile. She looked over her shoulder, studying the street for hats: black ball caps and straw sun hats. She was more confident than ever that they were out there. Someone was out there. She could feel it.

It was late enough in the day that they didn't really need the shade from the trees, but still early enough that the vendors remained at work and there were plenty of tourists and locals enjoying the hot, humid August afternoon. Enrico said that he lived with two other young men, including his brother, in an apartment on the far side of the park.

"This is how I get to work," he told her, motioning with his free hand at the pine trees that looked to Cassie more like lollipops and open umbrellas than the pines she could recall from her childhood in Kentucky. "Nice commute, right?"

"It is," she agreed.

"At the villa, there are so many lemon trees. So pretty. It isn't on the way, but sometimes I walk past it anyway. I make a detour."

He had said his apartment was small: the three men used the living room as a makeshift third bedroom, and there was no dining room, really. But it was on the second floor of a four-story building with a shared rooftop terrace, and he told her that the views of the neighborhood at sunset were beautiful. He assured her that his roommates, both waiters, would be gone, which she took to mean he was bringing her to his apartment for a drink on the roof before adjourning downstairs to his bed. Right now she was leaning against allowing him to bring her to either venue.

"May I ask you a question?" she said.

"Of course."

"Do you own a gun?"

He stopped in his tracks and released her hand. He brought his own hand up to her cheek and gently turned her face toward his. "A gun? This is Italy, not America."

"I take it that means no."

"My American grandmother is from Florida, and I follow the news. Why do you ask?"

"Never mind."

"No, please. Tell me. My uncle hunts. Wild boar. Deer. Not very seriously, but he goes to Montisi during the season. He has a *podere*—a little farmhouse—there. But he only lives two blocks from me here in Rome most of the time. His apartment? Much nicer than mine."

She resumed their walk down the path because now she felt

incapable of maintaining eye contact. He walked beside her, his hands behind his back. "I was thinking of a handgun," she said.

"You know you can't carry one in public places here. It's against the law."

"I did not know that."

"Do you have a license for such a thing? Maybe in America?"

"No."

"Have you ever even fired a gun?"

"Yes."

"Really?" He sounded shocked.

"It's been years, but yes. Not a handgun, a rifle. A Remington pump-action. It was my father's. Remember, I grew up in the country. I went hunting with him a couple of times, and I took a hunter safety course for kids."

"Kids?"

"Yes, kids." Then: "Do you think your uncle has a pistol? Or just a hunting rifle?"

"He has a pistol."

A ten- or eleven-year-old boy with wide eyes and a broad smile ran up to her and gave her a magnificent, niveous white rose, one of easily two dozen he held in his arms. She smiled and inhaled the aroma. It still smelled fresh. Enrico handed the child a couple of euros, and the boy ran off. In the distance was a woman with a straw hat, but it wasn't the same hat from the airport and it wasn't the same woman. Then Enrico asked, "Did you ever hit anything?"

"I wounded a deer. It was a bad shot. It took the animal far too long to die."

"Why are you interested in this? Why do you need a gun?"

She shrugged. "I might need a gun. Maybe I don't. I honestly don't know."

"Does this have something to do with that phone call you made to your sister back in the hotel lobby?"

"Yes."

"Tell me."

"You know, I could lie to you, Enrico. I'm a very, very good liar. I lie all the time. I lie to other people, I lie to myself."

"But you're not going to lie to me right now."

She smiled at him. "No. I'm not. But I'm also not going to tell you a whole lot. You could find most of it online. Just Google my name. But Enrico? I have a sense you're better off not knowing."

"I'm a bartender. I make people drinks. I make love to beautiful flight attendants—"

"You mean I'm not the first?" she asked, cutting him off to tease him.

"You are the first and the only."

"You're a pretty good liar, too."

"All I mean is that I have no enemies," he said.

"No, but I do. Or I might."

"Here in Rome?"

"Apparently. Maybe."

"So, you want protection, is that it?"

"Yes."

He put his arm around her shoulder and pulled her into him. "Then I will protect you."

"I'm not sure you can."

"But I will try."

She shook her head. "Nope. The best thing you can do is bring me to your uncle's."

"If he's home, he might not let me have his gun. His Beretta."

"Just for one night?"

"He'd be afraid I would get myself into trouble."

"And if he's not home?"

"You mean I just take it?"

"I mean we just borrow it."

"I have a better idea," said Enrico, his voice mischievous.

She waited.

"Spend the night at my apartment. With me. No one would have any idea you were there. And if somehow someone did? You would have two strong, young waiters and one strong, young bartender to protect you."

She thought about this as she walked, occasionally glancing around at the vendors with their gelato and the couples on their rented bikes or the tourists photographing the Roman temple beside the small pond. She saw two American boys in baseball henleys, the pair almost but not quite teenagers, running a little ahead of their parents. She saw a young man in shades standing beside a lusterless silver bike, and he looked back at her when she passed him.

She breathed in the air, lush now with the promise of twilight, and recalled Alex Sokolov's cold body beside her in bed and his blood in her hair. She thought of his neck and the white pillow sodden like a sponge with his blood. She envisioned the decomposition Ani had alluded to on the phone. After her conversation with her lawyer, she knew that she couldn't endanger Enrico that way. Moreover, she understood in the deep reptilian part of her brain, the core that controlled her body's most vital functions, that something inside her had been heat-blasted and now begun to harden. It was why she wanted that gun.

"Let me think about it," she said. "Let's go have a drink."

27

Elena stood before the hotel room mirror, appraising herself with her new black hair. She liked the look, she really did. Then she glanced down at her phone on the dresser and watched the blue dot on the app that was Cassandra Bowden. The flight attendant was strolling past the Temple of Asclepius in the Villa Borghese. Either she didn't believe she was in danger or she didn't give a damn. Knowing Bowden, it could be either. Elena doubted the woman was alone.

She drizzled a little honey onto the pecorino cheese she had ordered from room service, savored the sweet-and-saltiness of the combination, and then dabbed at her mouth with the napkin. She already had a room at the flight attendant's hotel. She would, exactly as she had in Dubai, be upstairs well before her prey returned. This time, however, she would be waiting for Bowden—and the bartender or whomever—in the woman's own room. If it looked like Bowden was spending the night elsewhere? Well, Elena would simply go there, too.

Unless she heard back from her handler, instructing her otherwise.

After she had climbed into the black dress, she brushed her teeth and filled her purse. They had sent her a package at the hotel with the tools she had requested: Two dozen pentobarbital tabs. One bottle of Stoli. A Beretta with a silencer and a clip. A dry-erase marker with an Arduino circuit board in the barrel to trip the hotel-room door lock. Wrist restraints that were lined with faux fur—a sex toy, but they wouldn't leave marks on the woman's skin the way handcuffs or even duct tape would. A stun gun built into a flashlight. And—just in case—a knife with a four-inch titanium blade that folded like a Boy Scout jackknife into the handle. It was, she thought, very similar to the one she had used on Alex Sokolov. She hoped this wouldn't actually be one of those just-in-case moments when she'd need it.

Everything fit snugly into her shoulder bag, along with her wallet, her compact, her lipstick, her sunglasses, and her phone.

She checked the app and saw the blue dot had stopped in a structure on a side street near the British School. She checked the building's address. It was—and this surprised Elena not at all—a bar.

28

Cassie was warm from her walk through the park, and she craved a Bellini. She thought of the tray of them she had seen at the bar in Enrico's hotel. But she didn't order one. She took a breath and ordered sparkling water instead. And then, because this was Rome, she asked for a cappuccino, too. She expected withdrawal—not physical, emotional—but she knew if there had ever been a moment in her life when she needed her wits about her, it was probably today. Tonight. Enrico, however, as if he had been put on the earth for no other reason than to tempt her, did order a Bellini. The two of them had a table in the bar's courtyard that an hour earlier would have been in the sun, but now it was shade and the air felt about as perfect as the air ever could feel in August in Rome. When their drinks arrived, she watched Enrico sample it.

"What do you think?" she asked.

He seemed to take the question more seriously than she had meant it. "I make a better one, but it's hard to screw up Prosecco and peach juice. But they should have pureed fresh peaches, not just opened a bottle of juice. It makes a world of difference." Then he leaned across the small, round table, his elbows on the wrought iron: "What kind of trouble are you in, *mio amore*? If you tell me, it might be easier for me to get you that gun."

She reached into her purse for her phone, planning to show him the article from the *New York Post*. She wasn't sure how much she would share after that. But before she had done anything, she saw that she had a text from Buckley. He wanted to know the difference between a Cart Tart and a Pop Tart, but admitted that he clearly had a fondness for both. The text was playful and perfect, and she found herself smiling. It was a relief to hear from him; she was a little undone by how happy his brief text had made her.

"Good news?" he asked.

"Yes. As a matter of fact, it is."

"So you no longer need that gun?"

She looked across the table at his Bellini for a long moment. It was so beautiful. Alcohol was so beautiful. The colors, the bottles, the labels, the glasses. The rituals. This bar served the Bellini in a highball glass with a red and green swirl at the lip. It was still almost full. She imagined Buckley reading the newspaper—the inky paper itself, a surviving dinosaur from the days before the digital asteroid had obliterated so many of its genetic cousins—at a coffee shop in the West Village.

Was it only ninety minutes ago, at the bar in her hotel, that she was fantasizing taking this young man back to her room? It was.

She opened the app on her phone for the web and found the story about her in the newspaper. Then she handed him the phone. "Happy reading," she said.

« «

When he was done, he placed the phone on the table and sat back in his chair, folding his arms across his chest. "So they think you killed this man?" he asked, his tone almost prosecutorial.

"They do," she answered, though she wasn't completely sure whom she meant by *they*. The media? The FBI? The Dubai police? Really, it could be any of them or all of them.

"But you didn't."

She almost told him the truth. She almost said that she had worried at first that she had, but she hoped that she hadn't—and now she was sure that she hadn't. But she needed to keep her stories straight. And so she answered, "When I left the hotel room, he was still alive. He was about to get dressed and get ready for his meetings in Dubai."

"So someone killed him after you left."

"That's right."

"And now you are asking me for a gun."

"I am."

He raised a single eyebrow. "I don't think you plan to kill me."

"No. Never."

He took a deep breath. He met her eyes. "I will get you that gun."

"Thank you," she said.

"You know, there might be Italian reporters who will want to talk to you. Do they know your hotel?"

"According to my lawyer, they'll find it. But no one approached me today in the lobby. No one, at least this afternoon, was staking out the front entrance."

"One more reason I am very glad we are going back to my apartment."

She felt a small pang at the way she was going to disappoint him. She looked down at her hands in her lap, gathering herself. This would all be so much easier if she could have a drink. Even one. But if she had a drink, she would have two, and then once more she would be in his arms and his bed. "We're not going back to your apartment," she said. "We can't. I can't."

He looked crestfallen. "Why?"

"I don't want to endanger your brother and your friend. I don't want to endanger you."

"So we'll go back to your hotel room?" She could tell that he hadn't really misunderstood what she was saying, but he was grasping for any small thread that gave him hope. She was flattered.

"No," she said firmly. She picked up the cappuccino and studied the swirl of milk for a moment, a little hypnotized by its allure. She took a sip. "We won't. I will. I'll go there alone. We'll get the gun, and then you'll walk me back to the hotel—the lobby. Please. And tomorrow morning I will leave the gun for you in a box or package of some sort when I check out. I'll leave it for you at the reception desk."

"I think you need me."

"Oh, I need a lot of things, Enrico. I really do. Trust me: The things I need? It's a very, very long list. But I can't let you take that risk. I just can't. And . . ."

"And?"

"Things have changed since last week."

"Because of the newspaper article?" he asked.

"Because there's another man."

"There wasn't last week?"

"There was, but it wasn't like it is now."

He nodded. His disappointment had deepened, but she had a feeling that he wasn't hurt. There was a difference. "I could still stay with you," he insisted.

"No. I wouldn't allow it. I won't stay with any of the other flight attendants for the same reason. It wouldn't be fair."

"Is there any chance you're worried for nothing?"

"There is," she said, but she didn't believe that. She thought of what her lawyer had told her when they had spoken that afternoon. She knew what she herself had sensed when she had been on that subway platform in Manhattan the other day. They were out there. They were. But for Enrico's sake, she continued. "That has certainly crossed my mind. Let's hope that's the case."

He took another sip of his Bellini and seemed even less satisfied by it now than he had been originally. She doubted he'd bother to finish it. "I have one more question for you," he said. He looked very serious.

"Ask me anything."

"Has it ever crossed your mind, maybe, you drink too much?"

« «

Her phone rang almost the moment that they left the bar and started the short walk to Enrico's uncle's apartment. She saw it was her sister and took the call, motioning to Enrico that she was going to stop and focus. She recalled reading Rosemary's e-mail on the plane last night over the Atlantic, and realized with regret that she had never responded. As soon as she had said hello, Rosemary started speaking.

"I just had two FBI agents at my house," she said, her fury evident over the phone. "Dennis just had two FBI agents and a pair of MPs show up at his office at the base. At. The. Base. How the hell bad is this, Cassie? What have you done?"

"I'm sorry, sweetie. I should have answered your e-mail. I just . . ."

"You just what?"

I just got sidetracked when I nearly tackled some woman at the airport in Rome who I thought I had seen in Dubai. I just got maced. I just lost track of time when I was interviewed by Fiumicino Airport Security. I just collapsed into a deep sleep. I just talked to my lawyer. I just convinced an Italian bartender to get me a gun.

But she said none of that. Instead she walked a few feet away from Enrico and said, "I just forgot."

"The FBI, Cassie. The FBI."

"What did they ask you? What did they ask Dennis?" She saw that Enrico was watching her. He looked concerned.

"They wanted to know what the hell kind of relationship you have with my husband. They wanted to know if you've ever discussed money problems with me. With him. With us. They wanted to know if you've been acting weird lately. Or ever. They wanted to know how much you drink. I could go on."

"Then do."

"They wanted to know if we ever saw you with strange people or with this Alex Sokolov person—the one who was killed. I guess, like you, he lived in New York. They wanted to know any stories you shared from Dubai. Or Europe. Traveling stories."

"What did you tell them?"

"I told them you don't have any relationship with Dennis, except he's your brother-in-law. At first I thought they were implying you two were having some sort of really icky affair—and maybe they were—but that wasn't it. At least that wasn't the main thing."

"We're not! He loves you. I love you."

"They were digging for something else. It was like they thought he was telling you things about work he's not supposed to tell anyone!"

"I promise you, I wouldn't understand a word."

"I don't think that was their point, Cassie. You know what he does is classified. He's in the Chemical Corps, for God's sakes!"

"What else did you tell them?"

Rosemary blew her nose. Cassie realized that as angry as her sister was, she was also scared: she'd likely been crying before she had phoned. There was far more terror than truculence in her tone. "I told them you drink too much, but you're not—as far as I can tell—as irresponsible as our father. I told them I know nothing about any strange people in your life because I don't know any of your friends. Or boyfriends. When I told them that, I think it sounded suspicious, but mostly it just made me sad. It dawned on me that I know nothing about your world except the sense that you travel to cool places and you bring my children sweet gifts."

Cassie wanted to lash out, to say something defensive about the fact it was really Rosemary who kept her at bay. But her sister was already so upset and Cassie knew that it was her fault that Rosemary was being dragged into her nightmare, and so she didn't respond. Instead she inquired only, "Is that the sort of thing they asked Dennis, too?"

"I don't know. He was at the base and couldn't talk. But I suppose so. They brought him to some conference room and just kept grilling him."

"Well, it sounds like he had nothing to hide."

"Nothing to hide? Dennis's work involves chemical weapons. You think he's just some goofy engineer geek, but that geek spends his days getting rid of our sarin and VX and some of the scariest stuff in our arsenal."

"I know."

"I mean, he's got a very high security clearance!"

"I get it," Cassie said softly.

"And now the FBI is interviewing him!"

"But he hasn't done anything wrong."

"I know that. You know that. But it's just . . ."

"It's just what?"

"It just looks bad. It just looks terrible."

"I'm sorry," Cassie murmured. "I am."

Her sister ignored her apology. "They wanted to know what you told me about this man who was killed. I told them the truth: you'd never even mentioned the guy because you never mention any of the legions you sleep with."

"It isn't legions, Rosemary. Come on."

"What am I supposed to tell Jessica and Tim?"

"I gather you don't think they'll be especially proud of their aunt?"

"Cassie, I love you. I really do. But what the hell have you done? This is different. I'm scared for my husband and I'm scared for my children. Tell me what sort of trouble you're in."

"I've done nothing," she said. She told herself this wasn't lying. This was staying on message. "I spent the night with an interesting man in Dubai. When I left, he was still alive. After that? I have no idea what happened."

"Except we do have an idea," her sister said. "Someone practically cut off his head. And as for him being interesting? I have a feeling the FBI would use a very, very different adjective."

« «

The front door was unlocked, and Enrico led them into the apartment without knocking. They walked through the dark, immaculate living room and kitchen, and out onto the terrace. His uncle was in a white dress shirt and light blue suit pants, no necktie, sipping Cointreau neat on the private terrace and reading the newspaper beneath a small pergola. His suit jacket was draped over the back of his chair. The terrace had a four-foot-high fountain with a goddess holding a pitcher, and two raised beds with tomato plants. There were lemon trees. It was a lovely, private oasis in the middle of a city.

Cassie guessed that Piero Bianchi was in his midforties, and when he stood to greet her she detected a wisp of verbena. He was Enrico's mother's youngest brother, and he worked for a bank. He was trim, like his nephew, but his hair had receded and what was left was more salt than pepper. Still, Cassie found the reality that she was much closer to Piero's age than to Enrico's disconcerting. Enrico had texted his uncle to make sure he was home, but he hadn't said why they were coming. He had told Cassie that she was not to bring up the gun or say a word about it. He'd said firmly that he would take care of it.

"And you're a flight attendant," Piero said when they were settled around the table. His accent was almost nonexistent. "I have friends who fly for Alitalia and American."

"Pilots? Flight attendants?"

"Both. But mostly the latter."

"I like the lifestyle."

"As do they. You're sure I can't get you two something to drink?"

"No. I'm fine," she said. She looked at Enrico, and he shook his head, too.

"Where is your base?"

"JFK."

"Among my least favorite airports in the world. It's a dinosaur."

"It really is."

Abruptly Enrico stood up and said he was going to the bathroom.

"So, tell me: how did you meet my nephew?"

"The airline was staying at his hotel. He made me an excellent Negroni."

"I'm not surprised. Someday soon, I believe, I will be bankrolling a bar for him. A restaurant and bar. First, however, he needs a partner who can cook. Can you cook?"

"My refrigerator is nothing but leftover Indian food and yogurt that's gone bad."

"I am guessing that means no."

"A very good guess."

He finished the last of the Cointreau. She stared at the empty glass when he put it down, and she had a feeling that her longing was so powerful that Piero could sense it. "Enrico's a good boy," he said, and Cassie couldn't miss the way he had used the word *boy*. She couldn't decide whether he was chastising her or teasing her—giving her a little good-natured grief—or merely referring to his nephew the way any uncle would, even when the child was a grown man.

"He is," she agreed simply.

"When he said he had someone he wanted me to meet, I was expecting something different."

"Something . . . younger?"

He gave a loud, reflexive laugh. "No. Italian."

"Really?"

"Of course not. I'm kidding. I don't know why, but I heard something in his voice when he called that led me to believe he wanted to tell me something important, and I was thinking this was it: I am about to meet a person who does something exquisite with wild boar or scallops or zucchini, and he wanted to start a restaurant with him or her."

"Sorry."

"Good heavens, why should you be sorry?"

"I'm not that person. You sounded disappointed."

"Not at all. But I am still trying to understand why he wanted me to meet you. Are you two dating?"

"No. We're just friends."

"Well, now: that does surprise me. Even if you weren't dating, I assumed there was more to the relationship than friendship. I know my nephew's hobbies well."

"Maybe in another life."

"Maybe."

A moment later Enrico returned. She noticed that he had untucked his shirt. He smiled at her, leaned forward, and pretended to scratch his lower back. She glanced there and saw that he was pulling tight his shirt with his thumb and forefinger so she could see the outline of the grip of the pistol he had slid into the back of his jeans.

29

Elena watched Cassie and Enrico emerge from the apartment's front entrance. The bartender's uncle stood for a long moment in the doorway beneath an overhead exterior light, the glass amber, as the couple strolled away from him down the street. He didn't wave because their backs were turned, and his shoulders were stooped and he looked a little sad. She wondered why. She tried to decide why Enrico had brought the flight attendant here. If he wanted to introduce her to his family, he would have brought her first to his parents, not to his uncle.

She hadn't needed any clandestine tools to research Piero Bianchi while she waited for them to emerge. She only wanted the basics. She learned he was a banker, though he didn't seem to have much to do with foreign currencies or hedge funds or international banking. Mostly he financed local real estate—new commercial construction inside the Roman ring. This was comforting, though not conclusive. After all, much of the fund Sokolov ran was in real estate. It was possible that the manager had told Bowden something about his day job and Bowden had told the bartender, and the two of them had now gone to Uncle Piero for a tutorial. Any banker with Piero's experience could answer basic investment questions or explain the bare bones of what Sokolov did at Unisphere.

But if Bowden had questions, she'd had plenty of opportunities to talk to bankers while she was home in Manhattan. Wouldn't that lawyer of hers have been tracking them down? Wouldn't Bowden have gone to speak to someone in America instead of going to the animal shelter or the zoo or hooking up with that actor?

No, Elena decided, the two of them had gone to see Uncle Piero for some reason that had absolutely nothing to do with the hedge fund.

She thought of something her father had told her: a smart girl is nobody's pushover and nobody's foe. A smart girl is both sword and smile. (At the time, she had considered countering that his ex-wife was all sword and seemed to do just fine, thank you very much, but she understood his message.)

Her handler in Abu Dhabi had postulated a theory to explain the connection between Sokolov and Bowden.

"Is it possible that this flight attendant is actually a whole lot smarter than the average bear?" he'd asked her. "Maybe she was working with Sokolov on the grift the whole time, and their inebriated debacle was a hoax."

"Play this out," she'd said to him.

"Okay. Bowden isn't even in the room when you phoned five-eleven. She got there just before you did, and she and Sokolov concocted the ruse when they were caught. They portrayed their meeting as just some drunken debauch."

"No, they were wasted," she assured him. "They weren't play-acting."

She told him her theory in return: Bowden had said something on the plane about what her brother-in-law did for a living, and Sokolov saw an opportunity. Here was a flight attendant who flew regularly into the United Arab Emirates, and she had a brother-in-law who was a major at an army base that was awash in chemical weapons. He was a destruction engineer. Perhaps the flight attendant could help them enlist or blackmail him. But Viktor already had his own asset inside the chemical weapons program; the FSB had their own courier with the airline. They didn't need her.

The irony, of course, was that back in the United States the FBI now had to investigate Major McCauley. Make sure that he hadn't violated his security clearance and told his sister-in-law something she might have shared with Sokolov. So they were talking to him. They were talking to his family.

Meanwhile, Viktor probably suspected—no assumed—that the flight attendant was either FBI and she was interested in Sokolov or she was CIA and hoping to use Sokolov to get inside the Cossacks. And even if she weren't? She'd still been in the suite. She may have been merely a sexually voracious flight attendant in the wrong place at the wrong time, but she may also have been something rather more dangerous.

And so Viktor fully (and rightly) expected that his redoubtable protégée would have killed the woman when she found her in the room.

But she hadn't.

Since Dubai, Viktor had been telling her they were worried that the flight attendant might reveal something compromising that Sokolov had shared while drunk. They had stressed that the flight attendant had seen her and, thus, could easily burn her. Certainly the crazy woman had recognized her at Fiumicino. So these were her fears, too. But there was something else going on, and it was now coming into focus. She had not merely failed Viktor by neither executing Bowden nor telling him initially that the woman had been in the room: she had irrevocably compromised his faith in her. Their faith in her. Their trust. They thought she had quite possibly spared an FBI asset or an actual agent. They'd never believe her, no matter how eloquently she explained the truth of what she knew or how many synonyms she found in English or Russian for the noun *drunk*.

They'd figured out that she was CIA; they'd figured out that she had turned.

Spies (and she always felt self-important and narcissistic when she thought of herself that way, but it was better than the alternative words, which stressed the more lethal aspects to her work) turned for a lot of reasons. Most of the time it was because they hadn't a choice: they'd been compromised or were being blackmailed, and changing teams was the only play to keep out of prison. Or, in some cases, to stay alive. The rationale for her turn in America had origins both prosaic and profound. Yes, once she was ensconced in Boston she could see more objectively the corruption that had spread plague-like in the new Russia, and she refused to succumb to that unique hybrid of fatalism and cynicism that marked her people. She wanted her new Russia to be better than the old one, and that meant undermining the old guard. But that alone wouldn't have been enough. There was also a man, a grad student five years her senior. An American. She was twenty-four, a young FSB agent. She would never know if the courtship had been recruitment all along, because in hindsight it never had been much of a romance: he'd been clear that they really couldn't be seen together in the event one or the other ever was outed. But he was the one who broke the news to her that her father had not had a stroke when she was twenty. They'd poisoned him with methyl iodide, selecting the pesticide because the cause of death would mimic a stroke. The Cossacks had done this. Viktor Olenin. In his old age, her father was becoming too outspoken and too critical of the president of the Russian Federation. He was becoming a liability, a loose cannon. He knew too much to live.

But he had lived, despite the toxin. Barely.

Now that young man was a poli sci professor in Berlin. Elena stopped visiting his public persona on the social networks when she saw that his German girlfriend had become his German wife.

She sighed. She wondered if Viktor's trust in her had begun to ebb even before she had chosen not to kill the flight attendant. If so, when had they come to doubt her devotion? Her fealty? It didn't matter. What did was this: they believed she had spared Bowden for reasons far worse than mere kindness. It was possible they might kill her even if she did take care of the flight attendant—or, to be precise, as soon as she'd taken care of the flight attendant.

And yet when she surveyed the chessboard, executing the woman still seemed a viable move for everyone. She'd expressed her concerns to her handler, and Washington was deliberating whether it was time to come in. But she was far and away their most deeply embedded operative in the Cossacks, the only one inside the group who could tell them what Olenin was doing. And that mattered.

And she felt a tug in her heart for Sochi. It was in her blood, her DNA. She wasn't prepared to give that up. Not yet.

Her father, as far as she knew, had never had a safe house: an apartment in Amsterdam or a cottage outside Johannesburg into which he could burrow. A secret chrysalis with food and money and yet one more passport, and from which he could emerge with new wings and a new identity. But just because she wasn't aware of one didn't mean that one hadn't existed. You never told your loved ones you had one. It was how you protected them. She herself had never set one up, and she couldn't help now but wonder if this bit of youthful hubris—*I'll never need one: I'm too smart and I have too many friends in high places*—wasn't now going to bite her in the ass.

She followed the bartender and the flight attendant at a careful distance. It was twilight, which was an easier time of the day to tail someone. Moreover, there were tourists and dinner crowds in this neighborhood, and she could blend in should Bowden suddenly turn around. But then, it was unlikely the woman would recognize her with her new hair color. She'd dyed it specifically because she couldn't risk a repeat of what had happened that morning at the airport.

She noticed that the couple wasn't touching as they walked, though it was still possible that they were returning to her hotel. Instead of cutting back through the Villa Borghese, however, they were strolling along the Via di Villa Ruffo, and so she assumed they would stop at a restaurant on the way.

Because they were dawdling, she had to dawdle, which meant that she also had to endure the occasional whistles and come-ons from young men as they passed on the sidewalk or as they drove by—slowing—on the street on their colorful Vespas. She smiled at the men whose remarks were less offensive because it was important not to make a scene, and she ignored the others.

It was in the Piazza del Popolo, as the bartender and the flight attendant passed a waist-high black fence with a beautiful cycloid of wrought-iron arches and neared the great obelisk in the center of the park, that she figured out why Enrico had brought Bowden to his uncle's. Piero had a little place in the country. In Tuscany. No doubt the fellow had a hunting permit. Perhaps even a concealed carry license. His nephew had brought the flight attendant to his uncle's apartment to get the woman a gun.

30

"So you're really not going to allow me to make you one of my perfect Negronis?" Enrico asked her as they entered the lobby of the hotel where she was staying. Instinctively she looked around to see if any members of the flight crew were present. None were. The lobby was so small compared to the Royal Phoenician—more living room than ballroom—the ceilings low and the decor modest. She noted the faux Renaissance tapestries on the walls and the fainting couch where she had sat that afternoon.

"I'm not," she said, though she glanced longingly at the bar as they approached the elevators, her ears alive to the clink of glasses and laughter and the music that occasionally bubbled up and over the bacchanal.

They had eaten dinner at a romantic trattoria with brick walls and lit candles in wrought-iron chandeliers where he was friends with the sous chef, and so they ate like royalty for almost nothing, which was about what they had for a budget. She had never had a panzanella salad so good, each tomato a different shade of orange or red. The house wines were excellent, Enrico told her, but Cassie insisted that she wasn't going to drink, and so Enrico didn't either. She sat with her back to the wall and sipped sparkling water, and stared at the entrance to the restaurant. She wasn't sure what she was looking for. She wasn't sure who she was looking for. She didn't honestly believe that Miranda—or someone—would appear in the dining room, but after Fiumicino she wasn't willing to sit with her back to the door.

It had been a lovely evening, though it had been and (she told herself) would be almost stoic in its denial: no booze, no sex. She was bringing him upstairs to her room so he could hand her the gun. The fact was that she knew more about firearms than he did. But he didn't dare bring out the Beretta at the restaurant, and so they had agreed they would retreat to her hotel room so he could give it to her there. She'd been clear that they weren't going to have sex, but she knew that he nevertheless remained hopeful. He was charming beyond his years; he was as unaccustomed to someone saying no as she was to saying it.

《　《

When they got to her room, she saw that the square red light on the desk phone was blinking. Instantly her anxiety rose. Enrico stood patiently by the window, his back to her as he stood bordered by the drapes, while she picked up the receiver and listened. It turned out that she had two messages.

"Hey, there. It's Makayla. I'm just checking in. How did I not think to get your cell? I wanted to make sure you're okay. Do you still want to have that drink? Do you feel up to joining some of us for dinner, maybe? I'm in room seven-thirteen. It's a little before five."

She made a mental note of the other flight attendant's room number and then listened to the second message:

"Hi, Cassie, it's me again. Makayla. Some of us are meeting in the lobby at seven thirty. Join us if you'd like. No pressure. Maybe text me when you wake up or get back from wherever you are," she said, and this time she left her cell number. Cassie wrote it down and texted back that she was sorry she hadn't gotten the messages. She wrote that she had gone for a long walk, but now she was back in her hotel room and she was fine. She was in for the night. She thanked her.

"Everything is okay?" asked Enrico.

"It is. That was just another member of the crew wanting to be reassured that I was safely back in my room."

"Good."

He picked up the paperback Tolstoy on the nightstand beside the hotel's digital clock. "Did you ever read Carlo Levi?"

"No."

"You should—if you like Tolstoy. He wrote beautifully about Italian peasants. My people, once. He had a soul like Tolstoy. 'The future has an ancient heart.' I think I have that right."

"Thank you. I don't expect I'll find him with the paperbacks at the airport."

"Look for him—when you're home," he said, and somehow his tone made the idea of home sound to her like an unattainable dream: a port she would not see again. Still, Enrico smiled and sat on the foot of the bed. He patted the mattress beside him, beckoning her. The bed was the unmade mess she had left it after her afternoon nap. She joined him there and he pulled out the handgun. He gave it to her and then reached into his front pants pocket for the bullets.

The gun was heavier than she expected, but she liked its simple solidity. Its heft. It actually felt sturdier than a rifle. And the smell—metallic, machinelike—instantly brought her back to the high school classroom those early autumn afternoons when she had taken the hunter safety course and been taught by a retired state trooper the three different types of magazines (tubular, box, floor plate with a hinge), and where the gunpowder sits inside a cartridge. Then she was back in the woods, with a whole other set of memories: the aroma of autumnal cold. Wet leaves as they began to merge with the mud. Decomposing trees. Damp clothes.

She thought of her father's breath, beery, when he would point out the deer tracks in the soft earth or the deer scat in the midst of the leaves just off the thin path.

The Beretta was a Model 92, all black. She released the magazine to make sure it was empty. She racked back the slide to make sure there was no bullet in the chamber, either.

"The bullets are so little," Enrico said. He poured four of them into her hand and rolled a fifth between his forefinger and thumb.

She took it from him. "I found them on my uncle's workbench when he was reloading the ammunition. The gun will hold all five of them?"

She examined the magazine. "Yes. This magazine probably holds three times that many rounds."

He shook his head. "I should have stolen more bullets."

"God, no."

Loading the magazine, she thought, was like loading a Pez candy dispenser one little sugar brick at a time. When she had the cartridges loaded into the magazine, she used the heel of her hand to tap the magazine back into place. She hoped she had done everything right. Then she placed it on the nightstand next to the telephone. She didn't want to get comfortable with the grip while he was there beside her on the bed. She wanted to do that when she was alone.

"So what do we do now?" he asked.

They had bought a large metal tin of Perugia chocolates on the way back to the hotel. The plan was that in the morning when she and the rest of the flight crew checked out, she was going to leave the tin for him with a friend of his who was scheduled to be manning the reception desk. The gun would be at the bottom, unloaded, beneath the chocolates.

"I'm going to thank you and escort you to the door."

"And eat the chocolates?"

She smiled at him. He was adorable. The perfect toy. "I'll make a dent in the box, maybe. There has to be room for the gun, right?"

"And you'll try to get some sleep?" he asked.

"I guess. If someone wanted to kill me, they had every chance this afternoon and this evening."

He took her hand in both of his and gazed at her. His eyes looked sleepy in the hotel room light. "But you're scared. You wanted a gun."

"I'm a heck of a lot less scared now."

"But tomorrow? And the day after tomorrow? And the day after that? What is your plan?"

She lifted his fingers to her mouth and kissed them once. Then she kissed them a second time. "I don't have a plan," she answered. "I wish I did, but I don't." The truth was, she had been living almost hour to hour since she had woken up in Dubai and found Alex Sokolov dead. First she just wanted to get away from the corpse and the likelihood of prison and reach Charles de Gaulle. Then she just wanted to land in America. Then she just wanted to find a lawyer. Then she just wanted to survive the FBI. Then. Then. Then . . .

But she couldn't tell him any of that because Enrico believed—or at least was pretending to believe—that Alex Sokolov had been alive when she had left the hotel room.

"Well, I have a plan," he said, his eyebrows raised, his face playful.

She shook her head.

"I'm not thinking what you think I am," he said.

"You're thinking you're so handsome that I'm going to fall under your spell. Well, you are that handsome, and I am under your spell. But I'm trying to do better. To be better. So, please don't tempt me anymore because I'm really not known for my willpower."

"No. I'm thinking that we turn on the TV and play video games or watch movies. I'm thinking that I call downstairs for a pot of coffee—for me."

"I can't allow that. I told you, I don't want you to take that risk."

"Can I tell you something?"

"Of course."

"I already talked to security. I told them the Cart Tart Killer is staying here and newspaper and TV people might try to sneak upstairs. They are going to be extra watchful in the lobby."

She sat back and appraised him. "Wow. You're good."

"You're impressed?"

"I am."

He picked up the gun and held it by the grip. "And we have

this. If we stay together and watch TV and play games? There's no one in the world who can hurt us tonight."

She took the gun from him. She worried that he might accidentally discharge it. "I wish that were true. But it's not." Then she stood and with her free hand led him to his feet. She walked him to the door.

"The chocolate box will be downstairs in the morning with your uncle's Beretta," she told him.

"Text me," he said.

"I will."

"And I will see you next week?"

"Yes, absolutely," she said, though she didn't believe it. She had a feeling she'd never see him again. Then she kissed him chastely on the cheek, thanked him once more, and said good night. When he was gone, she thought of what her lawyer had suggested and dead-bolted the door.

«   «

After he had left, she sat in the chair and turned so she was facing the door and practiced holding the Beretta with two hands. She closed one eye and stared through the sight, aiming at the peephole in the door one moment and at the handle the next. She flipped the safety on and off.

It was late here in Rome but nearing dinnertime in Manhattan. She texted Ani to see if there was news. Ani texted back that there wasn't. She texted her sister that she was sorry she had caused her so much worry—not just now, but over the years—and she told her she loved her. She texted her friend Gillian to thank her for all of the times she had brought her home and held back her hair while she vomited into the toilet. No, toilets. Plural. There had been toilets in bars, toilets in clubs, toilets in other people's homes. She texted Paula to keep her shirt on, a joke they shared about how impatiently they drank when they were together and how one or the other would often wind up with her shirt off those nights.

Cassie recalled holding back Paula's hair exactly the way Gillian had held back hers. She texted Megan to please wave to the Brandenburg Gate for her. She added how much she had always enjoyed flying with her. She put the words "filet mignon" with a hashtag after the text, a reference to the time that Megan was serving a particularly despicable, angry bore in first class. He had knocked his entrée, the filet mignon, onto the cabin floor, and complained bitterly as if it were Megan's fault. She had told him with a sincere smile, "Good thing we have extras." Then she had brought the piece of meat to the lav, rinsed it off with the undrinkable water there, reheated it, and returned it to him on his plate.

And she texted Buckley the answer to his most recent question:

> What's the difference between a Pop Tart and a Cart Tart? They're both sweet and they both get toasted, but a Cart Tart's not nearly as good for you.

She hoped her small joke would make him smile, but the truth of it made her cringe. It wasn't merely the acknowledgment of her drinking; it was the reality that she was poisonous; she always risked diminishing the people she loved or might someday love. Too often she forced them to make the same bad choices she did or she forced them from her life. Best case, she forced them to care for her. Today, though sober, she had gotten a kind young man to steal a gun from his uncle for her. She had needed Makayla to bring her to the hotel after she was pepper-sprayed. And she had attacked a strange woman at an international airport.

She wrote Buckley a second text.

> When I sent you that text (above), I meant it as a joke. But you need to know, Buckley, that it's true, too. It's the truest thing I have ever said. I'm not good for you. I'm not good for anyone. It's not just the lies or the fact I'm a drunk, it's who I am. It's what I am. So . . . don't ever wait for me. Don't expect anything of me. I will only disappoint you and I know you deserve better. And that, also, is true.

Would he understand this was good-bye? Perhaps not.

But he would when she ignored his next text and the text after that, either because she was doing what was right or because she was dead.

Finally she turned on the television and found the stations from America. She sat against the headboard with the handgun beside her and watched an old sitcom about brilliant young physicists who were socially awkward. She was going to watch anything but the news.

She was just starting to doze off when she was awakened by the deafening, shrill, high-pitched wail of the hotel fire alarm.

31

W ho really burned most of Moscow to the ground in 1812? Tolstoy seemed to believe it was the occupying French army and it was an accident: too many soldiers starting too many fires. Myriad small blazes igniting one massive one that drove Napoleon from the Kremlin—though only briefly. He would return and reside there a month before the long French retreat would commence. But Elena knew that her father and her father's friends thought otherwise: the Russians themselves, the few that remained in the city, set torch to the wooden buildings. Hadn't the Russian commander himself demobilized the firefighting corps? Hadn't he ordered that the firefighting wagons be wrecked? No one would ever know for sure where on the spectrum the inferno fell between suicide and sabotage, but Elena had grown up confident that it was the Muscovites themselves—citizens and soldiers alike—who had destroyed the great city.

Which, in her mind, fit the Russian character to a tee. She saw herself in the light from those flames. She knew her people, and she knew the way the West looked down on them: certainly the West had in 1812 and certainly the West did today. Hadn't she felt that when she had been a student in Switzerland and Massachusetts, hadn't she heard that in the derogatory comments in political science classes about serfs and gulags and oligarchs? Well, North Americans had their crimes, too: genocide and slavery and, yes, oligarchs of their own. So be it. She and her ancestors lived with a chip on their shoulders that made them at once defiant and fatalistic—and conquerable only by themselves. Always it had been Russians themselves who, in the end, vanquished or annihilated or finally broke Russians.

She was considerably more frightened of Viktor than she was of any man or woman she had ever met in the West.

« «

Her mind, as it did often now, meandered to Sochi and her father's dacha there. Her home there. Mostly it had been spared the madness of the Olympic construction, but the view of the mountains to the southwest had changed: you could see roads that had been cut through the forest in the distance, and in the winter you could spot the alpine trails that had been added when there was snow. Her father would have been appalled had he lived to see it. But the vista to the east was unchanged, as rustic and primeval as when Stalin had summered nearby, and she had a sense that despite his disappointment, her father would have adapted: perhaps he would have grown accustomed to sitting on the porch on the eastern side of the house instead of the one on the west, and arranged his days so he could bask in the sunrises instead of the sunsets. You didn't survive in the Soviet Union if you didn't adapt. You didn't thrive in the post-Soviet world if you weren't a chameleon. Certainly her father was. But he was also a realist and he was disciplined. It was one more reason why she had both respected and loved him.

And he was Russian: unconquerable by forces from beyond the border. The only person who had ever defeated him was his equally Russian wife.

« «

She read the message from Washington twice to be sure. Then a third time.

There was no ambiguity. She was done. Finished. They agreed with her: the Cossacks knew she'd been turned.

Inside she was an uncharacteristic riot of emotions. There was (and it pained her to admit this, because she liked to believe that she was above an emotion as pedestrian as fear) relief, because she herself was evidence of Viktor's brutality toward his enemies. She knew what loomed for her. But there was also shame, because she felt like a failure. She had failed the agency, yes, but more than that she had failed her father. She did what she did to fuck Viktor. And there were other discordant, confusing waves that broke over her, too, all of which began and ended with the unexpected fog that was her future.

Her orders were to get the flight attendant and get out. She was to get the two of them out.

She'd go ahead and pull the fire alarm as she had planned because she suspected that Bowden had a gun and she didn't really want the woman to shoot her the moment she walked into her hotel room. But the rest of her evening was going to be rather different.

So be it.

How funny that she'd just been thinking about her beloved Sochi. She felt a pang in her heart, knowing she'd never see Russia again.

« «

Elena understood that the blue dot on her phone could tell her more or less where the flight attendant was when it came to a street address, but it certainly couldn't confirm whether the woman had left her hotel room. The frog's heart was going to beat at this address, but it could not discern whether she was outside on the street or ensconced upstairs in her room.

And so she pulled the fire alarm on Cassandra Bowden's floor, but along a different corridor. Then she went quickly to the flight attendant's hallway and watched, occasionally moving with the herd as the guests emerged, hoping to blend in by looking as frazzled and sleepy as they. She was wearing a nondescript black hoodie and sweatpants.

It seemed as if most of the guests presumed this was either a drill or a false alarm, but she noted how most were obediently—albeit, begrudgingly—taking the stairs rather than the elevators to the lobby and exiting the hotel. Most had climbed back into their clothes, though none were as well dressed as they would have been just a few hours earlier. She saw women and men in blue jeans and sweatpants like her, their shirts untucked, their sneakers or shoes barely tied. She saw flip-flops. She saw women without makeup and men with their hair wild with sleep. She noted the couples who had clearly been having sex when they were interrupted, the evidence the way they looked at once sheepish and annoyed and clung a little hungrily to each other. She saw three children—all girls—and supposed they were sisters. The youngest was only three or four and was in her father's arms, using her fists to wipe at her eyes.

And she saw Bowden. There she was. Alone. She was still dressed in the sundress she had worn to dinner with the bartender, but the bartender wasn't with her. She couldn't decide what that meant, but it would make her job easier.

The flight attendant had slipped on her sandals. She had with her a shoulder bag, which Elena was quite sure now held a gun.

This time the woman hadn't noticed her. There would be no repeat of the madness that morning at Fiumicino.

It was then that her phone buzzed and she saw it was Viktor. She didn't dare ignore Viktor, even now. So she took her phone and retreated into the stairwell, secure in the knowledge that Bowden was gone.

"Yes?"

"Where are you?"

She told him, and he responded by telling her in great detail what he had enjoyed that night at dinner.

"I should go," she said.

"Yes," he agreed.

When she emerged, the corridor was clear, but the firefighters had not yet arrived to scan the hallway. She pulled the dry-erase marker from her purse and slipped the tip into the small hole with the power jack at the bottom of the lock on the flight attendant's door. There was a satisfying pop as the bolt inside it opened.

Then Elena slid into the room. Bowden had left the lights and the television set on. The drapes already were closed, which she deemed a lucky break. She was prepared to close them, but if she did there was the chance that the flight attendant would notice the change the moment she opened the door and either retreat or shoot. This was one less worry.

She surveyed the room carefully, noticing the open suitcase with the clothes rolled meticulously into tubes or folded and pressed flat. The woman may have been a mess in most ways, but she was one hell of a good packer. She saw the tin with Perugia chocolates on the dresser, the nightstand with her tablet and power cables, and the desk with a rather handsome pencil cup: it looked like the foot of an old Roman column. Like the vast majority of hotel rooms, the space was dominated by the bed, a queen with a faux headboard screwed into the wall. Most importantly, she noted the location of the two mirrors.

As she was positioning herself just inside the doorway to await the flight attendant's return, the woman's bathroom to her left, she felt the movement before she saw it and tried to turn. But it was too late. She knew that and was more dumbfounded by her stupidity than horrified by the realization that she was about to die. Someone had entered Bowden's room when she had gone to the stairwell: when she had been *drawn* to the stairwell by the phone call from Viktor. There was the strong arm around her neck, the crushing vise of the V of someone's arm against her larynx, as he pulled her into the bathroom. There was the agony of the knife in her lower back, the peculiarly sonorous grunt of her own gasp. She knew, despite the incapacitating pain, what was next, and it happened in seconds exactly the way she saw it in her mind: he withdrew the knife and ran it across her throat. Instinctively she tried to cry out, a reflex, but already she was gagging on blood—he had cut through the muscle and cartilage, exactly the way she had with Alex Sokolov—and so all she heard was the small sound of someone gargling with mouthwash. And, of course, this was not exactly the way she had executed Sokolov. He'd been asleep. Sound asleep. In her last seconds of life, in the midst of all that pain and all that surprise, she despaired mostly that they were killing her when she was awake.

32

Cassie stood in the crowd that had spilled out onto the street and the sidewalk across from the hotel and watched the fire trucks arrive and the firefighters race into the building. She was grateful that when the siren in her room had started to shriek and the alarm began flashing bright red, she had still been dressed. She had just started to doze off; she had just lost track of whatever was occurring on the sitcom. And so it had taken almost no time to slip into a pair of sandals and toss the gun into her shoulder bag with her passport and wallet and room key. She was glad this was August in Rome. It was the middle of the night, yes, but it was rather pleasant outside. She guessed there were close to two hundred people milling about, none of them alarmed in the slightest, most in some version of nightclothes or sweatpants. She was among the few women she saw in a skirt or a dress. For a moment she watched a gorgeous young couple nuzzling, and grew at once envious and happy for them. The guy could pull off a vandyke beard without looking like Satan, and she was clearly naked (or almost naked) underneath a bright orange shawl she had wrapped loosely around herself. They noticed her gaze and he smiled at her, so she quickly glanced down at her phone. She was scrolling through the spam that had come in when she heard her name and looked up. It was Makayla. She had climbed into a pair of black leggings and a white T-shirt. Cassie saw that she slept in braids.

"Well, this is fun," the other flight attendant said, joining her by the streetlight where she was standing.

"Were you asleep?" Cassie asked.

"I was. Sound asleep. I assume it's a false alarm."

"Yeah. I do, too. I don't see anything that would suggest there's a fire. No smoke. Nothing."

"Unless maybe it's something stupid and minor in the kitchen."

"That could be."

The woman leaned against the lamppost and surprised Cassie when she said, "It's times like this I wish I still smoked."

"You used to smoke?"

Makayla nodded. "I stopped when my husband and I decided we wanted to start a family."

"Was quitting hard?"

"Not at all. I thought it would be, but it wasn't. I just stopped. We said it's time for kids, and the next day, when I came out of an ATM before heading to the airport, I smoked what I knew was my last cigarette. There were nine or ten left in the pack, and I pitched them. I pitched my lighter. Of course, I'd always been a pretty casual smoker. I only started because of a high school play."

"You're kidding."

She rolled her eyes. "Nope. *A Raisin in the Sun*. I was Ruth. And the director had me smoking these stage cigarettes. They have chalk or something in them so it looks like there's smoke. But I had no idea how to hold a cigarette. So, after rehearsal one afternoon I bought a pack of real cigarettes to practice. It was kind of a drama diva move."

"When would you smoke?"

"You mean years later?"

"Uh-huh."

"Usually at times like this."

Cassie raised an eyebrow. "Fire alarms?"

"When I was bored. Or walking. Or after sex."

"Alex Sokolov was like that." She hadn't planned to say it out loud. She wondered a little why she had.

"The fellow who was killed in Dubai?"

"Yes. He only smoked when he was overseas in Europe or Russia or the Middle East. At least that's what he told me."

Makayla seemed to take this in. "How well did you know him? I thought you only met him on the flight from Paris."

"That's true. Not proud that I ended up spending the night with him. But, yes, that is when we met."

"Was he a good guy?"

Cassie saw another member of the flight crew approaching, a fellow a bit older than her named Justin who had pulled on a pair of blue jeans and a white oxford shirt. At least she presumed he had gotten dressed again. She wondered if he often slept naked when he traveled, like some of her friends who flew, because it meant not packing pajamas. Or maybe his body ran hot (like hers), and he liked the feel of cool sheets against his skin when he fell asleep. Maybe he liked the erotic charge. Certainly some nights she did.

"Evening, ladies," he began. "Nothing like getting a good two hours of sleep before the alarm goes off. The fire alarm, that is."

"Nothing like it," Cassie agreed. And then, perhaps because she had reached a stage where she just didn't give a damn any-more about what people thought of her, she continued to answer Makayla's question: "Yes. Alex Sokolov was a good guy. At least he was to me. Maybe he was up to something. Maybe he was involved in something shady. I didn't know him well, and I probably drink too much to be trusted to judge anyone's character. But I liked him." She turned to Justin and explained, her voice as deadpan as she could make it—the tone, she supposed, of a woman who knew all she may once have hoped for in life had now passed her by— "We're talking about the man I slept with in Dubai, the one who was killed in our hotel room. Excuse me, his hotel room."

Justin took this in for a split second. Then he put up his arms, his hands flat and framing his face, the universal sign for surrender. "I can stand right over there if you two would like to speak pri-vately. Far be it from me to interrupt," he said lightly.

"No," Cassie continued. "I don't seem to have any secrets any-more." As soon as the sentence had escaped her lips, however, she knew it wasn't true. It wasn't true at all. In some ways, it was the worst kind of lie because it suggested that her secrets and lying were behind her. But, of course, she was just living a different set of secrets and lies.

"Did you, I don't know, think it was going to go anywhere when you were back in America?" asked Makayla.

"My thing with Alex? Not really. But we did have fun that night. Maybe we would have seen each other again. Maybe not." She put her phone back in her purse, sliding it in beside the pistol. "Given my history, most likely not."

Justin looked uncomfortably down at his sneakers. They all noticed that he hadn't bothered to tie them, and so he knelt down, and Cassie imagined he was probably grateful to have something to do that did not involve listening to her discuss the sad end to her dalliance at the Royal Phoenician.

"My vice has always been drinking," she said now to Makayla. "I never smoked. I'm not sure I could quit drinking the way you just stopped smoking. Hell, I know I couldn't."

"Were you drinking when the fire alarm went off?"

"Alone in the night in the hotel room with a bottle of tequila? That could be me. But it wasn't. Not this time. I haven't had a drink all day—or night."

"There you go. You're fine."

She sighed. "No. I'm not fine, Makayla, I'm not fine at all. You saw me at the airport this morning."

Justin stood up and said, "What happened at Fiumicino had nothing to do with drinking. You were sober, Cassie." For a moment they stood in silence, and Cassie had the sense that he wanted to embrace her—to comfort her—but was afraid it would be construed as something less chivalrous. "I mean, you were sober, right?"

"Yes," she answered. "I was."

"There you go."

They watched two firefighters exiting the front entrance, followed by a gentleman in a black suit and a necktie the luminescent red of a New England maple leaf late in September. First in Italian and then in English he asked for everyone's attention. He introduced himself as the night manager and apologized profusely for the inconvenience of what was, happily, just a false alarm. He said everyone could safely return to their rooms or, if they preferred, first to the hotel bar, which was going to reopen for an hour for anyone who would like a nightcap—on the house. A free drink, he explained, was the least the hotel could do to apologize for dragging everyone out of bed in the middle of the night.

"I'm game," said Justin. "What about you two?"

But Makayla glared at him, her dark eyes daggers. Cassie couldn't miss what that stare meant. "I think we should all just go back to sleep," she told him.

"No, it's fine," Cassie said. "It really is. I won't join you, but if you two want to go, please don't let me put a damper on the party."

Instead Justin shook his head and said sheepishly, "You're probably right, Makayla. Wheels up will come a lot sooner than we think."

"Yes. It will."

And with that the three of them returned to the hotel lobby and rode the elevator together, all of them exiting on different floors, Cassie the last to leave on the sixth. No other hotel guests left with her on her floor. She guessed they were all at the bar.

When she got out, she stood for a long moment and stared down the corridor. The hallway wasn't as opulent as the Royal Phoenician, nor was it as long. But it was elegant: perfectly appointed for a lovely Italian boutique hotel. The carpet was a little frayed with age, but the patterns were reminiscent of a Renaissance tapestry. She thought of the clouds and sea in a Botticelli painting and imagined the work that went into making a color or dye five hundred years ago, the transformation of the pigments into the acrylic at the tip of the brush.

Then she started down the hallway. She felt a spike of unease, but she had lived with almost that sort of twinge since she had woken up beside a corpse, and so she disregarded it. She walked in silence down the corridor, lonely and alone, her room key in her hand, and stared straight ahead. She told herself that the air was not really charged and there was really nothing to fear, no reason to be morose. She was just going to a hotel room in the night by herself, as she had hundreds of times in the past, and there was no reason to be anxious or frightened.

After all, this time she was actually sober.

When that realization came to her, she smiled.

But the smile didn't last long, because when she turned the corner she saw a man and she jumped. For a split second she feared that her anxiety had a specific cause: it was every woman's fear when she's alone and sees a man in her path. He was about twenty yards from her room, and she almost turned and ran. But then she realized that it was only Enrico, and she relaxed. He was sitting in a small chair against the wall, his face in the shadow from the sconce behind him. There was a table with a hotel phone next to him. He stood when he saw her and went to embrace her, but she pushed him away.

"You just scared the you-know-what out of me," she told him.

"I thought I would be a nice surprise," he said, his tone apologetic. "I'm sorry. I didn't mean to scare you."

"God. It's best if I'm alone, Enrico. I told you that."

"And I was going to leave you alone. I was down at the bar when the fire alarm went off. I was helping them close. And I thought, my beautiful flight attendant must be terrified."

"By a fire alarm? No."

He shook his head. "By being outside in the dark—instead of safely in bed in your room."

"I'm back now. I'm fine."

"Then I will escort you to your room and leave you there." He held out his elbow, and she took it. Together they walked down the corridor. Then she slid her key into the slot and opened the door.

33

He had just finished dragging Elena's body into the bathroom and dropping it into the bathtub when he heard Enrico's voice in the corridor. It didn't give him time to rethink his plan. But at least he was ready.

The moment both the bartender and the flight attendant were inside the hotel room, the door shut behind them, he emerged from the darkened bathroom. He slammed the grip of his pistol into the back of Enrico's skull with his left hand and rammed the tip of Elena Orlov's stun gun against Bowden's gauzy little dress—high on the rear of her thigh—with his right. The bartender instantly collapsed to the carpet, unconscious, his shirt sponging up wet remnants of Elena's blood. The flight attendant grunted loudly, shuddered, and then went limp like a rag doll. Just melted against him. She stared up at him as he lowered her to the rug beside the bartender, and he could see the terror in her eyes. She would be able to speak soon enough, and he did want to talk to her. But first he had to reevaluate what he was going to do.

He dumped out the woman's purse and saw that she had gotten a gun. Perfect. He didn't care where she got it; he could use it. Elena had set the table rather nicely when she'd called the newspaper. The woman wouldn't overdose on the barbiturates the American spy had brought. Instead he would leave behind a tableau for the world in which it seemed evident that Cassandra Bowden had killed her Italian lover and her new, wealthy Russian friend from

Sochi, and then shot herself in the head with the gun she must have gone to such great lengths to acquire.

First, however, he had to transfer the silencer from his Beretta to hers.

34

The taser was excruciating, and Cassie wanted to scream—in her mind, she imagined a blue streak of expletives, a woman with a foul mouth and an impressive vocabulary unleashing it all in the throes of labor—but she could only moan, long and low. And then she was on her stomach on the hotel room floor, just outside the bathroom door, and there was Buckley crouching beside her.

Yes, it was the actor. Of course it was.

He was actually wearing that same black ball cap. Here she had been so obsessed with Miranda, and all along it had been a person she thought was sweet and well meaning and actually a bit of a puppy dog. It was a testimony to just how badly she appraised people and picked her friends, and it might have been comic if he weren't going to kill her the way that he or one of his associates had, she presumed, killed Alex. He was going to grab a handful of her hair, pull back her head to expose her neck, and cut her throat—probably poor Enrico's, too—and leave her facedown on the hotel room rug to bleed out.

Cassie hoped it wouldn't hurt, but she knew it would. She realized that she was most afraid of the pain, the sharp, brief, razor-like sting of the blade slicing into her skin, and maybe that explained why she drank. Pain came in all colors and sizes, much of it far worse than the pricks and aches and fever dreams that affected the body. This was the pain that gouged out great holes in the soul, hollowing out self-esteem and cratering a person's self-respect. This was the pain that caused you to gaze at yourself in the mirror and wonder why in the name of God you were here. Cassie understood that her life was a study in precisely this sort of palliative management. Or, to be precise, mismanagement.

Her tongue felt thick and heavy from the taser, and as she watched the contents of her purse spilled out in front of her, she tried to turn her guttural moaning into words. She had one sentence she had to say, and she wished it was the two words, *I'm sorry.* Or maybe something more specific: I'm sorry I didn't do more. I'm sorry I was unlovable or incapable of being loved. I'm sorry I never had children. Or even a cat of my own. I'm sorry, Rosemary, I'm sorry, Jessica, I'm sorry, Dennis, I'm sorry, Tim.

I'm sorry, Alex.

I'm sorry, Enrico.

God, Enrico. About to be killed for no other reason than that he was chivalrous. A young romantic who had walked her back to her room. She never should have let him. One more mistake of hers with consequences for others.

Would any of these people miss her? Would Megan? Gillian? Paula? Would anyone really and truly miss her? Supposedly, whatever we do that's selfish goes with us to the grave; whatever we do that's selfless lives on. She couldn't imagine a single thing she had done, a single act, that had even hinted at immortality. Her legacy? She had no legacy.

She could feel her cheeks were wet and she was crying, which she hadn't expected. She had been told over the years by pilots, usually when they were having a drink, that the last words of most captains before their aircraft augured into the side of the mountain or broke apart before breaking the plane of the sea were these: Mother. Mommy. Mom. That lovely woman who once upon a time had read to her from Beverly Cleary would have been devastated at the way her older daughter had followed so rigorously her husband's swath of self-destruction. Any mother would.

Finally she found just enough motor control to form a sentence. But it was neither the two-word apology that was bubbling up inside her nor the plea to spare her or Enrico the pain that loomed. It was the deepest truth of who she was because it spoke to how she had lived, and the plain unvarnished reality that we cannot escape who we are and most of the time we die as we lived.

She turned her head as much as she could so she could meet Buckley's eyes and asked, her voice still fuzzy from the shock and paralysis, "Please. Can I have a drink?"

He paused, seeming to give the request serious, genuine consideration, his eyes almost mystified, and for a long second Cassie believed that she had bought another moment of life. One last taste of the essentia, the ambrosia, the amrita that filled her veins and her soul and kept her pain at bay. But then he shook his head ever so slightly, almost wistfully, and attached a long, circular tube—a silencer, Cassie presumed—to the end of Enrico's uncle's Beretta.

FEDERAL BUREAU OF INVESTIGATION

FD-302 (redacted): MAJOR DENNIS McCAULEY, ARMY CHEMICAL CORPS

DATE: August 6, 2018

DENNIS McCAULEY, date of birth—/—/——, SSN #————, telephone number (—)————, was interviewed by properly identified Special Agents RICHARD MARINI and CATHY MANNING in a private conference room at the BLUE GRASS ARMY DEPOT in Richmond, Kentucky.

MANNING led the interview; MARINI took these notes.

After being advised of the nature of the interview, McCAULEY provided the following information.

McCAULEY acknowledged seeing his sister-in-law CASSANDRA BOWDEN on Saturday afternoon and evening, August 4, in New York City, and insisted that her behavior was "mostly" normal. She went with his family to the Bronx Zoo and then to a restaurant in lower Manhattan. He noticed that she was checking her phone more than most adults would throughout the day and during dinner, and "definitely seemed nervous about something."

He said he cannot recall ever seeing her without his wife ROSEMARY BOWDEN-McCAULEY present. He said the two of them have never e-mailed or spoken on the phone.

He stated firmly that he has never shared any classified information with BOWDEN, and BOWDEN has never asked him for any. He said that while they have discussed life in the military very generally and his background as an engineer, they always talked more about her job than his. He denied ever giving her papers, data, diagrams, flash drives, or e-mails that had anything to do with the disposal of chemical weapons or the remaining U.S. stockpile; he insisted that he never shared any information on sarin, VX, or any chemical weapons not yet destroyed in the U.S. arsenal.

He said he never took work home; he said there was no way that his wife ROSE-MARY could have shared any information with her sister or provided CASSANDRA BOWDEN with classified intelligence, because he didn't tell her anything.

He said he was shocked that his sister-in-law might have killed ALEX SOKOLOV, though he acknowledged that she has a drinking problem. He volunteered that he does not believe she is a Russian spy.

35

B ut Buckley didn't shoot.

Instead, almost as if it were happening to someone else, as if it were an out-of-body experience, Cassie saw him dragging her by her arms further into the hotel room and away from the door. Her dress had rolled up near her hips and she felt the rug burning her thighs. Intellectually she welcomed the discomfort: it suggested that feeling and mobility were returning. When they reached the bed, he let her go, dropping her unceremoniously onto the floor beside it as if she were a canoe dragged from the beach, and then sat down on the edge of the mattress and pointed the Beretta down at her chest.

"Yell for help and I'll kill you," he said.

Cassie tried to shake her head. She was indeed able to move it. "I won't," she murmured, her voice still mushy and hoarse. She tried to focus anywhere but on the tip of the long silencer at the end of the pistol.

"Tell me about Elena."

"Elena?"

Instantly he switched the gun to his other hand, grabbing it by the barrel, and rapped her hard on the shin with the grip. She closed her eyes and cried out reflexively against the pain, and when she opened them he was already aiming the weapon at her once more. She collected herself and whimpered, "I don't know who that is."

"The woman who came to Alex Sokolov's suite in Dubai."

"Miranda?"

He rolled his eyes. "Miranda," he repeated.

"We had a drink. The vodka she brought. Then she left."

He pounded her other shin with the gun, but either because she was expecting it or had just experienced precisely this agony, this time she merely grunted through her tears.

"What were you doing with her?"

"I told you, drinking! That's all!"

"Did she recruit you?"

"Recruit me?"

"Cassie, let me be clear: the only chance you have of walking out of this hotel room alive is if you give me the names. You knew Elena, obviously. Who else is embedded?"

"Embedded? I don't know what you mean, I don't understand any of this," she told him. She was crying now and didn't care. "Recruits? Embedded? I'm not a spy! I'm nothing. You know me. You know what I am. I'm just . . ."

"Why didn't she kill you?"

"I don't know! I'm telling you, I don't know anything," she whimpered.

He stared at her and seemed to think about this. Then: "I almost believe you. Almost."

"Because I'm telling you the truth."

"Tell me about your brother-in-law."

"He's in the army," she mumbled. "He's a major. He's stationed at Blue Grass."

"What else?"

"There is no what else."

He stood up, his feet on either side of her body, and aimed the Beretta straight down at her. "You are fast running out of time, Cassie. Why were you with Sokolov in Dubai?"

"We met on the plane, that's all there was to it," she mewled. "Please don't kill me."

"Why was he interested in you?"

Why was any man interested in her? she wanted to ask in return. The answer was simple: because she was a drunk and she was easy. And while a small part of her understood the rightness of sarcasm and self-loathing when she appraised her life, there was a gun pointed at her. And so she replied simply, "He wanted a good time. I guess I did, too."

From the corner of her vision she saw that Enrico had moved his head. She didn't dare turn her gaze on him because she didn't want to draw Buckley's attention to the young bartender, but Cassie noticed that one of his eyes was open. "He was just a guy on the plane," she went on, hoping to hold Buckley's interest. "Someone to drink with in Dubai. I didn't think I'd ever see him again." She didn't know if there was any way in the world that Enrico could creep over to him without drawing his attention, but the idea gave her hope.

"Did he mention the name of anyone else he was seeing in Dubai?"

"No. I mean, I knew he had a meeting, but I assumed it had something to do with his hedge fund."

"Did he mention anyone else who worked at the airline?"

"No, he didn't." She tried to watch Enrico with soft eyes: eyes that focused on nothing but took in everything. Her friend Paula had grown up with a horse, and it was how she was taught to ride: to see her surroundings without turning her head and thus confusing the animal beneath her by moving her body. Enrico had managed to inch a little closer to the bed from his spot outside the bathroom. Any moment, she supposed, he was going to dive at Buckley. When he did—if she could move quickly, which she was unsure if she could—she would try and help. She would attack too. Years ago she'd taken a voluntary self-defense course the airline had offered. She'd never needed to use anything she'd learned (or, alas, she'd been too drunk to realize that she should be defending herself), and she tried to recall what the instructors had taught in the class. There was something about pulling your assailant into you when he had his hands on you. Elbowing his head. Poking or punching his abdomen. She could do that. She would do anything to force the man by the bed to deal with multiple attacks.

"I'm about to go through your suitcase and your kit. I am going to empty everything onto the floor. Sensation should be returning about now. Do not get up off the floor, and do not try and stop me. Are we clear?"

She nodded.

But then Buckley swung his arm as if swatting someone with the back of his hand—he'd seen Enrico—and calmly pulled the trigger of Uncle Piero's Beretta.

36

The gun exploded, the silencer dampening but not eliminating the pop, and Cassie was aware that she had winced and cried out—and that Enrico was still alive. He had launched himself on top of Buckley, pinning him on his side on the mattress. There was a cut on Buckley's cheek, the gash already puddling red, and he was holding his right hand with his left. The wound on his hand looked far worse than the one on his face: Cassie could see blood streaming down the man's forearm, as well as the black burns along his fingers and thumb. His index finger was misshapen and either dislocated or broken.

Their eyes met and he snapped at her. "You don't even use decent fucking ammo!" And then Cassie saw the Berretta on the floor beside her, twisted metal shards rising like tentacles from the rear of the pistol, the silencer straight but dangling from the tip of the still-smoking weapon. They stared at each other, and Cassie understood that this was why Enrico was still alive. Buckley must have double-tapped and tried to shoot two rounds in quick succession. Had Enrico's uncle under-charged the top round she'd loaded into the magazine? Seemed likely. But it didn't matter. What did was that the bullet had gotten stuck in the bore—a squib—and that had caused the gun to explode.

"Call for help," Enrico said to her. "Call downstairs." He had wrapped his arms around Buckley, and they looked almost like lovers, and she recalled momentarily what it had been like when she had wrapped herself around him. Then she struggled to her feet, wobbly, her legs like licorice, but she held on to the side of the desk and reached gingerly for the phone.

"Don't," said Buckley, and he spat something—a tooth, Cassie saw—into the carpet. Cassie paused long enough for him to continue. "I'm telling you, you can't hide from us all. There'll just be someone else after you tomorrow."

Outside they heard guests in the hallway, some returning from the street where they had gone when they had been evacuated from the hotel, some drawn by the sound of the gun exploding. It was clear, however, that none had any idea what that noise was or where it had come from. She heard someone suggest that it must have been something on television and someone else argue no, it was too loud, and speculate that it had something to do with the air conditioning. Maybe something to do with whatever had triggered the fire alarm that had sent them out into the night in the first place. Neither guest sounded concerned.

Cassie continued to stare at Buckley. His right cheek was growing black and his right eye was disappearing into the swelling all around it. "Who are you?" she asked. "Tell me now: who are you really?" She kept her finger on the button for guest services.

« «

Say it like you mean it.

When had she said that, Cassie wondered, and then she remembered. She'd challenged her mother to reassure her that everything would be okay when Daddy was so drunk he couldn't navigate his way up the stairs and kept falling down as if he were battling a degenerative muscle disease. Apparently, her mother had not been especially convincing when she'd said everything was fine.

For a second, Cassie thought she must have said those words to an old boyfriend, too. Maybe he'd said he loved her in a joshing sort of way and she'd wanted more. Maybe she'd felt betrayed by the lightness of the way he'd spoken. Maybe she'd felt betrayed then, too.

No, that wasn't it.

Because that had never happened.

She'd never had a boyfriend who'd told her he loved her.

Never.

Cassie looked at the blood congealing on Buckley's fingers. Clearly this was a betrayal of a new sort, at once bigger and smaller than any she'd experienced before in her life. It was bigger because the stakes were bigger; it was smaller because she hadn't really known him.

She'd only gotten drunk with him a couple of times. She'd only had sex with him a couple of times.

Only. Only.

The sad truth was, she really hadn't known him at all.

« «

She watched Buckley try once to extricate himself from Enrico, wriggling and struggling to free his arms or his hands, and she started toward the men on the bed to help keep him restrained, but it was evident that Buckley was in a lot of pain and Enrico was deceptively strong. Buckley wasn't going anywhere. He ran his tongue through the slot where a moment ago he'd had an upper incisor. "It doesn't matter. My name, I mean," he said when the brief scuffle was done. He sounded—and the irony was not lost on Cassie—drunk.

"It does."

"Then it's Evgeny."

"Not Buckley?"

"No."

"You're not really an actor, are you? You're not really from Westport? It was all a lie, wasn't it?"

He rolled his eyes and then nodded.

"And that was you following me around New York City," she said, not a question this time.

"It was."

"You work with Miranda?"

"I thought I did. I didn't. Not really. Her real name was Elena. Elena Orlov."

"Was?"

"Was."

"She's dead?" asked Cassie, at once relieved and strangely, unexpectedly saddened. "God, how? Why?" She noticed the blood on the carpet by the door as she spoke, recalled Alex's on the sheets of that magisterial bed in Dubai, and had a feeling that the great stain this time was Elena's.

"Because she didn't kill you. That was the first clue. We have a feeling she was turned when she went to school in Boston. She was working for you folks now."

"America?"

"America."

"So you're Russian intelligence?"

"I'm nothing."

Enrico elbowed him hard in the back. He grimaced and then said, "Yes, FSB. I'm a Cossack. Google it." Then he said to Enrico, "You don't need to wreck my kidney, and you don't need to suffocate me. I think we've established I'm not going anywhere. So, let up on the chest, okay, buddy?"

"Call, Cassandra, call," Enrico told her. "Don't talk to this crazy person."

"No, Cassie. Don't call. Put the phone down," Buckley said. "You'll find Elena's purse in the bathroom. It's beside her body. And in that purse is a gun. Another gun. It's a Beretta that's already loaded, and so, thank God, you won't have to load it. You won't have to do anything. There's also a knife. Even if you really aren't with the CIA, I'm sure by now you have some new friends with the FBI in New York. Call them. Tell them to call their legal attaché in Rome. Tell them that Elena Orlov is here in this hotel in room six twenty-one. She's dead. Tell them Evgeny Stepanov is in room four zero six. I'm two floors below you. I'll be waiting for the FBI attaché there. Then when I've left your room, count to thirty, fire the weapon, and scream for help."

Enrico shook his head. "Don't do it, Cassandra. He's just going to run away."

"No, man, I won't. I have no place left to run."

"I want to know one thing," Cassie asked. "Is my brother-in-law clean?"

"As far as I know."

"So you have an inside elsewhere?"

"So it would seem."

Cassie put down the phone. She took her finger off the button for guest services. The she retrieved Elena Orlov's purse from the bathroom, careful at first to avert her eyes from the corpse in the tub, but then incapable of not glancing at it. There she was. Miranda. Elena. She was on her side, but Cassie could still see how deeply into her neck Buckley had run a knife and the blood that was pooling near the drain. She took the bag from the bathroom and in the hallway went through it. She wasn't sure what to make of half of what was inside it—the pills, the restraints—but she found the knife and the Beretta. She flipped off the safety on the weapon.

"Remember: that gun is properly loaded," Evgeny said to her when she returned.

"Go on."

"Point the gun at me. It's fine. You'll feel safer. Then your friend can let me go. He'll stand next to you. You'll hand me the knife. Or if you want to keep your distance, you can toss the knife onto the mattress. I think I've already left enough blood on the bedspread and the carpet, but a little more couldn't hurt. And my tooth is already there—on the floor. So there will be plenty for forensics. Then I'll go to my room, and you'll call your FBI contacts and tell them where I am."

"And hotel security?"

"No. Don't call them. That will lead to the Italian police and a real investigation. I want the world—at least my world—to believe you shot me dead. You killed me."

Enrico was shaking his head no, his eyes imploring her not

to do this. Cassie wondered if he'd even release Evgeny when she asked him to. He might not. She thought of all the mistakes she had made with her life—all the pain she had sown and reaped, all the things she would never have and never do—but she had a feeling now that listening to Evgeny wasn't going to be one of them.

"What about me?" she asked. "You said that even if I kill you or call the police, there will just be someone else coming after me."

"You'll be someone new. Your people will see to it."

"I assume by my 'people,' you don't mean the airline."

"Look, Cassie. Think about it. Do you really want to go through life as the Cart Tart Killer? I doubt it. Right now we share something I never expected when I followed you to that bar in the East Village: the need to start again."

FEDERAL BUREAU OF INVESTIGATION

FD-302: MEGAN BRISCOE, FLIGHT ATTENDANT

DATE: August 7, 2018

MEGAN BRISCOE was interviewed by properly identified Special Agents NANCY SAUNDERS and EMORY LEARY at the FBI office in Washington, D.C.

SAUNDERS conducted the interview; LEARY took these notes.

When asked point blank if she had ever acted as a courier or delivered classified documents or information to a foreign government, she broke down and said that she had. She admitted that she and her husband were both paid by the Russian Federation. He would use his security clearance as a consultant to bring her materials on, most recently, the U.S. chemical weapons defense program at the Edgewood Chemical Biological Center in Maryland, and she in turn would deliver them to her handlers overseas.

She asked for a lawyer, and the interview ended with her arrest and the arrest of her husband.

= = = = = =

Subsequent to the interview, BRISCOE'S home and garage in Centreville, Virginia, were searched, and two flash drives with classified chemical weapons information were found hidden in an electrical outlet box, behind the plate, in their master bedroom.

Epilogue

*REMEMBER THAT PERSON
YOU WANTED TO BE?
THERE'S STILL TIME.*

«

On the night flight to Moscow, Cassie brought the passenger in 4C his vodka and tonic and hovered over him an extra-long second, a noctivagant cat on the headrest of an easy chair. If she hadn't known who he really was—or, at least, what the agency had told her about him—she would have pegged him for a retired ice hockey star. The sort of red-haired Russian Adonis who as a very young skater had led his own country's team to Olympic gold and then taken the NHL by storm in his twenties. He'd clearly broken his nose at least once. His shoulders were still broad, but his hair was thin and his skin was leather. He used reading glasses. She guessed he was, much to her horror, her age.

He wasn't a hockey player, of course; he was Russian intelligence. Maybe a Cossack, but perhaps a part of the FSB's Center 18: the cyber spies. After she had absorbed all she could glean from his tablet—two e-mail addresses and some names she barely could spell—she retreated to the first-class galley and wrote down what she saw. She presumed she was giving the agency nothing they didn't already have. But you never knew. She liked this sort of walk-on role, which was about all they would offer her at this stage. She'd been sober two years now, but she had a long history of drinking to overcome, and so this special surveillance group was the extent of the leash. She had new hair and a new name. She had a new base. And when they needed a flight attendant, they used her. Apparently, they had an Aegean stable–sized pool of actors available for this sort of bit part. And she was good at the work: the circumlocutions of the functioning alcoholic were not unlike the daily subterfuge of a spy.

The irony to this particular assignment, of course, was that an awful lot of what the agency knew about the gentleman in 4C they had learned from Evgeny—or Buckley as she still thought of him sometimes. The passenger was a friend of Viktor's. Evgeny's knowledge ranged from drop sites to bank account numbers. He knew what everyone liked to drink and their tastes in women and men. He had a new identity, too, but they were still keeping him in a safe house just outside of Washington, D.C. His debriefing, given his history, could last a lifetime.

Cassie had seen him just one time since Rome. Four months ago, when Masha was almost a year old, a handler had brought them together at an apartment near Dupont Circle. It was maybe a block from the Carnegie Endowment, and the handler had made it clear that this was not where Evgeny lived. The purpose of the meeting was for the Russian to share firsthand what he knew about a woman whom Cassie was supposed to watch on a flight to Beirut. They never told her Evgeny's new name and he didn't volunteer it, but his hair now was short, a creamy mix of white and blond, and Cassie wondered if it was bleached or whether the chestnut she recalled when they'd first met had been the dye. Probably his natural color was the shade she recalled from that summer: the nights when they'd danced together at a grunge bar south of her apartment and walked through the West Village beneath a perfect half moon.

Or the night when he'd killed a woman named Elena and tried to kill a man named Enrico. The night when he would just as easily have killed her.

When they met in Washington, Evgeny had struck Cassie as neither happy nor unhappy: mostly he seemed comfortable and businesslike in his new role.

But when he smiled, she glimpsed the playfulness she remembered. Cassie had made a small joke about her boyfriend, a TV writer in L.A., and Evgeny confessed that he had watched a few episodes of the fellow's show. For a moment Cassie had been taken aback that he knew so much about her, even now, but then she had nodded. Of course he did. Then he'd said, "They really should stick to family drama. WASPy family drama. And if they want me to play the rebellious son who becomes an actor, I'm their man." His eyes went wide when he said that, and Cassie honestly wasn't sure if he was pulling her leg.

Before they parted, Cassie had asked if there was anyone he missed in Russia or America. She wasn't sure why: she guessed it was because they all presumed he was dead. He'd chuckled and said, "Trust me, you don't want to meet my friends. You just don't. They make me look pretty damn . . . American."

"What does that mean?"

"Wimpy." Again, she had a sense he was teasing her. But then he sat forward and folded his hands together. "How wimpy, you ask?"

She waited, wondering whether he was going to make a joke at the expense of the United States. But instead he continued. "So wimpy I am very, very glad you screwed up when you loaded that gun. I wouldn't have wanted you on my conscience."

"Because . . ."

"Because you are just too damn much fun. You're a mess—or, I don't know, maybe you were a mess—but you sure as hell were good company." Then he unclasped his fingers as if they were a balloon exploding and added, "And I have a feeling you're not nearly the shitstorm of a mother you probably figured you'd be."

She rolled her eyes. "Being sober helps."

"You named her Masha, right?"

She nodded.

"That can't possibly be a family name."

"Tolstoy. The young woman in 'Happy Ever After.' She's my happy ending."

"God, I remember you reading that," he said, his own happiness at the recollection genuine. Then: "You still dance barefoot?"

"I have other pleasures. Board books. Sippy cups shaped like animals. Teething."

He made a tsk-tsk sound with his tongue, pretending to reproach her. Then they parted.

Now, as she stood in the dimmed cabin light and looked at the notes she had written down about the passenger in 4C, she recalled—as she did rather often—the way Masha would nurse. She would latch on to Cassie and drink with the same fervor with which Cassie knew she had once drunk tequila. Those little baby eyes would grow intense, then sated, and it was in those moments that Cassie could see in them Masha's father, that enigmatic man who had loved Tolstoy and washed her hair ever so tenderly in a lavish hotel suite one night in Dubai.

She thought of that quote she'd seen on a blackboard outside a West Village boutique: "Remember that person you wanted to be? There's still time." She wasn't completely sure this was who she wanted to be, but she found the work offered the same adrenaline rush as drinking, but without the hangovers and humiliations. It gave her life purpose. She knew, however, that the person who had most assuredly saved her life was Masha, because Masha was the reason she had stopped drinking and Masha was warmth in the morning when Cassie was home and they would wake together, and Masha was a euphoric squeal when she would return to her from a trip. Masha was the word *moon,* her first word, and how with her authoritarian little pointer finger she had looked skyward at dusk at a sickle moon and elongated that single, lovely syllable almost into song. Masha gave her something she loved more than herself—something that didn't come in a glass with ice cubes or a paper umbrella or a straw.

Cassie opened the first-class bar on the flight, looked at the liquor bottles, as beautiful to her as Fabergé eggs, and reached for a can of Diet Coke.

Acknowledgments

"Nothing can be more limiting to the imagination, nothing is quicker to turn on the psyche's censoring devices and distortion systems, than trying to write truthfully and interestingly about one's own hometown," John Gardner taught us in *The Art of Fiction*.

I agree. I rarely write what I know. But I always do my homework, and I have come to love the research that goes into my books—partly because of what I learn, but also because of the new friends I make. In this case, I offer my deepest thanks to easily a dozen and a half people.

Jerrold H. Bamel and Tristram Coffin were my guides through how the FBI might be involved in this story. My sense is that each of them could someday write a gripping spy thriller. Tris is the former U.S. attorney for the District of Vermont. Jerrold is a retired FBI agent and now a corporate fraud investigator. He also makes some mighty tasty jam from mangos, pineapples, and key limes.

Carla Malstrom and Daphne Walker shared with me what life is like as a flight attendant at thirty-five thousand feet and at sea level. Chat with either of them for an hour and you will thank your flight attendants for all they do (and endure) the next time you board a plane.

Adam Turteltaub (a great friend from college), Khatchig Mouradian (my Armenian godfather), and Matthew Gilbert taught me about Dubai. Adam and Khatchig also read early drafts of this manuscript and offered valuable insights. I have dedicated books in the past to the two of them; I know I will again.

J. J. Gertler (another friendship that dates back to when I was eighteen years old) was my expert on drones and chemical weapons and National Intelligence. He is a professional national security geek, and it is a pleasure to have his name again in the Acknowledgments.

Jerry Everett, a gunsmith in Texas, read the first hardcover edition and was kind enough to assist me with the finer points of the Berretta.

Also helping me once more with a novel: Steven Shapiro, chief medical examiner for the State of Vermont, assisted with the autopsy scenes. Ani Tchaghlasian was my guide through the labyrinthine world of offshore money and OFAC laws, and the sort of fund one of my characters is managing.

My biking buddies in Vermont, Andrew Furtsch and Stephen Kiernan—again, I have dedicated books to them both—allowed me to bounce plot machinations off them over hundreds of miles. Stephen Gragg assisted with airport security. And while traveling with me on the backroads of Artsakh and in a bar in Stepanakert, Fred Hayrapet shared with me stories of what happens when a deal goes bad in places like Donetsk or Dubai.

I have to give a very special shout-out to Sarah Hepola. I fell in love with her hauntingly beautiful memoir, *Blackout: Remembering the Things I Drank to Forget*, soon after I finished the first draft of this novel. I keep a screenshot of page 214 of *Blackout* on my phone.

Among the books I read and enjoyed while writing this novel were: Heather Poole's memoir of being a flight attendant, *Cruising Attitude*; Patrick Smith's book about flying, *Ask the Pilot*; and Richard Whittle's history of drones, *Predator*.

I extend my deepest thanks to my remarkable editor, Jennifer Jackson (this is our sixth book together, and, yes, I dedicated a novel to her, too) and the whole team at Doubleday, Vintage, and Penguin Random House Audio: Maria Carella, Todd Doughty, John Fontana, Kelly Gildea, Zakiya Harris, Suzanne Herz, Judy Jacoby, Jennifer Marshall, Anne Messitte, Charlotte O'Donnell, John Pitts, Nora Reichard, William Thomas, and Margaux Weisman.

I am so grateful to my agents: Penelope Burns, Miriam Feuerle, Jane Gelfman, Cathy Gleason, Brian Lipson, Abigail Parker, Deborah Schneider, Hannah Scott, and Andrew Wetzel.

Finally, I am—as always—so appreciative of the counsel of my lovely bride, Victoria Blewer, and our daughter, the always amazing Grace Experience.

I thank you all.